RAPID RESPONSE

Jill S. Flateland

ISBN 979-8-9913102-1-5 (paperback)
ISBN 979-8-9913102-3-9 (hardcover)
ISBN 979-8-9913102-2-2 (digital)

First printing: June 2018
Revised 2020

This is an original Publication of Jill S. Flateland, 11350 W. 72nd Place, Arvada, CO 80005.

Website: JillSFlateland.com

Cover illustration by Kendra Petersen

Printed in the United States of America

10 9 8 7 6 5 4 3 2 1
Third Edition

Dedication to Byron Flateland

I dedicate this book to my handsome, fun-loving husband, Byron Flateland, who makes sure I have delicious meals set before me when I forget to eat. There are times when I get so wrapped up in writing that I need helpful reminders of upcoming appointments, meetings, or just to take time out for a break.

Byron has blessed me with his intelligence, humor, and love throughout my life. His honesty is unquestionable, although at times, I don't fully appreciate his feedback, but my superhero will stand beside me always. He is my greatest inspiration and the love of my life.

Fortunately, Byron is also a curious man who loves to travel. We take several weeks every year to experience new adventures. We've been to India, France, Great Britain, Italy, and Spain. More exotic trips included scuba diving in Indonesia's Raja Ampat, Bagon, visiting temples in Myanmar, Tiger's Nest in Bhutan, and a cruise up the Blue Danube.

We've visited eighty-four countries over the years, and we have barely touched the surface of the world. Wherever I go, I meet new people and learn about their culture. It's been thrilling to weave bits of their personalities, insights, and inspiration to create the soul of my characters.

Acknowledgments

My greatest blessings are our daughters, Kirsten Sielaff and Crystal Fletcher, their supportive husbands, Tim Sielaff and Jason Fletcher, and our grandchildren, Elsa Hana Sielaff and Wyatt Samuel Fletcher. I hope, in years to come, they'll enjoy reading these books.

As always, I have a unique blessing, my sister, Cindy. My love for her will last forever. Not only is she my sister, but she is my cherished friend. Thanks for always being there for me.

I would also like to give special thanks to my illustrator, Kendra Petersen, who designed this creative cover. Her creativity is amazing. I love the color scheme for this book series.

Thanks to my dear friend, Jeri Lou Maus, for her honest feedback and prompt edits. I'm truly blessed.

Last, but far from least, I give thanks to the 93rd Street Irregulars, my writer's group, who I'm privileged to call my sounding board for creating this novel. They helped to refine the chapters and make them flow.

Agent Joshtine Cordelia-Hastings Crisis Series
By Jill S. Flateland

Cordy's adventures continue in the second book of the Joshtine Cordelia-Hastings Series, *Rapid Response*, where she fights a bioterrorist attack. An astronaut unknowingly transports a potent virus, created without gravity on the space station, back to Earth. This virus is more deadly than our recent COVID-19 epidemic. Not only does it devastate the lungs, but it also attacks the brain. Risking exposure, Cordy rushes to find a cure when U.S. President Spendorf, his key advisors, and many members of Congress become infected.

If you've read, *Sweet Revenge*, you have already met Agent Dr. Joshtine Cordelia. She is a peculiar breed. At the age of twenty-three, she is adventurous, quick-witted, and energetic. She's any man's equal, although absolutely female. Her shoulder-length, strawberry-blonde hair is often pulled back in a professional French braid, which reveals a heart-shaped face, ivory skin, and alert eyes the color of a spring pond.

Her Irish-French heritage rings true when it comes to contrasts. Her father's Irish side makes her honest to her core, loyal, and unlike her father, slow to anger. However, once she hits that breaking point, watch out! It gives rise to a heart of a French lion. Just like her mother, she fights for what's right, refusing to admit defeat.

Rapid Response Character Summaries

<u>**Major Characters:**</u>

Dr. Joshtine Cordelia-Hastings, PhD (Cordy) – Lead Cyber Threat and Research Analyst, Former FBI Intelligence Analyst, MIT graduate with dual PhDs in computer science, and forensic jurisprudence and criminology.

Acting U.S. President Thomas James Harris, JD (Tom) – Vice president under Spendorf sworn in as acting president during Spendorf's recovery

Agent Braun Hastings – Commander for a Ghost Unit within the Joint Special Operations Command (JSOC), former FBI agent, negotiator, and SWAT commander, Cordy's fiancé

Special Agent Usher Hastings – Special Agent foreign affairs and FBI agent, former SWAT, Braun's brother

Chief Jackson – Former FBI Agent, Private Investigator, Braun, Usher, and Cordy's previous boss

General Rutoon – President Spendorf's past commanding officer in the U.S. Marine Corps, National Security Advisor, and trusted friend

U.S. President Isaac (Zac) Spendorf – Infected with Virus X and is near death

<u>**Secondary Characters:**</u>

Dr. Alex, MD, PhD – Head of Centers for Disease Control (CDC) Department of Virology

Dr. Quint Altari, PhD – Former Intelligence Agent, MIT graduate with PhD in computer science, Cordy's lead IT intelligence analyst

Agent Dun Bean – CIA Agent, code name Jelly Bean, working with General Rutoon

Russ Bracken – SWAT Team Leader of Federal Forces in Colorado, former Navy Seal Special Ops Explosive Breacher, served in Afghanistan, Cordy's past boyfriend

Dr. Bradley Brakinsky, MD, PhD Emergency Medicine – Medical Director of the Emergency Department at Holy Cross Hospital in Silver Spring, Maryland, Elizabeth's husband

Dr. Elizabeth (Liz) Brakinsky, PhD in Infectious Diseases – Secretary of Health and Human Services (HHS), Chairwoman of Rapid Response 7 Team (RR7)

Dr. Ryan Chugson, MD, PhD - Director of CDC, RR7 member

Ghim - North Korean astronaut on space station, heads up research team

Tip Granger – U.S. astronaut on space station

Agent Dr. Jacqueford Kelly, RN, DNP – Doctorate in Nursing, Nurse Practitioner, FBI, and RR7 member

Dr. Esthanne Jennings – Head of CDC Team creating Virus X Vaccine

Dr. Ivan Pendari, PhD – U.S. astronaut on spacecraft

Dr. Nat Ping, MD, PhD in Internal Medicine – Secretary of Health and Human Services (HHS), former Central Intelligence Agent (CIA) for counter-terrorism, and former Senate Foreign Relations Committee

Mordecai Ratinzky (Morty) – Russian astronaut on space station

Agent Loran Sloan – FBI Director and Braun's and Usher's boss

Joe Smith – Linda Smith-Tyler's half-brother, Rutoon's pawn, and not a Dr.

Linda Smith-Tyler – U.S. astronaut on spacecraft

Chester Tyler – Linda Smith-Tyler's son, School shooter

Maxwell Uliptos – U.S. pilot of spacecraft to International Space Station, first victim of Virus X

Guy Weimer – Secretary of Dept. of Homeland Security, RR7 member

Winston Willoughby – President's Chief of Staff

Carl Wyller – Secretary of Dept. of Defense (DoD), RR7 member

Officer Peggy Wyller – Police officer at Metropolitan Police Department 4th Division in Washington, D.C., Carl's wife

Abbreviations

AAA (Triple-A) – American Automobile Association

ASH – Assistant Secretary for Health

ASPA – Assistant Secretary of Public Affairs

BATT – Ballistic Armored Tactical Transport

B/P – Blood pressure

CDC – Centers for Disease Control and Prevention

CIA – Central Intelligence Agency

CMS – Centers of Medicare and Medicaid Services

DoD – Department of Defense

DHC – Department of Health Control

DHS – Department of Homeland Security

ED – Emergency Department

EMT – Emergency Medical Technician

FBI – Federal Bureau of Investigations

FDA – Food and Drug Association

FEMA – Federal Emergency Management Agency

FHTI - Future Hub Transit Inc

Ghost Unit – An elite mission unit for specialized tactics within JSOC

ID – Identification

IDI – Infectious Diseases & Immunity

IP address – A logical address assigned to each device to identify personal data

ISS – International Space Station

ICU – Intensive Care Unit

IV - Intravenous

IT - Information Technology

JLTV – Joint Light Tactical Vehicle

JSOC – Joint Special Operations Command

LCD – Liquid Crystal Display

LED – Light Emitting Diodes

LYA – Love you always

MD/Ph.D. – Doctor of Medicine/Doctor of Philosophy

MIT – Massachusetts Institute of Technology

MRSA – Methocillin-Resistant Staphlococcus Aureus

NASA – National Aeronautics and Space Administration

NCID – National Center for Infection Control

NIH – National Institutes of Health

NSA – National Security Agency

NVP – National Vaccine Program

NYSE – New York Stock Exchange

OPHEP – Office of Public Health & Emergency Preparedness

OGC – Office of General Counsel

OGHA – Office of Global Affairs

PE – Physical Education

RCV – Robotic Combat Vehicle

RN/DNP – Registered Nurse/Doctor of Nursing Practice/Nurse Practitioner

SOCOM – Marines Special Operations Command

STAT – Medical term from Latin word statim meaning immediately

STRATCOM – U.S. Strategic Command is one of eleven unified commands under the Department of Defense

SUV – Sports Utility Vehicle

SWAT – Special Weapons and Tactics

TOR – The Onion Router-a network that provides web privacy & hides IP addresses

U.S. – United States

WHO – World Health Organization

Washington, D.C. – Washington, District of Columbia

WW – Wild Woman

Table of Contents

Warning—Bio Attack

FBI Agent Dr. Joshtine Cordelia, known to most as Cordy, had enrolled in MIT at sixteen and earned dual PhDs in computer science and forensic jurisprudence and criminology. She had followed in her late father's career path and was now the FBI's lead analyst on cyber security. She knew risks hovered in plain sight. Most went undetected until disaster hit. Rumors of domestic and international terrorist attacks were on the rise, and each more deadly than the last.

It was 10 p.m. when Cordy had placed several encrypted files and a dossier of military secrets into her decrypter, translator, and analysis programs. It would take a few hours to run, so she headed for bed, hoping to catch some sleep.

As usual, that gnawing feeling grew with each passing hour until it roused Cordy out of bed and led her downstairs to brew a pot of java. *I know there's more in those files. What am I missing?* With a splash of cream added to her coffee, she took her favorite red Valentine mug to her office, opened her laptop, and logged into her darknet account. Two more files had been added to her search, which triggered alarm bells. "…a deadly agent worse than COVID-19 will strike the U.S. and sweep the globe…"

"What form will it take? Anthrax? Ebola? Or something worse?" Cordy muttered under her breath. "Who? When? Where? There must be some clues. I know it." Her mind jolted into overdrive as she thought of the millions of lives that could be lost. She dug deeper into the files.

For maximum security, Cordy worked all morning from her home when her wrist alarm vibrated, reminding her that she was due in the office in one hour. *Already? There is never enough time! I can't miss my meeting with Chief Jackson, and I can't stop my research.*

Being a control freak, she hated disorder and being uninformed. She clenched her fists as her mind spun, bouncing from one dilemma to another. *I wonder what the chief wants that's so urgent. Why won't Jackson just tell me what's on his mind? Does it have anything to do with this threat? Can we stop an attack?*

Retired FBI Agent Chief Jackson had mastered his career with extensive guidance by Cordy's father, Josh. Now Jackson was her mentor, ex-boss, and a private investigator. He also shared his office building with Cordy and had called her asking for 'a huge favor—one that he couldn't divulge except in person.' She had already postponed the appointment once, but he wouldn't have asked if it wasn't urgent. Cordy sent a quick text message: "Chief, I'll be there soon. Have you heard from Braun?"

Cordy compiled her latest findings without waiting for a reply and scanned the reports again. Fear clutched her throat—*millions, it said millions.* She still didn't know the type of bio-attack—by whom, how, when, and where remained a mystery. *It's time to brief U.S. President Isaac Spendorf. We have to confront this head-on.*

Cordy took measures to ensure the security of her updates to her boss. She transferred data from her protected web files to her TOR account, which concealed users' identities and online activity from surveillance and traffic analysis. Two minutes after disconnecting, she sent the data to ping President Spendorf.

Cordy sent one last text to her fiancé, Braun Hastings, a Commander for a Ghost Unit within the Joint Special Operations Command, known by most as JSOC, on a special assignment for the president. A sparkle from her diamond ring caught her eye as she logged off the darknet.

She smiled as she recalled last Friday night. *After four years, it happened right here. As I sat at my desk in disbelief, Braun finally committed, knelt on one knee, looked up at me, and asked, 'Will you marry me?'* He leaned closer and kissed her. If it were any indication of their life together, she welcomed it. Cordy hardly remembered what she had said, but couldn't wait to become his wife. *That was three days ago, and I haven't heard from him since. Why hasn't he called?*

They hadn't set a wedding date yet, and now wasn't the time to plan, but Cordy hoped to tie the knot soon. She'd even picked up a Bride's Magazine on her last trip to the store. She had barely perused the journal yet. *No time. Maybe next week, but every wedding gown seemed too frilly, too lacy, or just not her style.*

She checked her watch and groaned, *Focus, Cordy. I need to be at the office in 30 minutes.* Shoving her thoughts of Braun out of her mind, Cordy hurried upstairs to take a hot shower. Running late, she didn't bother to dry her hair, quickly dressed, and headed to work. Her mind was still racing like a cat chasing a laser light, trying to grasp the elusive news.

Tiny Deadly Treasure

Astronaut Maxwell Uliptos had just unstrapped himself from his sleeping bag attached to the wall of the International Space Station (ISS), which was located 240 miles above the Earth. Maxwell was thrilled to be returning home today. As he moved through the command center, he almost collided with Tip Granger, the station's engineer. He noticed that several computer parts were floating around, held by tethers. Curious, he asked, "What is going on now?"

"Good morning, Max. Unfortunately, our communication system crashed before today's launch deadline," Tip explained.

Max muttered, "This is just great! Another delay—I wish I had never piloted this trip. It's been nothing but one fiasco after another, starting before we even left Earth. I don't want to complain, but we were supposed to be here for only three days. It's been a month now, and to top it off, we can't even communicate with Houston. What else could go wrong?"

Tip didn't look up from the torn-apart communication center. "I know you're anxious to leave, and have worked all night on the latest glitch, but I'm making progress. I hope to reach NASA soon."

"Thanks. I appreciate all your help, but my son's wedding is in two days, and I can't miss it." Max moved closer. "Anything I can do to help?" Max grabbed the flashlight Tip handed him.

"Over here." Tip pointed to where he needed the light focused.

Max held the beam steady and spoke with a hint of despair. "I'm not sure what's bothering me. I used to love this job. Going from 3-G to 0-G was exhilarating, like a peaceful glide through space. But this trip is different. It feels like I'm on a never-ending rollercoaster ride. I'm not a teenager seeking thrills anymore. I have responsibilities back on Earth. Don't get me wrong, you're a great team, but I can't bear being confined in this space for much longer."

"I understand your concern, but it's important to remain calm," Tip spoke in his usual relaxed Texan drawl. "The ISS is aging with every passing day. I have already fixed this equipment three times since we arrived here six months ago, and I can fix it again. Give me the torch, and you can grab your morning coffee."

"I'm sorry," Max said as he handed the flashlight to Tip. "I'm not the best company today, feeling a bit on edge. I guess that comes with marrying off your only son."

"Don't worry, we'll get you home," Tip reassured Max. "The rest of your team, Ivan and Linda, are doing well."

"Yeah, that's because Ivan is a research biologist and loves every minute of working with Ghim. They couldn't wait to test the COVID-19 samples the National Institute of Health sent up with us."

Astronaut Ghim, head of the ISS research team, was a brilliant scientist from North Korea. Max recalled the first words Ghim said when he met Ivan: "Dr. Pendari, your fame precedes you. I'm interested in splitting DNA strands, too. Can you share your secret?"

Ivan had laughed. "Sure. Let's visit the lab, and you can show me your setup. Maybe you have some ideas on modifying the chains to prevent a virus from penetrating cells."

Ivan and Ghim had been inseparable ever since, as they tested and devised new research on numerous proteins, enzymes, bacteria, and viruses. After the last pandemic, NASA assigned Ghim to research new treatments for viral diseases.

Ghim came to the door with panic written on his face. "Has anyone seen that little red satin box? The one Morty's fiancé sent as a surprise present. Morty let me borrow it yesterday."

Tip shook his head. "That's not my area, and you know Morty won't go anywhere near the lab."

Ghim blew out a deep breath. "You're right. It has to be here somewhere. Where did I put it?"

Linda Smith-Tyler was the youngest and the only female on board. She was a Physical Education teacher who took two years off to train as an astronaut. This was her first trip to outer space. She was already up and exercising in the makeshift gym.

Max, the oldest and most experienced astronaut aboard the ISS, took his role as pilot seriously and had to get the team back to Earth safely. "I am proud of the team as we've managed one crisis after another, but I told NASA this is my last trip."

"We're glad you came, and we needed those supplies." Tip soldered two more wires together. "And every delay was legit. First, tropical storm Wendellyn made it impossible to land back on Earth as scheduled. Then, a coolant leak, followed by a telemetry data latency. But don't worry. I'm going to fix this latest glitch in the communication center." He tried the internet phone system, "Houston, this is Tip Granger on the ISS. Can you hear me now?"

Static came across the speaker, and a tinny voice answered, "Barely, I still think we should postpone another day."

Max clenched his fists. "Please, we can't delay! I will miss my son's wedding, and my new grandson will be there. He was born two days after we left for the ISS. We have to leave today. We can still make the timeline."

Tip kept testing with the NASA command station, assuring they could still make the launch window. He made a few more tweaks, placed the equipment back into the cabinet, and turned to Max, "The computer's fixed, and we might have approval from NASA to send you back home if you can get your team loaded within the hour, but you will only have a 15-minute window to launch today, so you better get going."

"Thanks, Tip." Max clapped his hands to get his team's attention. "Ivan, Linda, it's time to load. We must leave soon." He waited for a heartbeat, and with no response, he prodded again, "Ivan, change out of that hazmat suit and get your gear."

Ghim called from the lab, "We did it! We split a viral DNA. Did you know we grew MRSA without gravity, and it's three times more potent than a similar sample grown in Texas? I also want to split the COVID-19 samples. I wonder if it will respond the same way."

Mentioning Texas had Tip's attention. He chuckled. "It's a Good thing you reminded Ivan he's leaving. Knowing how wrapped up those two get when experimenting, they would be in the lab for hours."

The walls on the ISS were thin, and Ghim quipped, "Don't laugh. I'm sure we can find a cure."

Linda was a fanatic about exercising. She pedaled the stationary bike and glanced up at Ghim's comment. "Maybe you can also find a cure for Max." She grinned at her partner. "Let's face it. You're stressed out, gaining weight, and could use some exercise. Did you know that spending time in space causes the body to lose 1% calcium each month? You want to walk down the aisle at your son's wedding, right?"

Max rolled his eyes. "I'll get enough exercise playing golf after I retire. Come on. Tip's making a final check with NASA. I hope it's a go this time."

Tip smiled, "It looks like we have a deadline to meet—Gramps is looking forward to holding his grandson."

Despite the seriousness of their situation, Max couldn't help but chuckle.

Tip asked Ghim, "Did you find that box you were looking for?"

"Not yet, but I'm still looking."

All the chatter woke Russian astronaut Mordecai Ratinzky, nicknamed Morty, and he climbed from the sleeping bag hanging from the wall to join the rest of the team. He was the final member of the ISS crew and greeted everyone with a friendly, "Good morning, or evening if it's Moscow time. I've enjoyed your visit for the past few weeks, and I'm sorry to see you leave, but all good things must end."

"You miss your fiancé," Tip said. "I can tell when you're lamenting someone's departure and wishing it were you heading home."

"Yeah, but I talked to Anya last night." Max noticed Morty running his fingers over an ornate gold chain wrapped around his neck. It had been a surprise gift from his fiancé. She had tucked it into his duffle, and Morty found it inside a red satin box after boarding the ISS. Morty smiled. "I'll be home for Christmas. What's the weather like at Kennedy Space Center?"

"We're waiting for NASA to give us the green light," Tip checked his instruments, "but it looks like a go from here."

Linda was already at the hatch with her gear and nearly collided with Ivan, who nudged his duffle toward the opening.

Morty secured his bag of coffee. "Let me help."

"Thanks," Linda and Ivan boarded the spacecraft and grabbed the bags as Morty passed them through the opening. Linda secured the supplies.

Ivan buckled up, put on his headphones, and warned, "We're nearing the launch window."

Ivan's warning came across ISS' speakers.

Tip turned to Max. "You should leave within the next ten minutes. The next orbit will take 92 minutes, and the Earth's rotation will misalign your landing site if you wait much longer. We won't have another chance until tomorrow."

Max headed for the exit. "Can't wait. I'm not missing the wedding."

Tip and Ghim gathered around the hatch door to bid their farewell. Morty joined the ISS team and handed Ghim the satin box. "Don't forget this?"

Ghim frowned, "Where did you find that? Oh, never mind, here," Ghim handed the box to Max, the last astronaut to board the spacecraft. Ghim added, "This is—"

"Hurry, Max!" Ivan Pendari was already at the controls. "We just received the undocking command from Houston."

"Thanks." Max waved goodbye, moved through the hatch, and carefully secured the red box into a storage net attached to the wall.

After fastening their seatbelts, the crew closed the hatch and undocked before the initial departure burn propelled them into space. The crew contacted Houston, worked through the departure checklist, and followed commands. Ninety minutes later, the shuttle went through a 44-second blast, sending them into Earth's orbit. Everything proceeded according to plan.

The rocket was in a radio blackout, so Max and Ivan chose to relax and share their final meal. Max asked Linda, "Would you like to join us for dinner?"

"No, thanks, I'm not hungry." Linda kept pedaling the bike. "I want to work out before landing."

Ivan asked, "What's in the red box?"

"We've been so busy, I forgot about it." Max retrieved the gift from the net. "I wonder what's inside."

Ivan leaned forward for a closer look. "Open it and find out."

Curious, Max removed a sticker with fine print, which was too small for him to read, opened the box, and peered inside. "I think it's empty!" He covered the opening with his hand and shook it vigorously. *Nothing.* "Why would Ghim give us an empty box?"

Ivan took the item from Max's hand and examined it. He lifted an inner gray sponge cushion and wrinkled his nose. "It smells like damp jeans—reminds me of a fungus." He handed the package back to Max. "It's a nice box, the same color as that snappy silk necktie your daughter bought for you last Father's Day. You look handsome when you wear it."

"A box isn't handsome." Max pushed the cushion back inside and closed the lid.

Ivan nearly choked on his coffee. "I didn't say the box was handsome. I was talking about you in that tie you always wear, but the box is pretty."

"Who wants an empty box, no matter how pretty?" Max shoved it back into the storage net.

Ivan stretched. "Are you sure that box was for us, or was it for NASA?"

Max shrugged his shoulders. "I don't remember what Ghim said. Maybe Tip sent it to NASA as a joke, and Ghim didn't understand. You remember how upset Tip was with Houston after working all night on that communication center, and NASA wanted to postpone the return once more."

"Yeah, some joke, but it's not our problem. Leave it on the wall, and if NASA wants it, they can have it." Ivan pawed through the desserts. "Want a brownie or cheesecake?"

"Dessert?" He glanced over the dining area's partial wall at Linda, still slaving away on the bike. "Why not? I'll have a brownie. Leave the cheesecake for Linda. It's her favorite." They finished eating before locking the nose cone and engaging in the final Earth's reentry routine.

When they landed, Max was the first to exit the spacecraft. He was late for his son's wedding rehearsal in Washington, D.C., and he made no mention of the little red satin box in his final report, nor did NASA inquire about it during their debriefing.

* * *

After the rocket's journey, a crew chemically washed down the interior to prepare it for reuse. They also transported the forgotten box through the lock, ready for incineration.

Yoli Guntberg, the youngest member of the crew, expected another tedious cleanup task that would last all night. However, he was surprised to see a pretty red satin box among the debris. When he made sure no one was looking, he sneaked a peek and found that it was empty. The box was the perfect size to hold the delicate gold chain necklace he had bought for his wife's birthday. He quickly pocketed it and set the trash ablaze.

At the end of his shift, Yoli retrieved his car keys from his jeans and walked to his beat-up Ford. His was the last car in the secured, dimly lit parking lot. The only sound was the flickering of the lamppost, and he realized there were no chirping crickets or croaking bullfrogs from the nearby swamp.

Yoli got into his car and hoped it would start. It had stalled at every stoplight on his way to work, and payday wasn't until tomorrow. Jamming the key into the ignition, he flicked his wrist to start the engine. "Come on, baby. Don't let me down." *Not even a click.*

Yoli tried again with the same result. He reached under the dashboard, yanked the release latch, pulled a small flashlight from the glove compartment, and climbed back out of the car. Grumbling, he lifted the car's hood, flicked on the torch, and studied the engine.

Nearby footsteps paused. Yoli peered over the hood and saw a stranger standing on the sidewalk, watching him. *Where did he come from? How did he pass security? I was the last to leave work.*

The stranger stepped forward. "Working late?"

"Something like that." Yoli swung the beam from his light across the stranger's face. His spine tingled, and he backed away in defense against the unknown man. For some reason, he felt unaccountably threatened by the odd sight before him.

The man was sizable, nearly 6 feet tall, and had 50 pounds on Yoli, who was slight in build. The guy was dressed all in black, except for a white box with a red Jelly Belly logo sticking out of his front shirt pocket. He wore gloves and a mask, only revealing his eyes— bloodshot orbs that pierced the darkness. He stared without blinking and halted at the rear of Yoli's back bumper. "Car trouble?"

Yoli nodded, sweat breaking out across his forehead and armpits. He wanted desperately to run. *Is this guy on drugs? Does he plan to rob me? He looks like he's from outer space.* Other than the flashlight, Yoli had no weapon to protect himself.

The stranger locked those blank, cold eyes on Yoli as he walked toward him. Finally, the man asked, "You make a living cleaning up that trash?"

Yoli's gut clenched, burning bile in the back of his throat. "Trash? Oh, you mean my job. It's a paycheck." His heart beat wildly as fear raced through him. Yoli glanced around for an exit. When none was apparent, his trembling hand reached into his pocket to pull out his cell phone. His wedding ring caught on a loose thread, so he tugged harder, scattering his cell phone and the red box to the ground.

The stranger glanced down. "I wondered where that box went."

"Why is it important? The box is empty!" Yoli noted fury in those eyes.

"You think it's empty?" The stranger roared. "It's filled with evil and belongs to my boss, Dr. Joe Smith. I'm here to take it back."

"Take it!" Yoli bolted for the car door, hoping to lock himself inside.

Strong fingers caught Yoli around the throat. "This takes care of the final witness," were the last words Yoli heard before his neck snapped.

Braun Is Missing

Cordy was driving her 2022 silver Lexus to work when she got a flat tire on northbound Interstate 25, just before Fort Collins. This college town in northern Colorado was always bustling with traffic, so getting to the exit from the middle lane required some finesse. She signaled to change lanes, but four cars honked at her, and one driver even gave her the finger before a kind soul let her move to the right.

Not wanting to wait for roadside service, Cordy grabbed an elastic band from her purse and flipped down the visor's mirror. She scooped her wet, shoulder-length, strawberry-blonde hair into a ponytail, opened the trunk, and set to work. Though it wasn't the first time she'd changed a flat, Cordy's temper flared up when she saw grease on her favorite cream-colored suit.

She limped along on the spare tire at fifty mph and noticed the gas-low indicator light. *How long has that been on?* As it turned out, it had been ignored for too long. She ran out of gas as she turned onto the East Prospect Road exit. Disgusted, Cordy grabbed her cell phone to summon AAA, after all. That's when she noticed a new message from Chief Jackson. *He must have called while I changed that blasted tire.*

She hit replay, "Cordy, pick up." Jackson sounded distressed. There was a pause. "Have you seen Braun lately? I need to talk to you ASAP! Call me as soon as you get this message. It's a matter of life and death—his life."

Braun's life? I wondered why he hadn't called. I should have listened to my gut. She speed-dialed the chief, but it went directly to voicemail. She tried again, and when Jackson didn't answer, she left a message, and called AAA.

The chief returned the call while she was conversing with an auto repair service attendant. By the time she interrupted that call, she had disconnected both parties.

Fifteen minutes passed before a mechanic arrived with a container holding a gallon of gas, enough for her to get to a station, fill her tank, and repair her flat tire.

Cordy and the chief played phone tag for another twenty minutes. She forgot all formalities when she finally reached Jackson. "What happened to Braun? You sounded upset. Is he in danger?"

"Is your cell phone safe?" Jackson asked.

Cordy's heart skipped a beat. "Yes, and all my texts are encrypted. What aren't you telling me?"

"Not over the phone," Jackson said. "Meet me at noon at the same place we had lunch last week, and I'll tell you all about it."

"Can't you tell me—"

"Don't call back on this line. It's not safe!" Jackson disconnected.

It took longer than she planned to repair her flat tire, so it was already 12:25 p.m. when she drove into the parking garage across the street from Jack's Seafood Bar & Grill. She glanced around the walls, searching for security cameras—a survival instinct that had become a habit. She spied Chief Jackson, heading back to the parking lot as she sprinted down the stairs. "Chief, wait up."

Jackson met her at the entrance. "What took you so long? I already ate lunch."

"Sorry, I'm late." Cordy rushed on, "What happened to Braun?"

Jackson ran a hand through his ebony hair streaked with silver at the temples. She recognized the deep concern in his eyes—the color of fine whiskey flashed a glint of gold as he, too, glanced around the parking lot. As usual, he came straight to the point, but whispered as if someone was listening in the shadows, "Cordy, Braun is wanted by Homeland Security."

"What for?" The words caught in her throat.

"Shh," Jackson held his finger to his lips. "I don't know the specifics, but are you sure you haven't heard from him?"

"Not since last Friday," Cordy whispered.

"How was he?"

"Terrific!" Cordy exclaimed, holding up her left hand. "Braun even got on his knees to propose."

"It's about time Braun wised up." Jackson's brief smile didn't reach his eyes, but he seemed happy for her.

Then she remembered an incident just before he left her house. "Wait, now that you mention it, he got a phone call and stormed away like a lightning bolt with thunder at his heels about to erupt. I should have known then that something terrible was in the air."

"Who called?" Jackson asked.

Once again, Cordy felt in the dark. "I wish I knew. He refused to tell me, but he was pissed off."

"I'm afraid he's gone underground," Jackson warned. "This is serious business and very dangerous. If he's involved in what I think he is—"

"Involved in what?" Cordy asked, "Is this another undercover case?"

"Not undercover. I said underground." Jackson glanced over his shoulder. "If this backfires, he will need to change his identity and give up everything—even you."

"Even me?" Light captured a glint across her diamond as her hand flew over her mouth, covering a gasp. "He wouldn't." Butterflies took flight in her gut. "So I'll ask again, what aren't you telling me?"

"He found an enemy's mole inside President Spendorf's intelligence team," Jackson said.

"Who?" Faces flashed through Cordy's mind as she ran through a list of Zac's closest associates. None triggered an alert.

"Braun takes his work seriously enough that he wouldn't tell even me, so all I know is that it is someone high up the command, and if the wrong side catches him, they'll kill him," Jackson said.

"Braun will never give up without a fight." Cordy knew that for a fact.

"That's what worries me." Jackson handed her a manila file folder. "Knowing Braun, he'll go after that person alone without our help."

"Braun will protect the president with his life." Cordy saw the flash of gold in Jackson's eyes become brighter. "Braun called you in to help him, didn't he? Then he disappeared."

Jackson nodded. "Dr. Trent from CDC was in Denver for a conference, and Braun was to meet him while he was in town. Braun never showed, but someone got wind of the meeting and shot Trent. Flight for Life flew him to St. Anthony's Hospital. Trent's still in a coma in ICU."

Cordy frowned. "Why would anyone shoot a CDC doctor?" Then she remembered the encrypted warning she had sent to Zac. *Biohazard and CDC? Could they be connected?* "It's happening. The bioterrorist has launched his weapon, but when?"

"I don't know, but Braun's been missing for over 48 hours," Jackson said. "Are you sure you haven't heard from him?"

Her heartbeat shifted into high gear. "No, I—"

It was all she managed to say before Jackson stumbled and a loud shot blasted. Something slammed into the side of her head. She hit the floor, and everything went dark.

* * *

When Cordy regained consciousness, she was lying behind a dumpster on the ground floor of the parking lot. *What happened?* Papers lay scattered over the ground like someone had tossed them from the file, but there was no sign of the manila folder. *What else is missing? Nothing makes any sense.*

She gently touched her blossoming blackened left eye. A full-blown headache crashed over her. This day had been a doozy. Too bad she couldn't remember much about the past few hours. Unfocused thoughts rushed through her fuzzy mind—*something about Braun and Chief Jackson and a bioterrorism attack on the U.S.* She tried to recall what led her to this place. *Oh, right, Chief Jackson called.*

It was cloudy, rainstorms brewing, and getting darker by the moment. The place seemed deserted. A glance at her watch told Cordy why. It was 6:10 p.m. Hell's hammers beat an erratic rhythm in her head. Her grazed hands stung as she crawled to her knees, managed to stand, and staggered back to where she had met Chief Jackson four hours ago. *Did someone shoot the chief and then knock me out?* She couldn't remember.

Everything happened too fast. Cordy's brain wouldn't focus. Searching for clues, she found blotches of blood pooled on the cement at the front entrance to the garage. Jackson's car was parked where he left it. *Braun's missing, and now, so is the chief. She remembered him saying that Homeland Security was hunting down Braun or something like that. I had better call Homeland's director and find out why. Guy*

Weimer will tell me. Maybe I better check with President Spendorf first and keep Jackson's warning about Braun locked inside until I have more facts. But now, she needed to report this event.

Her fingers trembled, and she misdialed twice before she reached 911. It seemed like forever for the police and investigative team to arrive. While she waited, she perused the scattered papers and gleaned that the chief planned to rendezvous with Braun's brother, FBI Agent Usher Hastings, at 7:00 p.m. that evening. She doubted the chief would show, but maybe Usher knew where to find Braun. The brothers were close and tended to keep in touch with each other. It was her only hope at the moment.

She rechecked her watch and realized it had only been three minutes before the sirens sounded in the distance. Flashing blue and red lights rounded the corner and turned into the parking lot. An ambulance followed the patrol cruiser.

Two officers climbed from the car. The driver asked, "What happened?"

Cordy tried to sort out the details. "I met Chief Jackson early this afternoon. I heard a shot, and then someone slugged me, and I woke up behind that dumpster. Chief Jackson is missing, and there are blood spots." She pointed to the ground. "I think they are his."

A paramedic tried to examine her, but it wasn't her main focus. "I'm fine!"

"Are you refusing care?" the paramedic asked. "You said you've been unconscious for a few hours. That's not fine."

"I have too much to do."

"Let me at least get your vitals." The paramedic placed a temp probe over her forehead. "You may have a head injury." He shined a light across her eyes. "Pupils are equal and reactive."

Cordy pulled up her sleeve and let him take her blood pressure, pulse, and pulse ox. "I really am okay," Cordy insisted. "I promise if I have any symptoms, I'll report to the emergency department ASAP."

"If you say so, but you'll have to sign this waiver releasing us from—"

Cordy snatched the pen from his hand. "Where do I sign?" She nearly scribbled over his finger when he pointed to the signature line. "I'm sorry. I know you mean well, but this is important, too."

Ultimately, the paramedic offered an ice bag for her eye and handed her a list of head injury symptoms. "Read this, and if you develop any of these, get medical help immediately."

"I will do that. Thank you. The ice bag feels wonderful on my eye." Cordy folded the paper and stuffed it into her pocket. She turned toward the police officer, who stood beside her, waiting to ask questions. "I am fine. I need to find Chief Jackson."

After 50 minutes of questions, the police officer said, "Go home, Agent Cordelia, and rest. We'll contact you if we have further questions."

"Thanks for your concern." Cordy's legs wobbled, and her heart thumped, echoing through her head with each beat. She hoped to move out from under his scrutiny before her shakes took over completely. She planned to take two aspirins and return to work but needed to get off her feet, so she headed for her car. *Where are you, Braun? And where is Chief Jackson? What's going on?*

Usher Hastings drummed his fingers on the steering wheel while waiting for Chief Jackson. The pungent odor of rotting rubbish in a nearby dumpster made the time crawl. *Jackson is half an hour late. That's unusual for the meticulous man. What's keeping him?*

Checking the latest news, Usher turned on the radio while he waited. "...Astronaut Maxwell Uliptos has died. He was found unconscious in his apartment and rushed to the hospital yesterday afternoon. Cause of death is pending following an autopsy..."

Headlights flashed in his rearview mirror. *It's about time Jackson got here.* Usher switched off the radio. Instead of the chief's car, a silver Lexus came over the rise into the parking lot and pulled in next to him. He recognized his brother's fiancé getting out of the car, and felt his instincts jump into high alert.

"Cordy?" Usher's gut told him something was wrong. His brain told him, *Prepare for the worst.* He opened his car door, swung his long legs over the lower frame's edge until his feet touched the ground, and unfolded from his metallic-blue Toyota GR Supra Sports Coupe.

Cordy dashed to his side. "Have you heard from Braun?"

Usher asked at the same time, "Where's Chief Jackson?" Then, he took a closer look at Cordy. One blue eye stared at him. The other eye was swollen, puffy, and purple. "What happened to you?"

* * *

"Long story." A dull roar sounded in her head and echoed in the distance. She glanced toward his car and turned in a full circle, checking if they had company.

A motorcycle roared over the hill and nearly slammed into Usher's rear bumper. Braun shouted, "Get down. Van's coming in hot."

Relief flooded through Cordy's frantic brain. "Braun, thank God!" Without heeding Braun's warning, Cordy headed toward him. "Where have you been?"

Braun revved his motorcycle. "Not now."

Cordy persisted, "Why is Homeland Security—"

"They found me," Braun shouted. "Stall them!"

Usher shoved Cordy toward the car. "Gun's in the trunk!" He pressed his key fob, and the trunk popped open.

"Why do I need a gun?" Hearing another vehicle approaching, she darted behind Usher's car.

A black van swerved around the corner with firearms protruding through the open windows. Cordy snatched Usher's sniper rifle. She preferred a pistol or semi-automatic revolver, *but no, he packed a rifle* flitted through her mind as she did a quick calculation. *My luck, another dumpster.*

"LYA," Braun shouted. "Stay safe!"

Love you always. It was Braun's way of letting her know his feelings for her. Fear meshed with a deep tenderness, knowing that he cared.

"Cordy, get behind that trash bin and stay down." Braun skidded his bike toward Usher. "Hop on. We'll lure them away. Let's get out of here."

Usher tossed his keys toward Cordy. "Take my car. It's faster than yours."

She caught them in midair.

Usher didn't wait for an answer, drew his revolver, and hopped on the back of Braun's motorcycle. "Who are we running from?" He nearly lost his balance as Braun pulled back into the middle of the parking lot in front of an oncoming black van with its lights off.

Cordy didn't hear Braun's reply. She raced around the car and dove behind the metal trash container. Flipping down the cover, she heaved the bulky rifle onto the surface, using it as a support, and chambered the first five armor-piercing ammunition rounds. She adjusted the scope, putting the crosshairs on a man behind a gun protruding from the van's rear window. The butt of the rifle fit snugly against her shoulder as she settled in behind it.

Braun's motorcycle zigzagged ahead of the van, drawing gunfire from both sides of the vehicle. Cordy pulled the trigger, blasting bullets in an arc across the van's rear. The vehicle lurched to the right and came to a stop. Both front doors swung open, and two men dove out. One rolled, slowly rose, and he limped toward the curb. The other's body flew through the air as the van exploded.

A chunk of metal from the dumpster flew toward Cordy, followed by a sound like bees flying past. She couldn't tell where the shot came from. A revolver had landed on the ground near the blazing van. *Maybe it went off on impact.*

Her shoulder ached from the rifle's recoil, but her training had taken over—deciding on a course of action, she followed through without conscious thought.

Braun's motorcycle was no longer in sight. Cordy heard a siren in the distance. She wanted to find Braun and Usher and didn't want to be around when the police arrived, but she had to know who these men were and why they pursued Braun.

The limping man dropped to his knees at his partner's side. She didn't think he had a gun, but better to be safe. "Put your hands up."

One man lifted his hands into the air. "Don't shoot. I'm not armed. I'm only the driver." The other man lay prone on the ground in a pool of blood.

"What about him?" Cordy moved from behind the dumpster with her rifle aimed at the driver.

"I think he's dead." The man slowly turned toward Cordy. "Honest. I don't have a gun."

Cordy inched her way closer. "Who are you?"

"J…Jake."

"How many were in the van?" Cordy asked.

"Four. All dead, but for me," Jake said.

"Who's your boss?"

"Before I answer any more questions, I want a doc and a lawyer. I know my rights," Jake said.

The siren drowned out her next comment as the police stopped at a distance. An officer aimed his gun at her. "Drop the weapon."

"Don't shoot. I'm FBI Agent Joshtine Cordelia." She lowered her rifle. "Let me get my creds." Cordy held up her hands and slowly reached into her pants pocket. Her fingers pulled out a leather wallet, and she showed her ID to the officer. She read the man's name tag. "Officer Greene, I want the Evidence Response Team called for this case."

Flames and dark black smoke billowed thick clouds from the van's engine as the wind whipped up. The officer's partner called the fire department and secured the scene until ERT arrived.

"Okay." Greene turned toward Jake, who still held his hands over his head. "On the ground, spread eagle." The officer moved toward the pale-faced man with sweat dappled across his forehead and cuffed him. "We're taking you downtown."

The man obeyed and repeated, "I want a lawyer and a doctor."

"Duly noted." The officer patted him down and motioned for Jake to rise.

Jake limped toward the police cruiser. Once inside the squad car, Officer Greene pulled a spiral notebook and pen from his pocket. "What happened here?"

Cordy still wanted to follow Braun and Usher. Something terrible was going on, and she was again in the dark, but she had no choice and resigned herself to answering the officer's questions.

"Jake drove that van filled with assassins into the lot. They opened fire on two men on a motorcycle. That's when I got involved in the shooting." Cordy avoided bringing Braun and Usher by name into her conversation with the police—knowing Braun had indeed gone underground. Why? She didn't know.

When the officer asked, "Who were the two men on the motorcycle?" Cordy said, "Ask Jake who they were targeting and why."

Jake answered, "I told you that I want a lawyer."

After another 40 minutes of questions, Cordy was free to go home. It would be another long, sleepless night.

Witness from Afar

At the same time Cordy met Usher, Jake's boss, Dr. Joe Smith, was heading across Fort Collins with his nephew, Chester Tyler.

"Thanks for the lift. You can keep the Jelly Bellys. I got them from a friend, but they're not my favorite." Smith stepped out of Chester's car, waved, and climbed the stairs to a nearby restaurant. Joe Smith wasn't his real name, but it was the name he'd given the receptionist when he'd made the reservation. Alone in a secluded booth, Smith sipped cognac while thumbing through Facebook, or at least, that's what he hoped it would look like to anyone around him. He felt fine only an hour ago, but now he coughed intermittently and couldn't quench a tickle caught in the back of his throat.

The waiter approached in his crisp, starched, white uniform. "Will there be anything else, sir?"

"No, I have a conference call soon. I don't want to be bothered." Smith turned his face into his shoulder as he coughed once again. "I'll summon you if I need anything."

"As you wish." The waiter took his leave.

Smith opened a specially designed app on his phone. It was like a wide-range Zoom program that allowed him to communicate with others while getting an overview of their surroundings. He watched in fascination as a black van swerved after a man in a black leather jacket riding a Kawasaki Ninja H2R. The motorcycle skidded left and then right. The driver sure knew how to handle that hellcat on two wheels. Hopefully, Jake could keep up, but the van's driver seemed to be losing ground.

The Ninja took a sharp right and went up a hill. The van couldn't make the tight corner, and the front camera lost sight of the motorcycle.

"Come on, Jake. Follow him!" Smith let slip from his lips as he took a deep breath. He quickly scanned the room to see if he'd attracted any attention, but no one seemed to notice his outburst. *I can't wait to leave this cursed place—not enough air.* He pulled a hanky from his pocket, and a red satin box tumbled to the floor.

The van made a two-hundred-seventy-degree turn and drove up the hill into a semi-deserted parking lot, where Smith caught sight of the Ninja as a second man hopped aboard behind his target, Braun Hastings.

Where did he come from? Smith wiped the sweat from his brow and unmuted his speaker, "Jake, what's happening?"

"Don't know," Jake said. "Do you want to go ahead with the plan?"

"Kill them both if you have to," Smith ordered in a loud whisper that he hoped no one around him would hear.

The camera inside the van showed two men in the back seat and the one on the front passenger's side lowering their windows. They shoved revolvers through the openings and fired toward the Ninja. Several blasts came from somewhere to the van's left.

Jake ducked and swung the van to the right. The inside camera showed an active sniper in the passenger's seat, but both men in the back appeared dead.

Smith swore as he adjusted another camera mounted on the van's rear. It swung toward the dumpster in time to see a lean, strawberry-blonde-haired woman with a rifle. He gave orders to Jake, "Everyone, bail! You have five seconds before I detonate the van and destroy the evidence."

Two men ditched the van as it exploded, but only Jake survived the blast. It appeared that the Ninja got away. Smith allowed the cognac to burn as he downed the drink. Memorizing every feature of the woman, he'd get his revenge, one way, or another. "Waiter, check, please."

Epidemic Spreading

Cordy was shocked to find another flat tire, likely caused by a stray bullet. Thankfully, Officer Greene helped her change the tire before leaving the scene. At this rate, she would need to get another spare. She could have taken Usher's car, but arranged to tow it to his house.

There was no sign of Braun or Usher, so she headed home. She flipped on the radio during her drive, "…Astronaut Maxwell Uliptos has died." Having already heard that, she changed stations. "…health experts warn this epidemic could be the most deadly yet, feared to be a viral mutation."

Cordy pressed the scan button on the radio to listen to news updates from various stations, hoping to hear some good news. Instead, she heard more about the virus, "…D.C., confirmed 268 more cases—doubling overnight." "…112 deaths over three days. Half of the cases occurred within 12 hours of exposure." "The most recent flu/COVID-19 vaccine does not protect against this disease." "So far, there were more than 600 cases of this virus, while there were only 128 cases of COVID during the same period. If this spreads as rampant as COVID-19, it could claim thirty-five million lives worldwide."

A wave of panic consumed Cordy. *Could this be the very terrorist attack she had been meticulously researching? Was this the onset of a biowarfare-induced pandemic, far deadlier than my worst predictions?* The radio droned on in the background, its messages of caution and crisis blending into a cacophony of fear, "…shortness of breath, fever, a dry cough, or a headache, notify your doctor immediately." "The president is taking every precaution to avoid another crisis." "We repeat, all Washington, D.C., Maryland, and Virginia schools and non-essential businesses are closed. That includes restaurants and bars. Stay tuned for continued updates."

Cordy turned off the radio and called Braun's disposable cell phone. The number would only be active for another four hours, but it went straight to his voicemail. Cordy disconnected and texted, "Braun, where are you? I hope you've gone underground to track who is behind this viral outbreak because it's happening. According to my latest update, violent outbursts will be next. No one has linked the disease to bioterrorism, but they will soon. The Capitol is already in crisis. Call me! LYA."

Her mind raced as she pulled into her garage. *How far has the virus infiltrated? Has it reached the White House? Is the president in jeopardy? Has it spread outside the U.S.? How will it affect the healthcare system? What about the economy? We're still reeling from massive shutdowns during COVID-19.* There were too many questions for so late at night—no, so early in the morning. It was after midnight.

The message light on her home office phone flashed a bright orange glow. Cordy hit replay. "It's Braun. Usher is with me. We're heading for D.C. Check-in with Agent Kelly. She's working with the National Center for Infectious Diseases. As usual, her medical skills are her greatest asset."

The message was two hours old. Braun was probably on a red-eye flight when she tried to call his cell. Cordy wanted to know he was safe, but she could not track him as usual. *This has to change. Indeed, there must be some way I can keep in touch.* With her IT skills, she would find a way to keep closer tabs on her fiancé.

Agent Dr. Jacqueford Kelly, a seasoned Nurse Practitioner, was like a niece to Chief Jackson, and Cordy had previously worked with her. It's nearly 5 a.m. on the East Coast, so Cordy called—her mind in turmoil. *Should I tell her about Chief Jackson? What would I say? I don't have a clue where he—*

"This is Agent Kelly. How may I help you?"

"Hi, it's Cordy."

"Good to hear your voice. How's the chief? Been treating you well?"

"I don't know how to say this. The chief's missing, but that's not the reason I'm calling. I need to talk to you from a secure line. Call me back, STAT, as you would say—on an encrypted line only!" Cordy hung up and waited.

She brewed a pot of coffee, changed into her comfy green velvet robe, and still had time to check her emails before Kelly texted her.

"No time to call. All hell's breaking loose. New cases are spreading across the nation from D.C., to California. New York and Florida have been brutally hit, and violence has erupted on the streets. The New York Stock Exchange is plummeting. All White House activities are being diverted—Congress and the Senate are on lockdown. Number 1 is in bunker. VP is traveling overseas to get help. We're not in denial like with COVID-19, but we may still be too late. Don't try to fly here. We're shutting down airports. JK."

Don't fly? What about Braun and Usher? They're already in the air. If airports are shut down, where will they land? She tried calling Braun again, but still no answer. Fear went straight to her core. Exhausted, her mental reserves were almost non-existent. *Braun, stay safe.*

The president of the United States, Isaac Spendorf, known to his colleagues as Zac, sat at his desk in a stuffy, windowless bunker. Cordy, his top FBI research analyst, and IT expert had warned him about a potential bioterrorist attack six days ago. Less than twenty-four hours later, Astronaut Maxwell Uliptus fell ill and passed away due to an unknown illness. News of Max's death spread quickly due to his high-profile status. Within hours, similar cases followed in Washington, D.C., and Florida.

Throughout the week, the outbreak became more deadly, and by the weekend, the virus had already spread throughout the East Coast, which Zac confirmed with the National Institutes of Health and Centers for Disease Control. He had spent the past four hours analyzing the latest data—emails, Twitter feeds, and reams of statistics from the CDC, Homeland Security, and Defense Department—for his review and waited for his vital responses.

Zac took the pandemic seriously, unlike a previous president who was in denial, even months after CDC warnings. He held a televised conference to address the nation's growing concerns about the epidemic but couldn't answer many questions. The deadly disease hit close to home when two Congressmen and a Virginia Senator fell ill and were hospitalized, with the Senator in ICU on a ventilator.

Zac sent Vice President Tom Harris overseas to meet with World Health Organization members to get help. As a lawyer, Tom's negotiation skills were a great benefit. Also, it kept Tom safe in the event that, God forbid, Zac became infected.

The evolving epidemic wasn't his only concern. The JSOC Commander Braun Hastings had warned Zac there was a mole among his intelligence team—maybe even a terrorist—but he didn't know who. Zac needed to catch the culprit, eradicate this deadly disease, discover a cure, or go down as the worst president in history.

Zac logged off Cordy's TOR account, wondering what to do next about a crashing stock market, rising unemployment rate, and how to feed those needing food. He planned to create another economic and financial plan for the nation. *If this is anything like the last pandemic, we'll also require additional medical supplies, masks, gowns, and ventilators.*

No matter what Zac suggested, Congress would vote it down. The Senate could go either way, but this was worse than facing a war. Once he heard from Tom, he'd call General Rutoon to get his wise counsel. Rutoon had been Zac's commanding officer in the U.S. Marine Corps for fourteen years, and Zac made him his National Security Advisor. Rutoon was like a father to him, and Zac had to discuss options with someone he trusted.

Six laptops and a desktop sat in a row on a long desk, which faced two LCD monitors on the wall. Each monitor was split into several screens. "Geez, I hate computers. They're getting more complicated every minute. Whatever happened to paper?" he asked his Chief of Staff, Winston Willoughby, but he didn't expect an answer.

Winston did have a response, "Saving trees—besides, storage is a huge problem."

"Wish I was sitting under a giant oak right now. I can't stand being cooped up in these cement walls. Sitting here seems ridiculous. We're not being bombed."

"You did place the country under high alert and locked down the city," Winston reminded him.

"I did what had to be done." Zac blew out a deep breath and studied his surroundings. The bunker remained in the old World

War II bomb shelter, where Franklin D. Roosevelt spent many nights. Former presidents had renovated it over the last seventy years to accommodate more advanced technical changes. The concrete block was fifty feet underground. The walls were nine feet thick. Zac tapped a finger on his chin as if in deep concentration. "Maybe if I painted the ceiling blue, I could imagine it to be the sky. I'd even add a few fluffy white clouds."

The direct line from the vice president rang, pulling Zac back into the real world. "Morning, Tom."

"It may be morning where you are, but it's dinner time here." Harris laughed at his comment and then became serious. "Thought I'd let you know I've arrived in Geneva—any more orders?"

"Did you speak to the Director of the World Health Organization?" Zac asked.

"I have an appointment with Dr. Choy at 9 a.m. tomorrow," Tom said.

"We need all the help we can get." Zac leafed through several papers on his desk and found his notes for Tom. "Stick to the global health security agenda as we discussed before I had you whisked away."

"Is it as bad as you thought?"

"Worse, Tom—much worse. According to the CDC, this is a mutated virus. No human in the world has immunity to the disease. It could infect 7.8 billion people. Hospitals can't keep up with the number of patients. If it stays on course, we'll run out of medical supplies, masks, ventilators, and personnel in 30 days. This is just the beginning. To ride this out, we must slow down the spread and flatten the peak curve."

"I know you're always thinking ahead, and the outbreak started only a few days ago," Harris said, "but any hope of a vaccine or a cure?"

"No cure yet." Zac rubbed his aching forehead. He felt drained—all energy sucked out of him. "I don't know about vaccines, but we may get lucky. We hope those who survive the virus are immune from getting it again. If so, we might use monoclonal antibodies for newly infected patients, like during COVID-19. In the meantime, the Governors of New York and Pennsylvania are mandating social distancing and closing schools—going back to online classes. Florida should, too, but the governor refuses. I recommended all states monitor the rise closely and implement a work-at-home policy, but it will be up to their governors. Washington, D.C., Maryland, and Virginia agreed to uphold my request. I'm counting on you. Stay safe and keep me informed."

"I always do."

"Talk to you later, and make sure you're on a secure line." Zac disconnected the call and speed-dialed his trusted friend and esteemed confidant, General Rutoon.

An hour flew by as Rutoon answered most of Zac's concerns. "Dare the impossible," Rutoon said. "If you believe a mole is among us, I'll seek him out. Trust me. I'll trap him like all the enemies we fought in the Marines. You must focus on this epidemic. Lead the nation as an example. Be the driving force for change, and don't let anyone defeat your integrity. I will report back my findings by the end of the weekend."

"Thanks, General. You don't know how much I appreciate your help. Stay safe."

"You, too, my dear friend." Rutoon disconnected the call.

Feeling more energized than he had all week, Zac pressed the intercom button, "Winston, schedule another news conference for the morning."

Braun tapped Usher's arm. "Wake up. We're diverting to Logan International Airport in Boston. Dulles, BWI, and Reagan Airports are all closed until further notice. I'm afraid the FAA will cancel all air travel soon."

"Why?" Usher asked.

"If you had listened to the stewardess instead of your noise-canceling headphones, you'd know. The epidemic is spreading like wildfire." Braun held out a filtered mask. "Put this on before you're thrown off the plane."

Usher leaned forward and glanced around. "Everyone's wearing masks again? I suppose it's become a fashion statement."

"It's to ward off potent viruses."

Usher looped the elastic straps over his ears and placed the mask over his nose and mouth. "But you don't believe that for one minute. Do you? Something else is going on behind this epidemic. That's why we're heading to the Capitol. Not easy, with the state closing down and the city locking us out." Usher stuffed his headphones into its case. "Where do we start?"

"Better call Cordy," Braun said. "Then, we need to make our way to D.C., secretly. I must talk to President Spendorf. Agent Kelly will need to get us a pass into the city."

"Do we know how the microbes are spreading?" Usher asked.

"It could spread through the air or even the water, but there's no cure. I planned to meet with Director Trent from Colorado CDC, but he's in a coma in St. Anthony's hospital in Denver."

"Coronavirus-2?" Usher asked. "They won't call it that for long. Maybe it'll just be the new virus."

"No. More like lead poisoning. Someone shot Trent before our meeting. That's why I laid low and listened to the grapevine, but he's been working on a vaccine. Poor guy—he was perhaps our only hope, too."

"Is he expected to recover?"

Braun shrugged. "Don't know, he's still in a coma."

"Trent must have other team members working with him." Usher jotted a note and tucked it into his pocket. "Why not talk to them?"

"Everything has been hushed since two leading biochemists were killed last month after they announced a trial study to cure some lethal virus. I don't remember what they called the disease."

"Who's behind this?" Usher leaned closer to Braun's ear. "Any ideas?"

"According to Cordy's notes on TOR, she agrees that someone linked to our government is calling the shots, but she has no proof yet. It could be Iran, Syria, or any number of hostile countries. Believe it or not, the U.S. has made a few enemies. Before we can eradicate the disease, we need to contain it," Braun said.

"First, we need to identify the organism," Usher said. "That's where the CDC comes in, and it wouldn't hurt to have experienced members of the World Health Organization join in. Are there outbreaks in other areas around the world?"

"None that Cordy has tracked down," Braun said. "But if there's a threat, she's the best person to hunt it down. Her tenacity is one of her greatest traits."

"At least, after 2022, our front-line healthcare workers should be well-prepared to prevent the spread of this disease."

Braun nodded. "Only if we catch it in time and contain it."

Usher held out his palms to receive a squirt of disinfectant the stewardess was passing around. He rubbed his hands together.

Braun cupped his hands and also received a squirt. The alcohol-based solution made the whole plane reek like a hospital laboratory.

"Please, stow your carry-on luggage, fasten your seatbelts… landing in five minutes," sounded overhead.

Fifteen minutes later, Braun and Usher had deplaned and searched for a car rental agency. "What name did you book us under this time?" Braun whispered.

"B. L. Hardy," Usher said. "That's my name. I didn't book you as a driver. You're a serious risk, and it's time to change your disguise."

Sleep Eludes Cordy

Cordy lay in bed, awake and alert. Even if she drifted off, her brain wouldn't shut down entirely. Sometimes, her mind unraveled the most complex issues at night. Her subconscious worked all hours. She could go to bed with the worst dilemma imaginable and wake up with a simple solution. *Maybe I'll luck out again tonight.*

Three hours later, the walls of her bedroom closed around her. Sleep eluded her. As soon as her eyes closed, she saw Chief Jackson lying in a casket. His vibrant whiskey-colored eyes were now a dull void. That blank stare reflected her progress in this case. Bright crimson blossomed over the white satin pillow tucked under his head. Had she witnessed his death? *If he's alive, I have to find him. But how? And where is Braun? Usher had better take good care of him, or he'll have me to deal with! There has to be a better way to keep track of Braun.*

Her stomach growled. *Nothing except coffee since 5 a.m. the morning before will do that to a girl.* Cordy threw off the covers, went downstairs to put on a fresh pot of brew, and headed back upstairs to take a long, hot shower. *Chief, give me a clue where to find you.* The water turned cold before she opted to dry off and get dressed for the day.

She poured a cup of java into her favorite red Valentine's Day cup, added cream, and sat in her grandma's old rocker. Braun had given her that cup years ago. She loved the two white intertwining hearts, with Cordy written in a fancy script in one, and Braun written in the other. *Coffee always tastes better when I drink from this mug.*

She flipped on CNN for the latest news. "…Riots in the streets of Washington, D.C." "Panic buying has caused basic items such as toilet paper and soap to fly off the shelves. Unable to restock the items, most supermarkets and businesses remain closed." Cordy watched a video of people breaking store windows to enter buildings. When the police arrived, the people fled with whatever bread, canned goods, cleaning supplies, and other merchandise remained available. Some were children trying to get something to eat. *We must provide food for those who rely on one meal while in school. With all these closures, the kids will starve.* Cordy wouldn't let that happen. She sent a note to President Spendorf asking for additional aid.

The news showed squad cars surrounding an area with eerie lights flashing red and blue in the twilight. Every station had round-the-clock chatter, but provided little new information.

Cordy's mind raced. *Did Braun and Usher make it to Washington, D.C.? Are they in the middle of these riots?* She hoped they were safe, but communication had to be limited to secure phones only. *I should go to work early. Or maybe I'll swing by the police station first? Hopefully, the officers have uncovered something useful during Jake's interrogation.*

The ringing of her cell phone decided for her. "This is Fred Young at Saint Anthony's Hospital in Denver. I'm a nurse in the ICU taking care of Dr. Trent from the CDC. He's been in a coma for three days and still drifts in and out of consciousness, so he remains in critical condition. However, he's awake now and refuses to rest until he talks to Chief Jackson. The night receptionist referred my call to you. Is the chief available?"

Cordy felt a glint of hope. Maybe she would track down a cure after all. "No. The chief isn't here, and I don't know where to find him, but I'm heading up this investigation. I'd love to talk to Dr. Trent. Is he able to speak to me over the phone?"

"One moment." After a few seconds, Fred returned. "He wants to talk to you in person. You can stay for only fifteen minutes. If he needs more time, you'll have to wait another hour to speak with him again."

"Tell Dr. Trent that I'll be there in two hours." Cordy got out of the old rocker and slipped on her shoes. "I'm coming from Fort Collins. No. Wait. Make that three hours. I still have to repair a flat tire on my car."

"Is that the soonest you'll be here?" Fred asked.

"I'm sorry, but it is the earliest I can make it."

The nurse said, "I'll be sure to tell him. I hope he can stay alert that long." The call disconnected.

Fred Young turned toward Dr. Joe Smith. "I made the call, as you asked. Agent Cordelia says she'll be here in three hours. She's coming from Fort Collins and can't make it any sooner, but how can Dr. Trent talk with the woman? He's still in a coma."

"Leave everything to me," Dr. Smith said. "Trent had vital information to pass on to the FBI. I'll give her the message instead. What I have to share with Agent Cordelia is a matter of life and death. You've done very well. Your country thanks you, and our president thanks you."

Fred blushed. "I must take care of my patients now."

"Yes, take good care of Dr. Trent. I hope he survives this tragic ordeal. And remember, this conversation is top-secret—don't share it with anyone. Your country is depending on you."

"My lips are sealed," Fred said.

Dr. Smith flashed a superficial smile and muttered, "Yes, sealed for life and very soon."

"Excuse me?" Fred asked.

Smith shrugged his shoulders. "Nothing, I was thinking of something else." He pointed to Trent's room. "I believe the patient's IV is running low."

Fred glanced toward the transparent glass window and sliding door to ICU-7. The IV bag was nearly empty. "Thank you. I'll take care of that right away." The nurse logged onto the computer, picked up a new IV bag labeled with Trent's name, and leaned over to log off.

"One moment. Do you have the latest lab results?" Smith asked. "I noticed his sodium levels are still low."

Fred pulled up Trent's labs. "You can see for yourself. I'll be right back."

Smith pretended to peruse the results, flipped to a few other screens, and searched for a USB port. When he found it, he inserted a thumb drive.

* * *

By the time Fred returned, Dr. Smith had disappeared. Fred didn't think any more about the incident as doctors came and went in the ICU all the time.

Three hours flew by in the unit while Fred took vital signs, watched monitor rhythms, treated patients with meds, made rounds with another doctor, and was about to leave for a well-deserved break when a woman walked into the ICU and immediately caught his attention.

The strawberry-blonde stopped at the receptionist's desk in the middle of the unit and scanned the glassed-in rooms surrounding her. "I'm Agent Cordelia. Dr. Trent asked to see me."

"I'm Tracy. Um…" The receptionist leaned forward and peered through the glass window of ICU-7. "There must be some mistake. Dr. Trent couldn't have asked for you. He hasn't said a word since he arrived."

"Agent Cordelia, good morning. I'm Fred Young, the nurse who called you earlier today." He held out his hand and stepped in front of Tracy.

A frown etched the receptionist's face. "Why would you do such a thing? Dr. Trent's in a coma."

* * *

Agent Cordelia ignored Tracy and shook Fred's outstretched hand. "You can call me Cordy. Did Dr. Trent go back into a coma?"

"This way, please." Fred motioned her away from the desk and toward ICU-7, and whispered, "No, not exactly, that is…this is embarrassing. Let me call his doctor. He's the one who needs to talk to you."

"But you said—"

"I know what I said. Could you stand by for a moment in the ICU waiting room? I'll call Dr. Smith, and he'll clear this up shortly. Tracy," Fred called to the receptionist, "please page Dr. Smith and then take Agent Cordelia to the waiting room. We'll be with her in a minute."

Tracy dialed a number, "Dr. Smith to ICU." She stood and smiled at Cordy. "Follow me. May I get you a cup of tea or coffee while you wait?"

Cordy stared at Fred and then at Tracy. Ignoring both, she went inside ICU-7 to see Dr. Trent. "Hello?" Cordy moved to the bedside and tapped the patient's shoulder. "Dr. Trent, are you awake?"

Fred moved to her side and placed his hand on her arm. "He's still in a coma. Please go with Tracy to the waiting room. Dr. Smith can explain everything."

Cordy stepped closer to the window and scanned the ICU. Her training kicked in as a man in scrubs strode through the ICU toward the reception desk. *He must be Dr. Smith.* Tension rose as three men in black suits trailed close behind. They headed straight for Tracy.

"Where's Agent Cordelia?" the doctor asked.

Tracy's eyes widened and darted toward ICU-7, then back to the men. "She's…" Her whole body slumped in reaction to the force before her.

"Yes. Where is she?" the doctor demanded.

One man, dressed in black, stepped closer. His hand was in his pocket. He lifted it slightly, and a suspicious bulge pointed at Tracy. "Sit down. We'll find her."

"Fred? Dr. Smith is here," Tracy called in an overly loud voice and darted for her chair behind the desk.

The man followed Tracy, his hand still in his pocket. "She glanced over at that room." The man nodded toward ICU-7. "I'll stay here while you check it out."

Fred gasped, "What's going on? Who are those men?" He darted forward and closed the glass sliding door to ICU-7 before they reached the room.

"Get away from that door and stay down!" Cordy pushed Fred behind the curtain and watched Tracy move behind the desk. The threatening guy dressed in black continued to hover over her. *Tracy needs a distraction to hit the secret panic button under the desk.* Cordy slid the door open and deliberately approached the man dressed in scrubs. She held her hand out to greet him. "You must be Dr. Smith. I'm Agent Cordelia."

His other two minions moved up, one on either side of her. She felt something metal poke her in the back. "Come with us. I'll explain everything," Smith said.

"I'll go with you only if you promise to leave your weapons at the desk," Cordy said.

The guy behind Tracy pulled a small pistol from his pocket and pointed it at her back. Dr. Smith intervened, "We don't want a scene. No one will be hurt. We just want to talk to you."

Tracy's face paled, but she kept her composure, and the brave young lady cautiously slid her fingers under her desk. Three bongs sounded over the intercom, followed by, "Mr. Strong, ICU, Mr. Strong, ICU, Mr. Strong, ICU."

People rushed through the doors from every direction.

Smith gasped as Cordy ducked, grabbed the weapon at her back, twisted the man's wrist, and disarmed him. She pointed the pistol at the man behind Tracy. "Drop the gun."

A burly security guard slammed into the second man in black and knocked his weapon to the ground.

Smith moved behind Cordy, but she stomped her heel into his instep. Another muscular man dressed in a housekeeping uniform grabbed Smith, who had gone into a coughing fit.

The man behind Tracy dropped his pistol and screamed, "I told you this was a dumb idea!" He ran for the medicine room, slammed the door, and locked it behind him.

Cordy pulled a pair of handcuffs from her purse and slapped them on Dr. Smith's wrists. The take-down team subdued the other two men in black suits while the security guard followed the man into the medicine room. He used his master key to open the lock.

The trapped man threw a tray toward the door. The guard ducked, let the tray crash behind him, and wrestled the man to the ground.

Tracy called the local police as the hospital workers rounded up the gunmen and moved them to an empty room down the hall. Cordy escorted Dr. Smith behind the guard.

By now, Smith was wheezing. He spat up blood, and his lips turned blue. "Can't breathe. Please, I can't breathe." The heavy-set man collapsed onto the floor.

Cordy uncuffed one wrist. "He needs a doctor." She noticed something peeking out of Smith's coat pocket and pulled it free. It was two airline tickets, one from Miami, Florida, to Washington, D.C., and the other from D.C., to Denver, Colorado. She searched the rest of his pockets and came up with a thumb drive. Cordy couldn't wait to see what was on it. Her gut clenched as she snapped the puzzle pieces together: Washington, D.C., bloody sputum, fever, and cough.

Terror tore through her—*COVID-19? No, it's something far worse—the same symptoms as described on the news broadcasts, and I've been exposed to the deadly virus!*

She turned to the guard. "Isolate this man immediately! I think he's infected with the new virus. Then, everyone in this room, go directly to the Emergency Department for decontamination. It's better to be safe than dead."

In a Blink of an Eye

It was finals week for most Fort Collins, Colorado, high school seniors. Seventeen-year-old Luke Walker hunched over his new laptop on a table in the school library. His Toshiba had the latest apps, but today, they sat untouched. He was concentrating on studying for his history final. Luke had to ace this exam to keep his grade point average at a solid 3.64, which he knew was the required GPA for entrance into Colorado State University. Papers with sample questions lay scattered over the table as he searched for the answers one by one on Google.

His high school's last year had flown by—homecoming, Christmas, spring break, prom, Easter, and soon it would be graduation. Today was the senior's last day of classes. The school year would end next week, and spring fever spread like an epidemic. At least, that's what he blamed for his procrastination. He waited until today to study—the day of the test. The exam was in fifteen minutes.

The latest answer streamed via YouTube through his lime-green earbuds. Time raced by too quickly as he took a few notes and then moved on.

Luke checked his list—*only two more questions.* He frantically typed on the keyboard. His pen skipped while crossing off his completed items, so he shook it harder to get the ink to flow again. No luck. It had gone dry. He leaned over to reach below his chair and grabbed his backpack. The cord of his headset tangled in the cuff of his sleeve. He yanked his arm away and accidentally pulled the bud from his ear.

At the sound of the first popping noises, his head jerked up and banged against the table's edge. *Did Jana bring her fireworks to school again?* The principal had warned his sister sternly and swore he would expel her if she lit them inside the building.

The bell rang. It was time to get to class anyway. Annoyed, he slammed down the lid of his laptop and shoved it into his backpack.

Another crack sounded, and Karen Monroe, the love of his life, bolted into the library. She dashed in Luke's direction.

Why is she running toward me? First, she's my homecoming date, then she refuses to go to the prom with me, but she is heading my way.

"Oh, my God!" Karen choked out.

"What is it?" Luke whispered.

"He has a gun." Karen's voice shook in a high-pitched tremor. "I can't remember what we're supposed to do in a school shooting! All the drills and practice sessions seemed to go out of the window."

"Lockdown. Lockdown!" someone shouted.

"Head for the bathrooms!" According to their practice drills, if students were in the hallway during a break, they should run to the nearest classroom or hide inside a locked bathroom stall, stand on the toilet, and crouch down so no one could see them.

Many students were already in the hall heading for their next class. "They're already full," someone yelled.

The library was where students could go during a shooting, no matter what time of day. There were two doors to the library, and students poured through each. People murmured, "What are we supposed to do between bells?"

Someone shouted, "Shut off the lights!" The lights flickered off, but the sun shone through the high windows lining the outside wall.

Others yelled, "Hide under the desks." Students overturned tables, hid behind shelves, and ran for the back of the room.

The library doors barely closed, and they burst open again. A red-faced freshman screamed, "Everyone, get down!" Sweat beaded on his brow. The pudgy boy looked like he'd just run a marathon. His glasses sat askew on the bridge of his nose as he glanced around the room. "This is not a drill. Someone's shooting real bullets."

The panicked freshman ran for the library window and pounded on the glass so hard that it cracked. "Quick, it's the only way out!"

Screams filled the hallway. There was a sharp bang, then another, followed by a staccato of pops. More students ran into the library, pushing each other. "Hurry! Let me in!"

The room was getting overcrowded. Students ducked behind anything that gave protection. Laptops, papers, and books scattered to the floor as more tables overturned.

Karen's trembling hand gripped Luke's arm. "I'm scared!" Tears pooled in her eyes and trickled down her cheeks.

"It'll be all right." Although, he wasn't at all sure that was true. Luke threw his backpack over a shoulder and wrapped an arm around Karen.

It was so crowded now it was hard for anyone to enter. The librarian tried to open a large window behind her desk. When it didn't budge, she slammed a chair through the glass and broke out the panes. Students rushed to climb through the window to freedom.

Luke pushed Karen ahead of him. They were jostled left and right as people tried to move forward around them, all making for the open window. "Go," Luke shoved the wide-eyed Karen into the fray. I'll be right behind you the whole way."

Some students tried to help those around them, while others pushed ahead to leave the building. Luke knew it wasn't protocol, but desperation took over. He tried to open the window nearest him. The lock was halfway up, which was way above his head. He climbed onto a chair to open the latch.

"Run! He's right behind you. Run, run!" came from someone in the doorway.

Luke turned his head in time to see a girl in a yellow sweater dash through the library entrance. She screamed, "Luke, get down!" There was another pop. Her mouth opened, and she gasped, staggered a few steps, and then toppled to the floor. A bright red blotch spread rapidly over her back. Her arm jerked and then dropped. Other students lay on the floor in the hallway.

Luke eyed a dark-haired boy moving behind her with a rifle. *Chester Tyler?* The shock barely registered when Chester raised his gun and fixed crazed eyes on Luke. Panic rose in Luke's chest.

"Chester," some brave soul shouted and threw the book at the shooter, allowing Luke to dive off the chair. Those eyes darted toward the shout, and his gun swung in the same direction. The book hit Chester's shoulder but didn't stop the bullets from cutting in an arc as the gunman's arm swung from one side of the room to the other. The shots were deafening.

Luke landed behind a shelf of books as the bullets tore through hard-backed novels and pinged against metal shelves. Glass shattered. Many students huddled tighter beneath overturned tables. Chunks of wood blew through the air as Chester blasted his semi-automatic weapon. Then there was a click. Dead silence filled the room.

Or at least, it seemed silent. Luke's ears were still ringing with a high-pitched whine. A noise came from the hallway, sounding like an army marching. Their footsteps echoed and grew louder. There was a pop, and something or someone hit the floor. "Lab clear. Science room clear."

Luke didn't dare move. He could hardly breathe. It felt like hours that he'd been cramped in this small space.

Finally, there was a stir in the silent room as someone from the SWAT team announced, "Shooter down. All clear."

"Anyone hurt in here?" a familiar voice asked. Luke peeked around the shelf to see his history teacher, Mr. Martin, walk into the room behind three SWAT team members.

Chester lay crumpled on the floor. A bullet through the side of his head, and his rifle propped along the wall beside the library door. A pistol was in his right hand. A paramedic knelt by the body, placing his fingers on Chester's neck. He peered up at the SWAT team and shook his head. One member stood near the body, protecting any evidence and motioning for everyone to use the other library door.

Another SWAT member said, "Everyone who can walk on your own, file out behind your teacher. Medical personnel are tending to any injuries, so please let them do their job and meet your friends outside the school."

Luke's legs shook as he approached the door with other classmates to escape the room.

"Wait, Luke!" Karen caught hold of his arm and clung to him. He had to half-support her as she silently wept.

Luke wrapped his arm tighter around her. It wasn't easy, but he wanted to be strong for her sake. "It's over. We're safe now."

"It'll never be over. I'll always remember this," Karen sobbed.

The paramedic moved toward the girl in a yellow sweater, who had collapsed by the library door.

"Look, there's Bonnie!" Karen moved toward her friend. "Bonnie! Bonnie! Oh God, no!" she screamed as an EMT covered Bonnie's bloody body with a blanket covering her head.

Luke placed a hand on Karen's shoulder. "I'm sorry, Karen." He pulled her closer and steered her through the library door into the hallway, trying not to wobble on his jellied legs.

Medical personnel were working on several students lying on the floor outside of the library. "This way," Mr. Martin said. "We're going through the back door."

Karen sobbed, "She's gone. Did you see her back? She's—" Karen turned her face into Luke's shoulder and wept.

Luke knew her best friend had died. The adrenaline rush he'd experienced had drained every ounce of energy. Still, Luke wondered what had happened to his sister. He asked a few kids in the hallway, "Have you seen Jana?" Some stared at him in a daze. Others shook their heads. Although his legs felt like noodles, he forced himself to keep walking, his eyes searching for any sign of his sister.

People sobbed, hugged one another, and silently filed behind Mr. Martin as he led them out of the school.

Luke pulled Karen closer to the school's back entrance. Jana was nowhere in sight. His gut twisted with fear, but he hoped she was safe.

When Luke reached the door, a breeze hit his face. He closed his eyes and took a deep, shuddering breath.

Karen nudged him. "Isn't that your mom?"

Luke's stomach lurched when he saw his mother's car pull into the parking lot. She got out and ran toward an ambulance, shouting something. A policeman stopped her. He heard her say, "Jana."

Something's happened to Jana. Mom's frantic. Luke saw a group of Karen's friends hugging one another. "Olga, can you take care of Karen? Mom just arrived, and she's looking for Jana. I need to talk to her."

"Sure, Luke." Olga pulled Karen into the group.

Luke ran around crowds of students. Some were sobbing, and others stood with glazed eyes, *probably in shock.*

His mother brushed past an officer and kept running towards the school. "Where is she? Where's Jana?" she cried.

"Mom!" Luke dodged EMTs, teachers, students, and anxious parents. "Mom!" He waved his hand to get her attention as he dashed toward her. "Over here!"

She stopped, turned in his direction, and rushed into his arms. "Luke." Her whole body shook as she wept. "It's Jana. Someone shot her." Mom pulled away and peered at Luke. Mascara ran down her tear-streaked cheeks. "Have you seen Jana?"

"No. How do you know?"

"The secretary called." His mother wrapped him in a huge bear hug. "Oh, thank God, you're all right. We have to find her." She pulled Luke along the long line of emergency vehicles as they searched for his sister. A helicopter hovered, and a cloud of dust blew overhead.

"Mrs. Walker," the principal yelled over the chopper's roar as he ran across the schoolyard. "I tried to reach you. Jana's not here. A helicopter took her to Poudre Valley Hospital."

"How bad—"

"I don't know anything about her condition. They just said to call you immediately. I know she will want her mother. Do you have someone who can take you to the hospital? Perhaps Luke can go with you. Someone from the school will call to check on your family later today."

"Jana," Mrs. Walker buried her head in her hands. "My baby, my poor baby."

Luke pulled her closer.

The principal spied another parent. "I must go, Mrs. Walker. Sorry. You'll have to excuse me." He waved at another mother. "Mrs. Radcliff…"

"Where's Bonnie?" Mrs. Radcliff sobbed.

Several students ran toward Bonnie's mother. "We're so sorry."

Mrs. Radcliff's hand flew to her mouth, and she wept. "She didn't make it, did she?" An EMT came out of nowhere as the woman collapsed.

Luke tried to shield his mother from the view and guided her to the car. "I'll drive. You call Dad."

This is Not A Drill

A loud squawk came from the emergency department's radio. "Poudre Valley, this is Thompson Valley EMS. Do you copy? Over."

The triage nurse rapidly answered, "Poudre Valley. Go ahead, Thompson."

"School shooting. Multiple gunshot victims. Three ambos by ground transport, another by air en route. ETA: 3 minutes. Female, age 14, chest wound, maybe abdominal, too. Pneumatic anti-shock garment applied, B/P 80/50. Sinus Tach. 180/minute. Intubated with respiratory assist. IV Ringer's Lactate running wide open. Blood drawn for labs. Report on next case shortly."

The triage nurse called security. "Incoming chopper." She notified the supervisor of the impending casualties. Call the trauma team. We need more help."

The supervisor asked, "Is this a Code D? I don't have enough staff to send more nurses to the Emergency Department. How many were injured at the school?"

"Should the supervisor call a Code D?" the triage nurse asked Dr. Ashford, the ED doctor on duty.

He glanced over the triage notes, nodded, and took over on the radio. "This qualifies as a disaster. Call a Code D. Our team will meet the helicopter, but we need more doctors down here." He punched the radio button to dispatch. "You mentioned three more by ground transport. What do you have?"

"Make that four," the call center said.

The sound of a chopper landing on the helipad was just the beginning of the onslaught ahead. "We've called the trauma team, but we're only a level III," Ashford said. "Any other major injuries must go to another hospital. We'll take the four ambulances heading our way, but after that, we must divert all other emergencies. Stand by to report to the triage nurse."

Three bongs erupted over the intercom, followed by "Code D ED," delivered three times.

The emergency department team swung into immediate action. Two nurses dashed out to meet the chopper. A few minutes later, they whisked a gurney into the ED entrance to Trauma-1. The flight nurse was using an Ambu bag to breathe the patient. The girl's face was whiter than the sheets. Within seconds, they transferred the fourteen-year-old female gunshot victim to a trauma bed, started another IV line, and attached her to the hospital's heart monitor. The flight nurse handed over the Ambu bag to a respiratory therapist.

The triage nurse scribbled information about the next four victims as the ambulances approached the emergency bay.

The hospital supervisor arrived at the front desk to help direct traffic. Dr. Ashford called to the supervisor, "Susan, call every doctor available to get in here ASAP!" Ashford disappeared into the girl's trauma room, barking orders. "Type and cross-match—six units of whole blood."

A nurse started removing the anti-shock pants to check for further wounds.

"Don't touch those pants!" Ashford warned. They prevent further bleeding! Is the trauma team here? She needs an exploratory lap STAT."

Three bongs sounded overhead again, followed by "Every doctor in the house, report immediately to ED," which was repeated twice.

Sue entered the room. "Trauma team's here, but no parent to sign for consent to treat."

"We can't wait. She'll die," Ashford said. "Even if we get her to OR now, she still might not make it."

"Do we have a name?" Sue asked. Ashford shook his head. "I'll try to reach someone at her school." Sue headed for the door.

"Wait. I have a better idea." The trauma nurse scrolled through the list of contacts on the patient's cell phone and hit "Mom."

"The phone's ringing." The flight nurse shoved the phone into Sue's hands. "I have to go. There are too many injured."

"Hello, Jana! Oh, Honey, I was so afraid—"

"No, this isn't Jana. I'm the nursing supervisor at Poudre Valley Hospital. Your daughter is critically wounded, and we need permission to treat her."

"Look out, Luke!" A pause and heavy breathing came across the other end of the phone. "Can I talk to Jana?"

"Are you her mother?" Sue asked.

"Yes. How bad are her injuries? We are on our way, but the traffic is awful. I need to speak to Jana!"

"What is Jana's last name? Is she allergic to anything? What's her birthday?" Sue asked, trying to obtain critical information.

"Walker. Jana Walker. No, she's not allergic to anything. Why can't I—" An alarm sounded in the background. "What's that noise?"

"Mrs. Walker, your daughter is in cardiac arrest. I need permission to treat. Now! We must take her to the operating room before it's too late."

Sue put the phone on speaker as her mother shouted through sobs into the phone, "Yes! Yes! Please keep her alive. I'm on my way—six more blocks. Hang on, Jana. Mommy's coming."

Sue hung up. "We have permission to treat. Will someone co-sign?"

Dr. Ashford was defibrillating the girl. "Yes, but we may be too late. She needs blood." He upped the defibrillator to 300 watts per second and placed the paddles on the girl's chest again. "Clear!" He hit the button, and the girl's body jerked with the electrical charge.

"Sinus tach at 200 per minute," a nurse called out.

Ashford ordered, "Get her to OR STAT!"

Red Satin Box

The deadly virus silently festered in the red satin box in a dumpster in a narrow, rutted alley behind the restaurant where Dr. Joe Smith had eaten last night. A three-story brick building sat across from the shop where Mr. Barnes, the butcher, lived on the top floor with his family of five children: three girls ages three to seven and two older boys ages nine and ten. His wife ran a small coffee shop on the ground floor during the day. At night, she also ran a restaurant known for its fine dining on the second floor of the building.

Mr. Barnes furnished most of the meat served at the restaurant. It was convenient for his wife to cut across the alleyway for fresh beef, pork, fish, or chicken.

Troy, the oldest child, was a freckle-faced boy in a baggy, navy-blue T-shirt and jeans that barely stayed up on his narrow hips as he ran through the rutted path heading home from school. A shock of rusty hair poked from beneath his black baseball cap, worn backward with the brim over the back of his neck. Newton Elementary Baseball Team, stitched in faded gold thread, emblazoned above the rim.

His brother sprinted after Troy and tapped him on the back. "You're it!" He ducked behind an overflowing trash bin filled with meat carcasses, fish guts, and other rubbish. A larger dumpster sat alongside, which his father used for paper and recycled boxes.

Troy stopped mid-stride. He spotted something of interest in the trash. "Hey, Kevin, let's make a fort. We can use that big cardboard, and if I dig deep enough, I'm sure I'll find a few more boxes. Dad always cuts and folds them before throwing them away."

"I bet I find more boxes than you." Kevin brushed a strand of coal-black hair from his eyes and hefted himself over the rim to dig deeper into the bin. "Geez, Troy, it stinks! I don't want a smelly fort.

Look. Someone threw a slimy trash bag in here. Dad's gonna be mad. Oh, wait, what's this?" Kevin pulled out a small red satin box about three inches wide and two inches tall.

An orange, long-haired alley cat hopped from the trash heap and rubbed against Troy's leg, begging for attention. The back legs and rear of the mangy cat's fur were damp and matted.

Troy absently ran his hand along the cat's head as he watched Kevin brush the slime from the red box. "What is it?"

"I don't know," Kevin said. "I wonder if it opens." He tried to pry off the lid, but his fingers were too slippery.

"Let me try." Troy pushed the cat aside and held out his hand.

Kevin tried one more time, but the lid wouldn't give. He gave it to Troy. "Remember, I found it first."

"I know." Troy rubbed the box along his pant leg. He noticed a slit and wedged a fingernail along the edge. "I think it's opening." He tried harder.

Kevin grabbed the box. "I can do it." He stuck the top of the box between his teeth and wiggled the bottom until the box came loose. "It's empty, but it smells musty." With a shudder, he popped the lid back on the box.

"Musty, like what?" Troy asked.

Kevin sniffed the lid again, coughing like the box was full of hot sauce. He dropped the box to the ground and tried to catch his breath.

The cat whacked the box with its paw and sneezed, then batted it along the alley.

Troy pounded his brother on the back. "Take a deep breath!"

Kevin doubled over, coughing and sputtering. Then, he finally wheezed in a small amount of air.

"Kevin, are you okay? Your face is all red, and your nose is bleeding."

"Water," Kevin croaked as he swiped away the blood with his shirt sleeve.

Troy ran into the butcher's shop to get a glass of water. When he returned, Kevin was on the ground but breathing easier. Troy dropped to his knees to give Kevin some water.

The butcher came to the back door. "What are you boys doing back here? Your mother will be upset—"

"Hurry, Dad. Kevin needs help!" Troy called out as he shook his brother. Kevin, wake up. Can you hear me?"

Dad dashed toward the boys, pulled out his cell phone, and called 911. "Send an ambulance right away." He gave directions over the phone and answered several questions. "Just a minute, I'll ask. What happened?"

Troy blubbered through sobs, "We were just playing, and Kevin found something in the trash." Troy glanced at the ground, but the box was gone. He crawled on his knees to search. "It was here a minute ago. It's a little red box."

Dad wasn't listening. He cradled Kevin in his arms.

A siren got louder as the police and ambulance arrived. The flashing red and blue lights gave the trash cans an eerie glow.

Mom rushed from the back of the cafe. "What's going on?"

The siren piqued the neighbors' interests, too. A crowd gathered along the street and into the alley as customers filed from the coffee shop to see what had happened. Dad placed Kevin in Mom's arms and met the policeman walking toward them.

"Kevin?" Mom cried. "Honey, can you hear me? I love you, baby. Please open your eyes. Tell me you're—"

"Excuse me, Ma'am. My name is Greg. May I?" An EMT from the ambulance took Kevin from Mom and laid him on the ground. "What's the child's name?"

"Kevin." Mom had tears running down her face. "Is he going to be all right?"

"We'll do everything we can." Greg was too busy unbuttoning Kevin's shirt to talk more with Mom.

The ambulance driver brought some equipment and knelt next to Kevin."

Troy sat on the ground, too, but he scooted back to give the men more room to examine his brother. The cat came back and rubbed against Troy's legs. Stroking the cat's head comforted him as he watched the EMTs' every move.

Greg put a green mask over Kevin's face. The mask had a long hose connected to a small tank. Then, he put a few sticky patches on Kevin's chest and hooked him up to a machine that made blipping noises. "Harvey, draw some blood work when you start the IV," the EMT told the driver.

Harvey stuck a needle into Kevin's arm, drew blood into a syringe, and filled a few small containers. Then, he attached a long tube connected to a plastic bag full of liquid and securely taped the needle.

"What's he doing, Mom?"

"It's an IV to give him medicine."

"Is Kevin gonna be okay?"

"I don't know." Mom kept crying. Troy cried, too.

Mrs. Johnson, from next door, ran into the alley. "Can I help?"

"Yes, thank you." Mom swiped her apron over her face, and she seemed relieved. "Can you go upstairs and check on the girls?"

"Sure. Let me know if I can do anything else." Mrs. Johnson went inside.

Troy's father was talking to the police, and they glanced toward him. "Troy, this officer has a few questions."

The officer squatted next to Troy. "Can you tell me what happened to Kevin?"

Troy ran a sleeve over his teary eyes. His lips quivered, and he took another glance at his brother. *Kevin's face is white as mashed potatoes. He's too quiet. Kevin is always on the move and never sits still.*

"Troy, can you answer the policeman?" his father asked.

Troy was startled at his name. "Huh? Oh. I…" He sobbed. "Dad, I don't know what happened." Tears splashed as he blinked and dripped onto his pant leg. "He found a box in the trash and started coughing."

"Where's this box?" the officer asked.

Troy wiped at his eyes to clear his vision, looked at the cat, and then at the ground. "It's gone."

Kevin made a gasping sound, and his whole body started to shake. The EMTs ripped open small bags with syringes. They put a stick in Kevin's mouth, but he kept biting and jerking.

"What's wrong?" Mom asked.

"He's having a seizure," the policeman said. The EMTs worked frantically to get Kevin to stop shaking. Greg pushed something into his IV, and Kevin seemed to calm down. Harvey was talking on the phone.

"Mr. and Mrs. Barnes, we need to get him to the hospital," Harvey said when he got off the phone. He pulled Mom and Dad aside, and they had a brief talk.

Troy overheard, "… hospital's on divert." *What does that mean?* "…a school shooting." *Where? What school?* "…need room to land a helicopter."

"The alley's too narrow for a chopper," the officer said.

The next thing Troy knew, the police had asked the crowd to move down the street. The EMTs were moving Kevin onto a stretcher. A loud whap, whap, whapping noise came from the air and grew louder. Dust and wind blew over the alley. A helicopter hovered overhead.

The EMTs carried Kevin on the stretcher and moved to the street. The whole neighborhood must have come to watch. Troy followed the policeman as he cut through the crowd. "Stand back. Move. Let us through." The police cleared a space for the chopper to land in the street. The rotor blades spun slowly and stopped as a lady dressed in a navy blue jumpsuit hopped to the ground and helped load Kevin into the chopper.

Greg talked to the lady. "Who is she, Dad?"

"She's a flight nurse. She's taking Kevin to a hospital in Denver."

"Denver? Why Dad? We have hospitals here."

"Someone brought a gun to school and started shooting," his father said. "I don't know how many people are hurt, but the hospitals are all busy caring for the injured, so we're going to Denver. I'm going to fly with Kevin. Mom will drive to the hospital after she finds someone to take care of the restaurant. Help your mom and sisters while I'm gone." He climbed into the chopper after the nurse.

His mother took Troy's hand. "Let's go upstairs and check on the girls."

"Is Kevin going to be okay?" but his mother didn't answer. She dropped his hand and ran into the house, sobbing.

Troy felt as if the whole world lay on his shoulders. *What if Kevin dies? Why did he have to dig in that smelly old trash? I'm the one who wanted to build a fort. It's all my fault. I wonder what happened to that red box?*

He searched once more on the ground. The cat sat hunched in a corner, licking itself. It let out a loud cry and started twisting. Then it was chasing his tail. It ran around and around until it dropped to its side. The cat seemed to have fallen asleep. At least, Troy wanted to believe that. *I hope it's not dead.* He didn't want to find out. Troy ran into the house and up the stairs, worrying if Kevin would live.

Code Blue

The clock in the Emergency Room at St. Anthony's in Denver, Colorado, read 3:50 p.m. Agent Cordelia underwent decontamination after subduing Dr. Joe Smith in the ICU and getting exposed to the deadly unknown virus. A nurse took her to an ED room, where a physician examined her.

Dr. Hyatt listened to her heart and lungs. "I don't see any need to keep you at the hospital, so you're free to go home." He warned, "You might want to wear that mask even after you leave here and immediately report to your doctor if you develop a cough, runny nose, or other symptoms."

There was a knock on the door. "Come in," Cordy called out.

The receptionist cracked the door and poked her head into the room. "Sorry to bother you, Doctor, but Flight for Life just brought in a patient."

The flight nurse came to the door. "I need to give a quick report and get back to Fort Collins STAT."

The doctor stepped outside the door, but Cordy still could hear the conversation.

The nurse lowered her voice. "All our main hospitals are on divert—a school shooting, and I need to get back in the air."

"Okay," Dr. Hyatt said. "I heard you brought us a nine-year-old boy found unresponsive at the scene. How's his condition?"

"Critical. He had two seizures en route with decorticate posturing. Those tiny fists clenched so tightly into his chest that I could barely keep an IV running. His legs stuck straight out like rigid poles, and I could barely keep him on the gurney. He quit breathing, so I intubated him. Rales in both lungs. He's on a 100% non-rebreather oxygen mask, and his Pulse ox is only 82%. Pupils are unequal and non-responsive. Right pupil pinpoint. Left dilated. Vitals—"

"Doctor, in here quick!" someone called out in alarm. A loud bong rang three times, followed by "Code Blue ED, Code Blue ED, Code Blue ED."

The doctor and the nurse's voices faded. Cordy slipped from the bed and hurried to get dressed. *Fort Collins had a school shooting. I need more details.*

She had barely stepped into her shoes when a man in a white blood-splotched apron burst into her room. "Where is he?" His eyes darted around the room. "Sorry, I am looking for my son. A helicopter just brought him. I didn't want to leave my boy, but the nurse said I had to check him in first."

Cordy felt sorry for the flustered man. "The receptionist will know what room he's in. Come with me." She motioned for him to follow her to the desk.

A curtain to one of the trauma rooms was open just enough to see a small boy with dark hair lying on a cart. Nurses and medical personnel surrounded him. Hyatt glanced up. "Close that curtain."

* * *

Kevin felt light-headed, and someone was pounding on his chest. He tried to speak, but he couldn't make anyone listen. Odd machines beeped around him. Nurses and doctors were all around his bed. He saw his father rush into the room, and he felt calm. The burning feeling in his chest faded as he floated to the ceiling.

"Kevin!" His father yelled and grabbed his leg. "Please, doctor, you have to save him. He's just a child!" His worried face stared at the body in the bed.

"Dad, I'm up here!" Kevin tried to get his attention. The sounds faded, and a bright light shone. His grandpa called, "Kevin. It's time to come home. We've been waiting for you." Kevin smiled and reached up when he saw Grandma. She looked so young. Warmth wrapped him up like a cozy blanket, and they took him away.

* * *

Cordy stood next to the curtain, watching the commotion.

"Wait!" Kevin's father stepped over EKG paper, towels, and other debris scattered on the floor.

The doctor placed a hand on the man's arm. "I'm sorry. We did everything we could. His little lungs just gave out. The hospital chaplain is on her way. Is there anyone else we can call for you?"

A police officer entered the emergency room and stopped at the receptionist's desk. "I'm Officer Lee. I need to talk to Mr. Barnes." A woman came from the opposite direction and headed for the boy's room. Hyatt handed a gown and mask to the chaplain, stepped out of the room, and removed his gown, mask, and gloves into a double-bagged container.

Dr. Hyatt strode over to Officer Lee. "The chaplain just arrived. Can you wait until she talks with the father?"

Lee sighed. "If it doesn't take too long, I—"

Cordy's cell vibrated in her pocket—a message from Agent Kelly. She interrupted the men's conversation while holding out her ID. "I'm FBI Agent Cordelia, but you can call me Cordy. I just got word from the CDC." She held up her phone. "Anyone in contact with that boy must undergo decontamination or be quarantined. Before meeting the father, wear a mask, gown, and gloves while in the Emergency Department.

Hyatt agreed. "We don't know what we're dealing with, but it's deadly. I'll contact EMS to set up a HAZMAT unit for each ambulance. We must decontaminate everyone who's also come in contact with Kevin." Then, he notified his staff.

As Officer Lee put on a mask, Cordy asked, "May I have a word with you before you speak to Mr. Barnes? It'll be a while as he needs to remove his clothing and undergo a chemical spray before talking to you. His whole family will also need to be quarantined."

Hyatt returned with a gown and gloves for Officer Lee. "Put these on, and you can wait in the lounge. I'll have my staff post a "Do not disturb" sign on the door if you like.

"We'll need access to a computer," Cordy said.

"I'll arrange it." Hyatt motioned to the unit secretary. "Mary, take Agent Cordelia and Officer Lee to the staff break room and log them into the computer with guest access. Post a privacy notice on the door."

The unit secretary nodded. "Follow me." It only took a few minutes to set up access. Mary wiped down the computer and keyboard upon Cordy's request. "I'll be at my desk if you need anything else." She posted a privacy notice on the door and closed it.

Cordy pulled a thumb drive from her pocket and held it up for the officer to see. "I don't know what's on it, but Dr. Smith had it in his pocket. Let's see what secrets it might reveal."

Lee smiled. "I love a mystery. After you."

Cordy extracted another thumb drive attached to her keychain. With a few taps on the keyboard, she uploaded her OptiSnatch detection software into the USB port of the computer terminal she had been assigned. Once installed, the program immediately detected malware, quarantined the worm, and prevented further software damage.

Cordy plugged Dr. Smith's drive into the USB, and a "virus alert" popped up on her screen.

Lee hopped from his chair. "Did you just add a virus?"

"No, I just trapped one," Cordy said. "Don't worry, it's been quarantined, and my forensic program will repair any harm to the system. It's good we checked this out before it took over the whole hospital network."

"What are you doing now?" Lee asked as Cordy entered some more text.

"This thumb drive has an encrypted file," Cordy said, tapping the keyboard. "I'm making a backup and importing it into my analysis program."

Can't Stop Virus

This was U.S. President Isaac Spendorf's third address to the nation in as many days. After the press secretary's introduction, Zac stepped up to the podium, portraying more confidence than he felt. He squirted an antiseptic gel onto his palm and rubbed his hands together, explaining the need to follow CDC's guidelines.

The media interrupted—booing and throwing questions and denials out for discussion. Spendorf knew the spread of misinformation over social media and digital platforms during COVID-19 had eroded public trust and undermined the nation's response to the pandemic. At that time, the president had only hindered any attempt to control COVID-19.

Spendorf's brief message was delivered while wearing a mask. "We are working closely with the World Health Organization, and I have created an interagency task force to find a cure for this virus. There are seven key members, and Dr. Elizabeth Brakinsky with Health and Human Services is well-qualified to head the program. The team is called Rapid Response 7 or RR7."

The media launched several questions about the pandemic, how it would affect the economy, loss of jobs, more shutdowns, etc., for President Spendorf, who assured them he would keep the nation updated with any new developments. He returned to the bunker exhausted, but sleep was not on his agenda, and more dreadful news awaited him when he arrived.

His lead FBI analyst, Cordy, had left an urgent update while he was away. "A thumb drive found on terrorist Joe Smith in Colorado contains devastating news. Someone deliberately released an MRSA superbug enhanced with a fungus that attacks the brain and nervous system. The origin is unknown, but the deadly virus is spreading rapidly across Colorado. I'm sure this virus is the bioterrorist attack I warned you about."

Spendorf reviewed the latest CDC reports in greater detail. Cases were rising nationwide, especially in California, New York, Florida, Washington, D.C., and Virginia. The deadly disease had spread to every state in the nation except Montana. It has also spread globally to Europe, Asia, and Africa. The U.K., France, and Germany had banned flights to and from the U.S.

Zac moved from his office into the conference room, where he sat at a table and stared across several screens as numerous channels replayed some variation of his earlier speech. TV stations cut into their regularly scheduled programs to broadcast his message. Even the weather channel interrupted televising a tropical storm to deliver Zac's newscast. He listened to several snippets of his speech.

"My fellow Americans, we are facing a crisis much worse than the outbreak of COVID-19. I've heard your concerns, and we are working together to overcome the pandemic." "…this virus isn't our only concern. The stock market is plummeting, unemployment is rising, and the economy looks grim." "…COVID-19 epidemic caused more than 9 million deaths, more than 255 million lost jobs, and it was to be a once-in-a-century crisis—a false assumption." "We face the highest gaps in economic recovery yet—our GDP dropped another 6%, and the trade deficit increased by 22%."

Spendorf ran a hand over his damp brow. *That speech didn't offer any hope. I should have been more positive.*

He jotted a note for the following media blitz. "Remember, this isn't the first time we've faced peril. Previous generations fought World War I and World War II. The entire country came together, made sacrifices, and won those wars. This virus is a more modern war, infecting the youth and everyone in its path."

How do I include our teens? They have become a big problem. His pen jotted, "We're counting on you, including our younger generations, to step up to do your part."

What would I tell my son? The words flowed onto paper: "Stay at home. Don't sneak out to parties, socialize in person, or take unnecessary risks. Use your virtual programs to talk to friends."

He reread the notes. *Not enough impact.* So, he continued to wrack his brain for more potent words. Then it came to him.

"The key is to pull together as one. We are a strong country, and the economy and stock markets will bounce back. If we abide by the CDC guidelines, we will prevent the spread of this virus, but we can't succeed without your help."

I need a powerful closing. "I refuse to sacrifice the lives of our beloved citizens. Like all World Wars, we must work together to overcome what may seem insurmountable problems. Caring about each other is essential to prevention and recovery. Let me show you what we're facing."

He knew the statistics would change by the hour, but he pulled up today's graphs of the growing number of virus cases on the screen—by state and an overall total per day. A third column listed the COVID-19 numbers for comparison. The final column showed that today's caseload doubled again in the past eighteen hours. But in Washington, D.C., the number tripled during the same timeframe, with 40% hospitalized, 31% of those in ICU on ventilators, and a 7% mortality rate.

If this continues, the U.S. will have accumulated 150,000 deaths from the current epidemic in the first month. It took five months to reach that number of COVID-19 deaths. Math wasn't Spendorf's strong suit, but it was apparent something had to be done—NOW!

Zac intercommed his Chief of Staff, "Winston, put me through to the House of Representatives." Zac flipped to another screen to join a meeting already in session.

Winston Willoughby announced that Zac was on the conference monitor and wished to speak.

House Speaker Peach replied, "We heard all that bullshit you spread over the news a few minutes ago. Why? There's no deadly virus. It's nothing but the flu. This happens every year. Why get the nation all wound up over nothing? You're too old for this job."

"Didn't you see the graph?" Zac asked.

"Fancy," Peach said, "but I doubt even you can understand the meaning of all those numbers. I'm sure some CDC geek cooked it up for your little speech. Was there something special on your mind?" The screen blinked to black, indicating that Peach had disconnected Zac.

There is no use counting on Speaker Peach to support a bailout plan. Even loaded with the facts, it will be difficult to convince the House that there is a virus in the U.S., much less facing a potentially deadly pandemic or the need for a stimulus package. They'll wait until the stock market crashes. Of course, Peach is a loudmouth Texan Republican who will vote the opposite of anything I suggest, no matter the issue. Maybe I'll have better luck with the Senate, but first, I must check in with VP Harris.

"Afternoon, Tom, or I suppose it's your morning now. How did your meeting with Dr. Choy go?" Zac asked.

"Dr. Choy says WHO will provide any information and support we need. She suspects this virus is a bio-weapon. Has anyone else mentioned that other than Cordy?"

"No," Zac gasped at the thought of the word bioweapon being actually spoken aloud. "We don't know how far this thing has spread, and lately, I don't even know who I can trust."

"Dr. Choy reports similar cases across Europe, Asia, and China. She likes your plan for a rapid-response team. We have to be proactive and get our stock, gear, and additional personnel identified just in case we need them. I'll copy you on all her text messages and email you a full report."

"Good, now move on to number two on your list—the global health security agenda," Zac said. "Keep me informed. And Tom, if anything happens to me, you're in command, so stay safe and watch your back. The media is getting brutal. We have friends and fiends in our midst. Talk to you later and only on a secure line."

Agent Kelly was also having a hectic day in Washington, D.C. Her phone rang every few minutes with another update or demand for answers from the press, politicians, and medical personnel. Not only was this virus affecting the respiratory system like COVID-19, but it also attacked the brain, resulting in growing violence nationwide. YouTube videos of riots in the street, domestic attacks, and calls for more police kept popping up on the internet.

President Spendorf had called his top healthcare officials and security teams to combine forces into one national Committee called RR7. It stood for Rapid Response and seven for the number of members on the team. This group aimed to identify the source of the deadly virus, contain it, and develop a vaccine and treatment plan for this epidemic. They were also tasked with obtaining medical supplies, ventilators, suction machines, and adequate medications.

A panicked forensic lab technician phoned Kelly, "I can't kill this lab sample. I've heated, gassed, and frozen it. I even soaked it in bleach for a full twenty-four hours. It's still alive and reproducing. The coronavirus remained deadly when soaked in bleach for the normal twenty minutes, but eventually, it died after an hour. How can we contain such a contaminant?"

"I don't know yet, but thanks for the update." Kelly jotted down the concern next to twelve others she had already received for the day. "I'll relay your message to the team. We hope to have a reply soon." Kelly hated to silence her phone, but the meeting was about to start. She briefly checked the schedule to see who would be attending:

-Dr. Elizabeth Brakinsky, Ph.D. in infectious diseases, Secretary of Health and Human Services – Chairwoman

-Harry Barker, J.D., White House Counsel

-Dr. Ryan Chugson, Director of CDC

-Agent Dr. Jacqueford Kelly, RN, DNP, FBI, & CDC

-Guy Weimer, Secretary of Homeland Security (DHS)

-Carl Wyller, Secretary of DoD

-Dr. Nat Ping, MD/Ph.D. in internal medicine, DHC, former CIA for counter-terrorism, and Senate Foreign Relations Committee before that

Kelly took a seat and accidentally hit her phone's speaker button as she jammed it into her pocket.

"Kelly, this is Risa Grant. I'm calling from Holy Cross ED. We need help, STAT! I don't know who else to call, and you helped me in the past. I'm putting you on video cam so you can see what we're facing for yourself." Screaming in the background obliterated Risa's voice.

The conference room went quiet, and all eyes turned toward Kelly. "Do you have a screen where I can show this?"

"Done," a young female tech pulled up her laptop and patched it into Kelly's phone. The video went to an overhead screen showing a red-faced, stocky man darting toward a reception desk. "I don't have any insurance, but you have to treat me. It's the law." His veins bulged as he reached over the desk, grabbed the clerk by the collar, and lifted him from the chair. "It's the law. The law. The law. Law. Law. Law." The man head-butted the clerk three times as he spat out "Law."

A shriek went out as the clerk's nose cracked, and blood flew from his mouth. His front teeth broke into a jagged grimace. People scattered, trying to get away from the commotion. A male nurse examining an infant in respiratory distress stepped in to help the clerk.

The large man swore as he yanked the computer terminal from the reception desk and smashed it over the nurse's head. The nurse collapsed unconscious. The agitated man ran toward the nurse when someone stuck out their foot and tripped him. The bulky man sprawled across the floor, slammed into a row of crowded chairs, and started punching anyone in his way.

A security guard rushed toward the aggressive patient. "Sir," was all he got out before the man slammed a massive fist into the guard's stomach, causing him to wretch. Then, he banged the guard's head against the wall twice as he yelled, "Law. Law."

A police officer dashed into the room and tazered the patient, finally controlling the situation.

Risa turned the phone back to her ear. "This has been going on for twelve hours. We've had one violent patient in twenty-five, and it's getting worse. We need police backup. Our medical staff isn't equipped to handle this."

"Thanks, Risa. I'm showing the team your video as we speak and will get back to you shortly." Kelly silenced her phone and glanced up to see all eyes move from the blackened screen to stare at her. "It's been like this all morning," Kelly said. "The violence is escalating. We have to do something fast."

"It's worse than I thought." The tone in the chairwoman's voice and her expressive eyes, the color of steel, indicated she was surprised at the extent of the disease. She tapped the edge of her cup and glanced around the room. "This is serious. Let's get started. We have much to do, so I'll get right to the point. I'm Dr. Elizabeth Brakinsky, the Secretary of HHS. I'll be heading up this team as

President Spendorf requested. My job is to coordinate all pandemic activities and monitor our progress."

A man dressed in khaki pants and a navy blue shirt nearly dropped his laptop as he rushed into the room. "Sorry, Miss Lizzy Mae. Zac just called, and now I'm late. What did I miss?" His exaggerated southern drawl dripped like sweet maple syrup. A wide smile with perfectly straight, white teeth flashed across his face.

Harry was old enough to be Brakinsky's father, and Kelly noticed the tension go up a notch as soon as he walked through the door. *Being a lawyer, you'd think he'd be more careful in selecting his words.*

Dr. Brakinsky stiffened at the greeting but handled the affront reasonably well. "Mr. Barker!" She nodded an acknowledgment. "Have a seat. We're just getting started. I'm sure everyone already knows Harry Barker, White House Counselor. And Harry, my name is Dr. Elizabeth Brakinsky, not Lizzy."

"Yes, Ma'am," Harry snapped back and pulled out the chair closest to her. I forgot you're all grown up. I don't want to miss a thing." He glanced around the room. "Mornin', y'all."

"Good morning," echoed through the room.

Brakinsky bit the edge of her lip and then continued. "Each member of the RR7 will supervise a full team working under you."

"And who is working under you?" Harry asked as if this wasn't an insult.

Dr. Brakinsky glared at him, took a deep breath, and answered in a restrained voice, "I'll oversee a whole array of departments. The Assistant Secretary for Health, National Vaccine Program Office, OPHEP, OGC, ASPA, OGC, OGHA, FDA, CMS, and the list goes on."

"It sounds more like alphabet soup," Harry said. "And I think you forgot one—the CDC."

Brakinsky clenched her fists. "I'd like a word with you, in private, after this meeting."

Barker opened his mouth to speak, but seeing everyone glaring at him, he must have reconsidered.

Brakinsky cleared her throat and continued, "If you'd been here on time, you'd have seen how out of control this has become. And yes, you're right. Although the CDC also falls under HHS, it plays such a large role during an epidemic that Dr. Ryan Chugson, the new acting Director, will also be on our team." She nodded toward Ryan. "Will you please introduce yourself and state your duties?"

Sucking in his cheeks, Ryan made his face even more gaunt than usual. He'd been thumbing through the newspaper when she called on him and quickly placed it under his laptop.

"Ah, yes. I'm Ryan Chugson, but please, call me Ryan." He removed his gold wire-rimmed glasses, rummaged through his white lab coat pocket, and pulled out a tissue to clean the lenses.

Kelly thought he was stalling before answering the question. She'd be working closely with this man, someone she hadn't met before, and wondered what to expect.

"I'm new to this position, but I've been with the CDC for over twenty years. Most of my experience was in California. I moved to Washington, D.C., three weeks ago—as far as my duties?" He shoved his glasses back on his face and stared at the chairwoman. "We oversee testing of the disease, collect updated patient data, and are in constant communication with healthcare centers on the patients' status, lab results, treatment plans, and responses of each. We have a new software program creating a surveillance database that tracks each case, but I'm unfamiliar with how it works. Perhaps Agent Kelly can update me. I look forward to working closely with you and the team."

Kelly thought his was a cautious opening, but since he was new, perhaps he did not want to put too much on the table. *I'll need to get him up to speed on that database, but I can work with that.*

Brakinsky said, "Thank you, Ryan. Agent Kelly has a dual role here. Her medical background and FBI experience make her well-qualified. Do you have anything to add, Agent Kelly?"

"As usual, the press is hounding us for answers. You just saw how the virus escalates violence once it hits the brain. We're still researching the cause and haven't identified the source of the epidemic." Kelly nodded with her chin, "As Ryan mentioned, the CDC created a database of all known victims. As of an hour ago, 2,930 more patients are seeking treatment in Washington, D.C., which is rapidly growing, and 937 have died. The mortality rate is more than twice that of any other state, which has risen to 32%, even higher than those who die of MRSA, which is 28%. I'll keep you updated, but let's get to know the other committee members."

"Thank you, Agent Kelly." Dr. Brakinsky turned to a middle-aged man in a blue pin-striped suit, light blue cotton shirt, and red tie. Mr. Weimer, will you introduce yourself and tell us your responsibilities?"

"Thank you, Dr. Brakinsky. I'm Guy Weimer, Secretary of Homeland Security. I oversee all emergency response activities. Let me tell you, it's been a nightmare. People in Wisconsin, where I come from, would never act so foolishly. What's wrong with America today? They riot in the streets because we closed several airports and set roadblocks to protect our citizens. People refused to stay home as instructed. We're doing all this for their good. Why, if FDR knew, he'd roll over in his grave."

Dr. Brakinsky cleared her throat. "Let's get back on track."

"Yes. Let's," Harry cut in. "The president expects a report from me in ten minutes."

Guy nodded. "DHS works closely with the Dept. of Transportation and Dept. of Energy." Guy glanced toward Carl Wyller. "And we keep in touch with the Department of Defense, so I guess it's your turn."

Carl sat ramrod straight, shoulders back, "Yes, sir. I'm Carl Wyller, the Secretary of Defense and the Department of Veterans Affairs. My primary role is providing medical equipment and personnel during an epidemic. We also work closely with the American Red Cross. Doctors, nurses, respiratory therapists, and lab personnel are calling from all over the United States, volunteering their services as we speak."

Carl took a deep breath and continued. "Our problem right now is our hospitals' capacity can't meet the demand. Most have patients on gurneys tucked in every nook and cranny available. There aren't enough ventilators, IV pumps, monitoring equipment, and staff. It takes time to check professional credentials, so we're using our military medics to open new transport units and move into tents. We called in the National Guard to help rapidly convert gyms and schools into treatment centers. Doctors, military medics, and healthcare professionals are also in short demand, so the government waived the State Licensure policy so professionals can work in any State as needed without the additional paperwork and delays it usually takes to relocate. Our team is on top of the requirements and is working toward a solution."

A slender man with wavy white hair hopped from his chair. "You think we're on top of this epidemic? You have to be kidding!"

"Dr. Ping," Brakinsky said, "please, sit down. Dr. Nat Ping, head of the Disaster Health Committee and a former member of the CIA's counter-terrorism Committee, has been on the front lines of several epidemics. We value your input and feedback, but we also have an agenda for today."

Ping sat down briefly, so Carl continued, "Yes. As I was saying, people are rioting in the streets. Emergency rooms and doctors are turning patients away. We have no clue if this is a virus, fungus, or bacteria. How can we develop an antidote and then create a vaccination to prevent the spread of this disease?"

Dr. Ping piped up again. "What I fear most is biological warfare. There, I said it. It's on the table—terrorism to the max!"

CDC's Ryan said, "That could be true. We may be seeing multiple cases with different diagnoses and exposure to multiple organisms, and I haven't ruled out bioterrorism either. This Virus X, for lack of a better name, is undefined, and we're treating symptoms only. Tamiflu is worthless. The most popular treatments are Remdesivir, an antiviral, and dexamethasone, a steroid, but the drug companies can't meet the demand. We are trying to import Arbidol, an antiviral med used in Russia and China, and Kaletra, an HIV drug thought to block the replication of the virus inside the cells. None of these are enough. We need something more powerful. The best method is prevention. Everyone must wash their hands thoroughly with soap and water, wear masks, preferably an N95 respirator, and stay home to prevent exposure. Above all else, avoid getting exposed."

Dr. Ping said, "Misinformation will run rampant. It always happens that way. Dr. Chugson is right. Education is the key. Once we have the specifics of the disease, we must tell people how to protect themselves. Learn how it spreads, recognize early symptoms, and isolate victims. But that causes fear and panic. I worry more about how people will react rather than the disease itself. Then we must find a cure."

Agent Kelly got an urgent text message reminding her of her latest endeavor. "We recently created a rapid-response lab with advanced technology called an RRAT lab. This network provides 24-hour diagnostics and chemical analysis. We linked it to the U.S. EPA to detect and contain any human exposure to chemical agents." Glancing at the urgent message, she added, "A police officer found a small red box near a Fort Collins meat market, believed to have a potent virus ten times more powerful than Virus X. It's now in our lab for further research to determine the source of the box. It seems the owner's son found the container and became a victim of the virus."

"That's another concern—what to do with all the victims when it's 100°F outside?" Ping glanced around the room. "Don't look at me like that. It's a reality. I've seen it happen. Morgues and funeral homes can't keep up. Remember how New York to California had to use massive refrigerated storage units during the COVID-19 outbreak? The backlog of bodies took months to process.

Kelly's phone vibrated in her pocket for the fourth time during the meeting. She recognized the caller ID. "Excuse me for a moment. I have to answer this call." She got up and left the room. "This is Kelly. How may I help you?"

"It's Braun. Usher and I are in Boston. The bad news is we're trying to get to D.C., but every direction we go is blocked. No planes are flying. We rented a car, but major highways are blocked. So we can't fly or drive into the city. Can you help?"

"I'm in the middle of the most disorganized meeting I've ever attended. Give me two hours. I'll see what I can do."

"There's more bad news," Braun added, "I read a message from Cordy."

"Has she found the chief?" Kelly asked.

"I doubt it," Braun said. "However, she thinks she's tracked a key contact spreading this virus. She'll call you soon. Tell her LYA from me."

"What does that mean?" Kelly asked.

"She'll know. She's a real WW."

"World wonder?" Kelly guessed.

Braun laughed. "That, too, but I meant wild woman. I miss her more than she'll ever know. Don't tell her that, though."

Secret Signal

Wincing in pain, Chief Jackson rolled over and gasped at a catch in his side, another broken rib. Feeling bewildered, he attempted to remember what had happened while his shaky fingers touched a bump on his left temple. The last he remembered, he met with Cordy to warn her that Braun's life was in danger. *Then what?*

The world spun as he sat up. Black spots threatened to steal his vision as he eased himself to a standing position while holding his head. Cold concrete under his bare feet made him shiver. No shoes or socks in sight, but at least he was dressed. Jackson wondered where he was now.

He studied his surroundings. The cell was ten steps wide, twelve steps long, and twelve feet high. A faint light came from a window created by twelve-inch block glass on a three-foot wide slab. Cinderblocks made up the walls—rusty shackles, riveted near the ceiling, dark streaks running down the walls—*probably bloodstains.*

He guessed the empty prison cell was underground. A small ceiling trap door was in the far northeast corner. It was the only exit he could see. The opening was surrounded by wires stuck into a grayish-brown putty—*C4 explosives.* Cameras hung from the ceiling in every corner. A lens zoomed in and out as he moved around the room. Jackson slowly shook his head. His captors were probably watching his every move. *They won't let me live. I know too much. Why haven't they already killed me?*

Jackson was past his prime—in his sixties. He had survived because he lived by strict rules: strategize, re-strategize, map, and prepare for every possibility. When disaster hits, execute the plan that best fits the situation.

There was one flaw in this particular master plan. He worried about Cordy. *What had they done to her? She needed to track him, and being the best hacker he knew, she would reach him if given enough time. And if she is still alive.*

No! There was a second flaw—Chirk T. Transom, his ex-FBI partner, swore that Braun was a sleeper agent for Iranian forces or perhaps North Korea. The schmuck didn't even know the difference between these enemies. Chirk had demanded that Jackson turn Braun over peacefully. The Jerk, as Jackson used to call him behind his back, was dead wrong about Braun Hastings. Chief Jackson was hell-bent on proving Braun's innocence and agreed to meet Chirk. *Look where that got me—stuck in this cell with no way out.*

The mistake Jackson made was telling Braun he was in danger without assuring him of immediate protection. Jackson planned to pull Cordy in for the job, but it was too late. Chirk arrived early, and everything turned to shit.

It was stupid of me to think I could talk sense into my ex-partner. Where's Braun now? Is he still alive? Odds are against it if he truly sought such a powerful rival. *And how does Chirk fit into all of this? No, it can't end like this!*

Fortunately, Jerk's boys hadn't figured out how to remove his belt or wristwatch. Jackson hunched over, away from any cameras, and pressed the secret stem. He rubbed the cuff of his sleeve over his face and whispered into the device. Then, he pulled the stem. A warm glow beamed briefly under his sleeve. "Message sent. GPS on."

Cordy's thoughts raced like squirrels chasing one another. Nothing made any sense. Chaos was the only consistency. She had used NMAP, Acunetix, and various ethical hacking programs, which led to international files and warnings of a bioterrorist attack. It was her job to stay informed, get answers, and prevent the death of millions. Somehow, her rivals got wind of what she had been searching for, and attacks became personal. Her fiancé and Chief Jackson's lives were also at risk. Days of constant fear and lack of sleep made her raw with emotion—on the verge of tears one moment and angry the next. Today, she had missed every warning sign, had fallen into a trap set for her, and was nearly killed—in a hospital, of all places!

Focus! Cordy clenched her jaw as she stood in line at the hospital's billing office, speaking notes into her cell to help clear her thoughts.

"What do I know so far?" *I found evidence of a terrorist attack against the U.S. Homeland Security is targeting Braun as the culprit, but I know he is innocent.*

"Who?" *Dr. Joe Smith, not his real name, and probably others higher in the food chain are more likely suspects. Braun believes the source comes from someone on the president's advisory team. Braun is usually right, but no name has yet floated to the top of the list.*

"Where?" *Smith was in Washington, D.C., and then flew here, but initially, where was he exposed to the virus—North Korea? Syria? Libya?*

"Why? Was Joe Smith here to kill me? Or to kill Braun? Maybe even Dr. Trent?" *No, it doesn't make sense—too small a target. We just got in the way. Did Smith plant the virus, or was he just the messenger?*

"How did he do it? What mode of viral release did he use, and who is the target? Is this some form of a deadly organism to start a biological war that could wipe out millions?"

"When?" *It's already happening. Was it planted three days or two weeks ago? And for how long will this last?*

"Next," the receptionist interrupted her notes. Cordy approached the window to pay her emergency room bill before leaving St. Anthony's Medical Center. Something kept gnawing at her. The TV droned in the background with another update on the riots in Washington, D.C. A trailer crossed the bottom of the screen: "Astronaut Ivan Pendari has fallen ill and is being treated at Walter Reed ICU. A fellow astronaut, Maxwell Uliptos, died yesterday from similar symptoms."

Like a puzzle, the pieces started to fall into place. *Could the organism be from outer space? NASA's biotechnology group had been experimenting with growing cells in a non-gravity environment. Or maybe other countries are also experimenting.*

Cordy was no scientist, but she did recall that in February 2017, NASA had sent a sample of MRSA, an antibiotic-resistant superbug, on a Space X Falcon 9 rocket to the space station for research on the effects of no gravity on the organism. Scientists ran identical tests on a duplicate sample in Houston to compare results. Less gravity had increased the cell size, making the sample three times more dangerous in space. *What would happen if that virus escaped and arrived on Earth? Were they still experimenting with the virus years later? NASA may have wanted to do further testing after the recent COVID-19 outbreak. Has something gone wrong?*

She squirted antiseptic gel on her hands and rubbed them together as she left the hospital entrance. *Where do I begin? CDC? NIH?* Cordy focused on the next steps as she headed for her silver

Lexus. Too late, she noticed a man sitting in a parked dark blue truck in the row across from her car. There was a snowplow blade on his front grill. The driver glanced up, lifted a cell phone to his ear, and started his engine, but he didn't pull out.

Cordy turned to the left, heading away from her car, and spotted another man dressed in black trousers and a fleece jacket leaning against the SUV beside hers, reading a newspaper. He didn't bother to look her way, but as she moved, he folded the paper, touched his ear, and nodded.

Bluetooth! Cordy jabbed the panic button on her keys and ducked behind a minivan. The alarm startled the guy by her car. He dropped the paper, ran to the truck, pulled open the passenger door, and hadn't even closed it when the vehicle rammed the snowplow blade into her car. Shots fired, pinging off the minivan. The driver backed up his truck. She thought he would ram her Lexus again, but instead, he rounded the corner and headed her way.

A security guard ran from the hospital. *A lot of good he will be, unarmed. Is he trying to get himself killed?* Then she heard the whipping sound of a helicopter rotor growing louder overhead and realized the guard was heading for the nearby heliport. The whirring noise caused the driver to pause and look up at the sky. Cordy was surprised that the chopper wasn't the bright orange "Flight for Life" usually used by the Centura Health Care System. It was a MEDEVAC, a larger air ambulance probably sent from Fort Carson.

Cordy used the distraction, ran to the next row of cars to a sidewalk, and crept four car lengths beyond the minivan. She dropped to the ground and rolled under a white SUV. The truck driver tossed something from the window and screeched out of the parking lot. The minivan she had been hiding behind a few moments before exploded, wiping out a string of vehicles. Metal and debris flew into the air, and something crashed into the windshield of the white SUV above her.

Cordy's knees had taken a beating when she dropped to the ground, but she was alive and rolled out from beneath the vehicle, trying to avoid glass shards.

The security guard kept muttering "OMG" under his breath while rushing toward Cordy. "What the hell happened?" He knelt and gently lifted her by the elbow. "Are you okay?" He looked closer and added, "Better go inside and have the doctor examine your face."

Cordy felt her bruised eye and wiped away the blood from her cheek. "It's just a scratch."

The chopper circled the hospital and landed on the helipad. "Sorry. I need to meet that helicopter."

Cordy asked, "Why the MEDEVAC?"

"The hospital is sending an at-risk patient to Fort Carson." The guard rushed for the helipad.

It must be for Joe Smith or whatever his real name is. The wind blew wisps of hair and grit across her face. She took one glance at her crumpled Lexus and swore under her breath. *I need to find another way home. Can't I ever catch a break?*

Cordy hated being in the dark, grounded, with no laptop and only a burner cell phone that she should have disposed of hours ago. *I'll talk to whoever is in charge at Fort Carson, maybe even NASA. I need answers. Now!* She huffed out a breath and headed for the MEDEVAC. Before she took two steps, her wristwatch chirped, indicating a message. *Did something happen to Braun?* Cordy tapped the message button. It read, "Black ops alert. Braun's in danger." Fear jolted through her like an electrical shock.

She continued to read the message, "Call Bracken, and come get me—sent GPS. Chief." A map with a GPS tracker lit up.

Dang, Bracken is the last person I want to talk to. She had to admit that, with fifteen years of SWAT and sniper experience, Officer Russ Bracken was the best person to find Chief Jackson. Before SWAT, Bracken had been a Navy Seal explosive breacher. He also had a crush on Cordy. She had turned him down, not too gently, two weeks ago, and she hadn't given him the news of her engagement to Braun. *This call isn't going to go well.*

Cordy nearly speed-dialed Bracken as she turned back to the hospital. *Wait! No one can know where we're heading, especially if Braun is a liability. We will be the first to be targeted if I haven't already been singled out. I need an untraceable phone. I better warn Usher, too.*

Gathering Evidence

While Cordy headed back inside St. Anthony's hospital to phone Bracken, Agent Dr. Jacqueline Kelly was in Washington, D.C., gathering her laptop and briefcase, anxious to leave the disorganized RR7 meeting. Kelly had tried to keep everyone focused on the task, but Harry kept causing disruptions. When President Spendorf asked the lawyer to leave early, Kelly felt relieved. With Harry gone, the team made some progress until Braun called and needed her help. Checking her watch, Kelly realized it was time to call in some favors.

Brakinsky appeared frazzled as she gathered her notes. "I appreciate your help." Her steel-gray eyes rolled as she glanced at Kelly. "I feel like I'm herding cats!"

Kelly nodded. "Give us a few days. I'll stay in touch with any new developments." She headed for the door, her mind still on Braun and Usher.

Ryan stepped in her way. "Can you come to my office? We have a lot to discuss."

"Sorry, I have ten things I have to do at the moment. They've been put on hold far too long already."

"How about four o'clock?" Ryan asked.

"Make it six," Kelly said. "I might have two minutes by then."

"Six it is," Ryan shoved his wire rims back in place. "I want to know more about this CDC database."

Kelly's primary job was to work with Ryan. He seemed open to new ideas but was more analytical—interested in numbers and tests and probably could quote verbatim the latest articles in JAMA, the Journal of the American Medical Association. Kelly nodded and darted into the restroom to avoid further conversation. I must get Braun and Usher into Washington, D.C., ASAP!

At 5:55 p.m., Kelly walked through the entrance to the CDC— Washington, D.C.'s division. Pea-green paint covered the cement walls. Her heels echoed as she wove down the narrow beige-tiled hallway and ran up one flight of stairs to Ryan's office. It was ten times the size of her office, or cubbyhole as she put it, and was at one end of a brightly lit lab. Ryan wasn't in his office, but a partially eaten slice of pizza lay on a paper towel near his laptop. She glanced around the metal cabinets lining the wall behind his cluttered desk. A cot was in the corner with a shabby, indented pillow and a fleece blanket shoved to one side, half falling onto the floor. Ryan must be working night and day.

The Department of Virology was across the hall. A deep, resonant voice drew her closer. She stood in the doorway listening to a man in a dark blue lab coat speaking over the intercom. "What a coincidence. I think she just walked into my office."

Piercing brown eyes held hers. His olive complexion made his teeth flash when he smiled. "Agent Kelly, I presume. Come in. Ryan said you'd be here soon. I'm—"

"Dr. Alex. I'd know you anywhere. I've read all of your books." Kelly shook his hand in delight. "Will I be working with you?"

"Yes, I've been assigned to your team."

Ryan entered the room, breathing heavily. "I wish the elevator here was faster. I jogged up two flights, and opening the elevator door took the same amount of time. I see you've already met the other half of my team. I received a message from Walter Reed Hospital. Unfortunately, Astronaut Pendari didn't survive, and his family has requested an autopsy. I sent a team to pick up the body, ensuring they take contamination precautions to bring it here."

Kelly asked, "Is that the wisest move? Shouldn't we limit exposure?"

"We can isolate better than anyone and have all the equipment and serology capabilities. Fact is, I want to see this with my own eyes." Ryan's cheeks pinched as his mouth set firm. "Our team will ensure there's no breach of security or contamination."

Ryan's cell interrupted the conversation. "Did you get it?" His face turned pale. "What do you mean someone beat you to it? One moment, I'm putting you on a speaker. Okay, repeat that."

"The body is gone. The administrator says DHS was just here, and they released the body on the orders of Guy Weimer. Do you know him?"

"Yes, we know him." Ryan's fists clenched.

"Should we call him and get the body?" the attendant asked.

Ryan shook his head. "No, we'll take care of everything, but get a copy of Pendari's medical record. Surely, the family will grant permission. If not, call me."

Alex interjected, "Have they cleaned the room yet—any sheets, gowns, or other bedding? Don't enter the room without protection—a filtered mask, double gloves, you know the drill. Swab down exterior surfaces, bed rails, over-bed table, etc., and return with the samples. Be sure to double-bag everything. Oh, yes. Bring back any other evidence, such as IV tubing, ET tube, Foley catheter, etc. We may not have a body, but we can still gather a lot of info."

"Sure thing." The attendant said. "We'll bring everything to the lab." The phone call ended.

Ryan scrolled down his contact list. "I'll call Guy and see what they plan to do with the remains. We are on the same response team. Maybe they'll see fit to bring the body here for an autopsy."

Ryan's call went directly to voice mail. "Guy, this is Ryan. Call me as soon…" The message cut off. After three more attempts, Guy's phone wouldn't record any more messages.

Alex shrugged his shoulders. "It sounds like his mailbox is full."

Ryan paced the room, working off nervous energy. "I'm going to the lab to prepare for the incoming Pendari samples."

"Wait," Kelly said. "Two astronauts who recently returned from the International Space Station have died. Has anyone contacted the third one? What was her name again?"

"Linda Smith-Tyler. She's from Colorado," Alex piped up. "Maybe we need to check on the whole ISS crew, too. I'll call NASA and get her contact information."

"Colorado?" Kelly repeated. "I have a colleague in Fort Collins. She's reported a few victims with similar symptoms. Let me call her, and then I'll see how Linda's doing.

Kelly called Cordy, but the call went directly to voice mail, so she called Linda's home phone number. The phone rang several times before a recording of a frantic woman came on the line. "Please understand that my husband and I had no idea what Chester had in mind when he went to school today. We offer our sincerest condolences." Then, there was a dial tone.

Kelly's heart leapt into her throat, and she nearly dropped the phone. "Something dreadful must have happened in Colorado."

Kelly checked the Colorado news. Chester Tyler had gone on a shooting spree at his school in Fort Collins, killing twelve children before turning a gun on himself. *No wonder Linda sounded so upset. What a shock! She must be devastated.*

Kelly choked and nearly threw up at the news. *Children—they were all innocents, killed by a crazed teenager.* Forcing herself into her professional role, she fought back the sobs and tears that threatened to spill. *Get a grip, Kelley. You need to stay professional. What might have happened? Was Chester also infected with the virus? If so, how was he exposed?*

She gasped when it dawned on her that the virus or whatever superbug was causing this pandemic may have originated from the International Space Station. She needed more information—it was time to contact NASA.

Plan G

Braun was on the run from Homeland Security, which meant from any federal official, especially his colleagues in the FBI. His life depended on keeping up with his elaborate disguises. Flying from Denver to Logan International Airport in Boston as a first-class businessman, he needed a drastic character change. In a hurry, he shoved through the restroom door and tripped over a walking stick. It gave him an idea. He was the only one in the room.

Braun didn't have much time and went to work on his master plan. He wasn't an artist but started drawing a fake tattoo on his arm and neck. He knew Usher was checking Cordy's TOR account to get any updates, and then he would call Kelly.

After his quick makeover, Braun left the airport's front door and stood beside a shuttle sign, twirling the stick while watching for his brother.

Usher exited the airport with a cup of java in hand.

Braun avoided making eye contact, boarded the Thrifty Car Rental shuttle, and sat opposite Usher. They reached their destination in less than five minutes.

There weren't any customers when they arrived, but Braun wasn't taking any chances. His fake tattoo—an asp coiled up his left arm and neck, itched, but he didn't dare scratch it for fear it might smear. The snake's head appeared to have fangs around his right carotid artery. His tight T-shirt revealed washboard abs and muscular shoulders. Aviator glasses protected his eyes. He stood by the front door with the stick and the backpacks, waiting for Usher to rent a car. An attendant left the office to bring the vehicle from the parking lot.

When the car arrived, Usher slid into the driver's seat, placed the rental agreement into the glove compartment, and started the engine.

Braun tapped the windshield using the stick. "Mind if I ride with you a few miles? I'm a bit low on cash."

Usher nodded. "Sure, but I'm not going out of my way for anyone, so I hope you're heading in my direction."

"You can drop me off if we need to part." Braun glanced both ways. No one appeared suspicious as Braun climbed into the rental car.

Usher's eyes narrowed. "Nice, get up, but why do you have that stick?"

"I don't know," Braun said. "I tripped over it in the bathroom, and it seemed like it wanted me to take it. Who knows? Maybe it'll come in handy."

"Right." Usher rolled his eyes and dodged through traffic to I-90, closely watching the rearview mirror for anyone tailing them. Approaching Purchase Street, the traffic picked up.

Braun peered into the side mirror. A dark sedan with its lights off, parked on the side road, pulled out behind them. The lights came on after another car honked and wedged its way between them.

"Keep an eye on that sedan," Usher said.

"You saw it, too," Braun reached in his backpack for some Baby Wipes to wash off the tattoo. With a glance in the mirror, he seemed satisfied with the results and pulled a white shirt, tie, and brown suit coat from his bag.

"Before you change clothes, set up those AutoCams and send the feeds to Cordy, just to be safe," Usher added, "If anything happens to us, she'll track us down."

Braun worked quickly to get the camera feeds to Cordy and switched clothes.

Usher changed lanes. The dark sedan stayed two or three car lengths behind no matter where he turned or how fast he drove, but by now, they were on I-90, so it could be a false alarm. "I'll get off at exit 15-A. We'll need to lose that sedan and get another rental car if he's still behind us."

The sedan flashed its lights and left the Interstate at exit 14. A black van with a slight dent in the right front bumper crept up behind them, staying too close for comfort. It took another ten minutes to lose the van, take another exit, turn around, and book another rental car outside of New Haven, Connecticut.

This time, Usher took the toll road on the Massachusetts Turnpike. There was no sign of the dented van until Usher turned onto Wilbur Cross Highway. "There he is again," but the van passed him. The tinted windows blocked any view of the driver. "Go, buddy. I'm tired of you sitting on my tail."

Braun leaned forward. "That's not the only car to watch. I've been eyeing that silver Honda. We picked him up ten minutes ago."

Usher slowed way down. "Let's run a test." He got off at the next exit and paused at the stoplight until it turned yellow. Then, he drove across the road and got right back on the highway. The Honda followed through the intersection even after the light had turned red. Twelve miles later, the dented van was also behind them. "I don't remember passing that van, do you?"

"They aren't forcing us off the road, so we're okay for now. Better that we know where they are at all times."

Usher grunted, "I guess." He turned on the news: "Riots are spreading from Washington, D.C., to New York. Police are building roadblocks…"

Braun's burner phone chirped, indicating a message. "It's Cordy." He turned down the radio.

"What does her text say?" Usher asked.

"She visited Dr. Trent in the ICU, and some incident occurred. She didn't mention Jackson. Oh, I see I received a call from Kelly, too. She has arranged for a helicopter to pick us up in Philadelphia."

"Good," Usher adjusted the rearview mirror for another look."

Braun frowned. "That's not good! Didn't you hear the news? Roadblocks are going up throughout New York. Traffic is already slowing to barely fifty mph. We'll never make it to Philly. I think we better move to plan B."

"More like plan F," Usher said. "Your original plan was to fly directly to D.C., with Jackson. Plan B happened when he disappeared, so you're stuck with me. Plan C was to fly to Dulles, and we landed at Logan instead. So, we moved on to plan D, where we rented not one car but two. That left plan E when we were supposed to meet with the president four hours ago, but he's now grounded in the bunker, and there are riots in D.C." Traffic continued to back up on I-84. Usher was in the far left lane, trying to avoid the traffic jam.

"Look out!" Braun grabbed the dashboard as the dented van pulled up to the right side of their vehicle, cutting off a gray Mazda. A truck in the far right lane fishtailed, hitting the Mazda, sending it headlong into the rear end of the black dented van.

Usher stepped on the gas, passed the van, and headed for the right shoulder to avoid a collision. Breaks squealed, metal crunched, and tires skidded as vehicles piled up along the Interstate behind the van until traffic was at a standstill. That's when plan F changed to plan G.

While Usher called Kelly, Braun grabbed his moulage kit, made his face pale with fake beads of sweat on his forehead, and became an old, feeble man. "I'm ready. Flag down a trooper. The front and rear cameras are rolling. Hopefully, we'll catch whoever is trying to run us off the road."

* * *

Usher dashed from the car along the shoulder, where several police cars were headed toward the pile-up with sirens blaring. He waved a white hanky and shouted, "Help! My dad's having a heart attack!"

A man got out of the silver Honda, now three cars behind the van. He held up a cell phone as if taking a photo. He must have spied Usher and quickly turned away, but Usher saw the black patch covering his left eye.

Usher sucked in a breath. *Chirk the Jerk, in person. It's worse than I thought!*

Chirk dashed around the crunched Mazda and tapped on the black van's side window.

The van's passenger's door opened, and a uniformed officer stepped onto the road and glanced at Chirk. Shaking his head, the general made a slicing sign with his hand going right to left across his throat. Lifting his left hand, he swirled his index finger in a circle—a *wrap-it-up sign.*

Is that General Rutoon in the black van? Surely not. He's the president's National Security Advisor. The man ducked back into the van before Usher could get a positive ID, but the AutoCam captured everything.

The guy with the eye patch returned to his sedan. The two vehicles pulled forward, hugged the shoulder, and managed to drive away. Usher knew Chirk wouldn't have a shootout in the middle of this crowd.

A few people rushed to Usher's side to offer aid. A shrill whistle sounded over the noisy crowd. Blue and red lights flickered, and a siren died on the breeze as a state trooper pulled up near Usher. A tall woman with a dark ponytail draped over her shoulder climbed out of the cruiser. "What's the problem?"

"It's my dad. He's having chest pain and needs to go to the hospital, but we can't get through this traffic. Can you help us?" Usher pleaded. A tear slid down his cheek in desperation.

"Lead the way." The officer grabbed her radio.

Usher stepped forward and opened the passenger door. "Dad, everything will be okay."

A stooped, bald man feebly swung his legs over the car seat and lowered them to the ground. The chalk-colored makeup gave his skin a sallow look. "My cane, boy," quivered from Braun's lips.

Usher reached into the car and handed Braun the walking stick.

Braun placed a wrinkled hand over his left side and rocked a bit before putting weight on his feet. The cane slid, and Braun nearly collapsed.

Usher rushed to his side, as did the officer. "Easy now," she said. "I'm getting help."

Braun's face, void of color, made him appear ill and light-headed. He stumbled forward with Usher's arm for support. Sweat beaded on his forehead. Braun moaned. "Sonny, I think I'm going to die." He leaned heavier on his cane and slid to the ground.

"Dad? Oh, please hurry!" Usher knelt beside Braun.

The sound of whirring helicopter blades came from overhead as a Flight for Life chopper landed in a field nearby. As the EMTs worked on Braun, Usher pocketed the flash drive with the evidence of General Rutoon and Chirk on the AutoCam's recordings and arranged to have his vehicle towed. He would forward a copy to Cordy.

Then, he flew with Braun to the nearest hospital, where Agent Kelly promised to have a MEDEVAC waiting.

Time to Move On

Back in Colorado, Cordy anxiously waited to hear from Braun. She had set up a secure darknet website to ensure their conversations remained private, but had not received any message from him on her cell or her TOR anonymity email account. Usher's last message was ambiguous, saying, "D.C., closed! We're in Kelly's hands. I have AutoCam photos for you—will send soon." *No photos yet.*

Worried about her fiancé, Cordy refined one of her ideas for a tracking device that was sturdy and untraceable by others. It could double as a camera, a communication device, and also track deadly electronic equipment in the area. Cordy sketched her idea on a napkin until her food arrived and put it in her pocket to focus on eating. She planned to discuss her ideas with Dr. Quint Altari, her trusted colleague who could bring her vision to life with the proper specifications.

Cordy glanced at her watch. It had been forty minutes since she had asked Officer Bracken to pick her up from St. Anthony's hospital. She sat in the cafeteria, pushing a forkful of lasagna around her plate—hungry, but her nervous stomach prevented her from eating anything.

Bracken was a man who knew what he wanted, and for the past six months, he had wanted Cordy as a possession rather than a person. He vowed to protect her, but Cordy had to be free to make her own decisions and mistakes. She hoped that Bracken's crush on her wouldn't intensify after having to work together again. His bold determination made him successful at his job. Her best efforts to push him aside only made him more intent, which worried her. To Bracken's credit, he had taken her rebuff in stride and had been professional when she called in a favor to rescue Chief Jackson.

Braun had once tried to be Cordy's male protector, too, but she had kicked him out. They reconnected six months ago, and fortunately, Braun had sandbagged his protective training and instincts. She recalled Braun's struggles to accept her without judgment before her mind returned to the present. *Why hasn't Braun called? And where is Bracken?*

When she rechecked her phone, she noticed a text message, "Just arrived. I'm out front. Meet me in the hospital lobby, Bracken."

Cordy picked up her food tray, threw away the barely touched leftovers, and placed the empty dishes onto the conveyor belt leading to the kitchen. Chief Jackson's life was hanging in the balance, so she ran up the stairway instead of waiting for the elevator to the first floor.

Bracken was coming through the hospital's front door when she reached the lobby. His jaw tightened when Cordy dashed past him.

"You coming?" She didn't wait for him to open the door.

Bracken followed. Deep creases formed over his brow, and he jingled the keys in his pocket. "I nearly didn't come."

Playing with his keys again—he's irritated. Cordy turned around and blocked his way by stepping into his path. "Look, Bracken, I may be asking more than you're willing to give, but I trust you. You're bullheaded and stubborn, and we both know you'll find the chief."

"Yeah, deep down, I knew I'd take the job. I wouldn't trust anyone else to do it." His eyes blazed with intensity as he snatched her left hand and fixed his gaze on the engagement ring. "Braun won." He swallowed hard and stood straighter. "Let's go."

"Bracken, I—"

"No, I get it. I'm doing this for the chief!" He opened the passenger door, all business now. "Get in and show me the GPS settings."

Cordy opened an app on her cell phone. When Bracken was behind the wheel, she handed him her phone. "See the red dot? It's in the middle of the forest. All I can see on Google Maps is densely packed trees."

Bracken enlarged the map. "Look at this. There is a box-shaped structure located on the outskirts of the forest. Upon closer inspection, I see solar panels and a wind turbine. I think the chief is located in that area. However, as a precautionary measure, I want to notify the SWAT team as a backup."

"I wonder who owns the property." Cordy grabbed her phone to access the county's property database.

Bracken issued commands over the radio to Larimer County, lining up SWAT as he sped away—burning rubber in his wake.

Cordy lurched forward and nearly lost her cell as she braced herself against the dashboard. "Geez, you could have given me some warning!"

"Oh yeah, sorry, better buckle up." Bracken's grin was anything but apologetic.

Cause of Death

Agent Kelly stifled a yawn and took a few moments to regroup for a long night ahead at the CDC center in Washington, D.C. At this point, she had been working eighteen hours, and no break was in sight. Messages kept pouring in. Three more hospitals were over their capacity and were sending patients to the temporary medical facilities in schools and gymnasiums set up by Carl Wyller of DoD, who had been busy opening urgent care centers all over town, and in makeshift tents, too, and they just kept coming.

Ryan asked, "Have you ever seen so many patients?"

"In the past, flu season swamped medical clinics and the emergency department, but normally, we can clear them out in a day. Then COVID-19 hit, and now this."

"I wonder at what point the hospitals will just close," Ryan said.

"They have no more beds. Hospitals can't send patients home in critical condition." Kelly sighed. "Even with military backup, providing tents, and placing patients in closed schools as makeshift hospitals, we can't keep up. Besides, many patients are too violent to be placed in that environment. It's not safe—"

A man dressed in blue scrubs paused at the door. "The recovery team just arrived with Astronaut Ivan Pendari's samples, blood work, ET tube, oxygen tubing, IV equipment, and Foley catheter. Everything is double-bagged and loaded on a contamination cart. Where do you want it?"

"Take it to Dr. Alex's bio-lab." Ryan gowned up. I'll be there in a moment."

While Ryan and Alex took over culturing and analyzing the samples, Kelly reviewed the astronaut's medical record.

Two hours later, although it seemed only a few minutes had flown by, Kelly glanced up from reading the report when she realized someone was standing over her right shoulder. "Ryan, you look as exhausted as I feel. What have you discovered so far?"

"Pendari's brain must have been as soggy as a melon," Ryan murmured as he read over her shoulder.

"Yeah, brain stem herniation was the cause of death. Encephalitis is highly probable, but he died before they could do a scan to prove it. Have you heard back from Guy Weimer?"

"You won't believe this. They cremated the body before doing an autopsy. Guy said the infection was too dangerous for anyone else to be exposed."

Kelly blew out a deep breath in frustration. "I'm sure he thought he was doing the right thing, but what about Maxwell Uliptos? Can we get his autopsy report?"

"I knew you'd want access. It took some doing, but we have an electronic medical record and the autopsy report. Alex and I already reviewed the information and want a third opinion." Ryan pulled up a chair, turned Kelly's laptop toward him, and entered the necessary passcodes. "Take your time. Fresh coffee is on the way, along with a chocolate croissant. They're my favorite, so I hope you'll enjoy them." Ryan ran a hand over his brow and left Kelly to review the chart.

She started with the medical record and was analyzing Max's last day on Earth when a cup of steaming coffee caught her attention. She glanced up, expecting Ryan. Instead, weary, dark brown eyes met hers.

"Thanks, Alex."

"Do you take cream or sugar?" he asked.

"Cream, but first, I need a squirt of hand sanitizer." She placed a dab from the bottle on her desk before taking the cup. "I feel germy just reading over this medical information."

Alex laughed. "We have a bottle on every desk and refill them weekly. I'm ready to review these cases."

Kelly reached for the croissant. "I haven't read the autopsy report yet. Give me twenty minutes, and then we can discuss our findings."

"Sounds good, but it's already 2 a.m. Are you sure you don't want to sleep for a while?"

"No, it's not my first time working the night shift. Let's wrap this up and give our findings to RR7 in the morning." Kelly's phone pinged another text message. She flipped through the latest reports.

"More bad news?" Alex asked.

"Two thousand more cases are in New York, and three NYC hospitals are on deferral. Every state has an increased number of cases with the virus, including Montana, which was infection-free yesterday." Pausing to read more, she added, "Six Maryland hospitals are closed to any new patients. Two temporary school hospitals have also reached capacity, and the bodies are piling up for mortuary pickup. We can't keep going like this. After COVID, no one wants to shut down again, but the whole country needs to go into total isolation."

"I agree. I'll see if Ryan has any ideas. We'll meet in my office when you're ready. I have a conference room behind my desk." When Alex left the room, Kelly already had her nose in the laptop.

It took her 30 minutes to review Maxwell's autopsy report, which was quite detailed for being the first case diagnosed with the new virus. It was frightening. She had never seen anything like it in her twenty-two years as a nurse practitioner. As Kelly entered Alex's conference room, the two men were having an in-depth discussion. They turned to her with anticipation.

Ryan asked, "Did you notice any clinical differences between the two astronaut cases?"

Kelly pursed her lips. "They seemed to follow the same disease pattern, but I'm amazed at how quickly they deteriorated even with treatment."

Alex nodded. "Both men initially complained of a severe headache. Two hours later, they had a fever above 103° F and developed a massive cough."

Ryan added, "According to their medical records, both became confused and violent. Pendari was screaming nonsense and ripped a rail off his bed. Max hit a lab technician and tried to choke his nurse when she intervened. They both had to be restrained."

"I've seen things like this in the ICU," Kelly admitted. "But it usually takes a week to ten days to progress to ICU psychosis, not hours! Both developed a rapid-onset cough, producing profuse amounts of blood. Pendari was placed in a negative airflow room for protection since his immune system shut down, but he didn't last more than four more hours. Max was the first to develop symptoms, and he hung on five hours longer than Pendari did after his diagnosis, so the virus is becoming more aggressive."

"Right," Ryan agreed. "The symptoms advance faster once infected, and the virus attacks more people every minute."

Alex's brow furrowed. "The infection infiltrated the lungs, and both men soon went into full-blown pulmonary edema, lost consciousness, and had to be placed on a ventilator. Seizures developed during the night, and their spinal fluid specimens showed meningitis."

"According to Max's autopsy report, he died of massive encephalitis, so the infection crossed the blood-brain barrier," Kelly pointed at a cat scan. "It was so severe that it increased his intracranial pressure, causing temporal herniation through the sinus cavity, and the brain stem herniated through the foramen magnum. His systolic blood pressure continued to rise while the diastolic pressure dropped with a B/P of 220 over 30. His cardiac rhythm strips showed severe tachycardia, slowing from 300 to 20 beats per minute. Then his heart ceased to beat."

Kelly read another text message, and this one also sounded desperate: "Need more ventilators! We're out of suction, too."

"Forward it unto Carl. Vents and equipment are his responsibility," Ryan said.

Kelly forwarded the message. "I don't know where he'll find more vents. Last I heard, all Federal Reserve inventory is in use, and President Spendorf has added funding for private industry to produce more, but that takes time."

"It won't be soon enough." Ryan flipped to the lab results for both patients. "Look at these cultures. Both men had MRSA, Streptococcus pneumoniae, and bacteremia."

They had inflammation of the lungs and the bloodstream," Kelly mentioned as if thinking aloud. "That's a triple whammy not seen very often.

Alex added, "With similar symptoms and outcomes, I believe they were exposed while in flight. We know the virus grows three times more potent without gravity. Could they be the source of this infection?"

Kelly piped up, "If both astronauts were infected, why wasn't Linda Smith-Tyler? I know something happened to her son,

Chester, but what's different that she wasn't exposed or showing any symptoms?"

"What happened to Chester?" Alex asked. "He wasn't anywhere near the spacecraft."

"Good point. We need more research," Ryan surveyed several lab samples.

Alex frowned as he studied a series of X-rays.

"You've found something," Ryan said, "haven't you? I recognize that look."

Alex pointed to an X-ray. "The bacteria spread to the spinal fluid, causing meningitis, but what intrigues me is this odd growth in the lungs. It's a fungus. See several balls of fungus fibers, blood clots, and white blood cells in the air spaces of the right lung?" He flipped up another X-ray. "Fungus also infiltrated the sinus cavity. What do you suppose caused that?"

"That's something else we'll have to figure out." Ryan yawned.

Alex added, "We've cultured Pendari's IV catheter, which grew an odd bacterial chain on the agar plate, and we've only had the specimen for three hours. The Foley catheter hasn't grown much except gram-negative cocci. Although that's abnormal, I don't think that's the lethal ingredient."

Ryan held up three photos of the agar plates' growth at one-hour intervals. "Look at this unusual bacterial chain. It's rod-shaped, and the number has doubled over each timeframe. I don't know what to call this, but we must find out how to kill it. That's your job, Alex."

"Perhaps tomorrow we'll know more," Alex finished his coffee. "In the meantime, we need to get some rest. If we don't stay alert, we could miss something critical."

"I have a conference call scheduled at 5 a.m. with several bioengineers working with WHO. We sent them photos of the lab growth specimens, but two groups want to analyze actual virus samples."

"Which two countries?" Alex asked.

"Switzerland and France. It will be difficult to send a live virus," Kelly warned.

"We'll make it happen." Alex jotted a note on a sticky. "I want all the help we can get."

"There's an extra cot we keep for special visitors that you can use, Kelly, unless you'd rather venture home for a hot shower and your bed," Ryan said. "You have two hours before your conference call and four hours before our next RR7 meeting."

"I wouldn't trust myself to drive home," Kelly admitted. "I could put two chairs together and sleep just fine."

"I want to be on that call," Ryan said.

"Me, too," Alex agreed. "I'll put the cot in the conference room, and so we don't oversleep, I'll set an alarm."

Five minutes later, the lights were off, and Kelly heard snoring from Alex's office. She supposed Ryan was in his office, tucked away on his cot. It was her last thought before she, too, fell asleep.

Thirty minutes later, Kelly jolted awake when Braun called. "Usher and I made it to Washington, D.C. The MEDIVAC just landed outside of the CDC's door. We need to see the president ASAP."

"Okay, I'll make the arrangements with Winston, the president's Chief of Staff. He is the only person I trust to get you there safely. Meet you at the front door shortly." Kelly pulled her burner cell phone from her scrubs, sending an encrypted message to Winston as she headed downstairs. She opened the heavy door and let Braun and Usher inside while the MEDIVAC took off on another mission. "Coffee?" Kelly asked.

"Do you have any at this hour?" Braun studied her face. "You look exhausted."

Alex joined the group. "She didn't get much sleep. I guess we all could use a cup. Let's meet in the conference room."

Ryan soon followed with a pot of fresh brew and five cups. "You must be the Hastings brothers."

Kelly made the introductions.

Braun gulped half a cup and asked, "How bad is this?"

"It's not an epidemic as we thought at first. It's a pandemic," Kelly said. "The virus is spreading across South America, Europe, Asia, Africa, and the Middle East. I sure hope Cordy stays healthy. She was exposed to the virus in a hospital in Denver."

Braun paled. "My Cordy?"

"She went through decontamination," Kelly said. "Twice, so far."

Braun shook his head. "That sounds about right. She has to be in the center…"

Kelly didn't hear the rest, as a knock on the front door made Braun hop up from his chair.

Usher put his hand on Braun's shoulder. "A little gun-shy?"

"I'll get it." Kelly went to answer the door. "It's time to go. Winston sent a driver and a car."

"Thanks, Kelly," Braun borrowed a set of scrubs from the CDC as his latest disguise. He peered through the window before heading back outside. "Let's get this over with."

Three Strikes and You're Out

Chirk T. Transom kicked the door and slammed his fist on the table. Frustration twisted his face into a grimace. This third attempt to capture Braun had also failed. Chirk had successfully followed the general's orders to the letter until several days ago when he kidnapped his ex-partner, Chief Jackson. The brilliant plan to convince Jackson to lure Braun to turn himself in also failed.

"Stop interfering!" The general's words still rang in Chirk's head. "I don't want you to get wrapped up in this. Let Dr. Joe Smith handle the job."

That turned out to be another humiliation. Smith was to capture Braun during his meeting with Dr. Trent, but Braun was a no-show, and somehow Trent was shot.

"Still, Rutoon backed that worthless hack of a doctor. Then the schmuck died, and that's when the general finally calls me in!"

Rutoon swore, "Braun's going to be the death of us all. I have first-hand proof that Braun planted this superbug, and the president is on his hit list. We must protect Zac."

Chirk followed orders but wasn't happy to be stuck dealing with both Hastings brothers.

The general wanted Braun dead or alive. Preferably dead, but then, the idiot general aborted Chirk's third attempt on Braun's life when there was a nine-car pileup on the Turnpike.

Things were getting out of hand. Chirk opted to take cover and feared he would have to get rid of his ex-FBI partner, too. He was still determining if he could carry out the task. So, out of necessity, he had to make Jackson's death look like an accident. *Maybe I can try once more to get Jackson's cooperation.*

"You ready to talk?" Chirk spoke through a microphone connected to a speaker above Jackson's cot in his basement cell.

"Talk about what?" Jackson asked. "That dirty deal you pulled on me four years ago? That incident burns my gut."

"You still sore over that?" Chirk asked. When Jackson went shopping for a high-end laptop, he accidentally discovered a high-tech smuggling plot that sent weapons, equipment, and U.S. military weapons to Syria, and they used them against the U.S. Armed Forces. It was risky but beyond lucrative compared to Chirk's measly salary. "I wouldn't have gotten that promotion if you hadn't sent in the FBI."

"That promotion should have been mine, and you know it. I was the one who detained their shipment and found explosives. Instead, I ended up leaving the FBI."

Jackson's findings could have destroyed Chirk's career. Still, with fast thinking and inside information at the top, Chirk finagled a supervisor position out of the deal after claiming he'd discovered the smuggling scheme from Libya to Syria. Maybe Rutoon's recommendation helped. "Admit it. I'm smarter than you."

"Kidnapping me was your dumbest move yet," Jackson said. "Why did you do it?"

"Your buddy, Braun, is a bioterrorist, and I'm going to stop him. Dead or alive—it doesn't matter to me."

"You're a fool to believe that," Jackson said. "Braun's innocent."

"All evidence points to Braun. He spent months in North Korea, and then Kim Jong Un launched a long-range rocket." Chirk was so upset his voice cracked. "How else would they get access to that kind of weapon?"

"Braun was working undercover for the government, and none of us are privy to his mission," Jackson said. "I know he's no terrorist, though, and nothing you say will convince me otherwise."

"And what was he doing in Syria?" Chirk asked.

"Again, working undercover," Chief Jackson snapped. "Why are you going after Braun? What have you done that you're trying to cover up and pin on him?"

"I have proof that he planted that virus," Chirk said.

"What kind of proof," Jackson asked.

"I'm not at liberty to say, but I'm protecting our president. I'm under direct orders from the top, and my credibility is on the line."

"Really?" Jackson's tone dripped with sarcasm. "When no one can believe a word out of your mouth? That shocks me."

Chirk bit back his anger. "The general made it perfectly clear that Braun is guilty of planting this deadly virus. Homeland Security is also hunting down Braun. So, are you going to help me or not?"

"I think not," Jackson said.

"Fine, your life is on the line," Chirk vowed. He would silence Braun, with or without Chief Jackson's help. One huge problem—Chirk didn't want to off his stubborn ex-partner, so he'd give the guy one more chance before doing the deed. "Think about it. Maybe you'll change your mind after another day without food and water. I'll only give you twenty-four more hours."

"I won't change my mind," Jackson said.

Chirk already knew that. *Being caught between my boss and ex-partner is hell.*

Rescue Plan

Cordy was in Fort Collins, Colorado, feeling nervous energy spark through her as she faced the daunting task ahead. She knew she couldn't rescue Chief Jackson by herself and needed help. It wasn't easy, but she mustered the courage to call SWAT commander Russ Bracken, her ex-lover and trusted ally. She had faith in his team's abilities and knew they would do whatever it took to free Chief Jackson alive.

This was Cordy's first official assignment with the team. The last time she worked with them, she was an outsider who had to force her way in when everything went terribly wrong. Cordy was unsure if the team would accept her and wondered how she should portray herself. Every crisis was different, and from her past experience, Cordy knew that she could unintentionally offend Bracken. He was much like her, someone who had to be in control and make the decisions. He was a crack shot, a weapons expert, and led high-risk operations for a living. She knew logistics and wouldn't back down if challenged. They both had to make snap decisions during crucial moments without any warning. It was the nature of their worlds.

To calm down and feel more in control, Cordy studied the faces of each SWAT team member seated around the table. Bracken sat next to her with three SWAT members: Poncho, who was confident, macho, and Bracken's second-in-command; Chico, who was twenty pounds lighter than Poncho but agile, quick-thinking, and dedicated; and Kayman, tapping his fingers with nervous energy. This meant that there were four SWAT officers present, including Bracken. On the opposite side of the table were two men from the SWAT bomb squad: Sergeant Foley and the latest addition to the team, Bomb Disposal Officer Desmond. The last member of the group was an experienced medic named George.

Poncho asked, "This is a hostage situation. Should we try to negotiate? As far as we know, Chirk has not been a murder suspect in the past. What do we know about the man?"

"Cordy, do you have any more info on Chirk?" Bracken asked.

Cordy leaned forward. "He was Jackson's FBI partner four years ago. They had a falling out. Jackson believes Chirk absconded with over $5 million, which he stashed in an offshore account. However, no evidence has surfaced so far. The FBI promoted Chirk, and he became Jackson's boss. The incident angered the chief, causing him to retire and form his own private investigation company. Jackson still harbors suspicions about Chirk and was deeply disappointed when the FBI recently promoted Chirk to the Washington Army National Guard 19th Special Forces Group."

"Is Braun still working for the chief?" Poncho asked.

"No. Braun joined the chief initially." Cordy hesitated. "I'm unsure if I can say what Braun is doing now."

Bracken glanced around the table. "I'll vouch for my team. I know Braun is currently working undercover for the U.S. Joint Special Operations Command, JSOC. His brother, Usher, is still working with the FBI. Cordy here," he coolly nodded toward his one-time lover, "is the FBI's lead cyber threat and research analyst. The chief called her when Braun went missing. Then Chief Jackson also disappeared, and here we are. You know the rest."

"Is Chirk working alone?" Poncho asked.

Cordy thought a moment. "I'm not sure if Chirk decided to do this on his own or reports to someone higher up. If we subdue Chirk, we might get some answers."

"So, I guess the question remains, is Chirk a murderer?" Poncho asked.

"I think he would shoot to kill if he feels threatened," Cordy warned. "I doubt he's killed the chief yet, but his life is on the line."

"Subdue, as in maim, but not kill." Bracken rolled his eyes. "Does that answer your question, Poncho?"

"Yeah," Poncho agreed. "We do our best, but if a bullet becomes lethal, so be it."

Bracken nodded. "We have two teams. You know the drill: one bomb squad member with two SWAT officers. George, stay at the fence line unless we have any injuries."

Bracken stood. "I'll head up, Team One. Chico, you're with me. Kayman, you were nearly killed on our last raid. Are you feeling up to this task?"

"Count me in. I wouldn't be here if it weren't for you boys." Kayman absently rubbed his leg.

"Okay. Foley, you're my bomb man," Bracken nodded his way. "Poncho, you'll head up Team Two."

"Kayman, guess you're with me," Poncho said. "No getting trapped this time, right? You had all of us running to cover your ass the last time."

Kayman flushed. "Hey, rehab for four months, learning to walk again, and singing the blues ain't half bad, but I bet I can win hands down in an arm-wrestling contest."

Poncho smirked and spoke up, "Yup, that's more like it. All right, I suppose I'll be working with Desmond, the new guy on the block, as my bomb expert."

Desmond was taken aback, "I'm not new. I have served for six years in the army's EOD and IEDD, worked for four years on the Texas bomb squad, and have been with the team for six months now. It's time you treated me as a full-fledged member. I'm lookin' forward to working with y'all again." He smiled at his drawled remark. "I sense that my southern speak doesn't sit well with you guys." Desmond took a deep breath.

Poncho scowled. "We're all team members, Desi, but we've earned the right to be who we are today."

"No way will anyone call me Desi!"

Poncho held up his hand in defense. "Okay, Laddie, take it easy. We're a team. I'm your leader. Got it?"

"Yeah, Laddie is better than Desi, but my name is Desmond!"

Bracken patted the bomb man on the back. "Looks like you'll fit in just fine, Desmond. You're Poncho's right-hand bomb man. As he said, we work together as a team. That's final." Bracken looked fiercely at Poncho, and Cordy knew it meant to knock off these comments.

Cordy also noticed Poncho matched the glare, and the testosterone in the room festered to a boiling point and needed to be neutralized, so she tapped Bracken's arm. "What about me? Where do I fit in on this team as security?"

Bracken glanced at Cordy, closed his eyes briefly, and sighed. "You'll report to both teams, but you're assigned to Poncho."

Cordy quietly gasped. "What? He's not going to monitor my every move."

Bracken smiled. "You haven't changed. You have the most important job of all. Keep your eyes open, be ready to counter any booby traps Chirk triggers, and keep us informed of any danger lurking out there."

Cordy bit back her comments burning within, and seeing the men geared up, ready for action, she became all business. "This is for the chief. Let's check out Jackson's location."

The blinking GPS dot from Chief Jackson's watch tracked to a location on the edge of Rocky Mountain National Forest. Cordy had spent the last twenty minutes researching. "The Larimer County map shows a strip of private property, and according to Ancestry, it was once owned by Thaddeus Parker Rich."

Bracken leaned over her shoulder and glanced at the family tree she had built and attached documents she had pulled from archives. "What did you find?"

"The property deed shows it was owned by Chirk T. Transom's great-grandfather on his mother's side of the family. It has been passed down to Chirk through the generations."

"Let me guess. T stands for Thaddeus?" Bracken asked.

Cordy nodded.

"So Chirk the Jerk kidnapped the chief," Bracken said. "Now things are becoming clear as crystal. Chirk's also gunning for Braun. It makes sense that he'd go after the chief. They've worked together for years and are best friends."

"Can you get some BATTs waiting for us at the forest's edge?" Cordy asked.

"Already done." Bracken patted Cordy on the back. "Now pull up a blueprint of that building and a map of the surrounding area. Send a copy to our phones."

Bracken had requested a favor and was promised two transport systems would be waiting at the forest's edge. He called ahead to check on the progress of his request and headed back to his teammates for last-minute details.

"I sent the blueprint," Cordy said. "Did everyone get a copy?" Each man checked his phone and nodded.

Bracken took a few minutes to study the documents. "Take a good look at that building. Given who Chirk is, expect rigged enhancements throughout the place, probably strong enough to survive the next global war. It won't be easy to enter."

Cordy added, "Chirk has infrared cameras all around his property and a locked main gate."

"Let's plan how we get inside, unnoticed," Bracken drew a diagram on the board.

"I dug a bit deeper." Cordy tapped on her keyboard. "A security panel controls three entry points—the main gate, front, and back doors. Acme Electronics installed the system. I located an ID number for the property in Acme's database, but Chirk's iris scan activates them. We don't have access yet, but I'll keep trying."

"You mean retinal scans?" Bracken asked.

"No, iris scans, a photo of his eyes. He could easily take one with his iPhone."

The team members broke into a lengthy discussion while Cordy continued her search. She finally found a link to Chirk's cell phone. "Got it! He uses the same scan for his phone."

Bracken said, "Okay. We'll keep it simple. Team One will come through the front door. Poncho, take Team Two to the rear of the building, but the situation is fluid, so keep your heads up for changes."

"Will do," Poncho said.

Bracken pointed to Kayman. "Pack an extra set of night goggles for Cordy."

"I'll pack my own gear, thank you." Cordy grabbed a Kevlar flak jacket with ceramic inserts, a semi-automatic pistol, helmet, camo shirt and pants, gloves, protective pads, LED flashlight, and eyewear, which included a pair of night goggles. "Did I miss anything?"

Bracken cracked a grin and chuckled, "Gas mask and your laptop."

"Laptop accounted for." She searched the gear and tried on two masks before finding one tight enough to fit around her face. "Check. Are we taking the BATT or flying?"

"We'll fly to the forest land where 2 BATTs are waiting for us." Bracken adjusted his gear. "George, one BATT has additional medical equipment, so you'll stay there unless we need you elsewhere. Cordy, you have the toughest job, but your BATT is equipped with the latest communication and surveillance technology."

"So, I'm with George?" Cordy asked.

Bracken nodded. "Yup, you'll stay aboard to monitor all activities and keep our teams updated with any changes you observe. You'll be our lifeline."

Cordy opened her mouth to speak, but Bracken held up his hand and grinned when he told them what else he'd arranged for their hunt through the forest. "We'll have a drone with an infrared camera and a bomb sniffer to monitor the house. Find Chief Jackson and anyone else. If necessary, break through any security codes to make entry easier, and we'll secure the building, neutralize any resistance, and rescue as planned."

"Will each of you be wearing a body camera?" Cordy asked.

"Yes, and earphones," Bracken added, "any more questions?" The men gave a thumbs-up. "Cordy? Does this meet all your requirements?"

"Yes, sir!"

"Get your gear, and let's roll." Bracken grabbed his helmet, led the team outside, and they boarded a twin-engine helicopter.

The pilot greeted them with, "ETA, thirty minutes."

Violence Escalates

Carl Wyller, head of DoD, called Guy Weimer's motel phone and talked for nearly half an hour. "So do you think we did the right thing, having Pendari's body cremated? It sounds like you got an earful from Ryan."

"He'll get over it," Guy said. "We have too many irons in the fire, and we already know Pendari was infected. What good would an autopsy be?"

"I guess you're right." Carl pulled a few notes from his pocket. He noticed his hand trembling. "I've been busy all evening bringing military personnel to set up tents for treating patients. We've equipped every available school with isolation gear and cots. The military sent pharmaceuticals, chest tubes, IV equipment, and medical supplies to each facility by MEDEVAC. Hospitals are transferring patients."

"That should make RR7 happy." Guy's words seemed clipped.

Carl shoved the notes back into his pocket. "We're doing our part. I hope the rest of the team is as efficient. Sorry, I need to cut this call short. My wife still hasn't made it home, and she's been on duty for two shifts already. I think I better check on her."

"Peggy works at the Metropolitan Police Department, right?" Guy asked.

"Yeah, she usually works the fourth division, but nearly half the force has called in sick. She's spread thin lately, and the violence is only escalating."

"It's all over the news," Guy said.

"Peg got a Dispatch call from the sixth division and reported to work an hour early," Carl said. He checked his phone for messages, but there were none.

"Why did she report early?" Guy asked.

"Two police officers down, attacked while responding. Six citizens were shooting from different houses, and she was on backup to rescue the ambushed officers. I don't know what happened, but it spooked the whole neighborhood. Five dead, and one girl was only twelve. It worried Peg so much that she removed her Glock 19 from our safe and told me to wear it always concealed in a shoulder holster. It's her off-duty pistol. Then she loaded her Glock 17 service semi-automatic and reported to work."

"Dreadful." Guy paused. "Oh, I better go, too. My wife's calling. Something's happening outside." There was shouting in the background. "What the hell?" Guy yelled, and the line went dead.

Carl called out, "Guy! Are you all right? What's going on?" There was no response. Guy was staying at a local motel. *Surely, he must be safe.* Carl speed-dialed Peggy, but the call went directly to voicemail again.

* * *

Peggy's gun was ready as she aimed her flashlight across the hood of the parked squad car, watching a man holding something in his hand. "Is that a bat or a rifle?" she asked J.D., her partner of four years.

"Bat. It looks like blood smeared along one end," J.D. warned. The guy stood alone in the middle of the yard, shouted at three males, and ducked behind a porch swing. "He could be dangerous."

"Drop the bat," Peggy ordered.

The guy with the bat turned toward the cops. "It ain't me that you want. It's the couple over there."

Peggy swung her beam in the direction where the guy with the bat pointed. The front porch light was on at the house, every window lit, and the front door appeared closed. Nothing seemed out of place. "What do you mean it's the couple over there?" Peggy asked as she gradually stood from her crouched position.

J.D. clicked the radio transmitter attached to his vest. "This is unit six approaching four males at Parkside Terrace Apartments near Denver Drive."

Dispatch took a moment before responding, "Copy, unit six."

The guy with the bat headed toward them. Two men walked from behind the swing and ran down the steps to meet the bat guy.

Peggy repeated, "Drop the bat and stay where you are."

They stood still, but the guy with the bat held tight to the weapon.

J.D. rounded the car's hood and paused. "Who called 911?"

"I did," the man with the bat said. "Name's Colt."

"Drop the bat, Colt," J.D. said. "I'm coming over. My partner has a gun, so no fast moves. Just drop the bat on the ground."

Peggy beamed her light on Colt, who squinted, turned his head away from the beam, and dropped the bat. He stood with his hands in the air. "Lower that light. I can't see."

Peggy kept the light on the boys but dropped it from Colt's face.

J.D. walked closer and ordered, "Lift your shirts a few inches so I can see your waistlines, and slowly turn in a full circle. I want to check for hidden weapons. There are too many strange encounters tonight."

The guy still on the porch yelled, "Look out—"

J.D. flew backward and hit the ground as glass shattered, and a loud bang sounded from an upstairs window. Everything turned to chaos.

Peggy yelled, "Police, drop your weapons!" Shots continued from upstairs, and she yelled, "Take cover, boys."

The men in the yard ran and ducked behind the squad car beside her, and the shooting stopped.

"You got another gun?" Colt asked.

"No," Peggy shouted. "Wait here. I'm going to check on J.D."

Peggy hit the radio transmission button on her uniform. "Dispatch, officer down. Need immediate backup!"

J.D. was on his back, his torso in a pool of blood. He wasn't moving.

Peggy chanced a run and knelt next to her partner. "J.D., can you hear me?" He didn't respond.

Another round of gunfire ripped up the yard, and dirt flew into Peggy's face. She sprawled spread eagle.

Colt called from around the squad car. "You're going to get yourself killed!"

Peggy heard the cruiser's door alarm, glanced over, and saw the two other men leaning inside the car, searching for weapons. One yelled, "Look, man, a Taser." He grabbed the weapon and headed for the back of the house.

"Stop!" Peggy shouted and pointed her gun, but the man kept running.

"Let him go. His girlfriend is inside, babysitting, or at least, she was before all the shooting," Colt said. "We found that bat behind their house. I don't know whose blood is on it, but Larry's sure it's hers."

Torn between going after Taser guy, staying with J.D., or running for safety, she tried to arouse her partner.

Colt found a police shield and darted for Peggy. He held the shield in front of J.D. and knelt beside Peggy. "Where are you hit?"

Confused, Peggy said, "I'm not hit."

"Where's that blood coming from?" Colt pointed at her pant leg.

Surprised, she felt a burning sting above her right ankle. Blood oozed through her sock and onto her shoe. "I didn't even feel it until now."

Sirens sounded in the distance. During the commotion, porch lights flickered up and down the street, and people gawked out of their windows.

The ambulance arrived just ahead of another cruiser. An EMT dressed in a gown and mask ran toward them but ducked when Peggy shouted, "Stay down. J.D.'s been hit. I just got shot while trying to help him."

The ambulance driver called out, "Wait until I get there before making any moves. We've been so busy tonight that I need to reload my supplies tote."

Two officers pulled onto the grass in front of Peggy and got out. Ducking around the vehicle, they knelt next to Peggy. "What's going on? My boss is frantically trying to cover shifts. I got home from vacation this morning, and he begged me to return to work." His nametag read, K. Reed.

"We need to move my partner to safety," Peggy's voice quivered. "Your patrol car gives some cover, but the shots came from that upper window, and we're still exposed."

A paramedic ran toward Peggy's cruiser with a medical kit. He, too, was dressed in protective gear. He ducked behind the car and yelled, "What's your partner's name?"

"J.D." Peggy turned toward her injured partner. "Hurry. He's not moving and is bleeding. I'll cover you." She aimed her pistol at the house with the broken window.

The paramedic grabbed his medical box, dashed nearly 50 feet, and knelt by J.D. "He's got a pulse. We should move him while we can."

An EMT brought a stretcher from the ambulance. The two quickly lifted her partner onto the unfolded cot.

"We'll surround you as we move behind my cruiser on the street." Peggy raised the shield to protect Colt and nodded to Reed and his partner. "On the count of three—one, two, three."

The cops stood, and the EMS team lifted the cot. They darted behind Peggy's cruiser for safety. Reed and his partner had their guns aimed at the house, but no shots rang out.

When they reached the street, Reed stared up at the house. "We got word this afternoon that the station's jail cells are at maximum capacity. What do we do with the suspects?"

"We bring them to a collection point at station two," Peggy said. "A prison transfer van from the county picks up whoever we collect every hour and takes them to a makeshift jailhouse."

"How many will that hold?" Officer Reed asked.

"Five hundred or so, I'm just glad the county pitched in. I've brought in twelve so far today. How about you?"

"We've only been on duty thirty minutes. This is insane."

"Yeah, every call today has been an altercation, some minor, but they're getting more deadly," Peggy admitted.

"The hospitals are overwhelmed, too," the EMT added. "Some epidemic is running rampant. That's why we're all dressed in coveralls and wearing non-rebreather masks. I don't know, but maybe there's a link."

Peggy put her hand on J.D.'s shoulder. "Can you hear me?"

"He's unconscious." The EMT motioned for Peggy to move. "We need more room to work on him." The paramedic started an IV line, drew several blood samples, and hung a plastic bag of fluid while the EMT slipped an oxygen mask over his face and hooked J.D. up to the monitor. "Sinus tach at 180 per minute. B/P 60 palp."

"We're going on adrenaline only, and everything is total reaction right now, but I'm worried about J.D." Peggy caught something out of the corner of her eye and pointed toward the house, "Did you see that?"

Reed squinted. "What did you see?"

"A light flickered in the attic. It might be where they're hiding the girlfriend." Peggy hurried to the front of her cruiser. Her ankle throbbed with each step, but she had a job to do.

"You're limping," the EMT said. He tried to look at her wound, but she motioned him away.

"Help J.D.," Peggy said.

"Stay here." Reed inched forward. "My partner and I will walk around the house together from back to front and assess the situation from there."

"One guy took my Taser and headed for the back door, so watch out for him," Peggy warned. "I think his name is Larry."

Colt agreed. "And there were two other guys, but they disappeared when I ran to help the officer."

"Okay. When we reach the front, if we haven't met any resistance, I'll kick the door in, and we'll clear the main floor before moving upstairs. I wish we had another team, but it's up to us."

"His B/Ps dropping." The paramedic flipped the clamp wide open on the IV. "He's lost a lot of blood. Best scoop him up and take him to the nearest Med Center."

"Shouldn't we decontaminate him first?" the EMT asked.

The paramedic grabbed a bottle of solution. "I sprayed him down, but no time to remove his clothes."

The EMT pointed at Peggy. "What about her? A bullet grazed her ankle. She's been in action and needs treatment."

"When was your last tetanus shot?" the paramedic asked.

"Years ago," Peggy said. "I'm fine. Just take care of J.D."

"We will, but I'm going to look at your ankle. It'll take only a moment while my partner radios Dispatch." The EMT quickly cleaned and bandaged the wound.

The paramedic said, "Go to the ED and get a tetanus shot in the next 24 hours. We're moving J.D. to Holy Cross Emergency Department."

After the EMT finished radioing Dispatch, they lifted the cot and dashed to the ambulance.

Peggy barely noticed the backup officers running for the house with their pistols drawn. They slipped along the side of the house and disappeared.

The ambulance drove away before she saw Officer Reed motioning to her from the front door. "We're going in."

* * *

Officer Reed lifted his radio, "Dispatch, unit three. Two officers are entering a home on Denver Drive."

"Copy, unit three."

"Ready?" Officer Reed asked.

With a nod, his partner landed a hard kick next to the deadbolt. The front door slammed inward and was caught by a chain-locking device. He gave the door another boot as high as possible and snapped the chain. The door flew against the wall. The house was too quiet, especially after what had happened only moments earlier. Reed dashed forward. His partner moved along with him back-to-back, sliding into the living room as a unit. "Clear," the partner said, and they moved into the kitchen.

The back door was ajar. A man with a Taser lay on the floor. "Are you, Larry?"

His eyes were wide as saucers, and he barely nodded. A Taser dart was still in his leg—a pool of blood formed beneath Larry's shoulder.

Officer Reed knelt and placed his finger beside the man's carotid artery. "Pulse a little fast at 110 per minute."

The partner pulled out the Taser dart. "Call it in before we move upstairs."

"Dispatch. Unit three. Man down. Request backup, and we need immediate medical assistance."

"Copy, unit three."

Officer Reed released the radio transmit button. "Let's see what's going on upstairs."

"Find Tammy!" Larry whispered, "Be careful. Two shooters. Back bedroom."

Reed nodded toward the kitchen door. They moved into a foyer and paused at the bottom of a carpeted stairway. Blood splotches covered the landing, and the wall had streaks of brownish-red going up the steps from there.

Constantly shifting their aim between the railing banister above and the steps below, the two men ascended the stairwell until Reed's head reached the second-floor level. He paused and signaled that he was going to take a peek.

Before his partner could respond, a bullet exploded through the banister's spindles. Reed jerked back, searing pain cut across his forehead, and he lost his footing for a few steps, stopping when he plowed into his partner.

Bullet after bullet cracked above their heads. There was a rustling noise. Reed glanced up in time to see a gun appear between the spindles. He had no time to squeeze off a shot at the fuzzy outline behind the pistol, so he grabbed his partner and hurled them both over the railing, hitting the floor below.

Several more bullets snapped off, but the gunman was at an obtuse angle. Reed rolled off his partner and held his gun in a two-handed grip. "Drop the gun!"

A woman sprinted along the upstairs hallway, reached around a man dressed all in black, and raised a pistol.

Reed didn't hesitate. He shot a little wide. The bullet went just over her head. "Drop your weapons. The next one is dead center!"

She swore, ducked, and lifted the pistol again. The man next to her swiveled his gun in Reed's direction and fired.

Reed aimed and pressed his trigger repeatedly. The man jerked and fell to the landing. The crazed woman screamed and flew backward as a bullet struck her head.

"Reload," his partner yelled above the roar in Reed's head. "There might be a hostage." He turned and swiped a trickle of blood from Reed's cheek. "You've been hit!"

"What?" Reed brushed his hand over his forehead. His fingers came away smeared with blood. That's when he felt woozy.

His partner recognized the sign of shock coming on. "Lucky bastard. All you'll get out of this is a sexy scar! You'd be pushing up daisies if it had been just a little to the right."

Reed reloaded his Glock, but his hand shook. "We better check upstairs."

"You're not going anywhere until backup arrives. That woman looked at us like we'd personally tortured her. Who knows what else we might encounter."

A siren wailed, getting louder every second. "If we keep needing two backups for every rescue call, we'll run short of police in no time."

"Officer Reed?" came from the front doorway. "It's Peggy Wyller."

Peggy rounded the corner with a gun in hand, paused at the stairway when she saw the officers, and whispered, "You called for backup?"

"What the hell are you doing as our backup?" Reed asked. "I heard sirens. I thought backup would follow."

"It was only EMS. There are no police units available at the moment," Peggy inched closer. "You've been hit!"

"Like you, we're still functioning. We need to make it to the attic. Check on Larry. He's by the back door in the kitchen," Reed said.

Peggy left for the kitchen.

Once again, Reed led the way up the stairway with his partner. "Clear," Reed shouted as he raced from one bedroom to the next. A locked bathroom door led off from the master bedroom.

Reed's partner rapped hard, "Anyone in there?"

A tiny voice whimpered. "Please help. My sister is…" The sound muffled.

"Step away from the door. I'm going to kick it in. Are you out of the way?"

"We're in the bathtub," a boy called out. "We need more towels."

The officer kicked in the door. Bloody towels lay across the floor. He moved through the broken door, pulled back the shower curtain, and gasped, "We need medical help up here!"

Reed grabbed a towel from the top shelf. "Radio for more help!" He turned toward a boy about six years old, who held onto an older girl with multiple stab wounds to her left shoulder. A younger girl with a tear-streaked face sucked her thumb and sat huddled in a corner beside the tub. She was maybe three years old.

Reed wrapped the cloth over the girl's shoulder wound and held pressure. "What happened?"

The girl flinched but didn't say anything. Her eyes were glazed as if in shock. Reed turned toward the boy. "Can you tell me what happened?"

"Mommy came home with a bad headache," the boy said. "Tammy, she's our babysitter, let us watch TV. Mommy got mad. Tammy. Ummm." The boy cried and clung to his sister.

"It's okay," Reed said. "What's your name?"

"Randy, and it's not okay. Mom…Mommy hit Tammy with a bat." The child hesitated and took a shuddering breath. "She swinged her arms like this." He raised his arms and flailed them like a wild windmill. "Then Kat," he hugged the wounded girl closer and broke down crying.

Kat patted his hand. "Shh…"

"Daddy threw the bat out the window," Randy sobbed. "That made Mommy mad. She runned downstairs. We runned, too." Randy held his arms around Kat and rocked as he relived the horror. His breaths came out in small gasps, but he rushed on to tell the story. "Mommy comed back upstairs. She had Daddy's letter opener. She stabbed Kat. She stabbed and stabbed Kat. Kat…" The boy was panting.

Reed moved closer, and Randy screamed. "Daddy! Where's Daddy? Tammy's hurt."

"Where's Tammy," Reed asked in a calm voice.

"Runned away," Randy said. "Upstairs. She locked herself in the attic, but Mom stabbed Kat..." A mewing sound came from his throat, and he hiccupped. "Kat—she hit Kat! Kat pulled sissy and me in here. She locked the door. I screamed and screamed. Kat told me to shut up."

"Why is Mommy mad at Daddy?" the little girl asked. "They keep yelling." The girl stuck her thumb back into her mouth. Tears trailed through the dirt on her cheeks, and she swiped a sleeve across her runny nose before reaching out to touch Kat. Once reassured, she tried again. "TVs on. Why is Mommy mad at Daddy?" she repeated.

"Daddy must have put the TV on." Randy said. "He likes westerns. I hear guns like on Gunsmoke."

Kat squirmed from under Reed's blood-soaked hand and lifted her head from the boy's shoulder. She eked out, "Can't...breathe."

Reed called downstairs, "Are the paramedics here yet?"

Peggy yelled back, "Yes, in the kitchen."

"Send a paramedic up to the master bathroom. We have another victim."

"I'm on it!" Footsteps rapidly clomped up the steps.

"Where's Tammy? Is Tammy okay?" Randy asked.

Officer Reed waited until the paramedic arrived. His partner raced ahead for the attic. When Reed reached the attic door, a teenager lay on the floor, barely conscious. A small flashlight was in her hand. He called to the emergency crew, his own teenage daughter lying heavily on his mind. "Got another vic—head injury."

"Coming," the EMT called out. He dashed through the open doorway and dropped to Tammy's side. He checked her carotid pulse. "It's weak at 200 beats per minute." Her nose was broken, and blood flowed freely from her left ear. He checked her pupils. "This one's critical."

* * *

Peggy managed to make it upstairs behind the EMT. "I've never seen anything like this. Do you think she'll make it?"

"Call another ambulance crew," the EMT said. He was too busy starting oxygen and an IV and hooking the patient up to the monitor to make the call.

Peggy called it in. "Are we all clear here?" Peggy asked Officer Reed.

Reed nodded his approval.

She radioed Dispatch when her cell rang for the fourth time in the last half hour.

Officer Reed grabbed the radio. "I'll cover it. On a night like this, any call can be urgent."

Relieved, she hit the speaker of her cell. "This is Peggy."

"Thank God, you're all right," her husband said.

"Carl, I can't talk right now. Meet me at Holy Cross Hospital in one hour. I must call the ME and secure the place until the investigative team arrives."

"Are you hurt?" Carl asked in a panic.

"Today has been the worst day of my life. J.D.'s been shot, and I don't know if he'll make it." Peggy stifled a sob. "Just come to the hospital and take me home!" She disconnected the call.

Second Thoughts

Chirk was beyond frustrated and getting more afraid as time dragged on. Between Braun, the traitor, and the epidemic, he couldn't wait to leave Washington, D.C. Whatever this raging virus was, it was deadly, and he didn't want to become infected. No one seemed to know what caused the disease or how it spread, but most likely through the air or water. Chirk didn't drink anything the last day he was in the city for fear of contamination. He also wore a filter mask for protection from the air. Now that he was home, he only drank bottled water just to be safe.

Chirk fled Washington, D.C., before being exposed. He caught a private flight to Colorado and drove to his mountain hideaway on the southern border of Rocky Mountain National Park. It was like a private paradise among trees, deer, and other wildlife. No one would find him here—not even his boss.

The jailhouse in the basement safely confined Chief Jackson, who was apparently asleep after Chirk's last interrogation. The outdoor cameras picked up no activity, but it was 10 p.m. and dark. The little light that filtered through the garden-level windows made it difficult to see outside, so he switched on the infrared cameras throughout his property. He would monitor any activity from his office screen, secure the system, and head to bed. Tomorrow would be a long, dreaded day—he'd have to determine Jackson's fate.

Chirk's house was far outside of any targeted areas. He thought about President Spendorf, who was in a bunker in the core of the hot zone. There were no guarantees that he'd remain safe amongst the infected crowd. Zac needed to stay hidden away until this whole thing blew over. Chirk would protect the president, eliminate Braun and his meddling in overseas affairs, and maybe even get another promotion.

Chirk's gut clenched. *If this keeps up, I'll get an ulcer. What's eating at me?* The niggling, nagging feeling wouldn't go away.

After hearing Chief Jackson tell how Braun had worked undercover for the U.S. government and refused to believe Braun had anything to do with the bioterrorist attack, Chirk began having doubts about his mission. He knew enough to trust the chief's opinion, but the general was a force to deal with. *Of the two, the general held more power and made the difference between Chirk's life and death.*

In fact, if the general knew that Jackson was in his basement at this very moment, he would order Jackson's immediate extermination. *Of course, the general didn't know, and there was no way for the chief to escape. So why am I so worried? With any luck, Jackson will starve to death. It would be the easiest way to get rid of excess baggage.*

Chirk had never experienced hesitation about an operation before. He went back to pacing the floor. *Who am I kidding? The general might clean house, and I know too much to survive the ordeal. He can be ruthless when riled.* Chirk stayed as far away as possible when this happened.

Chirk went to his office to check the latest news and to see what his FBI buddies were doing about the viral outbreak. Reluctantly, he placed a call to his boss.

* * *

General Rutoon hated phone calls, especially after work hours. It was his job to rattle cages, not the other way around. He mumbled a greeting. The guy was a royal pain in the ass, but he praised President Spendorf whenever he could, except in private. Then, he'd called the president a buffoon. He sure had Zac spoofed.

"Heard anything about Braun?" Chirk asked.

"If I had, I'd have notified you," the general said. "Keep your pants on. He'll surface. When he does, we'll nail him."

"You're sure Braun's behind this virus? The chief—"

"What about the chief? I thought you offed him." The general's voice nearly pierced Chirk's eardrum. "That was the plan."

"Yes, sir!"

"Do your job. You have the mission packet. Read it, and don't call me again!" The phone banged in Chirk's ear as the general hung up.

"No, good luck, or hope to see you shortly?" Chirk spat into the phone, but he knew no one was listening.

He studied the screen with the general's detailed directions again, "Capture or kill HVI." That meant only capturing this high-value individual if he presents no risk. *Braun was a risk with a capital R.*

Needle in a Haystack

The twin-jet helicopter carrying two SWAT teams, a medic, and Cordy landed successfully in the lush woodland of Rocky Mountain National Forest. They were four miles south of their destination, Chirk's home, where Chief Jackson was being held hostage.

Cordy had her laptop ready to set up shop as soon as they boarded their armored truck. The crisp mountain air filled her lungs and cleared her head. It was at least ten degrees cooler than in Ft. Collins.

Bracken glanced at his watch. "I have 10:28 p.m. Watches in synch?"

"Of course they are," Desmond said. "Time is on our mobile phones, which are automatically synched."

"As I mentioned earlier, Cordy, you'll go with Poncho, Kayman, and Desmond. George will ride up front with your team." They headed to the larger, gray-colored ballistic armored tactical transport unit fully decked out with the latest technology while Bracken, Chico, and Foley boarded the other BATT.

Amazed, Cordy couldn't resist staring at the floor-to-ceiling screen display at her end of the truck. After setting her backpack on the table, she dug out her laptop and pulled up a chair.

"Buckle up," Bracken warned. He started the engine and took the lead. Poncho waited his turn.

Cordy snapped the strap across her lap, opened her computer, and barely logged on as the vehicle lurched forward. They were on their way to find the chief.

After logging into her TOR account, her first task was to check for any updates from Kelly or Braun. Kelly had left a message, "MEDIVAC has landed at D.C.'s CDC. Braun and Usher are safe and on their way to the bunker to speak to President Spendorf. Braun has evidence that General Rutoon is a traitor. However, Rutoon was Zac's war-time buddy and confidant, and he may not believe it. I hope Braun has enough proof to support his claim."

Cordy recalled General Rutoon. *I know he's Zac's security adviser, but where have I heard that name recently? President's cabinet? Counsel? No, it was on Dr. Smith's thumb drive.*

Cordy checked her latest program analysis, which ran in the background. Amid the chaos, she had completely forgotten about it. Upon reviewing the analysis, Cordy found several emails that had been sent from Smith's phone. Some of these emails had passionate overtones and discussed international governments and corrupt politicians in power. Rutoon was at the top of the list with a ten-page report detailing how the general had sold US military weapons to North Korea, Syria, and Libya, with some involvement from other unknown parties. Cordy automatically sent the files to Braun.

Excited about her findings, Cordy opened a screen for each SWAT member's body cameras. "How well do you know General Rutoon? I think he's involved."

Bracken visibly jolted. A frown crossed his face, and his Adam's apple bobbed as he swallowed.

"I can see you're worried. It's in your eyes," Cordy noted. "What's going through your mind?"

"Involved how?" Bracken asked. "Rutoon's the president's national security advisor and one of his oldest friends."

"I think he's behind everything, including Chief Jackson's kidnapping, false accusations of Braun being a terrorist, and who knows what else he's lied about? Maybe he even caused this epidemic, although that seems extreme. He's a traitor, an enemy of this government!" *Could Spendorf's trusted and dear friend be the culprit? Braun thinks so.*

Bracken appeared shocked as he spoke, "Are you accusing a trusted general of being a traitor?" He continued, "Rutoon holds a high position in the food chain, and we must focus on rescuing the chief right now. The general is not our concern tonight."

When Cordy began to object, Bracken interrupted her, "I understand your point, but we can discuss this later."

"Chirk knows the general," Cordy said, unwilling to let it go. "I wonder what role he plays."

"I guess we'll soon find out," Bracken replied. "I'm sending our plans."

Mission instructions popped up in the upper left corner of the screen, the blueprint floor plans of Chirk's home opened in the middle, and a map lit up the far-right corner. A GPS blue dot blinked their location and moved along, showing their progression as the BATT moved toward Chief Jackson's position, indicated by a stationary red blip.

Cordy glanced over at Poncho and George, now seated up front next to Kayman. Desmond was across the aisle.

His gaze fell on her as if studying how she fit in with this team. "Is this your first mission?"

"No," Cordy said. "But it's the first time I'm formally on the team. I had to worm my way onsite last time. It's not the best way to make friends, but a girl's gotta do, you know the rest."

"Yeah. I get it," Desmond said. "They're not too fond of anyone new on the team or willing to take any advice this new guy might have."

She leaned forward. "Do you have any advice?"

"Not yet, but I'm worried about this mission. I'm used to working with a team that respects my opinion."

"You'll be fine," Cordy said. "Bracken won't let you down. He hand-picked the team, so he must have confidence in your skills."

"Cordy, we have ten minutes. Can you decode the security panels?" Bracken's voice came through her earphones. She also realized Poncho got the message when he turned toward her and nodded.

"Working on it." Cordy turned back to the screen. "I've identified twelve cameras on Chirk's property and indicated them on the map. They show up as green dots. I'll freeze-frame the cameras and get the code to open the main gate."

"Just freeze the cameras," Bracken replied. "I want to take a look before moving onto the property."

Both vehicles paused outside the gate while Cordy secured their path.

Bracken did one final gear check and slid the night goggles over his head. "We'll walk the perimeter outside the fence to check for any breaches along the way. Team One will go left 500 yards from the main gate and check for explosives, trap wires, or any obstacles before proceeding. Poncho, take your team and go right the same distance, and then we'll return to our starting point."

"On it," Poncho said and moved forward. "Desmond, you go first. Check for bombs."

"Stay low and out of the camera's sight," Cordy warned. "Even if they have been freeze-framed, who knows when Chirk will reset the system again?"

"Will do, and get the drone ready to launch," Bracken ordered. "It's at least half a mile to Chirk's house."

"Copy," Cordy prepped the drone. "Give me the word when you're ready."

Bracken and Poncho's teams exited the vehicles, dressed in full gear. They moved in a quiet trek in opposite directions. Cordy spotted the men through night-vision cameras. Foley, being Team One's bomb man, led to the left. His moves were swift and silent. Bracken followed a few steps behind. He had a rifle slung across his chest and a semi-automatic pistol held low, barrel toward the ground. His head constantly turned from side to side, alert and on the lookout for any potential hazards.

Identifying Poncho in the grainy green night-vision image was more challenging as they trekked to the right. He was about the same build as Desmond, bulky but graceful. They walked in a soft, fluid, cat-like motion. She noticed that Kayman still had a slight preference for his left side. She hoped he hadn't returned to work too soon.

The quarter-moon reflected off the solar panels on the building's roof, but no exterior lights were on. The men continued to prowl, and both teams returned to the main gate fifteen minutes later.

"The house appears completely dark, inside and out. Send up the drone to be sure." Bracken's calm voice echoed in the BATT. *Why didn't he speak using her earphones?*

She noticed George was standing on them. *They must have come loose as I prepared the drone for launch.* Cordy plugged the buds back into her ears and sent up a drone with an infrared camera, a nanosensor sniffer for drugs, and explosive detection attached, which could pick up deadly chemicals for up to 1.8 miles. It flew with the grace of an eagle over the gate, razor wire, and security cameras while the men returned to the vehicles. The drone moved over the woodland and hovered above a clump of trees. A photo appeared on the screen.

Cordy warned, "Bracken, there's a cluster of animals, maybe deer, in the woods east of the main gate about two hundred yards from the fence."

"Team One will check it out." Bracken motioned to Poncho. "Team Two, return to the BATT."

"They're elk," George noted. "A herd of cows and a few calves. They could be dangerous—quite protective of their young at this age."

Cordy watched intently. "George says they're elk, and the herd could be dangerous. Be careful."

"Will do," Bracken motioned for Team One to advance toward the herd.

A few moments later, the drone reached the house. "I see two infrared bodies—one in the lower left quadrant. That's where the GPS dot for Chief Jackson is also located, so he's alive. Another hot spot appears to be upstairs in the right corner. I'm guessing that's Chirk's bedroom. Both images I'm getting are lying down," Cordy reported.

George opened the door for Poncho's team and relieved the men of their rifles as they entered the vehicle.

Cordy followed Bracken's orders, and the main gate slid open with barely a sound. "Gateway clear. I don't see any movement inside."

Someone tapped Cordy's shoulder. She glanced up to see Poncho at her side.

His brow furrowed. Poncho pointed to her headphones, which had fallen from her ear again when she reached over to activate the gate. *I need to be more careful, or I'll miss a command. Next time, I'll bring my wireless phones.*

Poncho clarified again, "Locate, secure, and capture if possible? Right?"

Cordy popped the bud back in time to hear Bracken say, "If we can capture, that would be our plan. If Chirk is amiable, I could announce our arrival and enter the house, but I doubt he'll come to the door with his hands raised in submission, so I hope to make this a surprise visit. We have a 'no-knock' warrant. Team One is going on foot. Poncho, you follow through the gate in BATT one, so Cordy and George will be closer to our teams if needed. Park in amongst the trees. Let's roll."

Foley moved forward through the gate, followed by Bracken and Chico. Once they cleared the gate, the men took off at a sprint toward the trees. Poncho followed a few yards behind in the armored truck.

"A light flickered upstairs. I think we've been spotted!" Cordy noticed another flicker. "There's a second light. Wait, they both went out. Now, I see a dim glow downstairs. More like a flashlight."

Bracken's voice cracked. "Close the gate and pull in behind that clump of trees. Maybe he'll think it's a false alarm."

Cordy did as ordered. The camera above the entrance swiveled back and forth but didn't seem to target their position.

Cordy kept a close eye on the cameras. A warning flashed when Chirk reset his security system, so she continued to jam any motion-sensor activation to undo his efforts. "That was too close."

Then, she saw an opportunity unfold. "Bracken, head for the elk bedded down on the grass up ahead, but stay behind the trees or a clump of rocks to remain safe. Get on your hands and knees so you look like one of the elk in case Chirk resets the camera again. The infrared on his camera will show the elk on his freeze-frame, and he'll never know we're here. Can you blend in?"

"Yeah. Has the drone located Jackson?"

"It's outside Jackson's window. I'm trying to get photos, but it's dark down there. I switched the drone's camera to a night-vision lens, but it gives only a fuzzy image. The explosive alert just came on."

Poncho moved closer. "Can you enlarge the image?"

Cordy made it big enough to fill the screen.

Desmond moved forward. "Bracken, you need to see this. It looks like an underground cell. Cakes of C-4 explosives line the window and the northeast corner of the ceiling where Jackson is being held hostage. I can't see any door for access—maybe a trap door in the ceiling."

Cordy moved the drone for a better view. "Yup, I see it, but there's no ladder."

"I'll be right there." Bracken arrived with his team a few seconds later to study Jackson's jail on the screen. They had a brief discussion on how to enter the cell.

"I recognize the layout," Cordy said. "It's much like our last encounter when we broke out Braun and Usher, except that was further underground. Do you think there's another entrance?"

"Send the drone in low and search for one," Bracken ordered.

Cordy sent the drone on the new mission.

Alarmed

Chirk lay in bed, drifting in and out of sleep, when his home security system pinged. *Something or someone is on my property.* He hopped from his bed, flipped on the bedroom light, and entered the hallway. All was dark, so he turned on the hall light. Realizing the lights would warn whoever was on his land that someone was home, he chastised himself, dashed back to his bedroom, and grabbed a flashlight. He clicked off the overheads and headed downstairs to his office. *Better check the exterior cameras.*

When he reached the office door, the security system appeared normal. "What the hell? That can't be." Chirk tapped each camera monitor throughout his property—*nothing.* The main gate remained closed, and no one was on the extended driveway to his house. On high alert, he swiveled each camera to get a 360° search—nothing. *Something pinged. I'm sure of it.* He rewound the tape to review the last ten minutes, but there was still nothing.

Chirk needed a closer look. A buzzing sound caught his attention upstairs. *Did I leave my bedroom window open?* He tapped the security system on his cell phone and raced upstairs to check out the noise. The bedroom windows were closed, so he went from room to room, searching.

Sweat dripped down his armpits, and a shiver ran up his spine. When he returned to his office, he checked on Jackson, who seemed to be asleep. At least he wasn't moving. Paralyzed with fear, Chirk's heart hammered against his ribcage. He rubbed his damp hands down his thighs, reset the alarm system, the exterior and motion-sensor lights, and remotely rechecked the locks on the front and rear doors. The sliding glass door above Jackson's prison cell remained locked.

Relief flowed through Chirk when the monitor rebooted, and he noticed an elk herd grazing along the southern woodland. The elk barked and made high-pitched noises, which seemed louder than usual. *It must be the birthing season.* He'd seen a few calves earlier in the day. "All that worry over some lousy elk!" Chirk blew out a deep breath. Since *I'm already awake, I might as well brew some coffee.*

Cordy sat in the BATT surrounded by the SWAT team gathered around her screen, reviewing an isometric drawing of the house floor plan and a map of the surrounding area between the gate and their target. "Chirk's information system has powerful firewall protection, but I finally accessed the gate and door. I'm ready whenever you are."

Bracken studied the screen for a few more moments. "Check out that dark area about ten feet away from Jackson's cell on the west side of the building. It looks like a tunnel or a mine."

Cordy sent a drone to check the area. The images popped onto the screen for review. "I doubt there is an outside connection to Jackson's cell." She zoomed in. "There's no sign of anyone in the area."

"Okay." Bracken pointed to the map. "There are explosives in the basement jail cell where we'll find Chief Jackson and potential for others throughout the house. Can you enlarge the floor plan?"

Cordy adjusted the image so everyone could get a closer view. "The drone sniffer ID'd explosive material in the basement." She hovered the mouse pointer instead of using her finger. "Here's the image of C4 packets lining Jackson's jail cell's window and ceiling entrance."

Bracken's two bomb experts were Foley, who had been with the team the last five years, and Desmond, the newest member of the SWAT team. "As assigned earlier, I'll head up Team One. Foley and Chico, you're with me. We'll take the front, clear the hallway to the closet and living room."

"Roger," Chico said as Foley nodded.

Bracken pointed to the house drawing. "Poncho, head up Team Two. Take Desmond and Kayman and enter through the back. Clear the kitchen, pantry, and dining room. Continue clearing until we meet at the stairway."

Poncho's team signified their understanding.

Bracken grabbed his gear. "Once the upstairs is cleared, we'll move to the basement. Stay sharp. Questions?"

There were none, and they geared up.

Cordy called after them, "Be safe. I'll use the drone to monitor the area and will keep you informed of changes."

Bracken loaded his rifle. "Let's walk the property before clearing the house. Both teams meet outside by the cluster of trees. We meet in two minutes."

Bracken motioned his team forward. The men left the armored vehicle, moved behind the trees, and awaited further orders.

The movement startled the elk herd, and they stood, lifted their heads high in the air, and rotated their ears. Several barked a warning. Some ran uphill, but not all.

"Look out for the elk!" Cordy called through her transmitter.

Two protective cows moved between the men and their calves. They pawed the ground with their front hooves and lowered their heads. One gave a shrill noise. In a nanosecond, five hundred pounds of elk charged through the trees straight for Foley. Instinctively, he jerked up his rifle.

"No shooting," Chico hissed as he raced toward the elk closest to Foley, trying to draw her attention away from the man. The elk clipped Foley in the shin and sideswiped him to the ground. Foley scooted back before he got kicked.

Chico moved between the second elk and Foley as it turned and pawed the ground, nostrils flaring. Chico quickly backed away, making himself appear as large as possible.

"Don't turn your back on the herd," George said through the headphones. "A charging elk has a hard time pivoting, so zigzag backward and duck behind a tree."

Bracken yanked Foley to safety.

The angry elk snorted but lost interest once the men retreated.

Bracken helped Foley get his footing. "Are you hurt?"

Foley was breathing hard and limped a bit, trying to stand upright. "I'm lucky, she got my boot, or I'd have a broken ankle. I'll have a few bruises, though. It's a good thing Chico said not to shoot. Instinct said to fire. It was heading straight for me."

Poncho's team took a wider berth around the elk and was already heading toward the back entrance.

"Everyone all right?" George asked. "Do you need any medical assistance?"

Bracken checked in with Foley, who shook his head. "No. We're okay."

"Most of the elk have gone up the hill," Cordy said. "There are a few still watching, so be careful."

"Thanks. Are we all set?" Bracken asked. "Those elk were noisy enough that Chirk is probably gawking out the window by now. I hope we haven't lost the element of surprise." He stared at the windows, but the curtains remained static.

Foley nodded. "I'm still in one piece. Let's get the chief."

"Lead the way." Bracken motioned the team forward.

Foley limped a few steps. Gritting his teeth, he balled his hands into fists and straightened. The limp disappeared as he sprinted toward the front door.

"Team Two ready," Poncho said.

Bracken whispered over the radio, "Team One is in place. Cordy, disarm alarms."

She entered the codes for the front and back door alarms. "Done!"

Foley checked the entry with the bomb detector. "Clear."

"Clear," echoed in Bracken's ears as Desmond did the same.

Bracken ordered, "On the count of three—One, two, three." Foley kicked open the front door as Desmond entered the back entrance.

Friend's Betrayal

President Zac Spendorf fidgeted behind his desk, crossing first one leg and then the other while studying the man standing before him. Zac couldn't believe the cold-hearted betrayal of his oldest and most respected friend, General Rutoon. The silence grew until Zac finally said, "Have a seat, General."

"If it's all the same, President Spendorf, I'd rather stand." The general stood ramrod straight at full attention.

"At ease," Zac's voice sounded fierce. His fists clenched until nails bit into the palms of his hands. He hated this. *Why would my friend put me in such a position?*

The general widened his stance and put his hands behind his back. "You wanted to see me. I'm reporting for duty as requested. I'm no longer your commanding officer. You are mine."

Zac's jaws clenched, and he seethed out a deep breath. "General, we've known each other for a long time."

"Yes, we have, so quit the bullshit, and say what you have to say." The general's smile didn't meet his eyes, but perhaps he was trying to lighten the load, knowing Zac would have difficulty getting to the facts. Maybe there was some remorse, as well.

Zac refused to stand and leaned forward on his elbows. "There's no easy way to say this, so I will show you. You'll recognize the players. Then I need to hear from you. Give me a reason—you owe me at least that."

The general kept his eyes glued to Zac's. Not even a flinch. Finally, he said, "Show me what you have."

"Sit down, General." This time, the words came out as an order.

The general pulled up a chair, and Zac handed him a ten-page report from Cordy and additional information and researched by Braun. "These documents prove you were working as a spy for three countries—Syria, North Korea, and Libya. And I'm sure you have worked for Russia in the past. This latest act is monstrous—deliberately infecting fellow citizens with a deadly virus."

Rutoon licked his lips but didn't say anything in his defense.

Zac had to calm down. He was so angry that colored spots floated before his eyes. "Braun, if you and Usher would do the honor of playing those recordings, I'd appreciate it."

The lights dimmed as Braun played back the evidence. The date, time, and GPS coordinates appeared in the upper right-hand corner of the screen. The first clip had been taken in haste, probably on a cell phone. The grainy image cut in and out as people climbed into cars. It locked onto a darkened room where several top North Korean military officers sat around a table with General Rutoon. It was like a mafia film. People spoke in several languages. Rutoon nodded on a few occasions, and then several papers passed hands.

Gray noise crackled in the background, and the image jerked to a new location like a lousy video splice. Rutoon stood before ten armored Humvees lined up at a military base. He handed over the keys to a North Korean official. Another truck filled with M-4s, laser illuminators, scoped optics, and explosive devices were among the trade.

When the recording finished playing, Zac held up a stack of papers. "I'm sure these look familiar. They have your signatures on them. What were you thinking? I never permitted you to sell weapons to North Korea. Congress wouldn't dare approve such an act. This is treason."

Rutoon sat like a stone. No expression.

"Where's the $15 million you received in return?" After a twenty-second pause with no response from Rutoon, Zac continued. "We found half of it in a private account in Ireland. But there's more! Run the second set of the evidence."

Zac scooted back his chair, stood, and paced as Braun put on the second video clip he had captured during the general's recent visit to Syria. General Rutoon met with high-ranking officials outside of Damascus. The topic of the conversation was biological warfare.

Zac slammed his fist on another pile of papers. "You exchanged $5.6 million for that escapade."

The general flinched. "I didn't take the money."

"No, you paid for it. Where did you get the funds? From weapon sales, I presume. I'm sure it was used to buy the deadly virus that nations worldwide are fighting to overcome. Now, explain why."

Rutoon folded his hands in his lap and straightened. "No comment."

"One of those astronauts on the International Space Station made it happen. Which one? And how did you convince anyone to do such a thing?"

General Rutoon stayed calm, but his brown eyes were dark as coal.

Braun adjusted the projector. "The last recording happened yesterday while you tried to kill me before I could deliver this information to President Spendorf."

The scene started with a long line of cars filing bumper-to-bumper on I-84. An accident caused the road to come to a total standstill. A man got out of a silver Honda with a cell phone in his hand. A black patch covered his left eye. A scar ran below the patch, puckering his left cheek. The man quickly turned away.

"Pause for a moment." Zac pointed at the screen. "That's Chirk T. Transom. I'd recognize that patched eye and scar anywhere."

The general didn't respond.

"Resume," Zac said.

Braun pressed the play button. Chirk darted around a motorcycle and tapped on the window of a black van. The passenger's door opened, and General Rutoon stepped from the vehicle. He glanced at Chirk and made a slicing sign with his hand going right to the left across his neck, nodded his head, and lifted his left hand. He swirled his index finger in a circle. Zac interrupted, "A wrap-up signal."

Chirk returned to his Honda, and the video captured Usher standing next to an officer, helping an elderly man from a car. A helicopter landed not far from the side of the road. A flight nurse deplaned and helped the elderly gentleman onto a stretcher. Several vehicles blocked the main highway, but the black van and Chirk's Honda headed for the highway's shoulder and drove away. The recording stopped.

"That old man you saw is Braun Hastings in disguise. I know you put out a kill order on him and Chief Jackson," President Spendorf said. "This is not the only incriminating evidence I have. As you told me yesterday, Braun is not responsible for the virus. He went undercover to collect the real culprit of biochemical warfare—you!"

Zac leaned over his desk. "Agent Cordelia sent Dr. Joe Smith's thumb drive with detailed information about your actions. It proves you smuggled a secret virus—a biochemical agent produced from a potent MRSA sample, harvested, enhanced, and replicated in space. During the latest Space Station mission, you had a specimen brought back to Earth disguised as an innocent red satin box. NASA denies requesting the sample. Yet, Tip Granger forwarded a message on NASA letterhead requesting that specimen. It was delivered to Dr. Smith, and the virus has now spread across the globe, reaching South America and the Middle East. Even Smith became a victim. Give me a reason why you did this."

The general didn't say a word. He didn't move to defend himself, nor did he have any reaction at all. It was as if he had turned into a statue—hard, stone-faced, and ruthless.

Finally, President Spendorf turned his back on the general. "I'm done. Take him away." He spun around and shook his fist. "I don't want to see your face ever again."

"So, we are done here," General Rutoon finally said. "Are you packing me up and shipping me off to Siberia?" Bitterness crept into his voice. "You've already condemned me. No trial, no jury, and no military honor. Fine. So be it."

"No military honor?" Zac spat out. "You're absolutely right." Zac ripped off Rutton's epaulettes. "As of this minute, I'm stripping you of all your stars. You are dishonorably discharged and dismissed! Get him out of my sight. Make sure the guard removes all his medals and return them to me."

"What about my pension?" Rutoon had the nerve to ask.

Zac's red face paled. His nostrils flared, but his commanding voice was calm and determined. "Oh, you won't need it. You'll be a guest of the United States Penitentiary System until the day you die!"

Once the secret service agents hauled Rutoon away in handcuffs, Braun and Usher received additional orders from President Spendorf. "Dr. Trent has been working on a vaccine using genetic sequencing.

I'm not sure how it works, but hopefully, it will prevent the further spread of this pandemic. Get that vaccine."

"Trent's in a coma in a hospital in Denver," Braun said. "I'm not sure if he'll ever regain consciousness."

Zac ran a hand over his face. "Then, find out who he was working with. Maybe they can find a cure."

"I'll talk to Agent Kelly." Usher suggested, "She might have an inside contact."

Braun tapped Usher's shoulder. "Why not have Cordy follow up? She's already in Colorado."

"Good idea. Should we present the information to the RR7?" Usher asked. "We met Dr. Ryan Chugson and Dr. Alex from CDC briefly."

"Yes, that's an excellent idea," Zac agreed. "They are definitely on our need-to-know list. You should attend the next meeting. It's scheduled for 8 a.m. Dr. Liz Brakinsky heads up the team. I'll have Winston notify her. Keep me informed if you need any help. Moving within the city is getting more difficult with roadblocks and the closure of public transportation. I'll assign two secret servicemen to drive you around town and accompany you to assure your safety."

"Thank you, Mr. President," Braun shook Zac's hand. "We'll keep you informed."

Zac moved from his desk and paused. "It's four hours before the meeting. Would you like a nap? You've been up all night, and we have plenty of cots in the bunker."

Braun had a short chat with Usher. "We still have a lot of work to do before the meeting. If you don't mind, we'd like to use a couple of computers to get another update from Colorado. Then I'll contact Agent Kelly, and Cordy can follow up on Dr. Trent's vaccine."

"Take the laptops on the side table. They're secure. I need to prepare for another news conference and make some tough decisions. I'm afraid I'll need to quarantine the whole country." Zac shook his head, sounding baffled. "Why'd he do it? What else has he done? I better plug some holes in the national security and Special Forces, too."

Braun logged into the darknet to notify Cordy of the latest information about General Rutoon and inquired if the chief had been rescued yet. He ended his message with LYA and stay safe. He got an instant reply. "LY2. SWAT is in Chirk's front yard." She filled him in on their status.

"Then we need to nab Chirk," President Spendorf was saying to Usher.

"That loose item is underway as we speak," Braun said. "Cordy is with a Fort Collins SWAT team. They're at Chirk's mountain home near Rocky Mountain National Park. Chief Jackson is on-site in an underground jail cell. C-4 plastic explosives surround the access point, and members of the bomb squad are on site. The situation is tense, but Cordy will keep us informed."

Zac, feeling exhausted, took a sip of his Morning Thunder tea, made a disgusted face, spit the tea back into the cup, and set down the mug. "That tastes bitter, like so much going on in the middle of the night, and sleep is a luxury we can't afford right now. But as soon as I hit that pillow, I plan to sleep like a hibernating bear."

Usher refilled his and Braun's coffee cups, black and hot all around. Then, he got on the phone with his FBI boss, Loran Sloan.

Busted

Cordy watched both teams enter the house on her multi-view screen. A solid kick above the deadbolts, and the doors flew open. Poncho was at Desmond's back as they entered the kitchen. She knew the first sixty seconds of subduing a suspect were the most dangerous. The team had to get in close contact, and Poncho stayed near Desmond.

Chirk dropped his cup of coffee. "What the hell?" He let out an angry hiss, bolted forward, and grabbed a kitchen knife from the counter.

Poncho aimed his pistol. "Drop it and get on your stomach, NOW!"

The hurled knife, directed at Poncho, went wild, bouncing off Desmond's shoulder, protected by a Kevlar vest, as he darted to protect Poncho.

A shot just missed Chirk's head, and Poncho snapped, "On your stomach, or the next one goes between your eyes."

A frown crossed Chirk's forehead. The scar beneath his eye patch stretched down his cheekbone into an angry purple pucker. "You wouldn't dare shoot me! The president will have your hide."

"Don't test us." Desmond grabbed Chirk's right arm and yanked it behind his back as Kayman whipped cuffs from his pocket and quickly shackled both wrists.

"Clear," came from the front lobby. "Need assistance?" Bracken called.

"Suspect restrained." Desmond spun the now-shaking assassin around and kneed him in the groin. "That's for the knife. Want to fight some more?"

Chirk dropped like a sack of potatoes, dazed. The patch had flown from his eye, exposing the socket as no more than a slit of skin. Blood trickled from his nose, and the broken coffee cup lay shattered underneath him.

"Enough! Spread eagle." Poncho nudged his feet apart and patted him down while Kayman aimed his gun at the back of Chirks' broad head.

"I want a lawyer." The jerk yelled again, loud enough for all to hear, "I want a lawyer!"

"Living room, clear," came from down the hallway. "Dining room, clear."

Poncho held his pistol on Chirk and stood guard. "Finish clearing the main floor."

Desmond and Kayman met Team One at the stairway.

"Is Chirk in the kitchen?" Bracken asked.

"Yes, Poncho's covering him," Desmond said.

"Clear upstairs and meet me in the kitchen. I'm going to chat with this animal, one on one." Bracken left both teams and then stepped beside the prone Chirk.

"Poncho, cover the door to the basement," Bracken ordered. "Wait until the teams clear upstairs. We'll descend the steps together."

Chirk shook his head, scattering blood droplets like a wet dog. "Don't go downstairs. Everything will blow. There are enough explosives to flatten the place."

"So you don't want to die," Bracken said. "I get that." He turned back to Poncho. "You have your orders."

"Yes, sir." Poncho headed down the hallway.

Bracken turned toward Chirk. "We know Chief Jackson is in your basement cell. Make it easy on yourself and hand him over to us."

"In your dreams," Chirk spat out.

"Pity." Bracken lifted Chirk by a shoulder and placed him on a ladder-backed kitchen chair. "Have a seat."

"Let me go, and I'll put in a good word about you with the president." Chirk's tone was mocking.

Bracken took out a roll of duct tape and bound each of Chirk's legs to the chair. He ran the roll around Chirk's chest and the ladder-back rungs. "I don't think you'll be going anywhere soon."

Bracken straddled a seat and placed his arms across the back. "Let's have a little chat. Why did you kidnap Chief Jackson?"

"No comment."

"Why are you tailing Braun?"

"No comment," Chirk said.

"Why are you following General Rutoon's orders?" Bracken asked.

Chirk gasped, and his eye widened briefly before catching himself and taking a deep breath. He pursed his lips.

"Yes, we know about the general. He planned everything, didn't he? You couldn't have done this alone, not without his permission. I hope you realize that the general will turn on you in a split second if given a chance. He's already in our trap. If you want a better deal, hand over the chief and start talking. I'll give you three minutes to think about that."

Cordy interrupted Bracken. "I just heard from Braun. He and Usher had an enlightening conference with the president in his bunker. Zac invited General Rutoon to attend an emergency council meeting. All weapons stayed at the door before entering the main meeting room. I can only imagine the general's shock at seeing Braun standing at the head of the room."

Bracken smiled. "Cordy, fill Chirk in on your latest update from President Spendorf."

Chirk glanced around the room. "Who are you talking to?"

Bracken removed an earbud and placed it in Chirk's ear.

Cordy repeated her message, "Braun's with the president as we speak, and General Rutoon is in custody at the bunker. I wonder what he'll have to say about you, Chirk?"

"But Braun's the traitor, not General Rutoon!" Chirk paled when Bracken shook his head.

"He duped you, but fortunately, Chief Jackson is still alive, so let's keep it that way."

"You'll never free him." Chirk's voice was barely a whisper. "No, it can't be. Not the general. He's Zac's best friend."

At Any Risk

At the Rocky Mountain cabin, Cordy sat in front of the BATT's communication center and monitored every move of the SWAT teams.

Bracken questioned Chirk in the kitchen.

"Upper floor cleared," Poncho shouted. The team met on the main floor, cleared the basement door, and prepared for the next bit of business—freeing Chief Jackson.

"Did we find another entrance to the cell from the outside?" Desmond spoke into his body cam.

Cordy answered, "No, but I think there's a common wall in the fruit cellar. It could become a portal. Be careful. Chirk might have rigged another explosive device. Do you want the drone to search before entering the basement?"

Bracken interrupted, "Chirk's not giving any answers. I put a camera on him. Can you watch him while we get Jackson?"

Cordy opened a corner of the screen. "Yes, but move the camera down so I can see what he's doing with his hands. They are cuffed, but he's rolling something between his fingers."

Bracken grabbed Chirk's left hand, holding a manual detonator that resembled a watch. "How did you get that?"

"It was around my wrist." Chirk smiled. "Your boys have ten minutes, then Kaboom!"

"Detonator activated," Bracken spoke into his body cam. "Not sure of the exact moment Chirk set the device, so subtract thirty seconds from the countdown to be sure we have enough time. Cordy, put the timer on your screen and call out every thirty seconds."

Cordy obeyed. "Nine minutes, twenty seconds, and counting."

Bracken yanked the detonator from Chirk's hand and set it on the counter. "Send in the drone ASAP."

"Open the back door." Cordy hovered the drone. "It's outside."

Bracken threw open the door. The drone moved through the kitchen, the hallway, and the basement doorway.

"Wait for the drone before we clear the basement," Bracken ordered.

"Nine minutes." Cordy spotted blinking green lights. "The drone found three additional explosives." She sent the drone's image to each of the men.

She watched as Bracken's brain cells fired rapidly, analyzing the situation without hesitation. Calm vibes seemed to emanate through him like ice flowing in his veins. Bracken's voice caught the team's attention, "Foley, you disarm the tripwire at the bottom of the steps. Desmond, disarm the fruit cellar door. And there's one more explosive inside the cellar, which we can't reach until we clear the door."

"Eight minutes thirty seconds," Cordy called out. Her stomach knotted in tension. It was an automatic response. When working with the SWAT team, she never knew what lurked around the next corner, and again, they faced uncertainty. Chief Jackson's life was in her hands. As were the team members. She watched Desmond's bulky muscular form follow the lean, sinewy Foley into the dim stairwell, their nonverbal cues communicating their readiness to take action. Both men walked cautiously down each step, their eyes darting up and down and left to right.

Cordy held her breath as Foley found the nearly invisible crush wire on the second to the last stair. One step on that wire and all would blow. He had to trace the wire to the switch leading to the detonator and separate it from the main charge. Desmond hopped over the wire and moved to the left to defuse the cellar door explosive he'd been assigned.

Foley traced the wire with his eyes only, avoided the switch, and peeled away the tape holding the detonator to a det cord.

Cordy knew this was the most dangerous time. Even if Foley disengaged the main charge, the detonator alone, if triggered, could blow off his hands.

He was able to separate the detonator from the cord. He quickly assessed the battery to be sure there were no other detonators. Finding none, he snipped the detonating lead. "Clear!" It took twelve seconds for Foley to disarm the stair bomb.

Cordy exhaled.

"Clear," Desmond said a few seconds later. He slowly opened the fruit cellar door, checking for another tripwire. There was none, so he reached to flip on the light.

"Stop!" Foley yelled. He held up an LED penlight. "The bomb's attached to the switch."

"Desmond, disarm it while we check on the chief." Bracken knew he should wait but had no time. His headlamp lit the room. He swung his assault rifle over his shoulder, slid through the doorway, and tapped the wall between the fruit cellar and Jackson's cell.

"Eight minutes." Cordy noticed Bracken's face tense, and then, he blinked. "Chief Jackson, can you hear me?"

"Oh, yes, I've been listening for a while now. The C-4 packets are fairly secure, but Chirk covered all the entrances, so come through the wall if you can. I've been hacking away at a few concrete blocks with my tools. I'm glad I had them hidden away in my belt. Knife blade busted, so I'm working with a corkscrew."

Bracken knelt closer to the floor. "Which ones are you working on?"

"Five blocks from the west wall. Second, third, and fourth up from the floor," Jackson added, "I'll stick my corkscrew through a hole I made in the mortar of the lower left block."

Bracken shined a light across the wall. "Yep, I see the tip. He removed a stub of chalk from his pocket and placed an X over each indicated block. "Okay, we'll focus on these." He tapped the lower left one. "This one is already loosened."

"Clear." Desmond heaved a sigh of relief and joined Bracken. "How thick is that wall?"

"Four inches," Chief Jackson said. My corkscrew isn't long enough to go through, so I had to flake off chunks of mortar before it broke through to the next room."

Chico carried a drill as he entered the fruit cellar. It appeared like a toy in his large hands. "There are several tools along the wall in the hall."

Kayman moved next to Chico. "I found a masonry saw." It turned out that the blade wasn't very sturdy, but it created plenty of dust as he cut through the mortar, causing the men to cough.

"Seven minutes," Cordy noted.

Chico reamed out the mortar in the corners of each targeted block.

The room got crowded when Poncho brought in a sledgehammer. "I'll wait until you've finished drilling out each corner, and then it's my turn to pulverize these suckers."

Cordy's voice grew tight with concern. "Keep the vibration low so we don't trip off the explosive."

"They're on the opposite wall," the chief said.

"Six minutes, thirty seconds," Cordy called out. Her heart fluttered, but the team joked as if they were friends having dinner.

Another minute passed. Cordy ticked off the time, which seemed to race by way too fast.

"Stand back." Poncho swung the sledgehammer at a cement block. It made a hole as a block crumbled, but it was hardly large enough for a cat to get through. He swung again, knocking out another block.

"Five minutes." Cordy's voice sounded strained. "Chirk's hopping his chair over to the kitchen counter. Someone get up there and stop him!"

"My saw blade busted, so I'll go." Kayman wiped a sleeve over his face to remove the dust and bounded up the steps. A loud thump came from the floor above them a few moments later.

"Kayman, need assistance?" Bracken called through his radio.

"I'm fine, but Chirk is out cold.

"Four minutes, thirty seconds," Cordy warned. "Kayman, go to the office and gather any evidence you can find, including the laptop and desktop computers."

"Set them by the back door, and we'll haul them away when we leave," Bracken said.

"Yes, sir." Kayman asked, "Is there anything special you're looking for, Cordy?"

"Just get the equipment, leave the cables, and walk through the office opening every drawer so I can get a good look," Cordy said. "But hurry."

Kayman gathered the equipment and found a couple of boxes on a shelf. He opened a file cabinet. Most files were color-coded. He held up a sample of each color for Cordy to view.

Cordy glanced at the tabs. Get all of the green and red-colored ones. They are government-related. The yellow files are personal. Leave them for now. Take the three orange files. I saw Rutoon's name on one."

Back in the basement, sweat dripped from Poncho's brow as he continued to hack away block-by-block with the sledgehammer. The hole grew to twelve inches by fourteen as Cordy continued the countdown.

"Put a ladder through that opening, and I'll climb up and disarm the explosives," the chief said.

Desmond passed one end of the ladder to the chief, who pulled it into the cell. "Just take a peek, and let us know what we're dealing with."

"One more whack and it'll be large enough for Foley. He's the skinniest," Poncho said.

"Two minutes," Cordy called out.

The hole widened. Dust caked the floor and covered Foley's clothes as he wormed through the opening into the room. Foley grabbed the ladder, leaned it against the wall, and climbed to the window. "The detonator is a collapsing circuit and has anti-tamper features. If one line is disconnected, they'll all blow."

"One minute, thirty seconds."

Poncho kept hacking away at the hole. It was finally man-sized. Chief Jackson was pulled through to freedom by eager, sweaty hands. Desmond scrambled after him in the opposite direction to help Foley.

"Get out of there," Cordy said. "We've got the chief. What else do you want?"

"She's right. Time to move. Now!" Bracken said. Chief Jackson found his shoes and socks in the hallway, grabbed them, and dashed up the steps barefooted. Chico dropped the drill and headed for the stairs. Poncho followed.

Foley yelled, "Hey, Bracken, I bet there's much more evidence tucked away in this place."

Bracken said, "It's your call."

Desmond glanced at Foley. "You in?"

Foley dug through his gear. "To the end."

"We're staying," Desmond said. "If this thing blows, it'll only be the two of us inside, and believe me. I'm not going to let this sucker be my last thrill."

"One minute," Cordy said. "Kayman has most of the files in two boxes by the front door and the computers."

"Good work, Kayman. Now grab Chirk and haul him outside," Bracken headed upstairs, still speaking into his radio. "We'll gather the evidence on our way out. Head for the BATT. Be there shortly." He hustled up the stairs.

Bracken gathered Chirk's laptop and shoved it onto a box of files. Poncho took the desktop computer, and Chico took the last box and went out the back door.

"Thirty seconds," Cordy warned.

In the basement, Desmond assessed the C-4 plastic explosive by the window and the line running to the ceiling door.

"Water gun?" Foley asked.

"Yup, that was my plan." Each pulled a high-powered saline pistol from their gear. Desmond said, "Usually, we have the bomb disposal robot pull the trigger, but here goes, three, two, one."

"Fifteen seconds," Cordy said.

Desmond blasted the water gun at the C-4 explosives around the trap door while Foley blasted the window explosives. The electronics separated from the packets.

"Ten, nine, eight," Cordy counted down.

Desmond continued to pump another hit to those lining the ceiling trap door. The electronics fell to the floor.

"Three, two, mmm." Cordy couldn't say one.

There was a slight popping sound when Foley pulled out the blasting cap, but they disarmed the explosives. "Clear," Desmond fist-bumped Foley.

"Ahh! Great job! What a team." Cordy exclaimed. She didn't even wait for everyone to return to the BATT before contacting President Spendorf. She felt drained and unable to move as the adrenaline stopped flowing. She felt drained and unable to move as the adrenaline stopped flowing.

Desmond climbed back through the hole in the wall and held his hand out to Foley.

"Thanks, we make a great team," Foley grabbed the outstretched hand and slid back into the fruit cellar. He motioned, "After you."

They left the fruit cellar, climbed the stairs, and dashed through the front door. Desmond took a deep breath. "Love that mountain air. It sure beats the Texas heat. I love working here."

Cordy also sent text messages to Braun and Agent Kelly, "The SWAT team rescued Chief Jackson, and Chirk is in custody."

The SWAT team met in the BATT and unloaded their gear.

Cordy entered the code to open the gate, and they exited the property. A helicopter waited to take them back to Fort Collins. Bracken handed Chirk over to a federal officer on board. "Book him. We'll start with kidnapping, but there's a whole laundry list to follow, and who knows what else the criminal evidence team will uncover."

What Makes Chirk Tick?

Cordy should have been in bed hours ago, but she couldn't wait to get her hands on Chirk's computer. A deep curiosity filled her as she opened one file after another. She wasn't sure how much more she could learn about a person by reading his emails and other folders, but she knew this man was full of surprises. He had traveled to twelve countries in the last four months.

She researched the man in detail after he kidnapped the chief and discovered that Chirk had joined the U.S. Marines two days after his seventeenth birthday and served for twenty years, starting out in aircraft communications. He took additional training in navigation and ended up as an electrical and weapon systems technician.

While in the service, he attended night school, earned his bachelor's degree in political science, and studied law.

When the war in Afghanistan broke out, General Rutoon became Chirk's commanding officer and had a strong influence throughout Chirk's life. Well-respected, the former law student headed some of the most dangerous raids and won a purple heart when he risked heavy fire by the Taliban to rescue most of his platoon, including General Rutoon. Chirk suffered injuries and was in a coma for two weeks. The doctors were sure he would die, but he surprised everyone.

After getting out of the military at thirty-seven, he wasn't ready to retire, so he fought hard to get back in physical condition to join the FBI. They didn't want him at first because he was at the maximum age, but his education, experience, and knowledge of weapons earned him a conditional letter of appointment. General Rutoon's letter of recommendation probably also helped get Chirk an age waiver. The FBI assigned him as a special agent. That's where he met Chief Jackson.

The two became partners, working overseas on several secret missions for the government. Chirk lost his eye while on a counter-terrorism attack in Pakistan. Cordy surmised that too many years of tension and violence had taken an emotional toll on Chirk.

After reading the numerous emails between Rutoon and Chirk, she knew the general had something hanging over the head of his protégé. Did he know about Chirk's smuggled funds? Not one email mentioned anything about a virus or about kidnapping the chief. Many messages mentioned Braun Hastings.

Several of Rutoon's emails stressed honor and loyalty. Others talked about integrity and justice. Was it to get Chirk to assist him? If not, why would Rutoon break all of these fundamental values?

One email especially caught her eye. "Braun has secret documents that could destroy the career of a top government official. Take any risk to stop him!"

Cordy wondered what government official Rutoon meant in his communication, President Spendorf or the general himself. As it turned out, from reading through his emails, she learned that Braun had several documents. But why was Chirk involved? Did he know those documents were about the general, or did he think they implicated the president of the U.S.? Why would Rutoon want to inflict such chaos by causing an epidemic? None of those answers seemed apparent in the light of what had happened. She had to continue searching.

Stifling a yawn, Cordy checked the darknet for any information from Braun. It was early morning in Washington, D.C. No news from Braun, but Kelly left a message. "You'll soon receive a message from Dr. Alex, head of Virology at CDC, to discuss a potential vaccine Dr. Trent worked on while in Colorado. Alex needs assistance from Trent's team. I will call soon. Braun, Usher, Ryan, and I will also conference in from wherever we are at the time. How's Jackson? Give him my love."

Cordy smiled and returned the message. "Chief has lost weight, but he's in excellent spirits. He sends you best wishes. Will have him on the 2 p.m. conference call, and BTW, stay healthy." Cordy entered several keywords into her computer for more background research as she headed upstairs for a quick shower and a brief nap before meeting with Chief Jackson at 7 a.m. Although exhausted by his ordeal, he was determined to study the paper documents himself. Maybe he had more information.

Before she reached the top step, her computer pinged. The alarm was loud enough that she padded back downstairs to get the update. Dr. Alex asked for three tasks, if possible:

"1. Meet with astronaut Linda Smith-Tyler and give her our condolences regarding her son, Chester, and her half-brother, Dr. Joe Smith, in person. She may have additional pertinent information as the only surviving astronaut from this mission. I don't understand why she hasn't been infected.

"2. Explore information on Dr. Trent's research team and their progress in developing a viral vaccine.

"3. If a vaccine is in the works, what is their ETA on completion?

"Talk to you at 2 p.m., Braun's reading over my shoulder and says, 'LYA,' whatever that means. He says you'll understand, and get some rest."

"Rest?" Cordy laughed. "Not enough hours in a day." She went back upstairs, hoping to get a few hours of sleep.

Will This Shift Ever End?

It was 5 a.m., and Dr. Brakinsky had been on duty at Holy Cross Hospital ED for nearly 20 hours when the ambulance brought in Officer Peggy Wyller. Her partner, J.D., was already in O.R. with a gunshot wound to the chest.

Brakinsky usually ran a tight ship. His normal hours were from 9 a.m. to 5 p.m., but nothing was typical today. The emergency department had a steady flow of patients, and the number grew as each hour passed. He'd treated over 240 patients, and the waiting room was still overflowing with angry people. The hospital called in extra police protection and stationed two officers in the reception area after an angry man nearly killed a male nurse as he examined an infant in respiratory distress. The nurse remained unconscious in the ICU. The restrained assaulter was in an isolation room. A police officer stood guard outside his room.

Aggressive behavior grew more rampant. To top it off, the police departments had barely enough officers to patrol the streets and answer 911 calls, let alone guard hospital staff.

Brakinsky hadn't seen his wife, Elizabeth, since she left early yesterday morning to run the RR7 meeting. He'd reported in with her two hours ago to say not to wait up for him. He'd be home whenever he got there.

Seven doctors had responded to the Code D situation earlier in the day. A pediatrician, a plastic surgeon, an internal medicine resident, and a cardiopulmonary surgeon were still on duty. Thank God for that because J.D. needed a pulmonary surgeon STAT. The surgeon inserted a chest tube to clear a collapsed lung. The trauma team had been working in the OR non-stop, and a second team arrived in time to whisk J.D. away for an exploratory laparotomy.

* * *

Peggy's ankle wound didn't warrant priority care, but she found a nurse to give her a tetanus shot. As she was leaving the ED, she ran into Dr. Brakinsky. "How's Officer J.D.?"

"The trauma team is doing their best," Brakinsky said. "Go home. Get some sleep. He'll be in the OR for at least another hour, and then, he'll be in recovery if he makes it. From there, he'll go to ICU. You won't be able to see him for another 12 hours."

"His ex-wife is in California, and his son is in Minnesota," Peggy said. "They can't fly into the city due to the ban on all flights. Put me on the emergency notification list. I'm the closest thing he has to family."

"Talk to the secretary. She'll take down your contact information and add it to his medical record," Dr. Brakinsky said. "Before you leave, go through decontamination. It won't take long, and then get some sleep. You look exhausted. I'm planning to head home, too, as soon as my relief arrives. It's been a long night."

"Thanks, I'll do that." Peggy stopped at the secretary's desk to give the information. A nurse directed her to the decontamination room. Peggy didn't want to leave her uniform behind but agreed to wear the hospital-issued coveralls.

The nurse double-bagged the uniform and instructed, "Remove the outer bag and toss the whole works into the washing machine. Use this soap to be sure to kill off any stray bacteria."

Peggy took the sample-sized container, left the decontamination area, and returned to the ED. When she glanced up, her husband was coming out of room 3. "Carl, what are you doing in the emergency department?"

Carl heaved a deep sigh. "I've been here for a while. Guy Weimer's wife called. I was talking to Guy when his wife yelled from the motel room's door, 'Someone is breaking into the car.' Guy disconnected our call, ran outside to stop the thief, and was hit over the head. Guy was unconscious. His wife called 911, and an ambulance brought him to the ED. She called me in a panic. Since they live in Wisconsin, she didn't know who else to contact."

"Is he going to be all right?" Peggy asked as she gowned up and headed for Guy's room.

"They're taking him for an MRI, worried about cerebral hemorrhage."

Two nurses moved Guy's cart through the door, bypassing Peggy and Carl.

Guy's wife cried and talked at the same time. "I don't know what I'll do if anything happens to him. They could have taken the car for all I care. It was just a rental. I told him to let the police handle it, but he said all his RR7 notes were in his briefcase on the passenger's seat. Why he'd leave anything in the car during all this chaos was foolish, but we never lock up anything back home. No one would touch our belongings."

Wrapping an arm around Guy's wife, Peggy said, "It's been a rough night for all of us. I don't think I've met you. I'm Carl's wife, Peggy. Do you have a place to stay?"

The woman pulled away. "I'm staying right here with Guy."

"Of course," Peggy said. "I only meant that you're far from home and might stay in Washington, D.C., for a while. We have plenty of room at our house. I think it would be safer."

"Oh, I'm sorry. I reacted badly, didn't I? Thanks for the invitation. My name's Joan, by the way. I can't make any decisions right now. Please forgive me."

"I understand." Peggy scribbled her home phone and cell number on the back of her business card and handed it to Joan. "Let's keep in touch. We want to know how Guy is doing. After going through that awful-smelling chemical spray, I think I'm ready for a hot shower and bed." She turned toward Carl. "Can you get my spare uniform from the car? I don't like this coverall."

Carl complied and returned to the Emergency department.

Peggy entered the restroom, changed clothes, and met Carl in the lobby. "Let's go home."

Welcome Home

Peggy stopped at the emergency room exit to squirt a dab of hand sanitizer from a bottle inside the door. She rubbed her hands together and waited until Carl pulled his car to the curb. Glad to go home, Peggy opened the passenger's door, sighed, and leaned the seat as far back as possible. "If I fall asleep, just leave me in the car. It'll be the best nap of my life."

"Don't worry, Peg. I'll wrap you in my arms and carry you upstairs to our comfortable bed. I don't want to spend another day worrying about you. When you wake up, we should visit your parents in Colorado. They would love to see you again."

"What, and leave this deadly place for paradise? There's no way that you can go now. You're on the president's special force committee. What did you call it?"

"The RR7," Carl said. "I know I can't go, but you'd be safe."

"I'm not going anywhere without you," Peggy insisted. "Do you have time to take me home before your next meeting?"

"We meet in two hours, but you're more important to me. I can't tell you how many times I paced the house, waiting to hear from you. The media is full of news of this deadly virus, and people are going insane. Look at Guy. Someone mugged him just walking to his car."

"You don't know the half of it," Peggy said. "I've seen people go crazy in their homes and injure their family members. They shoot police officers while doing their duty. I thought it only affected law enforcement, but look at the hospitals. There aren't enough medical personnel to treat the patients."

Her phone beeped. "Another Amber Alert. It's the eleventh one since midnight."

Carl said, "I think we should call this the 'lunatic virus.' Nothing makes any sense. I predict this is just the beginning, and I don't know how it will end."

Peggy didn't doubt him. Sleep pulled at her. She closed her eyes, but her mind wouldn't turn off—too many bizarre events in the last twenty-four hours kept replaying. Drifting off, an alarm inside the car jarred her awake. "Did someone just break into our garage?"

Carl turned off the remote alarm. "I doubt anyone could get inside. Besides, we're nearly home."

Peggy's eyes widened as they neared her neighborhood, and she was surprised at the number of people on her lawn. She recognized most of them. It was like they were having a sit-in while leaning against her maple trees. Many had rifles, sticks, or bats. Some stood in place, making repetitive motions, head nodding, and hand tremors. Others lay on the ground as if asleep. Sirens sounded in the distance, but no one even flinched.

A few people walked along the sidewalk like they were in a daze. Some had jerky body movements as they glanced her way.

Carl slowed before reaching the house. "My God, what are we getting into? Should I keep going, or do you want to face these people?"

"I don't like what I see," Peggy said, "and we can't rely on additional police backup. Keep going."

Too late, someone pointed in her direction, and the crowd got up from her lawn. They moved in mass toward the car.

"Peggy!" Jonah, their best friend and neighbor across the street, reached the car first and tapped the window with his knuckles. He didn't appear to have a weapon and seemed lucid. "Let me in your car, and let's get out of here!" He tried to open the back door. "Hurry, unlock the door. They're coming after you!"

Carl flipped the automatic door opener as another man swung a bat, smashing the front windshield.

Jonah leaped into the back seat and slammed the door on someone's hand when they tried to pull him back out of the car. "Go! Now! I'll tell you everything."

Carl didn't wait for another second. He backed up his car, and the wheels screeched. Someone hit the hood with a stick. Carl would have mowed them down if anyone were in the way as they spun 180° and sped away. He could barely see through the cracked windshield but continued to steer forward, sighting a small opening in the pebbled glass. Fortunately, the bat smashed mainly Peggy's side of the car.

"What happened?" Peggy dusted off fragments that littered the front of the dash and her clothes. "Why are all those people in our yard? And why are they going after us?"

"They're scared, angry, and I'm afraid some are infected. After the Heraldson incident, the whole neighborhood is in an uproar."

Peggy opened the glove compartment to get her sunglasses and found a bottle of Advil. Her head ached so much she took four and swallowed them without water. "What happened to the Heraldsons?"

"It was awful," Jonah said. "The whole family…mauled to death! You're a cop. They wanted your help, but no one answered at your house. The discussion grew so heated that someone tried to break into your back door to see if you were asleep. When they couldn't get in, they went through your garage but found no one at home. We have been calling for two hours for police protection, and no one is answering 911. The cell system is failing, too. We can't text messages anymore, and our calls are dropped. Too many calls, I guess. Did you know that?"

"No, but we couldn't get any police backup on my last call, so it doesn't surprise me." Peggy flipped down the mirror to check a few cuts on her face and was surprised at the bone-white image staring back at her. "Why are our neighbors angry with me? They even smashed our windshield."

Jonah shook his head. "You're a cop on our block. They want protection."

"I can't be everywhere, and I was already on duty protecting our community," Peggy said.

"Most of these neighbors are just agitated but not crazy, or at least that was what I thought until everyone started heading toward your car," Jonah said. "They wanted to talk to you about forming a neighborhood watch program."

"If they wanted my help, why come at us with bats?" Peggy asked. "Damaging our car doesn't make me want to help them."

"That part, I don't understand. I was afraid for you once your neighbors broke into your house. I doubt they took anything, but who knows how long that will last. The stores are closed, and many have been robbed. People are raiding each other's homes, stealing food mostly. Do you know what is going on?"

"I only know some flu or epidemic is going around. It causes people to become violent," Peggy said.

Carl cut in, "Lunatic bug! That's what I'm calling it."

"I thought you said it was 'lunatic virus,' but I like bug better," Peggy said. "Where do we go now?"

"Can you drop me off at my wife's work?" Jonah asked. "I don't want her to come home to danger. I'm taking her away from all of this. We'll take her car and get out of town, far away as possible."

"There are blockades everywhere," Peggy said. "I don't think you'll get very far."

When Carl reached the main highway, he exclaimed, "Seven a.m. is rush-hour traffic on a normal day, but there are hardly any cars on the road!"

"It gives me an ominous feeling like the whole world is in peril, and fixing it's up to us. The burden is too much." Peggy's work phone vibrated. "Oh, great. Work's calling me." She pulled the phone out of her pocket and stared at the ID. "I don't recognize the number. It's not the department calling. Should I answer?"

"No. It might be one of our neighbors. Let it go through to voicemail." It only took another five minutes to drop Jonah off at his wife's workplace. As Carl pulled back onto the main road, his cell rang. He took it from his front shirt pocket and handed it to Peggy. "See who is calling."

Peggy answered immediately. "President Spendorf, what can I do for you? Carl is driving, but I can have him pull over to take your call."

"Just put me on the speaker," Zac said. "I think the whole world is crumbling around us, and I don't know who to trust anymore, but I hope I can trust you. I have to talk to Carl immediately."

Peggy barely hit the speaker icon when Carl drove to the side of the road. "Good morning, Zac."

The president didn't attempt the usual niceties. "Have you heard from Liz Brakinsky? I've tried to reach her cell phone every five minutes for half an hour. It rings three times, then disconnects. It didn't even go to voice mail. Harry Barker can't reach her either, although I doubt she'd pick up the phone if she knew the call came from him. I hear Harry was quite disruptive at the RR7 meetings. I'm pulling him from the team. We have more important things to handle."

"Good idea," Carl said. "No, I haven't heard from Liz. Why do you ask?"

"I tried her home, and her husband answered. He's had a long day at the hospital and had been home only a few minutes," President Spendorf said.

"I know he's been busy," Carl interrupted. "We just came from there. He treated Guy Weimer after someone hit him over the head at his motel. They took Guy to nuclear medicine for tests. What did Dr. Brakinsky say?"

"He informed me about Guy. He'll be going to ICU," Zac said. "Liz wasn't there when he got home and probably never made it home. Neighbors vandalized their house—broken windows, raided kitchen cupboards, and someone even broke their fish tank. Glass was everywhere. He found their dog tethered in the bedroom to the shoe rack in the closet."

"I thought they lived in a gated community," Carl said. "Peg and I were attacked in front of our house, too. I guess nowhere is safe these days."

Peggy added, "Dr. Brakinsky mentioned that he spoke to Liz during the night to tell her he'd be home when he got there. Where was she at that time?"

"He mentioned that, but he spoke to her on her cell phone, so she could have been anywhere," Zac said. "She never mentioned a break-in, so he thought Liz had gone to work early. I thought you'd be attending the RR7 meeting soon and wondered if you could go directly there to check her whereabouts. Dr. Brakinsky is exhausted and tied up with the police but wants to hear when you find out anything."

"Okay. We're heading into town right now," Carl said. "I'll keep you posted."

"If Liz isn't there, contact me immediately." Zac added, "Oh yes, I sent Braun and Usher Hastings to this morning's meeting, so they'll meet you there shortly. Braun attended our team conference last month."

"I remember," Carl said.

Zac explained the problem the men had getting into the city. "It was so easy to run the country just a month ago. Now, everything is out of control."

"We're doing our best to help you," Carl said. "Are Braun and Usher joining the RR7 team?"

Zac cleared his throat. "Not formally, but they will update you on the latest developments. Then I have some loose ends to tie up."

Must be nice to be safe and hunkered down in your bunker," Carl said.

"You have no idea what I'd give to get out of these four walls," President Spendorf said. "I'm losing my mind."

"Don't ever say that," Peggy gasped. "I've seen too many people tonight that have lost their minds. We need you hidden away. Stay safe and run the country. Our lives depend on you."

"And I'm relying on RR7," Zac said. "We have to stop this epidemic and find a cure! You hear me, Carl?"

"Loud and clear. Talk to you soon." Carl disconnected the call. Resigned to a higher responsibility, he sighed, "I guess we won't be going to Colorado after all. I know you're exhausted. Take a nap while we meet at the Conference Center, then we'll rent a hotel room for the night."

Bad News Gets Worse

Cordy walked into Chief Jackson's office. The door was left open, but it seemed like the room was unoccupied. Good morning, Chief. "Are you here already at this hour? It's only 6 a.m."

The chief swiveled his chair, his voice almost inaudible as he muttered, "Here," while staring at his paperwork. Several files were scattered across his desk. "Nothing makes sense."

Cordy inquired, "Would you like some coffee before we begin working on this?" Without waiting for a response, she headed to the refreshment station to pour two cups of coffee—one black and the other with cream. She walked over to the chief's desk, moved a file out of the way, and put the black coffee within his reach.

The chief expressed his approval with a grunt and then took a sip.

Cordy squinted as she studied the diagram on the whiteboard. "What's this? You must have been up all night."

There were four boxes at the top labeled "Rutoon," "Smith," "Chirk," and "?" Under each header was a series of notes. Below Rutoon was the following list: North Korea, Syria, and Russia, with the names of key officials for each country.

Joe Smith had the longest list below his name: NASA, Russian astronaut Mordecai Ratinzky called Morty, North Korean astronaut Ghim, U.S. astronauts Tip Granger on Space Station, Maxwell Uliptos, Ivan Pendari, Linda Smith-Tyler, Chester—school shooting, autopsies-encephalitis, planted pandemic virus?

Cordy rubbed her aching head. "Can you clarify the purpose of this diagram? I think I understand, but I want to be sure."

"These all have the potential for a viral outbreak," Jackson said. "What I want to know is why plant a virus?"

"Rutoon's in prison. Braun had the goods on him. Maybe he'll tell us why—" Cordy started.

"Not likely," the chief cut in, "Chirk is a better bet, but I'd wager that he had no clue how deep Rutoon was into this debacle, nor to what extreme the general was willing to go. Chirk's a jerk, but I can't see him going on a killing rampage, especially infecting innocent citizens. I'm sure he believed he was protecting President Spendorf. He's been taken for a ride to hell, and it won't end well."

"You still care about him, don't you?" Cordy asked. "Why, after all he put you through? He tried to kill you. He would have killed Braun."

"Maybe, but he didn't remove my belt, where I hid my secret tools. He knows that I prepare for any situation. Maybe it was his way to save his own skin. Shit flows downhill, and most likely, Chirk will be the fall guy, lying in the gutter."

Under Chirk, the list included Braun Hastings, Chief Jackson, and Rutoon's goon, Joe Smith. It ended with 'hidden funds from Syria?' written in red.

"Why did you add hidden funds? Do you think he got a kickback from Rutoon?"

The chief frowned. "No, Rutoon wouldn't part with one lousy penny for anyone. I suspect Chirk smuggled funds from when I worked with him in the FBI. I couldn't prove it, but someday I'll find a few million tucked away in some account overseas with his name on it."

A second diagram had several more notes for Smith—Red satin box key source, planted virus in Washington, D.C., spread virus to Colorado, infected nephew, Chester Tyler, infected restaurant owner's son, arranged to kill Braun Hastings, shot Dr. Trent.

"I assume anything else goes under '?'" Cordy pulled out her computer to make additional notes. "There's more. We've barely touched the surface."

The chief said, "True. I set up a meeting with Linda Smith-Tyler. She's coming into the office in half an hour before she heads for a conference with the school principal." Jackson gulped his coffee.

Cordy added, "Dr. Alex from the CDC's Department of Virology in Washington, D.C., contacted me to request that we express our condolences to Linda. Then, he asked us to verify the progress of Dr. Trent's viral vaccine research. Kelly asked us to join the RR7 conference call with Dr. Alex, Ryan, and Kelly at 2 p.m. today. I guess that would be noon here.

"Esthanne Jennings worked with Dr. Trent," Chief Jackson said. "I spoke with her briefly after Dr. Trent was shot. She's an early riser. Let's give her a call." The chief thumbed through his cell phone contacts, tapped the number, and hit speaker.

"Good morning. This is Dr. Jennings. How may I help you?"

"Hello, this is Chief Jackson and my colleague, Agent Cordelia. Have you received an update on Dr. Trent's condition lately?"

"Unfortunately, he's still in a coma and on a ventilator, but his vital signs are stable," Dr. Jennings said. "In his absence, we're doing our best to stay one step ahead of this pandemic."

"That's why we called," Cordy explained Dr. Alex's discussion of a viral vaccine. "Can you join the conference call at noon today? I'll send you an invitation link."

"I know Dr. Alex," Jennings said. "Let me check my schedule." There was a pause. "Noon? I have half an hour. I'd love to help in any way possible, so we'll speak then. Sorry, but I was on my way out the door. See you at noon." Jennings disconnected the call.

Cordy's computer pinged. She found a file blinking from her TOR account, which wasn't from Kelly, Braun, or the president. Cordy jumped out of her chair. Her heart skipped a beat. "How did he get access to my account?"

"Who?" Chief Jackson's eyes widened with concern and glued to hers. A crease furrowed his brow, and he leaned closer to stare at her computer.

Cordy ran a hand over her face. She felt caged, trapped like a wild animal. "Rutoon. How did the general get access to my site?"

"How do you know it's from Rutoon?" the chief asked. "Not easy to do from prison."

"See the words Semper Fi written beneath the eagle over the world and the anchor. That's Rutoon's signature. I saw it in Chirk's files."

"Are you sure Rutoon's still locked up?" Cordy made an emergency memo to the president. "What federal prison did you send Rutoon to?" She sent an encrypted email and text to Braun, Kelly, and then tried Winston. She received no answers, and President Spendorf didn't respond even after five minutes. That was highly unusual. Normally, he sent a check mark signifying he had received the memo. Instead, a smiley face pinged onto her screen. It also came from Rutoon's site.

"He has immediate access to my encrypted account. Only three people have that: Braun, Kelly, and the president!"

Cordy grabbed the laptop and immediately shut it off. "He knows everything. He'll learn about Braun and Kelly's location and all my research on him and Chirk."

"Take a deep breath and calm down. We'll get to the bottom of this," the chief said.

"One of them exposed me!" Cordy gasped.

"None of them would have divulged access information," the chief said.

"Whoever it is, they are in big trouble!" She moved to Chief Jackson's laptop. "Are you secure?"

"You better check."

She inserted a thumb drive to update her program and began to scan his files. Cordy flinched when there was a rap on the doorjamb. "May I come in? I'm Linda Smith-Tyler. You wanted to talk to me?"

"Come in and have a seat." Chief Jackson stood and held out his hand. "This is Agent Cordelia."

Linda entered the room and shook his hand.

"Call me, Cordy." She barely glanced up, still freaking out about Rutoon's access to her computer. The last thing she wanted to do at that moment was to interview Linda. Cordy's laptop and access to her team were essential and her priority.

Chief Jackson pulled up a spare chair and motioned for Linda to sit. "Cordy, you set up this meeting. Come join us."

A hundred things buzzing through Cordy's mind drove her to distraction when she remembered Dr. Alex's requests. "President Spendorf and his entire team send their deepest condolences." She sat next to the astronaut.

Linda yawned. "Sorry, but these last few days have been horrific. My husband and I have participated in news conferences, delivered speeches at schools, and spoken with several police investigators. Attempting to rectify Joe's mistakes and having to apologize for our child's behavior has been an utter nightmare."

"I can't imagine how hard it has been for you and your family," Cordy agreed. "Sorry to call you down here for yet another session."

"Believe me, if I can help rid our country of this deadly epidemic, I'll do anything." Linda's eyebrow drew up with concern in contrast to the corners of her mouth drawn into a frown. Her voice had a somber tone thick with emotion. Then she cleared her throat. "I know this is rude, but may I have a cup of coffee? Black. I'm so tired I might drop off at any moment."

Cordy scooted off her chair. "No problem. I should have offered you a cup already." She swirled the pot. "When did you make this sludge?"

Chief Jackson laughed. "Maybe 2:30 this morning. Make a new pot. I'm sure we'll all enjoy some."

Cordy rinsed out the grounds and put a fresh pot on the coffee maker. "It won't take long." She sat back down.

"I can't believe my Chester could do such a thing. He was a straight-A student, loved sports, and participated in all school activities. Why?" Linda leaned forward. Her brow creased. "Can a virus cause someone to lose their mind? If so, I can't imagine how families are coping with this…this epidemic. And you think it came from the space station? How?"

Cordy placed a hand on Linda's arm. "I can tell this is haunting you."

"It's taking over my life! I want to help. It would mean my son didn't die in vain. Please tell me what you need. But first, I have a few questions of my own. Did anyone tell you how Max and Ivan died? I don't know why they were exposed, and I wasn't."

"I wondered the same thing," Cordy said. "Did you ever see a red satin box?"

"Yes. It was so small, yet it's become a big issue. Even the police mentioned the box, but I don't know what happened to it. I've wracked my brain trying to recall. The last I remember, that box was still hanging on the spacecraft's wall in a safety net." Her voice cracked. "I can't imagine what happened. Both Max and Ivan are dead, too. It's too much. I can't take it." A tear trickled down her cheek before she swiped it away with her sleeve.

Are these tied to one another? Cordy's mind tried to understand.

Linda dug a hanky from her pocket and blew her nose. "I'm sorry, but the police act odd around me as if I'm the one to blame. They even asked stupid and hurtful questions such as, 'Did I hate my son? Why would I infect him?' How could anyone who has a child be so cruel?" Linda breathed in a ragged breath. "I'm sorry. That's not why I'm here. I want to stop this madness." She clenched her fists and sighed. "Okay, I got that off my chest."

Cordy moved her chair a bit closer. "I know these are difficult questions, but we need answers, and you're the only remaining person we can ask."

"I understand. Yes, Max received a red box," Linda said. "Maybe it was supposed to be delivered to NASA."

"I contacted NASA, but they didn't know anything about the box, and it was only after speaking to Ghim that they realized the red box was aboard the shuttle and returned to Earth. Then, somehow, the box appeared in Fort Collins, and the police traced it to Dr. Smith. How did your step-brother acquire the box?"

"I don't know, and as I said, I don't know what happened to that box after we landed." Linda nearly shouted her answer. "Everyone keeps asking me that."

Chief Jackson got up and poured three cups of coffee. He handed one to Linda, another to Cordy, and returned to his seat. "Okay, you don't know what happened to the box," Chief Jackson said calmly. "What happened while you were on the Space Station?"

Linda sipped her coffee and set the cup on the desk. "We discussed the MRSA program in great detail. Dr. Pendari and Ghim were in the lab most days. It wasn't until we were about to leave that Max received the box. During the flight back to Earth, I saw Max open the box while the men ate dinner and found it empty. Max showed the box to Ivan and then replaced it on the wall. I recall I was exercising at the time. I told Max to use the bike, but he declined. I like to stay fit, but Max planned to retire soon, so he didn't bother. He said he'd make up for it on the golf course when he returned home."

"If Max opened the box and showed it to Ivan, and it was empty, how were they exposed to the virus?" Cordy asked.

"I don't know, but Max and Ivan were a team," Linda said. "I was the outsider. Perhaps that saved me, but Ghim gave Max the red box if I had to guess. He was proud of his MRSA findings and had been genetically engineering a cure, or so he said. He seemed very polite and mild-mannered. I don't think he would hurt a fly."

"What about the Russian astronaut, Mordecai Ratinzky?" Cordy glanced at the whiteboard for his name. "I think they call him Morty."

"Ah, yes. Morty is different. It's the only way I can explain the man. He laughs one moment and is serious the next. Overly cautious, he wouldn't touch the virus, afraid he'd become infected. Whenever we even mentioned MRSA, he left the area. His sister had died of SARS, leaving a deep impression on him. Tip wasn't too fond of the superbug either, but the U.S. sent the sample to space for research, so he logged any trial studies and reported back to Houston. Most experiments were Ghim's projects."

"Do you think Ghim acted under the orders of a North Korean official to send a sample virus to Earth to infect the U.S.?" Chief Jackson asked.

"No, I can't believe that. Ghim is for saving lives. He's searching for a cure, and he may even have come up with one."

Cordy perked up. "Do you think Ghim might help us?"

Linda took another sip of coffee and closed her eyes. "Ahh, that's delicious." She breathed in the coffee's aroma and leaned back into the chair. "I don't know, but Ghim mentioned that he'd run several experiments and had isolated the nucleus. I think that's what he said. I was involved in other experiments and paid little attention to theirs, if you want to know the truth. Has NASA talked to him about his research?"

Cordy's cell phone buzzed. She glanced at caller ID.

Is Braun calling you?" Jackson asked.

"No, it's Dr. Ping, the Secretary of the Department of Health. Linda, can I share the information we just discussed? He can follow up with NASA and Ghim."

Linda perked up. "If you think it will help us find a cure, please do. I want to help in any way I can."

"Thanks," Cordy answered, "Hello, this is Cordy."

Chief Jackson refilled Linda's coffee while Cordy entered the hallway to update Dr. Ping.

When Cordy returned, Linda was telling the chief about her last video call with her son while on the space station. "I'll always cherish those precious moments and will hold his memory dear in my heart. It just doesn't seem fair…" Linda took a deep breath and glanced up at Cordy. "I hope what I shared helps."

"Yes, thank you for coming. You've been very helpful." Cordy noticed flashing red lights racing across the chief's computer screen. Her gut twisted at the thought of Rutoon trying to breach her software. "Excuse me. I need to check this out." She logged onto the darknet account.

Chief of Staff Winston Willoughby sent an urgent message. "Need to talk to Braun Hastings ASAP. No calls are going through to his cell, and I have vital information regarding President Spendorf. Can you track him down? Need an immediate conference call."

Cordy sent a message to Braun from her secure satellite phone. It rang seconds later. "This is Agent Cordelia. One moment, I'm in the middle of an interview. I'll get Chief Jackson." Cordy turned the computer so the chief could see Winston's message while trying not to alarm Linda. She typed a message that only the chief could see. "We have a major concern, and Braun is on the line. Can you take the call?" She handed the cell to the chief.

"Hello, old friend." Chief Jackson scooted his chair away from his desk and got up. "I meant to call you. It's nice to hear from you again." He paced a bit before leaving the office to go into the hallway.

Cordy turned toward Linda and held out her hand, indicating it was time for Linda to leave. "Thanks for coming. You've given us important data. Dr. Ping will check with NASA to see if Ghim might have a solution to stop the virus."

Linda didn't budge. "What's wrong? I can see fear darkening your eyes, and that flashing red light is the same as we get when the president is in danger. It is the president, right? Has he been infected?"

Chief Jackson peered around the door and shook his head at Cordy.

She said, "No, the president's not infected. But we need to work on keeping him safe. I'm sure you understand. Thanks."

Linda's brows furrowed as she stood and glanced from Cordy to Chief Jackson. "Look, I know I'm not considered a top-secret agent, but maybe I can help. Tell me what's going on."

Chief Jackson disappeared back into the hallway.

Cordy paused, wanting to discover what Jackson had found out, but she didn't know how much information she could share with Linda. *Nothing if this involves the president.* "I'm not sure what the call is about."

Linda nodded. "I swear on my son's grave. I won't tell a soul."

"President Spendorf is working on a top-secret mission. We must find a cure for the pandemic. Your tip about Ghim's experiments may be a solution."

"And?" Linda tapped her finger on her thigh. Her hand flew to her mouth as she dropped back into her chair. "He's missing in action, isn't he? Mia? Max wrote Mia on a sticky and placed it on the Avionic panel. He said it was a reminder to call his family. Mia is the name of his soon-to-be daughter-in-law. Somehow, I had a gut feeling when he talked about her. I wondered if that was her real name." Linda's eyes closed as she pondered. "Max's daughter-in-law. Mia or MIA. Could it be a clue? Did he know something was going to happen to President Spendorf?" Linda opened her eyes. "Now, I wonder if Max even has a son. Oh, I'm sure he does. I saw his photo."

Cordy didn't know what to say. "MIA, that's an interesting theory, but it doesn't apply to the president. He's tucked away in the bunker for a few days, and I talked to him just a few hours ago."

Linda shook her head. "Maybe it's a coincidence, but I have a gut feeling. I have learned to heed that feeling. You had better check to ensure the president is still in the bunker. I know I've overstayed my welcome, so I'll leave, but if you need anything, call me immediately."

"I'll do that." Cordy stood. "Thanks."

Linda adjusted her purse strap over her shoulder, stood, and shook Cordy's outstretched hand. "Coincidence? No. There's no such thing. I need to check on a few facts. I'll get back to you." She bumped into Chief Jackson on the way out the door.

"Thanks for all of your help," the chief said, "And by the way, President Spendorf says he's sorry for your loss."

"Did you just speak to him?" Linda asked. "Of course, you did, the emergency phone call, right?" She blew out a deep breath. "I need some sleep. I'm getting paranoid." She dug through her purse, pulled out her car keys, and continued out the front door.

Cordy pulled Jackson into the office and closed the door. "What did Braun tell you?"

"President Spendorf assigned two Secret Service agents to take Braun and Usher to this morning's RR7 meeting. Something went amiss, and the agents were put on emergency alert. Braun will call when he has more details."

Cordy's cell phone buzzed. She glanced at caller ID.

"Is Braun calling back already?" Jackson asked.

"Yes, he just texted," Cordy answered, glanced at the message, and nearly fainted.

Chief Jackson reached for her. "What is it?"

"Braun says, 'They've been exposed to Virus X. Not once, but twice,' and Linda was right. The president is missing."

As Cordy headed to Chief Jackson's office, Braun and Usher were being escorted by two Secret Service Agents to the Conference Center in Washington, D.C., Braun nervously paced while waiting for someone from the RR7 team to arrive. When he spotted Carl Wyller from the DoD, Braun greeted him, and was introduced to Carl's wife, Peggy. "I'm glad you made it here early. This is my brother, FBI Agent Usher."

Peggy shook hands with the Hasting brothers. "It's nice to meet you."

Braun stepped aside for Carl to open the door. "Your husband mentioned that you're a police officer. Are you on or off duty?"

Peggy shared that she had worked for 18 hours straight. "I was eager to go home, but when we entered our subdivision, I noticed many neighbors were infected with the virus. Someone even broke our car's windshield, so we left to come here. I recall hearing that you and Usher had difficulty getting to D.C., after being rerouted on a red-eye flight to Boston."

"We had some snafus, but we made it," Braun admitted.

Carl tried the front door. "President Spendorf mentioned you would attend today's meeting. He's concerned about Liz Brakinsky."

"The door's locked," Braun said. "I was hoping Liz would be here already."

"She could be inside." Carl searched his pockets, found a key, and unlocked the front door. "The meeting room is the third door on the right.

The light was on when Braun opened the door. "Liz, are you in here? I have an update from President Spendorf."

Carl scanned the room for Liz, even checking behind the whiteboard, but she was nowhere to be found. "I wonder where she is," he mentioned as he turned on the kitchen light.

Peggy followed Carl into the room and began making coffee while they waited for the rest of the team to arrive. She searched through some drawers, found a coffee filter and grounds, and then filled the coffee maker with water. They agreed to wait for Liz to arrive before informing President Spendorf, who was already upset.

Usher entered the kitchen. "Where might I find a projector for Braun's presentation to the team?"

"We used one yesterday," Carl checked the front desk as he moved into the conference room, "but it's not here today."

Braun looked up from arranging the chairs. "We have another mid-morning meeting at the FBI, and I want to briefly discuss a few issues with Agent Kelly and Ryan Chugson before we leave. Can we add that to the agenda?"

"That's up to Liz." Carl paused a moment. "I bet she put the projector in the equipment closet." He tried to enter the room marked AV equipment, but the door wouldn't budge. "Something's in the way." He gave the door a nudge and found a black high-heeled shoe wedged beneath it. The heel split as he shouldered the door open, and Carl gasped. "Peggy, come quick! It's Liz. She's on the floor!"

Peggy dashed from the kitchen and nearly ran into Braun as she entered the narrow equipment closet and knelt at Liz's side. "Are you all right?"

Liz's eyes widened as blood trickled from her nose. She looked around, disoriented. The small room was crowded with people, making it difficult to move. Usher peered around the door. "I'll call Dr. Brakinsky."

Carl lifted Liz to a sitting position and asked, "Did you trip? You must have hit your nose," as Peggy wiped the blood from her face.

Liz dropped her head into her hands. "No, I don't think so." After a silent moment, she continued, "I came here for something, but I must have fainted."

"Seems like you have a fever," Peggy remarked. "Have you been coughing?"

"Some, but mostly, I have a headache." Liz stood with one heel broken and leaned on Peggy while Carl helped remove her other shoe. They then moved into the conference room and sat down.

Usher handed Liz his phone. "Your husband wants to speak with you." He gestured at Carl and whispered, "We need to call an ambulance. Dr. Brakinsky will meet them at the hospital."

Carl called 911 on his cell. The first attempt failed, so Peggy used her work phone. It took several rings before someone answered. Peggy gave the necessary details.

During the activity, Braun called President Spendorf to inform him that Liz was unwell. "She has symptoms of fever, cough, and severe headache. Peggy called for an ambulance. Dr. Brakinsky will meet them at the Emergency Room at Holy Cross Hospital."

"Is she infected?" Zac asked.

"Highly likely. Liz has early symptoms but no violent behavior. All of us have been exposed," Braun said.

"Wash your hands with that bacteriostatic gel," Zac instructed. "Don't touch your face until you've cleaned your hands, and keep me posted—by phone only. I don't want to catch that bug, virus, germ, or whatever you want to call it. Winston, get me…" He was already giving orders to his Chief of Staff when the call disconnected.

Agent Kelly and Ryan Chugson entered the meeting room. "Hello. There's an ambulance pulling up outside. Is everyone okay?" Kelly asked. She wore a mask over her face, latex gloves, and an isolation gown.

"Liz fainted earlier this morning," Braun said. "We're sending her to the emergency room. Her husband will meet her there."

Ryan distributed masks and gloves and instructed everyone to wash their hands with antiseptic gel. "We need to clean everything Liz touched with this solution. We'll provide gowns."

An EMT entered the room and started oxygen and an IV on Liz before moving her onto a gurney.

Liz's voice sounded muffled by the O2 mask. "Kelly, I'm turning the meeting over to you. The agenda is on the front table."

Kelly leaned over Liz. "I'll handle everything. You get well, and I'll see you soon." Then, the ambulance attendants wheeled her outside.

Kelly squirted liquid onto a rag. "I'll wash the equipment while the rest of you go to the CDC van for decontamination. Ryan, warn everyone else to stay in the hallway as they arrive."

When Braun and Ryan returned to the conference room, Braun asked if they had a few minutes to answer questions about Dr. Trent from the CDC in Colorado.

"Sure, ask away," Ryan called for Kelly to join them.

Kelly emerged from the kitchen, having just wiped down the countertops, sink, and coffeemaker. "I'm all ears," she said.

"Do you know Dr. Trent?" Braun asked.

"I've heard of him, but I don't know him personally," Ryan said. "He works mainly in research."

"Is this the same Dr. Trent that Cordy mentioned was in ICU?" Kelly asked.

Braun nodded.

"Cordy met Dr. Joe Smith when she went to the hospital. I didn't get all the details, since I was busy when she called. You should ask Cordy for more information."

As Braun paced, he explained, "I was to meet him in Denver to discuss Trent's vaccine research. Unfortunately, someone shot him before our meeting. Now he's in a coma. I wondered if you know anyone else who worked on his team."

Ryan tapped his finger on the side of his wire-rimmed glasses. "Kelly told us that Chief Jackson has a lead, and Cordy is following up. We're also collaborating with Dr. Alex, who heads our Virology department and is actively involved in research. I'll give him a call to get an update."

Braun asked for a meeting with him and Usher and inquired about his availability later today. "Usher, what time are you due at the FBI office?"

"Ten-thirty," Usher replied. "Maybe we could meet for lunch."

"I'll let Alex know," Ryan said. "If that doesn't work, maybe we can get together for coffee this afternoon. I think Kelly and I should join you."

"I agree, but we need to start this meeting," Kelly wiped her hands on a towel and headed for the podium. "It's already ten minutes past eight. Where is everyone?"

Carl announced, "Guy Weimer is in ICU, but I can update you on our progress. We know Liz's situation. The president removed

Harry from the team, and General Rutoon's indictment means that the attorney is needed for several legal matters today."

"That only leaves Dr. Ping unaccounted for," Kelly said.

Braun expressed interest in meeting Dr. Nat Ping, a former CIA Director whose lecture on counterterrorism he had attended. He hoped to hear Ping's theory on why a high-ranking official might unleash a pandemic on their own citizens.

"Dr. Ping now heads the Department of Health," Kelly said, "but he's been working closely with Agent Cordelia and has some ideas on the epidemic. He's the most experienced of us all when dealing with deadly diseases. I wonder where he is, but you have a busy schedule, so let's get started."

Peggy entered the kitchen and brought out the coffee pot and paper cups. "Is it safe to drink this coffee?"

"You went through decontamination. We disinfected the pot, so removing your mask for a sip is safe."

Peggy poured herself a cup. "That was my second time," she said, "I had to shower at the hospital before coming here. Do you mind if I join the meeting?"

Kelly smiled. "No, you can fill us in on the law enforcement side of things."

"It would be my pleasure, but first, let's hear from Braun and Usher."

Braun cleared his throat and moved to the podium. "Everyone, take a seat. This information comes straight from President Spendorf."

Usher waited for Kelly to wash down the projector he found on the equipment room's top shelf and inserted Braun's thumb drive.

"This is a brief overview of what we know so far about the super-infection we're calling Virus X," Braun said.

Carl laughed. "We've been calling it the Lunatic bug, but at least it now has an official name."

Dr. Ping hustled through the doors. "Sorry, I'm late!" He glanced around, slipped into the protective gear, and moved to the front of the room. "Good morning. Where's Liz?"

"She wasn't feeling well, and an ambulance took her to Holy Cross Hospital," Braun said. "Her husband is going to meet her there."

"That explains the mask and gowns. I'm Dr. Ping."

"My name is Braun Hastings, JSOC commander. This is my brother, Usher Hastings, an FBI agent."

"Sorry to disrupt your presentation." He fished through his pants pocket and produced a thumb drive. "I have a lot of information to share with the team."

Braun hesitated. "Is that drive secure?"

"Absolutely. I obtained the information directly from NASA," Ping confirmed.

Braun wished Cordy was present to check for viruses. He took a deep breath. "I'll need 30 minutes before you start, and then we must leave. President Spendorf sent us to update you on events unfolding at the White House."

Ping ran his hand through his silver, wavy hair. "Please, go ahead and present your information." He seemed slightly annoyed that he wasn't going first.

Braun smiled in understanding before updating the group on General Rutoon's activities. He ended with, "Agent Cordelia and

Kelly have been collaborating with Dr. Trent's team to search for a potential vaccine and cure. We should know more soon."

Thirty minutes to the second, Ping hopped back off his chair. "He's right! I knew it all along. Remember? I called this a bioterrorism attack. I just left a phone conference with Cordy and Chief Jackson, and we will solve this puzzle. Here's what we discovered so far."

Ping gave Braun the thumb drive to insert into the USB port. They opened a file about the most recent Spacecraft landing.

"According to Tip's report, the rocket carried a viral sample from the International Space Station. The ISS research team included three astronauts: Russian astronaut Mordecai Ratinzky (known as Morty), North Korean astronaut Ghim, and Tip Granger from the U.S. After the COVID-19 outbreak, NASA tasked them with modifying MRSA cells and searching for a cure in zero-gravity. The samples they collected are more virulent than those on Earth, and there is currently no cure.

"The ISS team sent a hazmat capsule containing a viral specimen back to their Texas lab after receiving a request from NASA. Tip provided a copy of the demand for proof. Ghim led the project, and Morty suggested shipping the capsule in a well-padded red satin gift box he found in his luggage after arriving at the ISS.

"Upon exiting the ISS, Ghim handed Max a box. Tip initially thought it contained the protected specimen, but upon further investigation, he discovered that Morty had secretly removed the hazmat capsule. Tip found the capsule had been double-bagged and placed back in the ISS lab. When questioned, Morty confessed that he was uncomfortable releasing a deadly organism to the U.S. and never felt safe around the virus. Fearing exposure, he double-bagged the capsule before replacing it in the lab. The ISS team was horrified to learn someone had exposed their virus worldwide."

"If there was no capsule in the box, how did Max and Ivan get exposed?" Kelly asked.

"Cordy spoke with Linda Smith-Taylor, the third astronaut on the shuttle. Max had opened the box, which was empty. He showed it to Ivan Pendari, and she believes that's how the two astronauts were exposed. Linda never touched the box, and she didn't know what happened to it after they landed back on Earth. Max didn't remove or include it in his report when he left the shuttle. Cordy said a Colorado police officer found the box, which is now quarantined in our lab."

"Ryan and I studied the autopsy reports, and Linda's explanation might be why Max got sick first," Kelly said.

Dr. Ping explained that Max and Ivan had compromised immune systems after being in space for a month.

Kelly asked. "Why was Linda virus-free?"

Dr. Ping said, "As I mentioned earlier, she wasn't around when the two men opened the box."

"Linda Smith-Tyler wasn't infected, but there was some incident with her son, Chester," Kelly said.

Ping answered, "Yes, an autopsy showed Chester developed encephalitis and became so violent that he killed twelve and injured sixteen more students at his Fort Collins school."

"How was he infected?" Ryan asked. "Especially after his mom was disease-free."

Ping leafed through his notes. "Linda mentioned her half-brother visited two days after she returned home. Chester drove his uncle to a restaurant in Fort Collins."

"Who was Chester's uncle?" Carl asked.

"The uncle went by the name Dr. Joe Smith, although that wasn't his real name, and he wasn't a doctor. He took his step-father's name after Linda's father died." Ping added, "Perhaps Smith lost the box in the restaurant because the officer found it across the street near a meat market. The butcher's son saw the box in his dumpster, was exposed to the virus, and died three hours later."

"Three hours?" Kelly asked, "I heard about the incident but didn't realize he died so quickly."

"Tip's afraid the enhanced virus leaked from the hazmat capsule into the box," Ping said. "It explains why those in direct contact with the box rapidly died. Linda was devastated to hear about Chester's shooting spree and to think her step-brother had infected her son, and the youth's death made it even worse. Now she's dealing with several deaths."

Carl asked Dr. Ping, "Did Joe Smith die?"

Dr. Ping confirmed, "He passed away while in custody at Evans Army Community Hospital in Fort Carson, Colorado."

"Why wasn't the missing box reported earlier?" Ryan asked.

"NASA denied requesting the specimen, and only after Ghim inquired about the sample's arrival at Houston did they hear about the box. Dr. Shep J. Shmito, MD/Ph.D. IDI signed the forged letter, and it appeared legit. Cordy figured out the name was an anagram for Joseph Smith. NASA did further investigation and realized the box was missing. Perhaps after finding the box empty, Max left it on board the shuttle. It must have gone through a decontamination chute because it was no longer attached to the shuttle wall where Linda last saw the box."

Braun added, "Smith's thumb drive files proved General Rutoon had forged the request on NASA letterhead and sent it to the

ISS team." Braun was impressed with Dr. Ping. He had done his homework. They would make a good team—Braun is investigating overseas, while Ping is researching the home front.

"Now we have to find out how to deal with this outbreak and contain it," Ping said. "What are the latest developments?"

Carl informed the team about opening five temporary medical facilities in schools and another in a gymnasium. "There are also six military clinics in mobile tents across the city."

"That's a start, but we need more," Ryan said. "Six hospitals have stopped taking new patients and transferred less critical ones to schools. It's hard to keep up with demand."

"We have plenty of beds," Carl said with confidence. "Any person can be cared for at an off-site location."

Kelly disagreed. "There will be patients that need a hospital's level of care. Although you and Guy worked late into the night, the hospitals still need more ventilators, suction machines, and IV supplies."

"My team is calling for more aid and supplies." Carl also told them about Guy's encounter at the motel. "They mugged him right in the parking lot. He's still in the ICU at Holy Cross Hospital. I'm hoping to get an update on his condition. Peggy, can you fill us in on the law enforcement side?"

Peggy sat staring at her cup of coffee. "They shot my partner." Tears dripped down her cheek. "Carl?"

"What is it?" Carl asked.

When Peggy didn't answer, Braun moved closer. Her hand shook. Coffee splashed onto the table, and she dropped her cup.

Braun grabbed Peggy's wrist as she began shaking. "She's burning up. I can feel her fever from here."

Kelly dashed to Peggy's side. "She's having a seizure." Kelly eased Peggy to the floor before she fell. "Carl, call for an ambulance. Usher, move those chairs away so there's more room."

Dr. Ping wadded a sheet of paper and placed it between Peggy's teeth to prevent her from biting her tongue. Then, he turned her onto her side and held her in position.

Usher cleared the area and then called his boss at the FBI. "I'm going to be late for our meeting. Fill me in when I get there, but I have no idea when that will be. We've been exposed to the virus twice already today." He disconnected his call. "The boss said to stay away! We'll keep in touch by phone."

Braun took the cell phone from Carl's trembling hand and dialed 911, but there was no answer. "Kelly, we have no emergency backup. Can we get Peggy to a car? We must take her to the nearest hospital." Braun realized Carl was still staring at his wife. "Carl! Get your car and take Peggy to the hospital."

"No, there's no hospital open in the area. We'll have to take Peggy to a makeshift urgent care clinic," Kelly said.

Braun nudged Carl's arm. "Where's the nearest facility?" Carl looked appalled at the thought. Maybe Peggy was the one person to refute his earlier comment that anyone could be treated at a makeshift clinic.

Carl appeared bewildered. "We have to take her to a hospital! She's critical. She's having seizures!"

Kelly cleared her throat. "Yes, she does need a hospital, but there aren't any beds."

Dr. Ping searched online for the nearest location. "Let's take her to Holy Cross Hospital. Maybe Dr. Brakinsky is still there."

By now, Peggy's seizure had stopped, but she was unresponsive. Kelly motioned to Braun. "Call the president's security guards to escort Peggy and Carl to the hospital. They're waiting for you by the front door."

Braun called the agents and phoned Zac to update him on Peggy's condition.

"I'll go with Peggy and Carl," Dr. Ping said. "They may need medical assistance en route. Make sure you shower with bacteriostatic soap as soon as possible. Discard your masks, remove your clothes, shower, and wear clean scrubs. Be sure to also scrub your shoes before going anywhere near other people. I'll use the decontamination unit at the hospital before leaving, and we should meet online from now on to minimize exposure."

"Good idea," Ryan said. "We need a secure meeting plan, though. The rest of us can shower at the CDC."

Kelly texted Cordy, "The RR7 team, Braun, and Usher are exposed to virus X. Two members are hospitalized, and Peggy Wyller is heading to the hospital. Talk to you soon."

"Everyone, vacate the meeting room." Ryan opened the door as Dr. Ping, and Carl carried Peggy to the waiting car. Braun and Usher straightened the table and chairs, washed their hands in disinfectant solution, and replace their gloves and masks. Kelly emptied the coffee pot, soaked it in an antiseptic solution, and disposed of the cups.

Ryan returned to the room. "Leave everything to be sanitized before anyone uses the space." He grabbed his notes. "Kelly, I'll meet you back at CDC." He left the building.

Braun's cell rang. "Commander Hastings. How may I help you?" He motioned to Usher to follow as he rushed out the door.

Kelly was the last to leave and posted a sign on the door, "Room Quarantined. Do not enter!" She locked the front door to the Conference Center and noticed Braun and Usher standing on the curb in a heated discussion. Braun held up his cell. "No taxis are running."

"Do you want to ride with me to the CDC building?" Kelly offered.

Braun didn't hesitate and climbed into the car. "Sorry. Can you take us to Secret Service Headquarters? I got an urgent message, and we're needed there ASAP."

Braun Hastings, JSOC Commander, felt his heart rate spike. "How did he manage to disappear from the bunker? It is supposed to be the safest place in the country."

"Who is missing?" Kelly asked. "Should I take you to the bunker instead?"

Usher glared at Braun. "I'm sorry, Kelly, he's overreacting. We're not going to the bunker. We're heading to SS headquarters as planned. The boss called a special meeting, and Braun doesn't like to be summoned without warning."

"He's right. The call caught me off guard." The fight-or-flight reaction to the news of President Spendorf's disappearance alerted all his senses. Braun felt edgy, but he had to reign in those feelings as he had no authority to share the information with Kelly. "Thanks for the lift, but could you step on it?"

"We'll be there shortly. I'm already going 70 in a 55 mph zone," Kelly's voice seemed strained.

Braun knew he had to harness the power of his nervous energy, narrow the hundreds of ideas racing through his mind, and direct them into a successful plan to save Zac. *Was Secret Service sleeping on the job?*

Usher placed a hand on Braun's arm. "Stay calm, little brother. We're almost to the security checkpoint."

Kelly slowed, rolled down her window, gave proper identification, and drove through the gates.

Being called *little brother* didn't sit well with Braun, but he waited until they cleared security before he snapped, "I am calm, just concerned. And you don't look as cool as my Ninja motorcycle either."

"Well, I'm downright worried." Usher had the door open before Kelly even pulled to the curb.

Braun's hand clutched the door handle. "Thanks. We may not be on the 2 o'clock conference call as planned."

"I understand." Kelly stopped the car. "Keep in touch, and stay safe."

"You, too." The chilled morning air sliced through Braun as he dashed from Agent Kelly's car. Pulling his suit jacket tighter around his torso, he followed Usher inside SS headquarters.

Usher flashed his ID, emptied his pockets of keys, coins, and a nail clipper into a cup onto a conveyer belt, and went through the scanner.

"Next." The security guard nodded for Usher to proceed.

Braun fished through his wallet and showed his ID. "Guy's in the hospital, so who's in charge?"

The security guard stepped closer. "Have you spoken to Secretary Weimer? I've been worried about him."

"Not yet. I heard Guy's in ICU, and I hope he gets well soon." Braun received an all-clear and pocketed his ID.

"Thanks for the update." The guard pointed to a short, haggard-looking man in a rumpled suit. "Head over there. Emil Schmidt, the Assistant Secretary of Homeland Security, awaits you, and none too patiently."

Schmidt chewed his thumbnail as he paced at the entrance. "What's taking them so long," he asked Chief of Staff Winston Willoughby. "You put out the alert an hour ago."

Winston checked his watch. "More like ten minutes ago, and you know they were at the Conference Center. That's a fifteen-minute drive on a good day." Winston turned his head and nodded. "Here they are. Good morning, Agent Hastings and Commander."

Braun didn't wait for formal introductions as he stepped up to Schmidt. "With all the White House and bunker surveillance, how did anyone get access to the president?"

Schmidt's hand jerked away from his flushed face. "I'll show you, but we're just as puzzled. The original security tape is missing, so we'll watch the backup until it goes blank."

Braun frowned. "Blank? How did that happen?"

"Come see for yourself." Schmidt motioned for the men to follow and moved into a small room.

Braun scanned the area. "Where's Kyle Benson? Shouldn't the Director of Secret Service be here?"

"He's on a temporary assignment." Schmidt pointed to four multi-screens stacked two-by-two in a square sat on a nearby table. "Each screen displays nine scenes at a time, rotating at five-second intervals from various sites throughout and around the White House, bunker, Pentagon, and the tunnel systems between each location."

Schmidt tapped the shoulder of an agent monitoring the screens. "Take a well-deserved break. We'll be in here for a while."

"Thanks." He grabbed his files and vacated his chair. "I'll be back in fifteen minutes."

Schmidt nodded.

"Impressive," Braun said, "but isn't there an emergency alert when the president goes missing?"

Schmidt demonstrated a sensor panel that displayed warning lights and enlarged screen images of activated sensors. "The camera captured Secret Service personnel footage 24/7 and estimated the time the president was kidnapped." He played the backup recording from the camera overlooking the SS counsel.

Schmidt stepped forward. "Watch closely. We train our personnel to detect the slightest threat. This is the third time I've watched the tape, and I'm still baffled."

The timestamp indicated 8:50:00. Two officials from the Pentagon met with President Spendorf. One screen displayed various angles of the meeting, while another showed the tunnel they used to leave at 08:58:00."

Braun watched the two men exit through the uncluttered tunnel, but he noted the dusty floors.

The third and fourth panels displayed different views of the White House perimeter. Braun focused on the president's screen views. At 08:58:12, Spendorf spoke briefly with Winston, took a phone call from VP Tom Harris, and hung up at 9:01:16. The president's guard, Marvin, was with him.

Schmidt pointed to the tape. "Marv spoke briefly to Winston and Spendorf, and then escorted the president to his room down the bunker's long hallway at 9:02:02. You can see Spendorf closing his door while Marv stood guard outside at 9:02:19, and that's the last anyone saw the president on tape."

Braun and Usher continued to watch the recording. Other segments showed regular activity—phones rang in the background. Winston Willoughby answered. Security agents helped themselves to coffee and chatted in calm conversations. Then, the lights flickered briefly on the tape.

"Pause for a moment," Braun said.

"What time is on the recording?" Usher asked. "Did the lights dim throughout the entire system?"

Schmidt nodded. "The tape registered a system-wide flicker at 9:05:00."

"The president met with General Rutoon, Usher, and me at 04:30:00. Rutoon was under arrest and left the bunker at 05:16:03. Are those events recorded on tape?" Braun asked.

Schmidt paused the recording on the large screen, pulled up another program on a laptop, and hit play. "Yes, see, even your times are correct. You and Usher left the building at 07:28:17. According to our log, you spoke to the president regarding Liz Brakinsky at 07:59:58. You called the president again at 8:45:06, informing him that Peggy was infected, and Dr. Ping was arranging her transport to the hospital. Marv was guarding President Spendorf when the recording ended at 9:02:19."

"Where is Marv now?" Braun asked. "I'd like to ask him some questions."

"We all would, but he's currently at Walter Reed Hospital. A knife wound to the chest and blunt trauma to the head. He never regained consciousness before going to the OR."

"Did anyone catch the assault on tape?" Usher asked.

"No," Schmidt said, "not that I saw, and no one reported the abduction. Just watch the tape, and then give us your thoughts." He paused the recording on the laptop and pushed the play button on the large screen to resume.

Two secret servicemen walked along a corridor. At 9:15:00, the lights flickered a second time, and a camera flicked on, showing a trail of Jelly Beans scattered from Spendorf's overturned cot in the bunker and along the tunnel floor to the Pentagon's exit.

"Pause the tape," Braun said. "Why are there no views of the president's sleeping quarters after Marv tucked him in?"

The Director heaved a sigh. "That was at President Spendorf's request."

Braun shook his head. His voice got louder. "What kind of surveillance team leaves the president unattended?"

Schmidt snapped, "He's always guarded. A camera outside his room gives Marv a live feed of the president's activities. Every 30 seconds, we see a 5-second clip of Marv watching that tape. At 9:15:30, the president's hallway camera went blank. We searched immediately, but the security tape and the president were missing."

Braun rubbed his chin. "What about the tunnel system? I saw a dusty hallway one minute and Jelly Beans covering the floor the next. How did they get there, and what do they represent?"

The Director appeared embarrassed and shrugged his shoulders. "Unlike the missing security recording of the president's corridor, the tape of the Pentagon tunnel system remained in place, but it went blank at 9:15:00. The Secret Service replaced both tapes at 9:18:50, so we're missing all recordings from 9:15:00 to 9:18:50 along with the SS backups. Winston called you at 9:18:57 when he found the open secret entrance door. I would have waited until we viewed the entire set of tapes again, but Winston refused to wait to contact you."

Braun heaved a sigh. "Who has access to the tapes?"

"I do, but someone else had a key. There's not a scratch on either camera box. No fingerprints and no clues."

"What was the last time stamp on your tape of the president?" Braun asked.

"As I already mentioned, the last reliable view of the president is at 9:02:19, when Marv stood outside the president's room." Schmidt moved closer. "It doesn't make any sense. The tunnel passage with the Jelly Beans can't be the route the president took. That tunnel goes to the Pentagon. Why would the president go to the Pentagon?"

"Do you have the Pentagon's security tapes?" Usher asked.

"Yes and no. None have President Spendorf on them. Spendorf shut down the Pentagon, so who would refuse to abide by his orders?" Schmidt sighed. "I guess I should check with their security agents for greater details."

Braun was appalled. "You haven't done that yet? President Spendorf has been missing for fifty-seven minutes!"

Usher placed a hand on Braun's shoulder, shook his head slightly, and mouthed, "Not helping."

Braun shrugged free, his temper rising, and forced his voice to remain calm, "Have you reviewed the entire set of security tapes independently?"

"I haven't had time, but my team is doing that now," Schmidt admitted. "We have hushed the president's disappearance, so only a handful of people know."

Braun tapped his cell phone. "Play the last recording again. I'm going to document each second."

"That's the first thing we did, and the seconds run consecutively without any freeze frames." The Director ran a trembling hand over his balding head. You can have a copy of our spreadsheet."

"Thanks, but I'm going to review for myself and compare notes." Braun fast-forwarded the tape, jotted notes, and asked Schmidt, "Did you send a copy to Agent Cordelia? She's the lead analyst for the FBI."

"Not yet—we're keeping this quiet. Winston called you as directed by President Spendorf earlier this morning," Schmidt said.

Braun noticed Schmidt hovering over his shoulder. "My notes concur with your timeframes."

Schmidt seemed relieved and backed away. "We would send a copy to the VP, if we knew where to send it. Do you know his whereabouts?"

Winston cut in, "You must find Harris and officially swear him in as acting president. It's legally required when the president is unable to fulfill his duties, and I don't want to bypass Harris to swear in the Speaker of the House, Lector Peach. Can you imagine this frail country in his hands? He'll send missiles to North Korea, Russia, and Syria in the next two hours. No questions asked. That would be a disaster."

Braun moved away from the monitors and glared at Schmidt. "What do you mean you don't know the location of VP Harris?"

Usher cleared his throat. "Braun, we'll do our best to inform him."

Braun forwarded a copy of the tapes and the following time grid to Cordy.

Time	Activities
4:30:00	Rutoon, meeting with Pres., Braun, and Usher
5:16:03	Rutoon was arrested and hauled away by SS

7:28:17	Braun and Usher left bunker to go to Conference Center RR7 meeting
7:59:58	Braun called Pres., informing him they found Liz Brakinsky ill and sent to hospital
8:05:04	RR7 meeting, and Pres. met with FBI and CIA
8:45:06	Braun called informing Pres. Peggy Wyller was infected
8:46:22	Pentagon meeting with Admiral Lund & Gen. Ames
8:58:00	Lund & Ames left via tunnel to Pentagon, tunnels dusty
8:58:12	Pres. spoke to Winston, connected a call from VP
9:01:16	Hung up call from VP Tom Harris
9:02:02	Marv escorted Pres. to his bunker room
9:02:19	Pres. last seen on tape
9:05:00	1st system-wide flicker, tunnels dusty, SS alert
9:15:00	2nd system-wide flicker, Jelly Beans scattered through tunnel floor, alert sent to Emil Schmidt
9:18:00	SS replaced all security tapes
9:18:57	Winston called JSOC Commander Braun Hastings per Pres. previous orders

"So *you do know* where to find the VP?" Schmidt's hand hovered over a familiar bulge over his right hip. "Where is he? I must find him immediately."

"No. We don't know," Braun snapped and paused. "Why the weapon? No one is allowed a gun here except the Secret Service Agents."

"Things are not as usual these days," Schmidt said, "but I'm prepared to protect the president, and right now, we need to find Harris."

"I have my orders if the president goes missing," Braun said. "I'm sure you also have orders, and mine don't include informing you." Unsure what Schmidt might do, Braun glanced at Usher and gave a slight nod.

Usher calmly reached into his pocket, speed-dialed his boss, and covered his mouth as if stifling a cough. "President's missing. Meet us ASAP at SS HQ."

Seconds later, the door to the small office whooshed open. Usher's boss, FBI Director Loran Sloan, strolled into the room. "Sorry to interrupt, but I need a word with my team in private." He motioned for Schmidt to leave the room, causing an abrupt argument. Loran glanced at his watch. "Okay, stay then. We'll leave."

Loran held the door open for Usher and Braun. When they left the office, Loran asked, "What did you find out?"

"Crucial security tapes are missing," Usher whispered. "One tape covered outside the president's quarters, and the other recorded the tunnel system leading from the bunker to the Pentagon. We need to get Tom Harris back into the country before we have an internal war on our hands."

Loran rubbed his chin. "Where do we start looking?"

"I'd start with that sealed file you get each day from President Spendorf," Braun said. "It's time to unseal it and follow his orders."

Cordy joined Kelly, Dr. Alex, and Carl on the planned noon CDC conference call. "Chief Jackson won't attend this meeting. He's working on another project."

"Dr. Ping has alerted us that President Spendorf is missing," Kelly rushed on, "and Braun and Usher aren't here either. I forwarded an encrypted message from Braun to your new TOR account. He didn't have the IP address, so he sent it here to pass on. Did you get it?"

"I'm downloading it as we speak," Cordy said worriedly. "Rutoon didn't gain access to my account through you or Braun. The only possibility is that he got it through the president. That means Zac is in danger, and I thought about missing this meeting, too."

"Let Braun and Usher do their jobs, and we have ours," Kelly said. "Virus X has mutated and spread to nearly every country. If this continues, the death rate could exceed a million worldwide by the end of the year. It took over two years to reach that number with COVID-19. Almost 30% of cases become violent, and that percentage is growing."

Dr. Alex added, "We're dealing with a virus and a fungus. Have you been able to contact Dr. Trent's research team?"

Cordy checked her second line. "Dr. Esthanne Jennings is heading up his team during Trent's absence, and she has agreed to join our conference call. She's on hold and available for thirty minutes. If there's no update on the president, I'll patch her in."

"Yes, let's bring her on the line. We can get an update later," Dr. Alex said, "I don't want to cut into her available time."

Cordy connected Dr. Jennings through her secured DarkVid program and introduced everyone.

"Dr. Alex, I'm pleased to meet you. I look forward to working with your team," Jennings gushed. She had admired his accomplishments for years.

"I'll cut through the minutia," Dr. Alex was all business. "Have you found a cure?"

Dr. Jennings leaned towards her screen, peered over her shoulder as if she was afraid someone was listening, and whispered, "I contacted Ghim, an astronaut who works with viruses on the Space Station. He gave us some suggestions. I think we're on the right track."

Alex asked, "How soon before we know the results?"

With more confidence, Jennings answered, "Our team inserted a stem cell into the MRSA nucleus to create a new core. The revised nucleus instructs the body's DNA/RNA to produce antibodies that counteract the virus. Our team used this process to produce a vaccine. With luck, this will halt the spread of the outbreak. We found high intravenous Vitamin C and Thiamin doses speed up the process."

"And how long does it take?" Alex asked.

Jennings beamed a bright smile. "The virus died within forty-eight hours."

Ryan sighed. "Unfortunately, many of those already infected may not live long enough for the cure."

Jennings admitted, "We haven't tested the vaccine on humans—only rats, pigs, and chimps."

Carl Wyller asked hopefully, "Can we get enough vaccines to give to our wives? I have medical power of attorney for Peggy. It may be their only hope. Dr. Brakinsky agrees. Liz is already at the violent stage."

Dr. Jennings seemed taken aback. "That's highly unethical! We only have a few doses."

Dr. Alex interrupted, "I don't mean to go over your head, Dr. Jennings, but this is life or death for thousands of people. We'll need willing volunteers under these circumstances. No one is immune. Three Senators are infected, and five Congressmen. One Senator has already perished."

Dr. Jennings hesitated and then nodded. "I understand. They would be volunteer test patients. Another concern is that it's one thing to create a few doses, but ramping up to make millions of doses in such a short time is difficult. And we'd have to bypass the FDA approval requirements because that takes way too long, yet I know how important it is to abide by the rules."

"True." Ryan added, "Any idea what fungus might have been added to the MRSA?"

"We need to research that more fully." Jennings sighed. "We haven't had enough time."

Ryan texted an attachment: "Here are our lab results so far. Your team may be able to identify it."

"I'll rush this order for more vaccine to our research team and get samples into the city, but with the roadblocks, access might be a problem." Jennings jotted something onto a sticky note.

"We'll find a way," Dr. Alex reassured her. "How soon will the vaccine be ready?"

"We have enough to treat fifty people, but we're unsure of the dose or the side effects. The vaccine is to prevent the virus—not a cure. As I mentioned, high doses of Vitamin C and Thiamine IV may have an impact. Have you tried Lopinavir? It helped treat Ebola, but we've never found a cure, and the med isn't an anti-fungal drug."

"It's worth a try," Carl said. "It will also allow my wife to move to a bed in a hospital ICU. We'll want to have the highest care to assure these trials are a success."

"How did you learn of the fungus?" Jennings asked.

"Both astronauts had fungus balls in their lungs, and the ME discovered fungal meningitis during Max's autopsy," Alex reported.

"Maybe try Voriconazole," Jennings suggested, "but I don't know the effective dosages. This is only a trial—our team refuses to take responsibility for any side effects."

"We're willing to take the risk," Carl choked back his emotions. "Without it, Peggy will die."

"I'll have the team prepare the vaccine, which will be ready by 5 p.m. tonight. Sorry, but I must run. I wish you all the best." Dr. Jennings waved farewell.

"We appreciate your help," Dr. Alex signed off.

Cordy disconnected Jennings' call. "Back to the president, Braun said the RR7 members are on the need-to-know list, so I can share his latest info. Rutoon escaped prison two hours ago, leaving three dead guards and four missing inmates. FBI has recaptured three of the four inmates, but Rutoon remains at large. Braun suspects Rutoon kidnapped Zac, as he is familiar with the bunker."

"That makes sense," Kelly said.

Cordy nodded. "He knows the floor plan, the location of every security camera, and the entrance to each secret tunnel."

"How did anyone get close enough to kidnap him?" Ryan asked.

"According to Braun, the president had gone to his bunker room to take a brief nap," Cordy explained. "When Winston came to wake him, Zac was missing, and his bodyguard was found stabbed and unconscious. Someone overturned the president's cot, and the hidden tunnel door allowing him access to the street across from the White House was open."

"Is that when the Chief of Staff called Braun?" Kelly asked.

"Yes. After investigating, Braun and Usher discovered evidence of a struggle in the president's bunker. Rutoon probably escaped through a tunnel to the Pentagon, but the details remain unclear."

Cordy also mentioned her conversation with astronaut Linda Smith-Tyler. "Chief Jackson is tracking down Max Uliptos' son. We have a few questions about Mia or M.I.A.," Cordy explained Linda's concern.

Dr. Alex cut back on the call, "I know you're worried about Zac, but we must get the vaccine here ASAP. Two of RR7's team are already infected."

"That's a great concern." Cordy asked, "Why are only Liz Brakinsky and Peggy Wyller infected? Are other members showing any symptoms?"

"Not so far," Kelly said.

Cordy frowned, "How were they exposed to the virus if the red box is in Colorado? Nobody from the RR7 touched that box."

"I found the virus in the wine," Kelly said. "Each of the members received a wine bottle as a gift. I recalled Carl's comment after someone had broken into their house, 'I didn't even get a sip of that fine wine President Spendorf sent. Peggy had a glass before turning in for the night, but I was too tired. Now I suppose it's gone.'"

"Luckily, I had not consumed any wine from my bottle," Kelly explained. "However, Liz had a glass. Her husband was working at the hospital and did not have any, nor did any other members. I sent a thank you card to President Spendorf, only to discover that he had not sent any wine. This is when I became aware and tested my bottle, which was contaminated."

"If the president didn't send it, who did?" Cordy asked.

"I'm not certain who sent the wine, whether it was General Rutoon, Joe Smith, Chirk, or someone else, but President Spendorf also received one," Kelly stated as she checked her laptop. "Winston had the bottles tested and found them contaminated, too. A courier from the Pentagon reported they sent over two dozen cases to high-ranking officials abroad."

Cordy asked for a list of cases and their locations in light of the rise in infections in France, England, and Germany as the virus spread from person to person.

"We're working on it." Alex rubbed his chin. "Do you have any ideas on how to smuggle Jennings' vaccine into the city? It's risky, but it seems to be our best option."

"Since I'm already in Fort Collins and the closest to Dr. Jennings, I'll deliver it at 5:30 p.m. to a secret rendezvous point where a jet can land and bring it to you."

"That's a great plan," Alex agreed. "In the meantime, Peggy and Liz might benefit from high doses of Vitamin C, Thiamin IV, and perhaps Vfend, or the generic form Voriconazole, as Dr. Jennings suggested to treat fungus."

Kelly hopped from her chair. "I'll get right on it."

"I hope all goes well." Cordy was already texting Dr. Jennings.

"Me, too," Carl added. "Hurry! I don't want to lose Peg."

"Don't forget to put the vaccine on ice," Dr. Alex reminded Cordy.

Her satellite phone rang. "It's Braun. Gotta go." Cordy disconnected the conference call. "Braun, it feels like I haven't spoken to you in ages. How are you? Have you found Zac?"

"Hold on," Braun rushed on, "I wish you were here. We need your help. Have you tracked Rutoon down through the darknet? I know you can track anyone, anywhere."

"No," Cordy said. "I was online with the RR7 team until you called, and I just got your earlier text."

"Find out where Rutoon is accessing his messages, and let us know immediately. Oh, yes. What clues do you get when you think of Jelly Beans?"

"Jelly Beans, as in the candy?" Cordy asked, but Braun had hung up. "Love you, too!" she murmured.

Jelly Beans

This is ridiculous. Why am I wasting my time? Cordy searched in vain, and she felt frustrated. No, she was downright angry.

Cordy glanced up from her computer search as Chief Jackson eased into his swivel chair. "Any word from Braun?"

Jackson's question triggered an eruption. "Yes! The blasted word is Jelly Beans!"

Jackson raised his hands. Palms outstretched as if in defense. "Whoa, what burr got under your skin?"

"Braun!" Cordy mellowed a bit and then laughed. "He told me to think about Jelly Beans. I've been looking up clues and realized it put me in a bad mood—all because of Jelly Beans."

Jackson was intrigued. His eyes twinkled gold flecks. "What was Braun referring to?"

"I guess something about Jelly Beans scattered down a tunnel between Spendorf's bunker cot and the Pentagon, but I haven't a clue what it means, even after spending the last half hour searching the net. I only found that the colorful candy has a hard-shelled exterior and soft interior."

"I already knew that. The chief laughed, "I've had enough Easter baskets full of sweets to sample them first-hand. I prefer Jelly Bellies. They're softer and sweeter."

"Another source refers to Jelly Beans as a hardcore man with a soft heart."

"That certainly isn't Rutoon," the chief added.

"In criminal slang, it means a weakling and a coward. Other Jelly Bean sources meant stupid or bean head. Not helpful, I know, and

I have too much on my plate to contemplate such stupidity. Perhaps something on Chirk's computer system will link me to Rutoon's site, but it hasn't so far, and I've been analyzing it bit by bit."

"What did you find out on the conference call?" Chief Jackson asked.

"Dr. Jennings is furnishing a sample vaccine, enough for fifty people. Liz and Peggy will be the first humans to take the drug. I hope it works, but Jennings is a skeptic. The vaccine is to prevent infection, not to treat it. I leave in an hour to pick up the med and get it to a CDC contact for delivery to Washington, D.C."

"A thought just hit me," the chief said. "What about Chirk's cell? Any reference to Jelly Beans?"

"I haven't researched that," Cordy admitted, "but I checked Chirk's finances. They seem clean."

"Keep looking." Chief Jackson got up, poured himself a cup of coffee, and sat at his desk. "I know there's a hidden account overseas."

Cordy rummaged through a box on her desk and found Chirk's phone. Ten minutes later, she had a list of phone calls to Rutoon. "Over two hundred calls originating from the same number bounced off a tower twenty miles from the Pentagon during the last six months. I wonder if all those calls are legit, but discovery would be too easy if linked to anything sinister."

"Track it," the chief said. "Rutoon is known more for his bark, not his brains."

"I'd love to know what he did with all that money." Cordy gulped the rest of her coffee.

"Now would be the perfect time for Rutoon to retire to some remote island and access his accounts," the chief said.

"He won't get far. Maryland, New York, and Washington, D.C.'s airports are already closed, and we put out a full nationwide alert from the moment we discovered Rutoon escaped prison."

"He has expert knowledge on smuggling secret officials across multiple borders." Chief Jackson added, "I'm sure he has several disguises and aliases, complete with passports."

Cordy's cell phone rang. "Agent Cordelia."

"It's Dr. Jennings. Can you get away?"

"I can hardly hear you," Cordy said.

"I know. Someone is following me and has been for a few days. I don't feel safe. Can you meet me at the café across the street from your office? Look out your window. You'll see me in a green sedan. I'll get out of the car and go inside to order a latte when I see you cross the street, but be careful."

Cordy dashed to the window. "Lock your doors! A man is moving toward your passenger side. Don't let him in. Chief, call 911. I'll stay on the line as I head across the street." A glint warned Cordy. "He has a gun!"

Jackson grabbed his phone. "Go! I'm calling."

"He just tried to open the passenger door." Jennings laid on the horn, ducked low in her car, and pulled into the street, barely missing another vehicle.

Cordy ran down the stairs and was out the front door in a flash, intent on stopping one more threat. She raised her pistol and yelled, "Stop and hit the ground!"

The man in a dark navy suit jacket dashed down the sidewalk, concealed his weapon, and darted into the nearest store.

Cordy pursued. "Everyone clear the building. Go out front exits." Customers screamed as the man knocked over carts, pushed people aside, and moved behind several aisles. Kids cried for their mothers.

People hid among clothes racks. Some called 911, and others were stupid enough to record the event on their cell phones. Many people scurried to the sidewalk.

Sirens sounded in the distance, and cops dashed for the building. A policeman spoke to a shopper as she ran from the store. She yelled, "He's inside and has a gun."

Cordy had cleared the first aisle when the officers entered the building. "Drop your weapon," a policeman demanded.

"I'm FBI Agent Cordelia. My creds are in my pocket."

"Drop your weapon," the officer repeated.

"Don't shoot." Cordy placed her pistol on the floor and held her hands high. "I'm getting my credentials." She waited until the officer nodded before reaching into her pocket and pulling out her card.

The officer checked her ID. "Sorry, can't be too careful."

Screams came from the other end of the aisle, "He's over here." Gunfire erupted.

Cordy hit the floor, rolling. She whisked up her pistol, but it was too late. The gunman lay on the floor. "Is he alive?"

An officer knelt beside the man, checked his neck for a pulse, and shook his head.

"Does he have any ID?" Cordy asked.

The officer checked his pockets. "No, there's nothing to ID except his fingerprints. I'll call the medical examiner."

By now, news vans blocked the road. Cordy wanted to leave the building before a news anchor caught up with her. She redialed Dr. Jennings. "The man who chased you is dead. Do you have any idea who he was?"

"No, but I want to get rid of this vaccine before someone kills me for it." Jennings agreed to meet immediately at the coffee shop.

Cordy felt light-headed. Her hand shook when she fumbled for a business card to leave with the officer. She took a deep breath, ducked behind a crowd gathered around a news van, and headed for the shop while surveying her surroundings.

Jennings parked her green sedan on the other side of the road below Chief Jackson's window. She climbed from her car, looked both ways, and quickly crossed the street. She grabbed Cordy's arm and leaned close. "Who did you talk to besides the RR7 team?"

"No one," Cordy said.

Jennings adjusted a scarf around her head and covered half her face. "How did anyone know I would be here?"

Cordy motioned toward the shop's door. "Do you want to go inside?"

Dr. Jennings quickly scanned the street and nearly stumbled while heading for the door. "I don't want to stay on the sidewalk."

Cordy opened the door and glanced around the coffee shop. People were too quiet for it to be a coffee house. "It looks safe." She gently grabbed Jennings' arm and led her inside. "Let's order our drinks and sit by that beam where we can watch the window."

A steady buzz picked up as someone spotted an officer outside. Cutlery clanged against plates, a hiss came from the steamer, and everyone was back to the usual day chatter, so Cordy ordered their drinks and moved to the pick-up line.

Dr. Jennings' white-knuckled fingers clung to her purse. "I can't believe someone would threaten my life. I'd rather face a virulent virus any day."

"Who did you talk to?" Cordy asked. "Your secretary or a colleague?"

"Neither, I Instagrammed my husband to say I was swinging by your office before heading home." Jennings frowned. "Could someone be tracking my Instagram?"

"Did your husband answer?" Cordy asked.

"No, but he doesn't usually bother." Jennings' voice rose a notch. "Why?"

"Just wondering."

"Do you think my husband's in danger?" Jennings' breathing grew more rapid.

"I'll check to make sure he's okay." Cordy sent a text message to Chief Jackson and cc'd Bracken to check on Jennings' husband.

"Just take the vaccine. I want out of here." Jennings shoved the vaccine toward Cordy, nearly dropping the bottle, and headed for the door.

Cordy grabbed her purse strap, pulled her back in line, and shoved the bottle back into Jennings' bag. She ordered their drinks.

A man in a black cowboy hat entered the shop. He'd been sitting in a car parked behind the green sedan when Cordy had looked out her office window. Most people in the coffee house were students, workers, and hipsters, so this guy stuck out. His eyes darted around the room.

Cordy moved in front of Dr. Jennings and nudged her behind a pillar to wait for their order. "Don't make it obvious, but peer around the post. Do you recognize the man who just entered the café?"

The man removed his cowboy hat, revealing a military buzz cut. How he positioned his body alerted Cordy that he likely carried a firearm under his jacket. If a gunfight broke out, civilians could get caught in the crossfire. Cordy stared at Dr. Jennings. "Ever see him before?"

"No, but I want to get out of here." Jennings reached into her purse once more.

The man removed his sunglasses, slid them into a pocket, and headed their way.

Cordy pushed against Jennings' hand and whispered, "Not now," while staring at the man. She sat at a nearby table as he walked by. "Are you up for a chat?" Cordy patted the chair next to her, then stretched her legs and crossed her feet to appear relaxed. She hoped her actions conveyed a non-threatening manner.

He waved a dismissing hand in her direction.

"Sir, I'm talking to you," Cordy insisted.

When Dr. Jennings arrived with their drinks, he changed his mind and decided to sit down. She asked the man, "Do I know you?"

"I doubt it, but I do know you." The man placed an elbow on the table and leaned forward. His other hand drifted to his jacket, evidently intent on staying close to his weapon.

A female police officer entered the shop. "Who called 911?" The man's brow furrowed when she asked Cordy. "Did you call?"

"Not me. Why would I need 911?" Cordy breathed deeply to stay calm, unsure of what might transpire in the next moment. She paid attention to the man's micro-expressions. He seemed in control, alert, and aware of the officer's threat. He scooted his chair back and stood.

Tension filled the air, and the room went instantly quiet. The music raised a few decibels in the silence. The officer walked closer to their table. "Did you call 911?" she asked the man.

"Yes, I did." He smiled. "Someone threatened Dr. Jennings' life, and I'm here to protect her."

Cordy knew Chief Jackson had called the emergency number and jumped from her seat. At least she knew he was a liar. "Under whose orders?"

"President Spendorf's. If you allow me to reach into my pocket, I have proof. I'm with the CIA. You're with the FBI. I believe the doctor is safe. No need for additional law enforcement."

The officer turned toward Cordy. "Is this true?"

"I'm FBI Agent Cordelia, but I have no idea who this man is."

"Agent Dun Bean." He pulled out his wallet and showed his credentials. "And I guess I'm done here." He laughed at his little joke."

"Was that your partner the police shot in the clothing store?" Cordy asked.

"No, I was tailing him." Bean put away his ID.

"So, you know who he was," Cordy asked.

Bean shrugged. "Got a hunch, but not sure. Did they ID him?"

"No ID," Cordy said. "For some reason, I have a hard time believing you. Why didn't you intervene when he came up to Dr. Jennings' car?"

"It was tough, but I had my orders to observe." Bean snubbed Cordy and turned toward Dr. Jennings. "May I escort you home?"

"Not so fast." Cordy stood, caught her foot on the leg of the chair, and stumbled against the man. "Sorry." When she straightened up, his weapon and a phone in his pocket found its way up her sleeve. "When did you last hear from the president?"

"I got a text message."

"The question was, when did you hear from him?" Cordy placed her hand in her pocket and dropped the items from her sleeve.

"Yesterday afternoon."

Not possible. The president didn't know about Dr. Jennings. "One more question. When would you have stepped up to her defense?"

"That man didn't pull a gun until the doctor drove off," Bean said.

"Not true," Cordy said. "I could see the gun from the upstairs window across the street."

"Guess you had a better view. I didn't see a gun, or I would have acted." Bean turned toward Jennings. "It's my job to escort you home."

"Thanks for the offer, but I'm not going home. Agent Cordelia will escort me back to my office." She stood and nudged Cordy toward the door as if she were running late. "We have to make a pit stop on the way home. I'm nearly out of gas."

Bean clutched the doctor's arm but quickly let go when the officer stepped between them. "Your ID checks out, but this woman has the right to refuse your offer, or would you like to talk to my boss at the police station?"

"Thanks, officer, but I prefer to return to my official duties." Bean shoved his hat on his head, followed the women out of the café, and allowed the door to close behind him.

Cordy clasped Jennings' elbow. *Unusual name: Bean, as in Jelly Bean.* "I don't trust the man. He may follow us." They quickly crossed the street. "Let's take my car from the rear of the building, but first, I want to check his cell and get the ID on this Glock. I'll make sure you get your car back this evening."

When they reached the other side of the road, Jennings pulled away and slipped the vaccine vial to Cordy. "Just take the vaccine."

The outer pack stung Cordy's hand. "That's cold!" She moved the vial to her pocket.

"Sorry, I should have warned you. It has to stay on ice," Dr. Jennings said. "I reviewed the lab work Dr. Alex sent and enhanced the sample further this afternoon. It probably won't cure, but it may prevent further complications or maybe weaken the virus. We haven't had enough time to test for results."

"What about side effects?" Cordy asked.

There haven't been any major ones—nausea and diarrhea in 5% of the rats, 2% in the pigs, and none in the chimps, but they haven't received this enhanced serum. I would have liked more time to experiment, but that's impossible. If this works, the team agreed to work around the clock to create more vaccines. Have Dr. Alex contact me when he gets the samples. If possible, I want to explain how to enhance the nucleus with Liz and Peggy's stem cells. It might be a cure. If not, it could save their lives."

There was a commotion in front of the coffee shop. "Hey, where's my gun?" Agent Bean shouted.

Cordy smiled. "We'd better get as far away from here as possible." As Bean turned his attention toward them, she pulled Dr. Jennings into Jackson's building and flipped the lock on the front door.

She heard Agent Bean pounding on the door as they dashed for the elevator to the basement car park.

Cordy took several detours to ensure no one followed her car to Dr. Jennings' home.

Mr. Jennings was mowing the lawn when Cordy and his wife pulled into the driveway. He dashed to the front porch and wrapped his arms around his wife, his concern so intent that he neglected to greet Cordy. "I've been so worried about you. Thank God you made it home."

Dr. Jennings opened the screen door. "A bit frazzled at first, but I'm fine."

"Are you sure?" her husband asked. "I heard that one man is dead, and another man followed you, saying he's with the CIA. Chief Jackson questions that, though. I'm not letting you out of my sight. By the way, where's your car?" Reassured that his wife was, in fact, unharmed, he finally noticed Cordy standing silently at her side. "I'm sorry, I was so upset, I just realized you're not alone. I didn't mean to be rude."

"No problem," Cordy introduced herself. "Your wife had a challenging day, and with someone tailing her, we left the car downtown. It's parked under Chief Jackson's office window, so he'll watch it."

"Come inside for a cold drink before heading back out in the heat." Dr. Jennings led the way to the kitchen and dropped her handbag on the table. She opened the fridge and took out a pitcher of lemonade while her husband took three glasses from the cupboard.

Mr. Jennings turned toward Cordy. "I understand you're delivering a vaccine sample to Washington, D.C. I'm glad my wife doesn't have to go."

"I won't feel safe until the vaccine gets in Dr. Alex's hands and I hear from him directly." Dr. Jennings poured the drinks and handed one to Cordy and another to her husband. "We'll pick up the car after dinner tonight."

"Yes, I'm definitely going with you," her husband had no hesitation, and as if an afterthought, "I'd love to take you out for a nice meal, but most restaurants are closed."

"I think going out of town for a while would be an excellent idea. Do you have a safe place to get away?" Cordy rummaged through her purse. "I'll activate a burner phone so you can keep in touch with Dr. Alex wherever you go."

"It's a plan." Mr. Jennings became serious. "Officer Bracken called and arranged for a patrol car to circle the area every hour so our home is safe. I'm to call if anything happens out of the ordinary." He turned to his wife. "But you do need a vacation. You've worked non-stop since Trent landed in the hospital."

"When all of this is over." Dr. Jennings patted his hand and sipped her drink.

It's nice to see a couple so dedicated to each other. I hope Braun and I will have that same bond. Cordy activated a phone and handed it to Dr. Jennings. "Lay low and stay safe. I'll deliver the vaccine."

"Dr. Alex can still reach me if needed on this phone, right?" Jennings sounded relieved.

"Right, and unlike your current cell phone, it won't be traced by Bean." Cordy gulped down her drink. "Thanks for the lemonade. It hit the spot, but I need to go." She had barely backed out of the driveway when a patrol car passed her. She recognized the officer and waved as he passed. *At least, Bracken would keep the Jennings safe.*

Cordy reached the drop-off point fifteen minutes early and parked at the edge of a small private field, large enough for an unmarked government jet to land. It gave her a few moments to check out Agent Dun Bean.

Bean graduated at the top of the Academy class in 2010. He climbed the career ladder and served under General Rutoon starting in 2012. He completed tours in Serbia, Colombia, and Russia before leaving the military in early 2020. He'd operated undercover ops for the government, going off the radar for extended periods.

She discovered the gun was unregistered, unusual for an agent, but he was indeed a rising star with the CIA. His cell phone revealed a code name she recognized as Jelly Bean. *The Pentagon must have fought hard to conceal this encrypted file.* Cordy put the record through her portable scanner, activated a new throw-away phone, and sent the scan to Chief Jackson for more scrutiny.

The chief texted, "Give me a moment. There's something familiar about his face. I've met him. He's dangerous—better beware! Braun, too. He's like a bloodhound, and he will track down whoever Rutoon orders him to."

It seemed like an eternity since she had last seen Braun. Now, he was in the epicenter of a viral pandemic, searching for a missing president who had disappeared from the bunker—the most secure place in the nation. Fear made it hard to breathe. *What had Braun gotten into this time?*

She felt like she was on the brink of disaster nearly every hour this week, never knowing where, when, or if she'd see Braun again. *Is this what it will feel like to be married to my secret agent? I must find a way to keep tabs on him.*

Lost in her thoughts, Cordy absently twisted the diamond ring on her finger, wondering if her life would ever return to normal. A warm tear ran down her cheek. *What's wrong with me? I have to be strong. Braun is counting on me. Worse yet, the president and the whole country are depending on me.*

Rolling her shoulders, Cordy moved her head from side to side to release the tension. She checked her watch and saw that it was already 5:48 p.m. The plane was delayed, and no messages on her phone indicated why no one had shown up yet. She double-checked all her data, and everything seemed correct. According to the GPS, she was at the right location.

Her newly activated cell phone rang. "Cordy, Bean was in Rutoon's covert operations program," Chief Jackson warned. "Started his career as a veterinarian, became a highly trained sniper, specializing in security systems manipulation, advanced urban combat, and a master of deception and disguise. He's completed his missions 98% of the time. Braun was his first miss and hopefully will be his second."

"Why is Bean here in Colorado when Braun is in D.C.?" Cordy asked.

"My guess is he's after you. Did you deliver the vaccine?" Jackson asked.

"Not yet. The plane's late."

"I'll call Kelly and see why there is a delay," the chief sounded worried. "You need to watch your back. Drop off the vaccine and then disappear!" He disconnected the call.

A loud rap on the passenger's door quickened Cordy's pulse. The air rushed from her lungs as a man with a goatee, and long, dark brown shaggy hair peered through the window. "Officer Cordelia,

I'm here for the vaccine." He tried the passenger door, but she had locked it.

His voice gave him away. Cordy started the car engine, threw it in drive, and shouted, "Stand back, Agent Bean." The engine roared to life, and the car lurched forward.

Bean had somehow opened the locked passenger door with a flick of his wrist and slid into the car as she pulled away. He hung on tight, scrambled into the seat, and buckled up. "I can't believe you recognized me."

"What do you want?" Cordy continued to drive onto the airfield, hoping someone would spot her.

Agent Bean smiled as he scooped his cell phone from the glove compartment. "I knew you took it. Where's my gun?"

"I don't have it," Cordy said.

"That's okay. I have a spare. So what did you discover?" Bean grinned as if this were a game.

Rutoon's Revenge

President Isaac Spendorf sat in a wooden chair. His eyes blurred, and he felt dizzy. Metal cuffs around his wrists and ankles caused numbness. Chains bolted the cuffs to the floor. Half a glass of wine sat on the rectangular table in front of him. The room had a high ceiling, bright white lights beaming overhead, and navy blue drapes covering the two front windows.

General Rutoon entered the room and addressed Zac, "So you're finally awake. I've been waiting to talk to you alone, but I didn't expect sevoflurane to last that long."

"So that's what was on that rag." Zac's words slurred. "It was sweet and made my brain fuzzy."

"Side effects. I had to give you extra doses before entering my little getaway."

"They'll find you soon," Zac warned.

"Doubtful," Rutoon replied. "I left a hint in the tunnel to the Pentagon. It'll look like his doing."

"Who, Chirk? I know he's in Colorado, and the Secret Service will track your property deeds," Zac informed.

"This location is untraceable—a gift arrangement. It makes it a perfect place to hold this discussion. You asked me why I planted the virus. I'll tell you, but never with Braun and his brother in the room."

"Unfortunately, kidnapping me on top of all you've done so far won't help your case," Zac said. "You know your career is over."

"Oh, yes. I'm well aware of that."

"Why, Rutoon? Tell me why you've done this."

"The real question is, why did you assign me to that arrogant, inexperienced team?" Rutoon asked. "I no longer have the time or energy to babysit your boys, especially those snobby brats you called your Elite Task Force. They thought I was washed up as a General, too old to make rational decisions, and too soft to make hard demands on our allies."

"I had no idea you felt this way." Zac's headache worsened, and his vision blurred. "Why didn't you tell me earlier? You've always been reliable."

"You sent my experienced teams to Iran, Colombia, and Afghanistan, where I worked them hard to prepare for the worst. We successfully took down drug lords and military leaders. They completed all assignments. However, the Yemen assignment was different. The soldiers were inexperienced, coming straight from farms in Kentucky, Tennessee, Georgia, or the oil fields of Texas. I requested more time or to merge them with more experienced soldiers, but you still sent them into combat."

"You know that I don't make the final decision as to who went or who stayed." Zac yawned. "That's up to the military commanders."

"However, you instructed the military to extract the leader of an extremist group that is more powerful and dangerous than the Taliban. I put together the plan and ran them through the drill once again. Ordinarily, we'd go through the plan repeatedly until we get it right, tweaking it as we go along, but not this team. Oh no. Twice was all they needed. The arrogant bastards wouldn't listen to me— reported me as inept."

"I didn't know that." Zac closed his eyes to keep the room from spinning. "I would have listened to you if you'd made a plea, but you didn't."

"No, I didn't have a choice. You removed me as their leader and placed me on Special Ops to negotiate with the North Koreans. What were you thinking? Do you believe the U.S. could negotiate with North Korea? Like they were ready to put down their nuclear weapons just for the asking? So, my inexperienced team went overseas without me. They were to train the Afghan military and police, ramp up rapidly, and provide assistance on the ground."

"They did just that." Zac could hardly hold his head upright.

"They encountered security breaches, and most of the team returned in coffins. I failed as a leader and commander. No one would listen to me. Now, I must show the brass how inept you are as president. See how it feels? You'll never be able to stop this epidemic!" Rutoon's voice echoed in Zac's ears.

"You seem confused, Rutoon. Our goal will always be to save lives," Zac muttered between coughs, struggling to catch his breath.

"Thirsty?" Rutoon pushed a glass forward. "Sip your wine. It'll ease your cough."

Zac's cuffed hands barely reached the glass. The tickle in Zac's throat annoyed him, but he spotted a slight smirk on the general's face and decided against a sip. Swallowing another cough, he added, "You've lost all focus on your responsibilities to this country."

"Our country will survive. I'll see to that," Rutoon continued, sneering. "Perhaps the political giants who've ruled the nation for decades will die, but that can't be all bad. Others will rise to take their place. We've needed an overhaul for several presidential terms now."

Zac's chains rattled as he moved his elbows onto the table and leaned forward to ease his breathing. "You're destabilizing our nation. Must protect allies." The words came out in wheezes.

"Don't worry," Rutoon said. "As usual, I've covered all the bases. This epidemic will hit Syria, Afghanistan, and Russia within the week. So you see, you can lock me up, maybe even kill me, but I'll get revenge."

"How?" Zac asked.

"I had a backup plan. When you called me to your office and placed me in prison, I couldn't make a call to cancel preset triggers. So you're to blame for that, too. No call, and the prototypes were shipped automatically."

"What prototypes?" Zac gasped and breathed through pursed lips.

"The key is in the wine," Rutoon answered.

"So you sent the wine to RR7!" Zac took a few deep breaths.

"No. You did!" Rutoon jabbed Zac in the ribs.

His cough got worse. "I don't understand."

Rutoon gloated and leaned forward. "It was so easy. People don't think twice when someone from the White House asks a favor. They even picked up the shipments from the Pentagon. Of course, the bottles went through security, but they were no danger to our country."

Zac couldn't quit coughing. Sputum sprayed from his lips and splattered Rutoon's face.

Rutoon backed away and wiped his sleeve across his chin as anger boiled inside him. "You're going to help me escape," he demanded.

"Impossible!" Zac fisted his hands. "Not without killing me!"

"That's the whole idea." Rutoon motioned to the wine on the table. "I've already forced half of that drink down your throat.

I imagine you already feel the effects and will burn up in twenty-four hours. I'll be your hero again and have you escorted out of the country for medical treatment in Paris. Then onto a private island where no one will find you—somewhere you will rest in peace."

"What about Tom Harris?" Zac asked.

"Maybe we should call him," Rutoon said.

"Can't. No number." Zac refused to endanger the nation. Harris had to live. He'd become the next president soon. Zac's eyes drifted closed like a curtain falling.

"Doesn't matter," Rutoon said. "He's not part of the plan. By the time the vice president reappears, you'll be dead. You might as well take another nap. I have to make final plans."

Zac forced his eyes open even though the room kept spinning. "You won't get away. Every airline, port of entry, or cruise line has your photo, fingerprints—"

"Did you think I would be escorting you? Guess again." Rutoon laughed and turned his back.

President Spendorf's face fell onto the table, breaking the wineglass, lacerating his left temple and forehead. The blood and wine pooled together and dripped down the corner of the lacquered tabletop.

Emergency Packet

Chief of Staff Winston Willoughby handed Braun a manila envelope. "This is for your eyes only. These are direct orders from Zac in case anything happened to him. Of course, you can share it with Usher and Loran, but it's your responsibility to carry out these orders."

The manila envelope had a bright orange sticker, and the tab read, "Packet-A—For Commander Braun Hastings only. Share with those who need to know. FBI—use Packet B."

Braun tore open the Packet-A envelope and spread the five-page document on a desk in front of Usher and Loran. Braun filed away facts like a computer as they flowed from each page to his brain. It was surreal to see Zac's graceful handwriting on the entire document.

Braun memorized the few pages of instructions, clearly hearing Zac's voice as he read. He also noted the extreme concern that made the task urgent: "Locate VP Tom Harris and swear him in as acting president ASAP to prevent Speaker Lector Peach from taking over the country."

Usher and FBI Director Loran Sloan struggled to keep up as Braun flipped through the document detailing Vice President Harris' global efforts to seek aid in fighting the pandemic, including visits to the Director-General of the World Health Organization in Ethiopia, a G20 Health Ministers meeting in Berlin, and seminars in Great Britain, Paris, Geneva, and with China International Health. Harris should arrive in Syria for peace talks later today.

Usher reread the last page. "I wonder what Spendorf ordered in Packet B."

"That's for me." His boss, Loran Sloan, opened the second envelope. "President Spendorf is worried about the meeting in Syria."

Loran pointed at the document. Zac had written, "Warning: Avoid conflict at all costs! Stay safe." Also tucked inside the envelope was a satellite phone with a sticky label attached to the back that read, "Dial 1 for emergencies only." Loran added, "I'll round up the FBI team, and let's get moving."

Braun seemed unsure. "Zac penned these instructions shortly after apprehending Rutoon."

Usher asked. "Are you wondering if they're still current?" He pointed to the margins of Plan A orders. "The president jotted several handwritten notes beside these paragraphs summarizing the results of Harris' meetings."

"It's not totally up to date," Braun said. "The last note sums up the Ethiopian meeting. I hope all went well in China." Braun thought for a moment and ran his finger under the final destination. "Harris is scheduled to arrive in Syria for peace talks today. That's where we're heading."

Usher asked his boss, "Can you track Air Force Two? We need to meet him somewhere safe."

Sloan took a deep breath. "Vice President Harris chose to fly in the B-21 Stealth bomber instead of the usual C-32, the current Air Force Two. Members of Congress will complain about the cost, but it's a safer plane. We'll need to get to Syria quickly."

Braun tapped the cleft of his chin while deep in thought. "CCTV had a short news clip earlier today. There's rioting in Damascus, and according to his itinerary, Harris will land there in three hours. He's flying straight into danger." Braun spoke into his cell, "Hey, Google, what's the flight time between Washington, D.C., and Damascus, Syria?"

Google replied, "The quickest route from Washington, D.C., to Damascus is twelve hours and fifteen minutes."

"I'll see if we can get a government jet." Loran handed Braun the satellite phone—"for emergencies only. Be back shortly."

"I'd say this is an emergency." Braun logged onto the phone.

Usher nodded as Braun dialed one.

The phone rang four times before Harris answered. "Evening, Zac. Sorry to make you wait, but my cell vibrated, and I had to find a quiet, secure place to answer."

"Vice pres—" Braun started.

"Listen. Don't speak yet. Air Force Two is spacious, and I love the executive suite, but we're entering a war zone. Secret Service agents everywhere I turn, and I can't get a moment's peace."

"Vice president," Braun tried again.

"Two men and a woman have been following me for two days," Harris whispered. "I don't know their names, but I have photos. I saw them in Ethiopia and again in China. The air hostess gave me a note at the beginning of today's flight. These men tried to access the plane before our departure, but Rafe, my Secret Service guard, deterred them."

"Mr. Vice President, I'm sorry to interrupt. I'm JSOC Commander Agent Braun Hastings, calling from Washington, D.C. You were no doubt expecting to talk to President Spendorf, but he's missing, which is urgent."

"What do you mean, missing?" Harris gasped, and then, with only the slightest quiver in his voice, he added, "What do you need from me?"

"I'm acting under the president's direct orders and understand you're heading for Damascus, which is under siege. We're coming to get you and must swear you in as acting president ASAP. Peace talks are important, but this is a priority."

"Zac's missing?" Harris whispered, his voice sounding strange as he tried to grasp and accept the bad news.

"Yes, where should we meet? I doubt we'll get there until after midnight tomorrow. Can I contact someone closer to meet you? It can't wait."

"Zac's missing or dead?" Harris asked. "I have separate directions for either event."

"Missing at the moment," Braun felt exhausted just thinking about the long flight before boarding the plane. "As I mentioned earlier, we need you to be sworn in as soon as possible before the hot-headed officials in D.C., make Speaker Peach our new leader."

The phone went silent for a moment, and then static took over. "Hello? VP Harris, are you still there?" Braun asked.

An echoing voice broke through the static as if coming from an overhead intercom, "...a change...plans. Divert... Damascus International under attack." Then, a woman's voice clearly stated, "Vice President Harris, you need to sit down and fasten your seatbelt."

"Mr. Vice President," Braun paused as Loran stood in the doorway. A crease ran across his forehead. His shoulders slumped, and he appeared ten years older than when he left a few minutes ago. "What's happening?"

"Gotta go! Sending a text." VP Harris disconnected, but not before Braun heard more static in the background.

Braun pocketed the emergency phone. "It's not going as planned—we may not have a president or a vice president to swear in."

Loran stepped into the hallway. "Inform Winston while I arrange your flight with the Secret Service. They may need backup. Usher, you're going with Braun. Make arrangements with your Syrian contact."

"Yes, sir." Usher stayed behind and made a few calls.

Braun followed Loran into the hallway and saw Winston engaged in a heated discussion with Schmidt. *He must have gotten word about the VP already.*

"Give us time to swear in VP Harris," Winston shouted.

"He's in a war zone." Schmidt's finger poked Winston's chest. "If you can't get Tom Harris here in the next two hours, we're swearing in Speaker Lector Peach."

"And give him the football?" Winston asked. "This could get out of hand."

Braun cleared his throat. Both men turned toward him.

"Any more news?" Winston asked hopefully.

Braun moved behind Winston and lowered his voice. "We just got word Air Force Two is making an emergency landing somewhere in Syria, and it's not Damascus as planned."

"I guess that makes our decision easier." Schmidt smiled at Braun. "We'll handle everything."

Winston's forehead broke out in sweat. "I was afraid of this happening."

Braun warned, "We can't get VP Harris here in two hours, but we can swear him in as acting president, even while he's overseas. We can capture the ceremony on video for the whole nation to see."

Schmidt paled. "We can't wait. It won't fly with Congress."

"It has to," Winston said.

The shouting caught the attention of everyone around the two men, and people started weighing in on the argument. Voices escalated into a heated discussion.

Schmidt fisted his hands and yelled above the crowd, "We need a president here in our country to fight off this deadly disease!" His nose was nearly in Winston's face. "Speaker Peach is ready, willing, and able to fulfill the position."

"So is Harris!" Winston didn't step away. "The law states that we must swear in VP Harris immediately."

More people crowded around, adding their opinions. Braun couldn't get another word in.

"I'm taking this before Congress ASAP!" Schmidt shouted, "We can't wait any longer to swear in Harris."

"It is protocol." Winston's face turned beet red.

"Congress has to approve first. I know where they stand," Schmidt snapped back.

"No, they don't have to approve VP Harris." Winston pushed past Schmidt, seething with anger. He pulled a thick document from a bookshelf and leafed through it. "I have the rules right here."

Kyle Benson, the Secret Service Director, entered the room. "What's all the yelling about?"

"Found it!" Winston shoved the document in Schmidt's face and tapped at the location. "See right here…"

Schmidt scanned the pages. "Keep reading. The twenty-fifth amendment, Article 4, Congress may by law provide, and transmit within four days to the president pro tempore of the Senate and the Speaker of the House of Representatives their written declaration that the president cannot discharge the powers and duties of his office." Schmidt pointed and raised his voice. "Thereupon **Congress** shall decide the issue, assembling within forty-eight hours for that purpose if not in session."

Loran and Usher stood in a cubicle across from Winston and motioned for Braun to join them. "Hurry, we must find VP Harris!"

Kyle grabbed Schmidt's arm, his voice filled with authority and the power of his position, "Listen, you've forced your way into my headquarters, kept me in the dark about the president's disappearance, and now you're breaking every rule to swear Peach in as president. Over my dead body! Get out of my building! You have no business in here."

"Let's check this book to clear any misconceptions." Schmidt found his proof in the index and showed it to Benson. "Secret Service reports to Homeland Security. See, I told you so."

"We have four days!" Winston shouted.

"That's only four days for Congress' approval! We're not leaving the U.S. without a president for another day," Schmidt swore, "You idiot."

The arguing crowd didn't seem to notice Braun leaving the rowdy group. He entered the cubicle and closed the door to block out the noise.

Loran clenched his fists. "I can't believe Harris is flying to Syria. Not now. Get him out of there!"

Braun's satellite phone pinged. He swiped open a text message from VP Harris. "I just got word that several Syrian key officials are dying with similar symptoms as in the U.S. This virus is spreading, and the victims are violent, I'm afraid we're heading into unknown territory. ISIL forces have attacked the Damascus Airport. Air Force 2 is landing before we reach the airport. I don't know the location yet. Check with air traffic control. They'll have direct contact with our pilot. Here are the promised photos of the two men and the woman tailing me. I've activated GPS on my watch and phone. Blue is my watch. Green is the phone in case I become separated from either of them."

Loran was hustling the Hasting brothers for a jet that just landed outside the Secret Service Headquarters.

"Usher, you board, I'm right behind you." Braun raced to the top step of the jet, found his seat, and forwarded the photos to Cordy. After buckling his seatbelt, Braun texted her about evolving events, "Keep us posted if you locate Harris on GPS. Usher and I are leaving for Syria in six minutes."

Cordy didn't immediately answer.

"No Cordy yet," Braun updated Harris' coordinates and leaned toward Usher while pointing at his tracker, "There's no evidence of a green tracker, but maybe Harris' phone is off for the flight. Perhaps it will appear after Air Force 2 lands."

"A blue dot just popped up. VP Harris is over Al-Qisa, Syria," Usher said. "I'm running facial recognition of the photos through our new software database."

"What about the local police in Rif Dimashq Governorate?" Braun asked. "They may know who these people are. Should I contact them?"

Usher frowned. "The Rif Dimashq area is questionable, but I reached my Syrian contact and sent copies of the photos. He's gathering a small team of respected soldiers. We'll meet with them when we land. Hope VP Harris stays safe until we get there."

Braun tried again to reach Cordy and left a text message, "Taking off now. Miss you much. Talk to you soon. LYA, Braun."

Agent Kelly was overwhelmed with tasks at the CDC building, including managing phone messages, updating infected patients, and serving as a liaison for international health services. Despite delegating some tasks, she needed help scanning emails, typing responses, and tackling new issues as they arose.

Her eyes burned even with frequent doses of lubricant. Her laptop screen's illumination cast a pale glow directly contrasting with the overhead yellow fluorescent lights.

Ryan, the CDC director, sat in the next room reviewing the latest statistics. Several technicians filtered through the office, giving up-to-the-minute results on cultures and cell kill rates and monitoring the spread of the virus into West Virginia, Kentucky, Massachusetts, and Vermont. Pennsylvania's governor called in the National Guard for riot control.

The day remained hectic, and there was no end in sight. Kelly's cell phone rang, snapping her attention away from her work. On the first buzz, she answered the direct line from Colorado: "Good evening, Chief. I hope this means the vaccine is on its way."

"No, the plane hasn't arrived yet. Any idea why there is a delay?" Jackson asked.

"Perhaps it was difficult to get out of D.C.," Kelly said. "Dr. Alex is on that jet. He wanted to speak with Dr. Jennings but couldn't reach her. We've tried to contact Cordy to let her know our plane is on the way."

"Cordy is waiting at the drop zone, and she has the vaccine," the chief said. "However, there was an incident earlier today—"

Kelly rushed on, talking over the chief. "Guy Weimer from Homeland Security called from the hospital. He got word that a CIA Agent went to Colorado shortly after President Spendorf's disappearance. He's…" Her voice had a dramatic uptake as her brain finally registered what the chief was saying, "An incident?"

"That wouldn't be CIA Agent Dun Bean, would it?" Chief Jackson asked.

"I think that's his name," Kelly said. "Anyway, it was perfect timing. The FBI and CIA are wasting no time and working together. We are so busy here."

"Kelly," Jackson tried again to explain to no avail.

"Dr. Alex's team is working on collecting stem cells from key people, such as Liz, Peggy, a few senators, and infected congressmen. Braun's escorting the vice president back into the states and swearing him in as temporary president in Spendorf's absence, and—"

"Kelly! Agent Dun Bean isn't working for the government. He's gone rogue, and the CIA hasn't done a damn thing about it," the chief shouted. "He has a different agenda, and I doubt it's to ensure the vaccine gets into proper hands."

"Are you sure?" Kelly asked. "I talked to him over the phone. He promised to meet Dr. Alex when he landed in Fort Collins. He said he'd met Dr. Jennings…"

"So, he knows about the rendezvous point?" Chief gasped and ran from the office, dialing on another cell phone while trying to keep up with Kelly's conversation.

"Officer Bracken here."

"This is Chief Jackson. Cordy is at the drop-off point with the vaccine, but there's no plane yet. Thirty-six minutes late, and Cordy's not answering her phone. CIA Agent Dun Bean has attempted to intercept that vaccine twice already, and he's Rutoon's minion."

"I thought Cordy might be in danger, Bracken said, so I have Chico, one of my best men, on-site, posing as a mechanic. He has eyes like an eagle, and it's a good thing since I am twenty minutes out. I'm on my way, though—how about you?"

"Give me thirty. I need to pick up Dr. Jennings." Chief Jackson disconnected Bracken—Jackson switched phones. "Kelly, I'm on the run. Check-in with Dr. Alex ASAP. Find that plane, and make sure it doesn't land until we grant permission."

"Already on it." Agent Kelly disconnected.

* * *

On a tiny, dimly-lit airstrip near the Fort Collins-Loveland Municipal Airport, Cordy sped across an open field. Before she could spin away, Agent Dun Bean jumped into the passenger seat.

"Listen, I am armed and willing to shoot," Bean threatened. "Where is that vaccine?"

"You could shoot me, but you'd be no closer to getting the vaccine, would you?" Cordy reached into her pocket and hit the record button on her phone. At least, if he did shoot her, there would be evidence to convict him. "Agent Bean, it seems we are at a stalemate. I am driving, and you can't get what you need unless a plane lands, so stop threatening me to get that vaccine."

"Lady, you know too much already, and it would be so easy to leave you here with a bullet in your head. In fact, I'm mad enough. I could shoot you just for the fun of it."

Cordy needed help and noticed her throwaway phone to the chief had slipped between the door and her seat. She reached down and entered *3 to speed-dial Jackson. "Listen, Bean, why are you here? What is it you want?" She spoke loud and fast to cover Jackson's response if he answered.

"President Spendorf needs help," Bean said, "and I have orders to bring that vaccine immediately. So, for the last time, where is it?"

Cordy snarled right back at him. Her mind raced, calculating the risks and the possibilities while assessing the danger from her crazed assailant. A plan flashed through her mind. "I'm on my way to get it."

"I thought you already had it."

"No, Dr. Jennings needed more time to increase the sample size," Cordy lied.

"Are we going to meet Dr. Jennings?" Bean asked.

"She's too busy, but one of her colleagues will bring it. Cordy took the fastest but roughest route across the tarmac.

"I don't believe you." Bean leaned back and swiped through several programs on his phone to check his messages. He paused before putting in his code name. "What do you know about viruses?"

"Nothing," Cordy snapped, waiting for Bean to open his messages. She had activated the speaker on his phone earlier in the day.

"Then, I'll wait to talk to Dr. Alex." Bean tapped the latest message from Rutoon. It blasted, "Zac's dying. Can't transport. I need that vaccine. See you—" Bean cut off the speaker and held the phone to his ear. All color drained from his face, and he shoved something hard into Cordy's side. "Yes, you know what this means. Stop the car. We're going to get out now."

He had found his spare gun. Cordy was about two hundred yards from a gray mechanic's shed. She beeped the horn as she turned off the key, hoping to attract some attention from anyone nearby. "Sorry, I bumped it."

"Sure you did," Bean said. "Now get out nice and slow, or you'll die in less than a heartbeat."

Cordy removed the key to her car with her right hand, grabbed the phone connected to Jackson with her left hand, slid it into her jacket pocket, and opened the door.

A siren sounded in the distance.

Bean bounded from the car and was at her door, instantly pulling her upright, the gun still aimed at her chest. "Head toward that abandoned shed. Hurry, and don't turn around."

Cordy's eyes locked on the barrel of the gun aimed at her. A surge of adrenaline had every nerve cell in her body on high alert. She wanted to run but didn't dare turn her back on that pistol. "Okay, Bean, what must I do?" The tremor in her voice startled even her.

"Give me the vaccine," Bean said. "I know you have it. Where is it?"

"I told you, I don't have it. Jennings needed more time."

"Let's not play games," Bean said. "You're unarmed, less than five feet away, and totally at my mercy, so you'd better hope you have that vaccine on your body, or you're a dead woman."

Cordy's mouth was dry as a bone. She blew out a ragged breath. "You hear those sirens? You can kill me, but you won't get the vaccine. I also know Rutoon has President Spendorf. How did you fit into his capture? Chloroform? I know you're a vet. Anesthesia is nothing new to you."

Bean's eyes darted toward the shed and back to Cordy. "Simple anesthesia is old school. Sevoflurane. You know that I can't let you live. Pity, I was beginning to like the challenges you set up for me."

"So, Zac's infected?" Cordy tried to keep him talking, hoping for an opportunity to get away.

"Guess so. I doubled the dose in the president's wine, but I'm not the one that made him drink it."

"Why the Jelly Beans in the tunnel hallway?" Cordy asked. "Wanted some recognition for your part in the scheme?"

"That wasn't me." Bean ruthlessly grabbed Cordy's arm and dragged her toward the shed as a siren ground to a halt.

"Let go of me!" Cordy yelled.

"Shut up, lady. We'll hide here till they leave. Not a word out of you."

Cordy saw movement behind the glass in the shed. She wrenched her arm away from Bean's grasp.

"Get down," a man shouted.

Bean panicked. Gunfire split the air, and Cordy flew backward, her chest on fire, but glad she wore her Kevlar vest.

Bean's automatic pistol continued to fire even though he was on the ground with a hole between his eyes.

As soon as Bean's gun silenced, Chico dashed from the shed. "Cordy, are you hit?

She reached for his hand. "Thanks." A groan escaped her lips as she eased onto her side.

"Breathe, nice and slow." Chico held firmly to her hand. "It's going to burn like hellfire."

The first breath was torture. Cordy gasped and quickly let it out again.

"Slowly inhale, hold it briefly, and breathe out through your mouth," Chico reassured her. "Kevlar vests are lifesavers, but you'll have a whopping bruise." He eased her to a sitting position.

Cordy realized her knuckles were white as she held Chico's hand in a death grip. He didn't flinch. "Sorry." She relaxed her hand.

"Take another breath." Chico breathed with her. "Now, let it out."

Bracken's cruiser's brakes screeched as he reached the shed. He was already running toward Cordy before she stood up. "You're bleeding!"

Cordy eased into a standing position and released Chico's hand. She rubbed her forehead, and it came away with a streak of blood. She felt numb. "I didn't notice."

"How's your vision?" Bracken held up three fingers. "How many do you see?"

"Three."

He handed her a hanky.

"I'm sure it's just a scratch." Cordy put pressure on her head wound.

Bracken nudged Bean's foot. "Is he dead?"

Chico checked for a pulse and then patted Agent Bean down. "Yeah, but not before he got off a few shots first."

Cordy dabbed at her oozing wound. "Chico, get his phone. Bean got a voice message from Rutoon."

Chico removed the cell phone from Bean's pocket. "Here, Cordy. Do your magic. I bet you'll find out where they stashed the president."

Chief Jackson drove up with Dr. Jennings in the passenger seat and her husband in the back. The chief threw open the door, shouting, "Don't ever do that again. He nearly killed you!"

Mr. Jennings strained to get out of the car, holding a red and white cooler in his hands. He turned to his wife, pale and shaking with anger, an annoyed expression on his face. "Honey, I don't like your work, and I never want you in danger like this again."

Dr. Jennings ignored him, walked to Jackson, and calmly placed her hand on his arm. "What is the delay?"

The chief was still scolding Cordy, "Did you hear me? He tried to kill you!"

As though she hadn't heard him the first time, Cordy turned to Bracken, who explained the delay. "Air traffic control kept the plane circling until we resolved a few problems."

Bracken walked toward the shed. "I'll contact the tower. They can land now."

Dr. Jennings took the cooler from her husband. "My team worked all day, so I brought another vaccine vial. There are detailed instructions inside."

"How many more doses?" Cordy asked.

"Another fifty," Dr. Jennings said. "Do you still have the original vial?"

"I'll get it." Cordy walked to the car and brought back the bottle. "Should I add it to the cooler?"

"Hand it to me." Dr. Jennings pulled a pen from her pocket. "I want to mark this as the first vial."

The sound of a jet grew louder as the plane landed on the tarmac.

"The chief told me that Dr. Alex is on the plane." Dr. Jennings smiled, and her eyes gleamed with joy. "I can't wait to meet him personally. I am a big fan."

Bracken came from the shed to meet the plane and greeted Dr. Alex as he descended the steps.

Alex motioned to Dr. Jennings. "Sorry, we don't have much time to talk. The pilot will refuel, and then we'll head back to D.C."

Dr. Jennings gave a brief overview of the vaccine. She was all business with Alex but pleased to offer her report after all their work. "This is the first time we'll test it on a human, so I'm not sure what will happen. Call me with any questions, and I want to know the results."

Dr. Alex nodded. "Thanks for everything. You have no idea how important it is to find a cure. It could save thousands of lives. Once proven, and approved by the FDA, we'll be able to go into mass production."

"It's not a cure," Jennings reminded him, "but with the enhancement, it may prevent death."

Cordy thumbed through Bean's cell phone. "Listen to this message from Rutoon." She hit the speaker button, "Zac's dying. I can't transport him, and I need that vaccine. See you this Friday. Chirk's gone underground, so eliminate Braun and his brother, then meet me in Virginia at 0600 to get rid of our resident president."

"Where in Virginia?" the chief asked.

"I don't know yet," Cordy said, "but that vaccine may save President Spendorf's life." She turned to Dr. Alex. "How long do most people live after infection?"

"Forty-eight to seventy-two hours," Dr. Alex said. "Liz is approaching her last hours. She's already at the violent stage. We put her into a coma while giving her the most potent broad-spectrum antibiotics and massive doses of Vitamin C and Thiamin."

"What about Peggy?" Cordy asked.

"She's only a few hours behind Liz," Dr. Alex said. "We moved her to ICU and induced a coma before she had any anger issues. If you're ever in the D.C., area, Dr. Jennings, look us up."

"If this vaccine works, I'll be there when they clear us for travel. I want to see the results for myself."

The pilot appeared at the jet's door and waved, indicating the plane was ready for a return flight, so Dr. Alex wished everyone farewell.

Dr. Jennings hugged him and walked arm in arm with her husband back to the chief's car.

"Call as soon as you land," Cordy said. "I hope to have President Spendorf's location by then."

"I'm going to visit Chirk," Chief Jackson said. "If anyone knows where Rutoon is hiding, he does. Perhaps he'll cut a deal and cooperate."

Bracken walked Cordy to her car. "Can I hear the message you sent to the chief? He was distraught with you."

"Yes, and I also recorded Bean's conversation while in the car." She held up both phones, grinned, and then played the recordings. When she finished, Cordy started the engine. "I want to get back to searching Bean's phone. The chief and I have to find the president. He has only forty-eight hours to live, and Bean said he'd doubled the viral dose, so maybe not even that. I pray the vaccine works."

Cordy climbed behind the steering wheel and quickly texted Agent Kelly. "Virus vaccine is heading your way. Let me know when it arrives." She barely started the engine when her cell phone rang.

"This is Chief Jackson. Braun left you several messages. He needs your help tracking down Harris, and I can see why. Turn on the radio. The VP is missing, and Speaker of the House, Lector Peach, just announced he's in charge. God save us all!"

Cordy punched the radio button. "...and I, Lector Peach, promise never to hide from my countrymen. As you can see, President Spendorf wasn't even safe in the bunker. Our vice president has flown overseas. Who knows where he is during our country's darkest hour? We are facing doomsday, and I'm your savior. We must fight back against this deadly epidemic. Burn the infected bodies in a mass grave, remove all contaminated persons to a remote and safe area, pick up our lives, and move on. I'm relocating all White House duties to Texas, where we can live, breathe, and conduct the nation's affairs..."

Chief Jackson interrupted, "We must help Braun find the vice president and bring him home ASAP!"

Chirk sat on the edge of his mattress with his head in his hands and awaited trial. The hours had passed slowly while in maximum security at Larimer County Jail, and he was already going nuts living within a six-by-eight-foot single cell. Isolated from other prisoners, he had nothing to do but wallow in guilt. At first, he felt like a failure for letting General Rutoon down. As time progressed, he became angry, realizing Rutoon used him as a pawn for personal gains.

No visitors came his way. He ate his meals alone. A tasteless dinner was served on a plastic plate on an overbed table tucked away in one corner. He didn't even get real flatware to cut the tough old bird or whatever meat they served for the meal.

Three walls were nothing but cement gray. The fourth wall had metal rungs running across both sides. A barred metal door in the middle locked from the outside. A stainless steel, one-piece combination sink, and toilet sat in the corner across from his bed. There wasn't even a window to look outside to determine if it was night or day. Dim lights stayed on in the hallway twenty-four hours a day. Chirk was refused a cell phone or any phone calls except from his lawyer.

That was the only good thing about his incarceration. He had an excellent lawyer, young, in her thirties, but tough as steel. Ms. Liberty Marshall, or Ms. Marshall as she preferred to be called, followed in her father's, grandfather's, and several uncles' footsteps. She told Chirk, "I can trace my ancestors back to Chief Justice John Marshall, so don't lie to me. I'll know instantly, and believe me, I'll call you on it every time."

Marshall had snappy, whiskey-colored eyes, much like Chief Jackson. It was what Chirk noticed first when she blazed into his room. He couldn't think of a better way of describing her actions. Full of energy, she had already done her homework. He had only met with her once earlier in the day but trusted her. If anyone could devise a plan to lighten his sentence, she could.

He recalled her words. "That stupid stunt you pulled, capturing the chief, will cost you, but your friend General Rutoon will get you killed."

"What do you mean?" Chirk had asked. "He's the president's best friend. He'd do anything to protect Zac."

"What world are you living in?" Marshall snapped. "My inside sources tell me Rutoon has embezzled funds, sold weapons to North Korea and Syria, launched bioweapons in our country and is directly behind this devastating pandemic. President Spendorf stripped him of his stars and dishonorably discharged Rutoon before hauling him to Federal Prison."

Chirk's insides twisted. He suspected things weren't adding up. "When did this happen?"

"Within the last forty-eight hours, probably while you were being evicted from your little cabin in the woods." Marshall shoved a file in front of Chirk. "Read it for yourself. His arrest is in all the papers. I even have a CNN news clip."

Chirk took a few moments to read. Then something caught his eye. "I had nothing to do with providing weapons to any foreign—"

Marshall squinted at him. "Not true!"

Chirk insisted. "I never—"

"You furnished weapons to Syria when you were with the FBI." Marshall pulled another file and shoved it under Chirk's nose.

Chirk read over the first page. "Where did you get this?"

"Doesn't matter, Chirk."

"But I didn't deliver weapons," Chirk insisted. "That report is fabricated. Maybe I unintentionally let a few weapons slide out of the country, but I wasn't directly involved."

"Another lie!" Marshall pointed to the document. "You're right there beside Rutoon. But that's not the half of it. Rutoon broke out of prison, along with four inmates. They killed three guards, and Rutoon returned to the bunker and kidnapped President Spendorf. He knocked out Zac's bodyguard and knifed him in the chest. Marv is still in a coma. Rutoon also infected the president with the deadly virus."

"I don't believe it!" Chirk said, but his gut continued to knot. "Does anyone have proof?"

"Yes," Marshall said. "They have a phone message directly from Rutoon."

"They who?" Chirk asked.

"Your ex-partner, Chief Jackson, and his team."

"If anyone could find out the facts, it would be Chief Jackson." After learning the truth about Rutoon, Chirk felt like a fool. The chief will no longer call me Chirk the Jerk, more like Chirk the Chump. Blood rushed from his head. Everything turned black.

When Chirk opened his eyes, he was back on his cot. His lawyer was gone. His jaw clenched until he thought he'd cracked a molar. "Rutoon, I'm going to take you to hell and back! I don't know how, when, where, or what it will take, but I do know who—ME!"

* * *

A correctional officer walked to his door at 9:38 p.m. "The warden says you can have a visitor."

Chirk became curious and nervous. "Who would visit me?" Chirk asked.

"He says he was your partner at one time." The guard opened the cell door. "I'm cuffing your wrists and ankles."

Chirk sighed. "Must you use these to see Chief Jackson? It's too demeaning."

"Do you want to see him or not?" the guard asked.

Chirk nodded. He hoped the chief would be forgiving, but being his past partner in the FBI, he doubted it. "Might as well get this over with—Jackson won't take no for an answer." Chirk pulled his shoulders back and glared at the guard.

"Don't try anything foolish like trying to get away. Your bright orange jumpsuit is an easy target." The guard led Chirk to the interview room where Chief Jackson and Agent Cordelia were waiting.

Ms. Marshall stood just inside the glass door. She had changed from her standard navy business suit to a rust-colored midi, free-flowing dress. A belt hugged her around the waist, showing off her slender figure and lending her womanly curves a diminutive pixie look that emphasized her youth. She seemed to be anything but his assertive lawyer, whom he had met with only hours before. It worried him.

The door opened, and he walked inside the interview room, noticing the inch-thick bulletproof glass wall on one side and the solid cement on the other three walls. It was intimidating and claustrophobic. Chirk straightened his posture, raised his head, and walked straight for Chief Jackson. He sat in the remaining metal chair, bolted to the floor like the other three.

The guard locked his ankle cuffs to the floor and closed the door from the outside but remained within view from across the hallway—there was no way out until he was released.

"Have you met Ms. Marshall?" Chirk asked.

Cordy nodded. "We met her by the metal detector. She agreed we could tape your interview. Is that all right with you?"

"I want to hear it from her lips," Chirk said. "I'll do as she recommends." His cuffs rattled against the small, equally-secured metal table.

"I approved the taping of the interview on the condition that I get a copy by morning," Marshall said.

Chief Jackson agreed, switched on the recorder, and returned his attention to Chirk. "Did your lawyer tell you about your old buddy, General Rutoon?"

Chirk's one good eye narrowed, puckering the other cheek under his patch. "Yes. She even showed me several papers and the latest news clip on CNN. That bastard lied to me. I would never have followed his orders if I'd known we weren't protecting President Spendorf. Instead, he's trying to kill Zac!"

Jackson leaned closer. "Why should I believe you? You're in this conspiracy up to your eyeball. First, you try to kill Braun. When that failed, you beat up Cordy and left her for dead, then kidnapped me."

Chirk turned his head toward Cordy. His jaw dropped open. "I didn't beat you up. I tried to save you by knocking you out rather than shooting you."

"Thanks for sparing me," Cordy spit out. "I guess I hadn't noticed. Either way, I was out cold and woke up with a shiner and a headache."

"Sorry about that." Chirk did seem appropriately contrite.

"Let's get to the point," Ms. Marshall said. "You mentioned you might be willing to negotiate a deal. What do you have in mind?"

"Under the right conditions," the chief said.

Chirk's demeanor changed from defeat to hope. "Yes, Chief, I know you. What do I have to do in return? You never give anything away for free, but you always stick to your promises."

"Tell me everything, including why you were after Braun," Chief Jackson said.

Cordy held up her hand. "Let me check the recorder to make sure we get everything." She replayed the last few words, set the device back in the middle of the table, and hit record. "Start talking."

"Rutoon's orders. He told me that Braun had damaging information against a top White House official."

"Meaning himself, no doubt," Cordy interrupted.

"I guess, but I thought he was referring to President Spendorf. Rutoon was Zac's best friend. He always found a way to improve their relationship. Zac needs this, and Zac expects that. Whenever Speaker of the House, Lector Peach, came on the news to slam Zac's latest accomplishments, Rutoon strongly defended the president. I have a tough time swallowing that the general would allow anything to happen to Zac, much less try to kill him."

"Ms. Marshall placed her hand on Chirk's arm. "You know the truth. What are you going to do about it?"

Chirk swallowed. "It's up to me, is it?"

"We're here to help you if you help us," the chief said. "Remember when we used to sit around throwing out ideas and hoping something would stick? I want to try that in this situation. Cordy, you go first."

"Rutoon called Agent Bean to say he infected President Spendorf with a virus, and Zac's dying," Cordy said. "Bean was to meet Rutoon somewhere in Virginia to bring the stolen vaccine and, in Rutoon's words, 'To get rid of the resident president.' Do you know where in Virginia?"

Chirk licked his lower lip. "He once mentioned that he had a house overlooking the Potomac River, but that would be too close to D.C."

"Where?" Chief Jackson asked. "If we can locate President Spendorf before it's too late, I'll drop charges against you involving my kidnapping."

Cordy pitched in. "I'll also drop my assault charges, but only if we get to the president in time."

Chirk shook his head. "That sounds too good to be true, but I'm not sure I can find his house's exact location. He bragged that he never had to pay a finder's fee for the estate, so I'm not sure who holds the title."

Ms. Marshall asked, "Will you drop all charges if Chirk cooperates and finds the president?"

"You have my word, and it's on this tape," Chief Jackson said. "But how will we track down Rutoon? He won't stay in the country for long."

"I have an idea," Cordy said. "I want to replay Rutoon's conversation with Bean." She dug Bean's phone from her pants pocket, placed it on the table, and pressed play. The recording repeated, "Zac's dying. Can't transport. I need that vaccine. See you this Friday. Chirk's gone underground, so eliminate Braun and his brother, then meet me in Virginia at 0600 to get rid of our resident President." Cordy paused the tape. "We need to call Rutoon tomorrow at 0600. Chirk, do you know Agent Dun Bean?"

"I've met him a couple of times," Chirk admitted.

"Could you impersonate Bean and make that phone call at 0600, or should I?" Chief Jackson asked. "That would be 0400 our time, since Virginia is two hours ahead of Colorado."

Chirk fidgeted in his chair, only this time, with seeming eagerness, not shame. "Let me call him. I want to hear his voice admitting this was a sham. Don't worry. I won't fowl up." Chirk turned toward Chief Jackson, "Please, Chief, let me renew your faith in me. One problem: my voice doesn't sound anything like Bean's."

Cordy interrupted, "What if we used a voice scrambler? Rutoon shouldn't be too surprised if Bean used one, but I doubt Rutoon still has that phone number. I guess we can try it as a last resort."

"What else is on the tape Rutoon sent," Ms. Marshall asked.

Cordy pressed the play button. "Bean, check in with me before destroying the vaccine first thing in the morning. One of us might get infected." The call ended.

"I'm prepared to cut a deal," Marshall said. "We'll listen in on the call and jot any urgent notes for Chirk to discuss as needed. I'll draw up an agreement, and we can meet back here at 0330."

"Let's be ready to call," Cordy said, "but I'd wait twenty to thirty minutes to see if Rutoon calls Bean. Rutoon will want to know if Bean has the vaccine. I will run a GPS tracker on this cell, so we must keep Rutoon on the call long enough to locate the origin."

"How long will it take?" Chirk asked.

"Keep him on the line for at least thirty seconds," Cordy said. "The longer, the better. If you think you're losing him, entice him with an offer he can't refuse. You know him best. Come up with something."

"I'll try anything," Chirk said. "Thanks, Chief Jackson. If this works, I will owe you my life. I guess this is the second time you've rescued me."

"Make that the third," the chief said, "but who's counting."

"When?" Chirk asked.

"The SWAT team could have taken you out in a nanosecond," the chief said.

"True," Chirk said. "What did you find looking through my files?"

Cordy smiled. "You have a sophisticated firewall. It wasn't easy to discover information. I still haven't found any secret financial accounts hidden away overseas. Chief Jackson says you must have squirreled away a large sum while working with him."

Ms. Marshall nodded, "That's detailed in the second file I handed you. Have you read it?"

Chirk nodded. "I read that lying statement and told you it's a fabricated report. It wasn't me taking funds. That was Rutoon using my name. He had access to my social security number, too. I don't know how to prove it, but I will clear my name."

"See you at 0330." Chief Jackson escorted Cordy out of the interview room, leaving Chirk alone with his lawyer.

Five hours and thirty minutes later, they were back in the interview room waiting to call Rutoon, or better yet, to receive a phone call from the ex-general.

Chirk was jittery, nervous energy pouring from every cell. A chain around his ankles jingled as he tapped his foot against the floor. The guard had removed his handcuffs so he could make the call. "Will I be released when the president returns to the bunker?"

Ms. Marshall frowned. "No one said you would go free. Chief Jackson agreed to clear your assault on Agent Cordelia and his kidnap charges, but your murder attempt on Braun Hastings still is on the books. We'll have to see what else we can work out, but you should be grateful to your ex-partner for now."

Chirk made an effort to smile, but it left a hollow feeling. He might still have to live out his life in prison. "I will get Rutoon to divulge as much information as possible. He'll make the call short if I know him. He won't want any possibility of a trace, and he'll use a burner cell. One use, and he'll discard it, so the GPS tracker has to work fast." He glanced at Cordy for acknowledgment.

"I'll do my job," Cordy said. "You do yours. We'll have you on speakerphone, but I'll mute our end. Only Rutoon and you will be on the call."

* * *

Agent Cordelia had always been vigilant with computer security, but inside the prison, it was hard to use her unique skills without drawing undue attention. She downloaded a high-powered GPS tracker onto Bean's cell before handing the phone to Chirk. "Remember, act like Bean. Pretend you want him to get off the phone quickly, but keep him on the call until I hold up my hand, indicating I've located Rutoon."

"Got it," Chirk said.

"Also, I'm recording the call and tracking any passwords he uses to get access to this phone."

"Who else is Rutoon working with?" Chief Jackson asked Chirk. "We know he relied on you and Agent Bean, but he probably has a handful of others."

Chirk thought for a moment. "He doesn't trust many people. I didn't even know about Bean's involvement."

"I just thought of something," the chief said. "You claim you never took any funds while we worked together in the FBI. You believe it was Rutoon, so did he know Haya or Aqib?"

Chirk's eyes darted toward his lawyer. "They were the young couple who smuggled U.S. explosives to Libya. They hid weapons inside their merchandise. Rutoon might have known about the scam, but I never told him."

"VP Harris sent three photos of people following him," Cordy said. "I ran them through NICS and a facial recognition program." Cordy motioned to two of the pictures. "I confirmed this is Haya, and I got a 96% match for Aqib, but no hits on the third photo. A judge acquitted the couple after a lengthy trial. I already forwarded a text to Braun's phone, but we have no identity for the second man. Do you recognize any of these people?"

Chirk reacted only after staring at the photo for several seconds, stroking his forehead, and tapping his foot. Then, he confirmed a positive ID. "They're a bit older, but I remember that Jade tiger necklace."

"Are you sure you've never seen this second man?" Cordy held up the photo in question.

"No, I don't know him." Chirk became excited. "See, I told you I didn't take any funds. It was the general all along. He made frequent trips to that part of the country and was in Syria during that time. Where should I go with this, Chief? Rutoon will probably call within the next fifteen minutes, and I'm not sure how to verify that information."

"Find a way to bring up the funds," the chief said. "I know we're pressuring you with last-minute changes, but if you want to clear your name, make a plan."

Chirk closed his eyes briefly and took a deep breath. "Yes, I'll think of something."

Chief Jackson said, "You always were a shrewd businessman, confident, and quick-thinking. We're relying on that intellect. No shenanigans, or this deal is off the table!"

"Right, Chief, I had lost all self-worth a few hours ago and even contemplated suicide," Chirk admitted. "Now, I have a reason to live, get my life back, and save a man I truly respect, President Zac Spendorf. We have to return him to the White House. Lector Peach is a disaster. Zac needs to heal this country."

Chirk turned toward Ms. Marshall. "I'm ready to talk to Rutoon. No, make that. I'm ready to get even. He won't get away with this!"

Ready To Roll

Rutoon hated leaving his luxurious red stone mansion overlooking the Potomac. It had been "home sweet home" for over a year. The highlight of his office was a dark Honduran Mahogany desk with a lighter wood inlay in a floral design. A glass top protected his treasure. Everything was in order. He had destroyed all paper files and carefully packed his laptop computer.

The house appeared vacant—except for one room. President Spendorf lay on Rutoon's king-size bed. His old friend turned enemy no longer required restraints. He would rest in peace. Well, it would be where Zac would die. Rutoon couldn't stand watching Zac's fever-struck body shaking uncontrollably.

Rutoon ran a sleeve over his sweaty brow. He rose early, took the hottest bath he'd ever taken, soaked until he was a prune, and even used diluted bleach to wash any virus from his skin. Fresh air was what he needed. He hauled his briefcase to the front door and set it next to his luggage.

Exhausted, he poured two fingers' worth of Kentucky whiskey into a Waterford crystal glass and rested in one of his wingback chairs. His head throbbed as he glanced at his watch for the fourth time this morning. It was 0610, and he still hadn't heard a word from Dun Bean. He'd given orders to intercept the virus vaccine and return to Virginia. After Zac's coughing fit last night, Rutoon worried he had been exposed to the virus. He downed the whiskey, knowing it wouldn't kill a superbug—he needed that vaccine now.

Bean was to be at the mansion at 0600, so Rutoon had waited, but time was wasting. Bean hadn't even reported that the vaccine was in his possession. Fidgeting with his burner phone, he decided to call Bean. An automated system answered as expected. Rutoon gave several passwords to authenticate himself.

"Morning, General. How may I assist you?" The voice sounded like it was on a scrambler.

It was new for Bean and shook Rutoon enough for a long pause. "Bean, explain why you're late."

"Vaccine is safe. How's Zac?" came from the phone.

Indeed, it has to be Dun Bean. No one else knows about Zac. "He's dying cell by cell. Won't be long now, so why are you late?" Rutoon asked again.

"I'm being tailed. Get off the phone now and leave the country."

Rutoon couldn't leave the country. Not yet. Cold sweat dripped down his back. "Bring me that vaccine!"

The idiot wasn't listening to Rutoon. What was he saying? "… and by the way, Chirk's in prison—perfect for covering our asses. You should deposit a large sum of money into one of his accounts. Let him take the rap for kidnapping the president."

"Hang on!" Rutoon's voice rose in anger. "Are you blackmailing me?"

"Money's not for me. It's for Chirk."

Rutoon's brain raced. "I need to get out of the country. And I must have that vaccine!"

"Make it at least six figures. Chirk hasn't touched a dime of any payoff he has received. Can you believe that?"

Rutoon chuckled. "You know that sum of money you're referring to? He couldn't touch even a penny. I took it!"

"So, you know what account to put the million into?"

"Wait a minute, you said six figures," Rutoon hissed.

"Don't you think a million is worth your freedom…and mine? I'll line up half if you do the same," came from the phone. "Unless—"

Rutoon started coughing. What was the temperature in the room? His collar felt too tight to breathe, and his shirt stuck to his back.

"What's the account number so I can forward my $500 thousand?" the caller asked over the phone.

"I'll have to call you back," Rutoon choked back a wheeze. "When will you bring me the vaccine?"

"Call me as soon as you have everything ready. It better be within the next four hours," came over the phone.

Rutoon heard a click, and the call disconnected. "How dare you threaten me?" In a fit of anger, he destroyed the cell phone. His heartbeat thundered in his ears as he picked up his suitcase, walked out of the front door, and headed down the street. Bean's warning of the virus' potency echoed as Rutoon mentally cursed his stupidity in getting so close to Zac. His blond toupee made his head feel hot, and the fake whiskers itched. He couldn't wait to leave the country and tear off his disguise.

A distant siren startled him into a mad dash through his gate. Panic set in as if all his military training had left him. What was he doing out in the open? Rutoon had to force himself into some semblance of calm even though every molecule in his body told him, "Run!"

Agent Cordelia raised her hand as Chirk asked Rutoon for an account number to place his money. Not waiting any longer, Chirk ended the call with a threat of his own, "Better be within the next four hours," and disconnected.

"Got it!" Cordy said. "The GPS coordinates show Rutoon's only thirty minutes away from the White House."

"You were terrific, Chirk," Chief Jackson patted his ex-partner on the back. "You got much more out of Rutoon than I thought possible. How did you think of blackmail?"

"It's what he did to me," Chirk said. "I knew he would find a fall guy, and I made the most logical person. Bean's dead. How did you keep that information from the media?"

"Friends in the department," the chief said. "But it remains secret only until Rutoon's in our clutches and President Spendorf is safe."

"Can I see Zac?" Chirk asked. "I mean even via video. I suppose he's in no shape at the moment, though."

Ms. Marshall tapped on the interview room window and motioned for the guard to open the door and escort Chirk back to his cell. "We'll talk soon. Get some rest." The guard replaced the cuffs removed from Chirk's wrists so he could take the call and led him away.

Cordy called Kyle Benson, the Director of Secret Services, and Loran Sloan, head of the FBI. Sloan immediately summoned a SWAT Team to the GPS location to rescue President Spendorf. "I'll send a car to pick up Dr. Alex. He needs to meet us ASAP with a treatment plan to save Zac."

It took several minutes for Cordy to reach Agent Kelly, so she texted. "Located President Spendorf. SWAT en route. A car will meet Dr. Alex at the CDC. Have him bring the vaccine and emergency treatment."

Agent Kelly returned a message, "Sorry for the delayed text. Dr. Alex is en route to treat the president. We're seeing mixed results with the vaccine, despite our efforts to enhance it with Liz's stem cells. However, there is a ray of hope in Peggy's successful treatment, which has effectively lowered her fever. Unfortunately, we've also experienced some losses, with two senators from Maryland and New Hampshire, and a Pennsylvania House Rep. is on the critical list. I'll provide an update on Zac's progress once we begin his treatment."

Narrow Escape

Sirens grew louder and unnerved Rutoon. People milled around on the streets, but few cars were on the road. It gave him an odd feeling like something was about to explode. Then, three squad cars squealed as they turned the corner to his block.

Rutoon ducked behind a hedgerow. His legs were like noodles as he crouched low, moving quickly toward a fence. He stumbled and nearly lost his toupee. *Better to lie still than attract attention.* He took the time to catch his breath.

The police cars whizzed by and pulled up to his estate gate. He'd gotten out just in time. They would be too late. President Spendorf would probably already be dead; if not, he would be soon. Zac would be the officer's priority.

Now wasn't the time to turn paranoid. *Maybe Bean was right. Chirk was already in custody. This is the president, after all. The government had to hang his death on someone. Chirk's already a sitting duck. Why expose anyone else? I'll have to reassess my funds, maybe even put the mansion in Chirk's name. Not a bad idea. Sorry, Chirk! But you'd do the same if you were in my shoes.*

Rutoon had to get away, which meant now, while the officers focused their search on his estate. His heart hammered in his chest, and he wheezed with every breath, but he had to run with this blasted bag and briefcase tucked under his shoulder. He traveled down alleyways, slid behind fences, and dashed from tree to tree, constantly glancing around. He'd made it eight blocks and no police cars yet.

Rutoon leaned against a light post tucked behind a giant rosebush to breathe. He pulled another burner phone from his suitcase, activated it, and texted his lawyer, "I'm granting you Power of Attorney effective immediately. Put my finances in order as we've discussed, and sign over the deed to my Virginia home to Chirk T. Transom. He sent Chirk his contact information, including his social security number. Text me if you have any questions. I'll be out of the country for a while. Rutoon."

He had arranged for a car and driver to pick him up ten blocks from his neighborhood so that no one would associate him with the area. It felt more like ten miles when he finally reached a car parked on a side street. The driver sat in the front seat of a black sedan. He wore a mask and face shield and didn't leave the car to help with Rutoon's luggage.

Rutoon peered up and down the road, but there were no other vehicles, so this must be his ride.

"You getting in, or what?" the driver asked.

"Aren't you going to open the trunk?" Rutoon held up his bag.

"There's a virus going around," the driver snapped. "You can't be too careful these days, so keep it in the back seat with you. The door's unlocked. Climb in."

Rutoon nodded and sprawled out on the back seat. "Wake me when we reach Pittsburgh."

"You know it'll cost extra to smuggle you across the State line," the driver said.

"We already discussed that," Rutoon murmured. "You agreed to take me."

"Pay upfront," the driver insisted. Rutoon pulled a wad of cash from his wallet. "Here. Now, let me sleep."

Cordy received a call from FBI Director Loran Sloan. "The SWAT team found President Spendorf unconscious in a mansion bedroom near the White House," Loran explained. "The team is taking Zac to Walter Reed Hospital for treatment. There's no sign of General Rutoon."

Cordy said, "Yes, I heard Dr. Alex is at the hospital. He has the vaccine and will know what to do."

"Any news regarding VP Harris?" Cordy waited anxiously for an update.

The Director replied, "Top Syrian leaders are succumbing to a rapid-acting disease, probably Virus X, but there's no proof yet since they have no diagnostic labs. Damascus is under attack, and the airport has closed. The VP's jet made an emergency landing, and Harris is no longer onboard."

"Do Braun and Usher know where to find Harris?" Cordy took a deep breath, worried about her fiancé. "I haven't heard from either since they left the country. Not even by text."

"Neither have I, but I sent a message to both of them, and we contacted the Secret Service about five minutes ago to let them know President Spendorf arrived at Walter Reed. Unfortunately, he's in no condition to run the country, and Peach has taken it upon himself to take charge in the VP's absence. Congress is backing Peach since he's in the States, and I don't know how to shove the ogre back in the can."

Help Is On The Way

Agent Kelly, CDC Director Ryan Chugson, and Dr. Alex were on a conference call with Dr. Jennings' team in Colorado and a small team of WHO biologists from several countries.

"We have been working with bioengineers to separate the MRSA DNA," a Swiss engineer reported. "Vancomycin alone doesn't touch the virus. Three out of four mice died of heart disease within a few days. All ended up with a deadly bone infection."

"That's interesting news, and our team is working on re-engineering cells of Virus X by separating the helix into two single strands of RNA," explained a Swiss engineer.

"What happens when you add Vitamin C?" Kelly asked.

The virologist from Amsterdam replied, "High doses prevent viral cell growth, strengthen cell walls, and inhibit viral replication. However, monitoring red blood cell counts is important as it also increases iron absorption. And Vitamin C kills the superbugs."

"What dosage rate?" Agent Kelly asked.

"We used 35 mg. Vitamin C per kg. body weight per day, so an average of 2,000-3,500 mg. IV for a person weighing 57-100 kilos or 125-220 pounds."

Dr. Alex asked, "Anything new on the horizon?"

A French biologist added, "We tried ADEP. It's a new drug that wakes up a person's immune system and fights off the virus. It worked well in chimps, but we haven't tried it in humans."

Ryan asked, "Any side effects?"

"None to date, but we've only been testing for two months at various dosages," the biologist replied.

A team from China shared graphs and extensively discussed their research. "Some biologists have researched stem cells, but Virus X is not pure. We found mycoviruses."

"Yes, same here." Alex agreed. "Both astronauts had an atypical fungus attached to the Virus X DNA, which infected the lungs."

"So, the patients have a fungus ball in their lungs?" a Swiss engineer asked."

Dr. Alex reported, "Yes, and we've had minimal success treating the deadly fungus with the newest Echinocandins. The fungus alone is not contagious but deadly.

During the presentation, a biologist from France presented a series of X-rays. "We found that administering high doses of corticosteroids along with IV Vitamin C, thiamin, and Vfend with an Echinocandins (Anidulafungin) proved the most effective treatment. As evidence, you can see the fungus disappeared by the second day."

"It always fascinates me that we all share the same form of DNA, whether a virus, bacteria, or plant, and we each find different ways to treat complications." Dr. Alex said.

Director Choy, the Director of WHO, asked about the recovery of two victims of the RR team.

Agent Kelly reported, "Liz Brakinsky's vital signs have stabilized since using Dr. Jennings' initial vaccine. We modified the vaccine based on a Swiss engineer's recommendations for Peggy Wyller, who is now off the ventilator and gaining strength, although she is still confused sometimes."

"How's the president?" Dr. Jennings asked.

"President Spendorf is still in a medically induced coma and on a ventilator, but we see less lung congestion." Dr. Alex added, "Thanks for all your input, and keep us posted if anything new develops. So far, anyone vaccinated before being infected has remained healthy. We need more doses to inoculate the masses."

"Yes," Dr. Jennings seemed excited, "we have 22 companies working on it, including some overseas in Amsterdam, China, and Paris. While the vaccine is not fully tested, it is working. Some U.S. companies are ramping up in California, Colorado, Pennsylvania, Massachusetts, Texas, and Georgia."

Agent Kelly reported, "We found contaminated wine that contained Virus X and caused an outbreak in Damascus, Syria. General Rutoon had shipped the wine to several other countries, but our government notified all their officials to decline shipments. Fortunately, there are no signs of infection, and the vaccine will be available to their citizens."

Dr. Choy added, "I plan to travel to Syria to open a plant there, but religious conflicts make it challenging. I'll inform you of my progress."

"Thanks." Dr. Alex reviewed an update on the most recent data on the vaccine treatment. "I'm working on a hybrid stem cell generator to individualize treatment for each patient. I would appreciate any input."

Both the Swiss engineer and the French biologist agreed to assist.

Dr. Alex's face lit up, and he appeared ten years younger as he quickly summarized the results, "Thanks for the great teamwork. The infection rate has dropped in half in the U.S., Switzerland, France, and China. Other major European countries are also making progress since using the vaccine, and the death rate is leveling off. Still, it's not fast enough, so I've identified a few variations in our patient's genomes that prolong the therapy's effects. I'm still researching the cause and effect of various doses and would appreciate your help. I'm forwarding the data to you. Maybe you'll find a link that will help rid this pandemic."

Finding VP Tom Harris

Vice President Tom Harris spent a grueling week traveling between countries, leaving him jet-lagged and disoriented. His eyes involuntarily closed during his last meeting while his head throbbed with each heartbeat. He boarded Air Force 2 and flew to Syria, but he was diverted from landing in Damascus because the area was under siege. Finally reaching Al-Qisa, Harris could rest, but he didn't sleep.

His thoughts were sluggish at sunrise as he lay on a cot, drenched in sweat. Despite the rotating fan's squeak, the air didn't reach his skin. Harris' memory failed him, wondering what happened as the light pink of dawn filtered through the broken blinds. A faint sound of a morning prayer echoed, reminding Harris that he had flown into Syria.

Upon hearing a knock, Harris opened his eyes to find a stranger, a petite woman in a white dress, entering the room without waiting for an invitation. She removed her sunglasses and greeted him as vice president.

The VP slid from the bed and threw on his robe. "Guess I slept in. Where's Rafe?"

"You mean that lean, blue-eyed, handsome hunk I passed in the hallway?"

Harris laughed, "I never saw him quite like that, but he might have blue eyes."

The woman plumped the pillow, pulled the sheets up, and made the bed. She straightened a tipped glass on the bedside table. "He says to meet him for breakfast in five minutes on the outdoor patio."

"Thanks. I didn't catch your name," Harris said.

"Nope, I never threw it." She smiled and left the room.

He later recognized her as the woman following him, but he was still clueless when she swept through the door.

"You must be Rafe," Harris heard her say from the hallway. "Vice President Harris will meet you shortly. Would you like a full breakfast or just coffee?"

"Harris will have black coffee with steaming hot water, an overeasy egg, and multigrain toast if available," Rafe requested. "Just black coffee for me. I'll make my own protein shake later."

"You got it, handsome."

Rafe poked his head into the room. "How'd you sleep?"

"Terrible, but I heard you snoring clear out in the hall."

"That bad, huh? As Zac would put it, 'like a hibernating bear.' At least one of us caught some z's."

Harris pointed at the door. "Who's your admirer?"

Rafe approached the bed and pointed to a small electronic bug under the pillow. He placed a finger over his lips and then spoke loudly, "I don't have a name, but she seems nice enough." Rafe retrieved his bug detector.

Harris stepped into the bathroom to wash up and get dressed. When Harris returned, Rafe had found an electronic bug behind the bedside table, another along the doorjamb, and one inside the phone receiver.

"Mind if I use your bathroom?" Rafe checked the privy and found another device under the medicine cabinet. He disposed of all but the one behind the table as a tease and radioed a code to warn the team, "How's Rover?" The reference to the imaginary beagle had been tested many times in the past. The security team had been alerted.

Harris got the message. "Let's eat. I'm starving."

As they entered the hallway, Rafe spotted a bug on the underside of the top stair railing. He inactivated it but left the device in place.

Unsure if there were more bugs, VP Harris whispered, "That little minx is quite the housekeeper."

Rafe pulled a pen and notepad from his pocket and wrote. "We'll use this plant as a decoy and make sure she gets special information as needed."

Harris wrote, "Hope she doesn't spike the coffee."

"I'll taste yours before drinking mine," Rafe scribbled. "But I won't touch the egg."

The two men spoke about their pets and family while feverishly writing back and forth.

Rafe whispered into his radio attached to his hip pocket, "We'll dine on the patio."

"It's a clear day," came across the radio.

* * *

Cordy traced the blue GPS signal from VP Harris' watch as it zigzagged in a Z-formation, similar to going up and down stairs. She wished for a body camera on Harris to locate him. Once the signal stabilized, she messaged Braun, "Located VP Harris," and sent him the coordinates. "What's your ETA?"

"Fifteen minutes." Braun sent a phone number to call and picked up on the first ring. "Not much time to talk, but hearing your voice again is great."

Cordy cleared her throat to mask her emotions. "When did you land?"

"Usher met with his contact and five police officers an hour ago. The police know where Harris is staying, and they have been monitoring the building since the VP arrived last night. Haya is present, but there's no sign of the other two men."

"Are you safe?"

"As safe as it ever gets in Syria," Braun said.

"Wish you wore body cameras so I can see what's happening."

"No such luck," Braun replied.

"Will VP Harris hold peace talks with the president of Syria?" Cordy asked. "It is one of Zac's highest priorities."

"I heard that the Syrian president arrived an hour ago. Sadly, several officials and colleagues have contracted the virus, and seven have lost their lives. Three top officials couldn't travel due to the virus. It was discovered that they received a case of infected wine from President Spendorf. Thankfully, the Syrian president was not infected with Virus X since he doesn't consume alcohol. Harris is scheduled to meet today to address civil rights violations, chemical warfare, and the viral outbreak will also be discussed during the meeting."

"Cordy said, "We need to initiate a vaccine program ASAP.""

Braun warned, "A deadly outbreak is eminent because members of ISIL will refuse the vaccine."

"Perhaps the president will set an example for his people by getting vaccinated. As a trained physician, he understands the importance of this vaccine," Cordy said. "Mention that to VP Harris when you see him."

"I'll do my best, but no promises."

"Hurry back to the States," Cordy said. "Peach is making a farce of our government. He ordered all infected patients to be shipped to Barrow, Alaska. Fortunately, even Congress refused to follow that order. Instead, bodies are piling up in a mass grave in New York City, and Peach plans to cremate the whole lot at noon today."

"Can't Congress control him?" Braun asked.

"Peach Twitters all day long," Cordy said. "No one even knows when he's telling the truth or lying. Just bring back VP Harris. We're doing everything we can to get President Spendorf back on his feet, but it'll be months before he's healthy enough to return to the office."

"The odd part is that VP Harris thinks he's the acting president," Braun said. "Which is logical, but Congress is only listening to Peach. Harris has no say in what's happening inside the country, yet he's meeting the president of Syria under his new role. Hopefully, Peach's stupid rulings won't scare other nations."

"Guy Weimer tried to have an interview with President Spendorf to televise over CNN and FOX News, but Zac wasn't coherent enough to make any sense, so it was a failure. Thank goodness, it wasn't a live feed."

"I guess that means Guy is back from the hospital," Braun said.

"Yes, but he hasn't gotten any smarter." Cordy blew out a deep breath. "Even Carl Wyller has wised up after Peggy became ill. He's finding out the facts before spouting off."

"We are almost at the meeting place where the elders, Governor, Colonel, Chief of Police, and the Syrian president will meet Vice President Harris." Braun rushed on before disconnecting, "Security measures are in place, and the Secret Service guards are collaborating with Usher's team to ensure safety before the arrival of any personnel."

"How large is Al-Qisa?" Cordy asked.

"Total population is around 41,000 people," Braun's voice sounded choppy. "Our jeep is rumbling down a hole-pocked road, which is getting narrower by the second. There are dusty ridges baked into a once muddy path. I see about a dozen jeeps parked up ahead and several men in turbans carrying AK-47 Kalashnikov rifles. Better sign off now. This is a burner phone, so no calls, and don't text again until you hear from me. Usher's GPS tracker is orange, and mine's purple."

The two lights came to life on Cordy's screen. "Be careful," she whispered, but he had disconnected the call.

Rutoon lay in the back seat of his getaway car. The chauffeur drove him up the wall with constant questions.

"Why are we taking only these back roads?"

"To avoid the roadblocks," Rutoon said.

"Why are you leaving D.C.?"

Rutoon scratched at his fake beard for the umpteenth time. Bits of the beard shredded and collected under his fingernails. He itched all over like his skin was crawling with bugs. "I already told you. I'm meeting my family in Pennsylvania."

"What if I get pulled over?" the driver asked. "What should I tell them?"

"Just show them my pass card." Rutoon broke out in a fit of coughing. He bolted upright and could hardly catch his breath.

"That's a nasty cough," the driver said, "Turn your head into your shoulder. I don't want to catch whatever you have. I told you there's a virus going around."

"I don't have a virus!" Rutoon demanded. "Allergies!"

Sweat drenched his toupee, making it almost impossible to keep it on his head. Rutoon noticed the driver staring at him through the rearview mirror. "Watch the road!"

"Of course, sir." The driver's eyes diverted back to the road. There was no traffic to speak of.

"Can you please go faster?" Rutoon asked as he searched through his bag for a stocking cap. He struggled to put it on without dislodging his wig. Finally succeeding, he checked himself in the rearview mirror and rested his head on the cool window. "It's too hot in here. Turn on the air conditioner?"

"The fan's already on high," the driver said.

"Not the fan, stupid," Rutoon said. "Turn down the temperature. Put it on the coolest air possible and force it back here."

The driver fiddled with the knobs, and colder air blew through the rear vent.

Rutoon wanted to kick off his shoes, cuddle under his goose-down quilt, and sleep. The down blanket might be too hot, but he loved to have it near him.

"Is it cool enough for you now?" The driver smirked into the mirror.

"Would you shut up? I'm trying to sleep."

"Fine," the driver snapped back. "I won't mention that police car that's following us."

"What?" Rutoon turned and looked over his shoulder to both sides of the car and ducked low. "I don't see one."

"Not yet, but if you don't quit barking orders at me, I'll find one," the driver said. "I just realized you're at my mercy. I could drop you off at the side of the road, and no one would find you for hours."

Rutoon's headache went up a notch. "You wouldn't dare."

"Don't test me," the driver said.

Rutoon considered strangling the man. He could throw the guy onto the road and drive himself. He took a few deep breaths and noticed his vision blurring—*not a good idea.*

A chill snatched away Rutoon's breath. His body began shivering. "Turn up the heat. I'm freezing."

The driver turned his head and stared at Rutoon. "Heat! Now you want heat? You've got the virus, don't you? I knew it!" He slammed on his brakes and pulled to the side of the road. "Get out of my car!"

"Oh n-noo! I-I'm f-f-fine! Rutoon stuttered. His whole body shook. "Please, keep going."

"That's more like it," the driver said. "No more crazy orders. Lay down and shut up. I'll wake you when we get to Pennsylvania."

Rutoon nodded. "I've already paid you."

"I know, but if I come down with that virus, I'm suing you for every penny you own."

"Fair enough. I'm not infected." Rutoon dug through his bag again, pulled on a sweatshirt over his damp clothes, threw his coat over his legs, and then curled up on the back seat. His eyes couldn't stand the bright light, and the world spun.

* * *

Forty minutes later, the driver asked, "Mr., are you awake?" There was no answer, so he pulled onto the side of the road, stopped the car, and got out. He surveyed the road. No one was in sight, so he opened the trunk, found a pair of old garden gloves, and put them on. Then, he opened the back door. He searched the man's wallet and suitcase and took whatever was of value. Moments later, he pulled the stinky, sweaty old man out of the car. The man was dead weight.

Rutoon barely groaned as the driver laid him on the side of the road in a pile of tall grass.

The driver placed the luggage next to Rutoon and stepped back. Satisfied that no one would see him while passing by, the driver climbed back into the car and drove away.

Peace Talks

It was a typical sunny day outside of Al-Qisa, Syria. The temperature was 36°C or for VP Harris, a humid 96°F. A rare gust of wind whipped up dust from the road. By noon, it would exceed 100°F, making it too hot for the black suit and dress pants worn for the meeting.

Peering over the railing of the building's patio, Harris noticed a crowd gathering across the street near a three-story building. "Is that where we're meeting the president?"

Rafe downed the rest of his coffee and patted his mouth with a napkin. "Looks like it. I can see our agents. They seem poised for our arrival." At least six Secret Service agents, including one woman, stood at ease with their suit jackets open and hands in front of their chests, ready to grab their Sig Sauer pistols at any sign of danger.

Harris glimpsed a man silhouetted on top of the roof with another sniper poised and watching from the opposite end. A SpectroDrone circled the area with high-powered laser cameras and an explosive detection system. "I have to give you credit. Usually, it takes months to prepare for a meeting like this, but we landed here by accident, and our Secret Service Team has already secured our location."

"I believe that's the president's jeep approaching," Rafe said. "Shall we greet him?"

VP Harris buttoned his suit coat. "I'm sure I'm not the only one who wants to get back home."

Rafe moved through the patio with a communications radio in his hand. Two officers snapped to attention as the door swung open, leading outside. Meeting the Syrian president, who was stepping down from the vehicle, was hardly a stroll.

"As-Salaam Alaikum, Sabah alkhayr," VP Harris held out his right hand and gave three kisses on alternating cheeks, which the Syrian president reciprocated.

An interpreter motioned for the two men to lead the way into the meeting hall.

"Kayf hal asratak?" the Syrian president asked. The interpreter repeated in English, "How is your family?"

"They are well, and yours?" Harris replied.

The interpreter smiled and relayed the message, then stepped forward. "They are also fine. Would you like some tea?"

Harris swallowed and hid his disdain for the beverage, "With much sugar."

The Syrian president belted out a deep laugh. "You need not drink tea for me. Perhaps coffee would be your preference?"

"Shokran." Harris rubbed his forehead, which brought another burst of laughter. This time, other officials joined in.

The interpreter introduced VP Harris to the Minister of Foreign Affairs, the Minister of Defense, and two elders. The interpreter motioned to the Head of the President's Guard. "This is Major General Khaled. He is honored to meet you formally."

There was a medium-sized meeting room across from the main entrance. It had a large round table surrounded by folding chairs. Khaled pulled out a chair, and the Syrian president sat at the table. He gestured for Harris and the others to take a seat.

The Syrian president spoke, and an interpreter translated his words into English for the VP's benefit. "Thank you for coming on such short notice. We have not always been on the best terms, but I wish this to change. What can you tell me about this deadly virus attacking your United States? I'm afraid a few similar cases have erupted in our country."

During a briefing, Vice President Harris informed the president that the CDC has a vaccine with an 88% effectiveness rate if administered within 24 hours of infection, but the supply is limited."

"A doctor from the WHO discussed producing the drug in Syria. How did the virus enter our country? Are other nations affected? Will the death rate continue to increase?"

"I believe it is too early to determine the outcome of this disease," Harris said, "We must work together to eradicate it. This could be the beginning of mutual agreements on other pressing issues." The meeting started positively.

* * *

Braun Hastings monitored movement and activities at the peace talks from a small niche 100 meters away. He needed the meeting to end, as it wasn't safe for Harris to stay. Braun used his handheld spotting scope to observe two Secret Service snipers on the rooftop of the building across the street where the VP stayed last night. However, he was still determining if they were positioned close enough to prevent an incident inside the building.

Usher's team surrounded the area and lay prone behind ridges, low-lying buildings, and shrubs.

Only one road ran through the town, and heavy fighting occurred less than fifty miles away. According to Usher's police contacts, Damascus was already under the military control of ISIL, who had recently joined forces with Al Qaeda. Braun wasn't taking any chances.

The Syrian president hadn't wanted to travel far for a meeting.

Rafe had warned Braun, "We're on high alert. During breakfast, I saw Syrian fighter jets flying overhead on their way to attack ISIL rebels in Damascus, so I stationed an Apache helicopter on the rooftop as a precaution for VP Harris' safety."

Three Humvees approaching from a distance caught Braun's attention. It also triggered an immediate concern with Major General Khaled, who swung his AK-47 over his shoulder and motioned for three heavily armed officers to follow him. They piled into an armored truck and drove out to intercept the intruders, blocking the road.

A U.S. drone hovered above the vehicles but didn't identify any explosives aboard.

The Humvee drivers stopped in a line. Doors opened, and men stepped out, positioning themselves at the back. A heavily armed man stood next to each vehicle, facing the Syrian officers, who still had their rifles drawn. None of the convoy members had raised a weapon.

Braun kneeled, aimed at the convoy leader in his scope, and steadied his right hand over the trigger. He saw the agents on the roof aiming as well.

Usher's interpreter silently moved to Braun's side, equipped with a radio linked to Major Khaled's frequency, so he could translate and respond to any orders. "That convoy isn't ours. Let me tell you what they are saying."

Khaled asked, "Why are you here?"

"The first driver's name is Omar. The convoy is here to speak to the Syrian president. Omar has the ISIL Commander on his radio, who agreed to a cease-fire in Damascus and wants the government to call off their air strikes."

"La!" Khaled spoke in Arabic. "He won't back down and wants to talk to the ISIL Commander."

Braun shifted his rifle to cover Omar as he moved toward Khaled.

The interpreter said, "Omar refuses to hand the radio over and says the ISIL Commander will only talk to the Syrian president. Omar gave Khaled three minutes to bring the president outside."

"Or what?" Khaled asked.

Omar said, "We take the president to our Commander." The second and third drivers moved closer.

"Not likely. We have you surrounded." Khaled motioned to the rooftop. "You'll never get to the president."

Omar said, "We want peace. Do you deny us that option? I want to hear it from the president's lips, not yours."

"Who are these men?" Braun asked the interpreter. "Should we take them out?"

"No," the interpreter said. "Wait for the Syrian president to make the decision."

"Do they know Harris is here?" Braun asked the interpreter.

"I'm sure they do, but stand down."

Everything inside Braun's brain went against that order. One of the sentries on the rooftop touched the side of his head for a few seconds. Braun was sure that the sentry had just received orders through an earpiece. The man moved to the far edge of the roof as two secret service agents and four Syrian police officers holding rifles marched from the meeting place and headed for the convoy.

Usher and his men were on the periphery, awaiting orders. All guards inside would be heavily armed to protect the VP and the Syrian officials.

Braun saw the Syrian president trying to leave through a screen door, but a policeman stopped him. During a heated argument, the president shouted at the marching men and gestured for a policeman to bring the radio.

The policeman turned on his heel, marched out of the building onto the street, and spoke into a communicator. "Bring me the radio. The president will speak to your ISIL Commanding Officer, but he's not coming outside. I will bring the radio inside to him. I want the rest of your men to climb into their vehicles and back away. Do it now."

The Syrian president gave a few more orders, and the rooftop guards crouched lower.

"What did he say?" Braun asked the interpreter.

"He wants VP Harris and the other men inside the warehouse to take cover in a safe place before anyone comes inside with the radio. Rafe is guarding Harris."

Khaled ordered one of his officers, "Frisk Omar before we head back to the meeting room."

Omar clutched the radio and held his arms over his head, allowing the officer to pat him down. "He's clear," the officer said.

"Let's go." Khaled motioned Omar to enter a waiting vehicle and turned to his officers, "Stay and ensure these vehicles retreat."

As Khaled and Omar drove back to the meeting room, the uninvited guests reluctantly moved the convoy back another mile.

Usher's men moved closer to the rear of the meeting room and pulled out a map. "Why do they need a map?" Braun asked the interpreter. "Don't they know the area?"

"These Turks come from Pakistan."

For the first time, it dawned on Braun. None of their men had first-hand experience in this land—not Usher's backup team, Harris' Secret Service agents, or the interpreter. Only by reading a map could they figure out the most accessible route to freedom, but it might not be the safest. *How could I have missed this tidbit of information?* "I need to speak with Usher NOW!"

The interpreter signaled for Braun to take cover behind some Humvees before running to the back of the building. Although this exposed Braun for fifty yards, most potential enemies were at least a mile away.

Braun zigzagged along the path to find Usher and plan their next move. He spotted Usher's men ahead and hoped to reach them without an incident to create an escape route.

Usher stood behind a tree. After a quick discussion, Usher said, "I'll have my men narrow the distance to the convoy. Stay close to the VP and make sure he boards that helicopter if danger arises. If trapped, we'll find another way out."

Braun headed back toward the VP but stopped short when Haya crossed the road between the hotel and the meeting room.

* * *

Haya balanced a tray of cups, a teapot, sugar, and a cream pitcher between her hands. Steam wafted above the cups. Haya knocked on the door, glanced through the screen, and smiled at the president. "May I come in? I have your refreshments."

The Syrian president nodded to a guard who opened the door.

Rafe stepped forward as the guard took the tray and set it on a chair inside the meeting room door.

"That will be all," the Syrian president said to Haya. "It would be safer for you to return to the hotel." He nodded to a guard who was holding the door. "Escort her back to the hotel and be sure she's safe. We don't know what to expect."

Rafe moved between Haya and Harris.

Haya pulled back her silken headdress, narrowed her eyes, and refused to budge. She turned toward the Syrian president. "I'm not afraid. You have many guards here. I will serve the tea for you, my Excellency."

The Syrian president jerked his head toward the door guard. "You have your orders. Hurry. They'll bring the radio soon."

The guard saluted, his heels clicked as he walked across the highly polished tiled floor toward Haya to follow orders.

"I'll go. I can take care of myself," Haya dashed past Rafe, the guard, and out the front door. She nearly collided with the approaching vehicle.

The Humvee screeched to a stop, and Omar jumped from the passenger's door. "Miss, are you okay? He could have hit you."

Haya briefly grabbed his offered hand, slipped him a hidden knife, and quickly pulled away, "Watch where you're going!" She fled in front of the vehicle and ran into the hotel.

* * *

The guard assigned to escort Haya stood in the road, confused, turning toward the hotel and back to the meeting room. The Syrian president waved him away, so he hurriedly walked toward the hotel.

Rafe moved beside VP Harris and whispered, "Don't eat or drink anything."

The Syrian president was impatient. "Hurry and bring that radio. You delay our talks."

Omar moved to the front door and was introduced to the door guard. "He's the convoy's lead driver," Khaled said. "I'll stay outside with Omar while our president speaks to the Commander. Then, I'll take the radio and Omar back to his troop." Khaled reached for Omar's radio to deliver it to the Syrian president.

Omar turned toward Khaled, still clutching the radio. "I want to talk to the president."

"You aren't allowed to get near him, given that no one here is trustworthy. Just give me the radio. You don't get to take it in. You are uninvited here, and I don't care who sent you." He grabbed the radio and shoved it into his assistant's hands. The assistant inspected the radio, then went inside and handed it to the president.

"Salaam Alaikum," the president said into the radio.

There was much static, and the president repeated his greeting. "Who am I speaking to?"

Nothing Goes As Planned

Braun had discovered that Haya and Aqib had negotiated their freedom from prison last year by offering up key Syrian officials during a chemical weapon probe. They provided a video as proof of two attacks on Syrian citizens by the rebels. Braun suspected the couple was also on the rebels' side, but were they a threat to VP Harris?

Braun needed answers to many questions. *What was the likelihood of Haya on site today, and why had the couple followed VP Harris? Were they working with General Rutoon? Had they delivered the tainted wine? Had they only provided it to Syrian officials, or had bottles of wine also reached Afghanistan and Russia?*

Braun startled when gunfire erupted from the hotel and turned in time to see a guard duck behind the Humvee. His eyes flew open, and a scream, cut short by Omar's sharp blade slicing his throat, died in the dusty breeze.

Omar hopped into the Humvee, which was still running, and drove around to the back of the hotel.

Braun raised his rifle and bolted to the rear of the hotel, along with four other agents, following the sound of rapid gunfire. Rafe had promised he'd get the VP aboard the waiting helicopter on the roof at the first sign of danger, so Braun put that out of his mind as he ran toward the corner of the hotel. He needed to discover how Haya and Aqib were involved in this attack.

Omar yelled, "Hurry, Haya! Aqib is waiting."

The first thing Braun noticed as he rounded the corner was the smell of blood and gunpowder. The Syrian policeman assigned to protect Haya lay sprawled on the back steps in a pool of blood.

Shadowy figures moved along the tree line several meters to the right. They wore gas masks and carried assault weapons.

Haya flipped a mask over her face and headed for the Humvee.

Braun yanked a gas mask from his vest pocket and hit his radio transmitter, giving orders, "Gas masks on now. Seven men armed with canisters and weapons. Haya and the driver are at the rear of the hotel. I want Haya alive."

"Roger," Usher said. "Rafe, do you have the VP loaded yet?"

"No, the Syrian president is laying out peace guidelines, and VP Harris doesn't want to miss this opportunity," Rafe said.

"Have him send an e-mail," Braun said. "We need to get Harris out now, fully geared with a gas mask. As soon as I fire, all hell will break loose. Do you read me?"

"The convoy is slowing down," Usher said. "I'm going to strike before the men leave their vehicles."

"Roger." Braun motioned for the agents to take the men advancing from the bushes, and he'd take the vehicle Haya was heading for. "I want a coordinated strike in ten seconds," Braun said. The agents next to Braun dropped to their knees. "Three, two, one!"

Bullets ripped through the air, tearing apart the Humvee's windshield and the upper dashboard. Bright red splotches on the driver's side confirmed the driver hit. Haya bolted from the vehicle, running back into the hotel. A bullet pinged off the metal, hitting her in the leg. She dropped and rolled, then continued limping toward the back door. A trail of blood followed behind her.

The agents fired methodically at the figures hidden in the bushes. One rebel tossed a gas canister through the air, spraying a mist toward Braun. It was the only canister to hit the air.

Braun moved briskly to the driver's door, still firing. The side window was nothing but glass shards. Red stains streaked the steering wheel and dashboard. A bulletproof tactical vest protected the driver's chest, so Braun fired a bullet through the driver's head before opening the door.

He caught movement in the rear of the truck and ducked just in time as a bullet whizzed by his ear. Unable to determine how many people were in the back of the truck, Braun returned fire with a volley of shots. Braun came from the passenger's side to peer inside when the smoke cleared.

A small armory of gear sat in the back, covered in blood. Braun hardly recognized Aqib's body hovering over a laptop. He managed to wrestle the computer free of the dead man's grip, grabbed a shirt lying on the floor, and wiped off most of the grime and gore before shoving the laptop into his backpack.

Gunfire erupted to the east, where Usher and his men opened fire on the convoy. Then, to Braun's surprise, he heard gunshots from the meeting room. "Rafe, is the VP safe?"

Braun raced toward the meeting room. "Rafe, come in!"

There was no response. Another shot rang out.

"Usher, to the meeting room, STAT! VP under fire," Braun said as he pushed through the entrance to the building. He vaulted over a dead body and recognized him as the second man in VP Harris' photos.

The president's guard stood over Haya's body with a gun in his hand. "I had to shoot. She was going to kill the VP. I had to shoot."

Braun glanced around the room and spotted the Syrian president crouched by the wounded Minister of Foreign Affairs, who had a bullet in his shoulder. "Where's Harris?"

"On the roof," the president said. The Defense Minister lay on the other side of the room. He had suffered a leg wound, and one of the officers attended to him. The elders had disappeared.

Braun moved to check the men's injuries. "We'll fly you to the nearest hospital."

"No, I'll make sure they get medical assistance," the president said. "I'm sorry I sent a policeman to protect that woman. I heard that he's dead, too."

Braun nodded. "Anyone else hurt?"

"The VP is safe. Rafe took a bullet in the chest," the president said.

"I thought he always wore a bulletproof vest," Braun said.

"He did, but when all the shooting occurred, he demanded Harris wear it instead. It did save the VP's life," the president said.

Usher dashed through the entrance. "Convoy clear."

The helicopter blades whirred to life from the rooftop. Braun's eyes scanned over Usher. "You all right?"

Usher nodded. "Let's hitch a ride before the chopper leaves." They dashed up the steps to the roof.

One of the elders and an interpreter held the trap door open. "The president said you were on your way. VP Harris agreed to send us the vaccine as soon as he gets back to Washington, D.C., but first, they're heading to Tel Aviv to get medical treatment for Rafe."

"Thanks," Braun said over his shoulder. Usher hunched low and waited until the helicopter pilot motioned them aboard. Braun turned toward Rafe. "How bad is it?"

Rafe stifled a groan.

"Trouble breathing?" Braun asked.

"A little," Rafe said. Braun checked the wound and listened to his chest. He watched both sides of his chest rise with each breath. Braun poked at the area to see if the skin crackled, a sign air was leaking from his lungs. "There's a slight amount of swelling, but not bad. I'm going to put this ammo pack over the wound as direct pressure to prevent further bleeding."

"He took a bullet for me." VP Harris' voice was unsteady. He appeared pale and sweaty. "We have to save him."

"How long before we reach Tel Aviv?" Braun asked the pilot who had maneuvered the flight off the roof.

"Roughly 215 miles as the crow flies, so a little over two and a half hours," the pilot said. "I've called ahead, and an ambulance will meet us."

Braun turned to the crew, "Got any morphine?"

"Med pack in the back," the pilot said.

Usher was closer to the rear, rummaging through a medic bag. "Yup, a year's supply. IV equipment, too."

Braun took Rafe's pulse and did an initial assessment, checking fingernail beds, pupils, and vision.

"What did you get?" Usher asked.

"Strong at 120 beats per minute," Braun said. "Needs fluid. Anyone here a medic?"

When no one answered, Braun held out his hand, "We'll work as a team."

"It's not the first time, and probably won't be our last." Usher handed him a syringe and a bottle of Morphine. "I'll start an IV of

Ringers. Sorry, Rafe, I'm not that pretty blonde you nearly fainted over when she drew your blood work last year."

"You would remember that," Rafe said and attempted a laugh but choked it back with a moan. "Just do your stuff."

Braun drew up the Morphine, spiked a bag of Ringer's, and connected it to the IV tubing. "Let me know when you're ready."

Usher hit the vein on the first attempt and connected the catheter to the IV tubing. He held everything firmly in place until Braun taped the catheter down.

Braun gave Rafe 10 mg. of Morphine IV. "Sweet dreams. If it doesn't ease the pain, let me know. There's more where that came from."

Once Rafe was asleep, Braun placed a call to Cordy. "We're safe and on our way to Tel Aviv."

"Tel Aviv, why?" Cordy asked. "Was VP Harris injured? Are you hurt? What about Usher?"

"Relax, we're fine," Braun said. "Rafe was shot in the chest, so we're were flying directly to the hospital. How are President Spendorf and the RR team?"

"Zac's getting antsy," Cordy said. "I'm not sure if it's the confusion that leads to violence or if he's on the mend and can't stand to be grounded. Liz has a left-sided weakness but is stabilizing. Peggy is off the vent but fades in and out of consciousness. She's not out of the woods yet. I have some good news. A policeman found Rutoon's body alongside a road not far from the Pennsylvania border. An autopsy showed that he'd been infected with Virus X."

"There's justice in the world after all," Braun said.

"When will I see you again?" Cordy asked.

VP Harris piped up, "Ask her if she can bring a vial of vaccine to Tel Aviv. I promised the Syrian president we'd get him enough doses to cover his family, top officials, and anyone he believes is infected."

"I heard that," Cordy said. "How long will you be in Tel Aviv?"

"Everyone here is exhausted," Braun said. "We'll swear in VP Harris as soon as the chopper lands. We even have a news crew meeting us there."

"There may be a problem, Braun," Cordy warned. "Acting President Peach may not step down so easily. What's the law on this? Will it have to go to the Supreme Court?"

"I doubt it," Cordy said. "Guy Weimer and Carl Wyller have been tracking Peach's activities. He's dangerous. I want him out as much as the next, but how?"

"We'll figure it out," Braun said. "So, how about catching a flight to Tel Aviv? I'd love to see you. You can be here by this time tomorrow."

"I'll talk to Dr. Jennings and get enough vaccine for all of you and the Syrian president," Cordy said.

"Have you been vaccinated?" Braun asked.

"Definitely, and so has Chief Jackson."

Rafe gasped, "I can't breathe!"

"Gotta go, LYA." Braun didn't wait for a reply before disconnecting the call.

Rafe's lips were purple. His skin had broken out in a cold sweat, and his pulse was up to 180 per minute. "He's bleeding out."

Usher grabbed an oxygen mask and tried to put it over Rafe's face.

"Get away. I can't breathe." Rafe tried to sit up. He was pulling at his IV.

"More Morphine," Braun said as he was already drawing up another dose. "Lie down! You've opened your wound."

Usher and two other agents held Rafe down while Braun administered 10 more mg. Morphine IV.

Rafe's chest was puffy over the right side around the bullet wound. Every time he took a breath, air seeped between his lungs and skin.

"Damn, he has a sucking chest wound—collapsed right lung," Braun said. "If we don't stop the leak, we'll lose him." Braun rummaged through the medical bag, came up with some saran wrap, and taped the edges to seal off the wound. "Give me a #14 gauge IV needle."

Usher found the needle and some Betadine. He washed Rafe's chest around the 2nd rib from the clavicle on the right side. "Okay, hold him still."

Braun inserted the needle just under the second rib. He knew he was in the right spot when a distinctive pop sounded as the trapped air rushed free, allowing his collapsed lung more room for expansion. "Turn him on his right side and make sure he keeps that O2 mask in place," Braun asked the pilot. "How much longer to Tel Aviv?"

"Still forty minutes," the pilot said.

"That long?" Braun said.

"I've pushed this bird to its upper limits. We can't go any faster."

Braun glanced at Usher. "Let's hope we can keep him breathing."

Reporters swarmed the area as the VP's rescue helicopter landed in Tel Aviv. Two paramedics pushed through the crowd to load Rafe onto a stretcher, urgently calling for an OR STAT.

Rafe wouldn't leave Harris until Braun threatened him. "If they don't fix your lung, you'll never return to duty."

Harris placed his hand in Rafe's. "Thanks for saving my life. Now, get well. Do you hear me? I'm not ready to train a new bodyguard, even if I am acting president. That's your job."

"Right." Rafe signaled for the paramedics to take him off the helicopter. He tightly grasped Braun's wrist as they approached the door and warned, "Bring him home safely, or I'll show up at your doorstep. It won't be pretty."

"You can count on me." Braun placed his other hand over Rafe's as he promised not to fail him. The EMTs moved Rafe from the helicopter through the crowd to an awaiting ambulance.

Braun scanned the crowd from the doorway. Satisfied all was safe, he stepped aside.

VP Harris approached the podium to thunderous applause. The U.S. flag waved in the breeze while a brass band stood to the left of a small raised wooden platform. Reporters yelled questions.

A judge in a black robe approached with a Bible and motioned for silence. "Are you ready to take the presidential oath?"

"Yes, sir, I am," Harris said.

The Judge leaned in and whispered, "I have special permission from your Chief Justice to swear you in as acting president of the United States. Although I am not a federal judge, I am a U.S. citizen with a law degree from Harvard. I now serve as a Supreme Court Justice for Israel with dual citizenship."

Vice President Harris nodded in gratitude.

The Judge moved to the microphone. "It is my honor to witness today the swearing-in of the acting president of the United States."

The Judge held up a Bible, and Harris placed his left hand on it while raising his right.

"I, Thomas James Harris, solemnly swear to execute the office of President of the United States faithfully and to preserve, protect, and defend the Constitution of the United States to the best of my ability, so help me, God."

The Judge extended his hand. "Congratulations, Mr. President." A band struck up Hail to the Chief, and massive applause rang out.

President Harris didn't stick around for questions. His bodyguards immediately escorted Harris to an awaiting armored limousine and headed to the Tel Aviv Sourasky Medical Center to check on Rafe.

Braun and Usher followed behind in another car. When they arrived at the medical center, Rafe was still in the OR. President Harris and his team settled into a private waiting room until the OR doctor could update them on Rafe's condition. In the meantime, Harris contacted Winston Willoughby to issue an expedited official order.

Winston informed Harris, "Agent Cordelia will arrive in Tel Aviv at 0300 with four vaccine vials. Dr. Chugson suggests all agents get vaccinated, and I booked Cordy a room in your hotel." Winston chuckled when he added, "I recommend one of the agents meet Cordy at the airport. I'm sure Agent Braun Hastings will be eager for the assignment."

President Harris laughed. "I'm sure you're right. I'll ask him in a moment. While I have you on the phone, arrange for Rafe Seaman's transfer to Walter Reed Hospital when his condition stabilizes. He's still in the PACU, but a Recovery Room nurse stopped by a moment ago. Rafe made it out of surgery. I'll know more after talking to his physician."

Harris disconnected the call and turned to Braun. "This is your first official order from your president. Meet Agent Cordelia's plane at 0300 at the airport and bring her back to the hotel. Can I count on you to do that?"

Braun stood up and gave a crisp salute. "It would be my honor, sir."

Impeach Peach

Back in Houston, Texas, Lector Peach held his own news conference. Reporters flocked to hear him, expecting a formal resignation from the Presidency, and offering a smooth transition to Acting President Harris.

So when Peach blurted out, "I'm the president! How dare he usurp my power?" The announcement caused excitement and confusion that soon led to an uproar of angry people.

Peach was delighted by the response initially, believing the people were angry that the government was trying to replace him with Harris. That was until someone threw a rock at him and yelled, "Impeach Peach!"

"This way, Speaker Peach." A secret service agent rushed him through the crowd to a waiting limo as the chants echoed louder and more rocks flew his way.

"I'm not the Speaker," Peach shouted to the agent over the din. "I was President Peach when I arrived, and I'm still the president until I declare otherwise." He refused to get into the car. The argument ended abruptly as the crowd converged with yells and shouts, and the agent forced Peach into the armored vehicle.

As the armored limousine raced through the crowd, police surrounded it with escorts in front and back.

The agent handed his cell phone over to Peach. "The Chief Justice is on the speakerphone. He demands to talk to you."

"I knew it!" Peach beamed and grabbed the phone. "Yes, your honor. I'm here to accept the official presidency. I'm sure that's why you've called."

The Chief Justice hesitated, "By the authority vested in me by the U.S. Constitution, I formally swore in Vice President Harris as acting president. Thank you for your service in his absence. You may now return to your normal duties as Speaker of the House."

"What?" Peach's eyes narrowed into an intense stare. He saw red. "This can't be happening. I'm the president!" Peach stared at the cell phone and screamed, "You can't take away my presidency. I've worked my whole life for this."

"Speaker Peach, calm down," the Chief Justice said.

"No, I won't calm down." Peach clenched his teeth and slammed the phone against the window, shattering the device. His whole body shook as he ranted nonsense. "I'm president."

The secret service agent ducked as Peach swung a fist at his face. "Let me out of this car! I must speak to my people." Peach pounded on the door, but it wouldn't budge. Then, he grabbed for the agent's gun. The men struggled until Peach started gasping for air. "I can't breathe. Get me some air. Open the windows." He clutched his chest. Peach's neck veins bulged, and his heartbeats roared in his ears. "Help me!"

The agent radioed to the police car in front of the line. "Take us to Kindred Hospital Houston Medical Center. I think Speaker Peach is having a heart attack!"

"That's president," eked from Peach's lips. Then, he slumped onto the agent.

The quick-thinking agent checked Peach's neck. "No pulse. Hurry." He began CPR as best he could in the cramped limo.

Sirens blared as the procession of cars turned into the hospital lot. A team of medical professionals rushed out to meet the limousine. Within seconds, Peach was on a gurney and rushed inside the ED.

Twenty minutes later, after extensive resuscitation efforts, the doctor pronounced the death of Speaker Lector Peach.

The news hit the streets like wildfire. The police had their hands full, but law and order prevailed on Houston's streets by nightfall.

A Day to Remember

Agent Cordelia's hands tried to contain the bouncing knee that kept time to her rapid heartbeat as the aircraft jolted to a stop outside of Tel Aviv's Ben Gurion International Airport. It was the busiest airport in Israel, and she wasn't sure where she would find Braun.

Her feet felt like blocks of wood after sitting for nearly twelve hours. She never could sleep on a plane, and now she was worn out to the point she felt nauseated, but she couldn't wait to see her fiancé again. It felt like years since they'd last set eyes on one another.

Nor could she wait to see his face when she gave him her gifts. She made them, especially with Braun in mind—a tracking pen with an electronic bug sweeper, a few extras, and a tie tack with a camera for two-way communication. Cordy had worked hard to design the devices and then handed the plans over to her trusted expert craftsman, Dr. Quint Atari, to craft the end product, but she would never have to worry about Braun's whereabouts ever again.

It took forever to taxi and deactivate the safety precautions. Hearing the ding overhead, Cordy wrenched open her seatbelt and joined the crowd in the aisle, waiting for the plane door to open. Her wedged backpack was bulky from the thermal cooler nestled inside, and she removed her bag from the overhead luggage rack only using brute force.

It took twenty minutes to go through Immigration and Customs before she could hunt down her fiancé. There was a large crowd next to a coffee shop, but her eyes only noticed a handsome blond who stood a head taller than all the rest. She flung herself into Braun's open arms.

"You made it." Braun held her as if there were no tomorrow before he moved her to arms' length. "I've been doing a lot of thinking. I've missed you so much that I can't wait any longer to make you mine."

"I've missed you, too." Cordy pulled Braun closer. "It has been forever."

Usher came up behind Cordy and gave her a gentle embrace. "Good to see you again. We're glad you're safe." He held out a box wrapped in silver paper. It's from Braun, but he dropped it the moment he saw you."

Cordy took the gift. "I have one for you, too, but you'll have to open it later when we're alone." She shook the silver box and listened, disappointed that it didn't rattle. "Should I open it here?"

"It can also wait until we're in the air."

Cordy opened her backpack and crammed the box inside. It was a tight fit. Her clothes were nestled inside a plastic bag next to her laptop, Braun's present, and the serum box took up most of the room. She couldn't rezip her backpack. "What do you mean, in the air?"

"There's been a change in plans." Braun smiled that lopsided grin she loved and felt her gut flutter. "Acting President Harris has arranged everything. We leave within the hour."

Cordy let out a groan. "We're leaving tonight?"

Usher handed Cordy his communicator before she could ask any more questions. "The acting president wants to talk to you."

Harris' face entered the screen on Usher's device. His voice was crisp and clear. "Welcome. I hope you had a nice flight."

Cordy's cheeks burned with embarrassment. "I had no idea you would be here." She turned and glanced around the airport. The crowd was thinning. "Where are you?"

Braun cleared his throat. "He's waiting on Air Force One."

Cordy nodded and spoke into the device, "Congratulations, Mr. President."

"Thanks," Harris said. "We just heard that Lector Peach is dead, so we're heading home tonight before Congress gets any more bright ideas."

Cordy gasped, "What happened?"

"Peach heard from the Chief Justice that he had me sworn in as acting president. Peach became upset about returning as Speaker of the House and suffered a heart attack. He died on the way to the hospital."

"I'm sorry he's gone, but it does take care of one problem," Cordy said. "I was afraid he wouldn't step down quietly. President Spendorf will be glad to hear from you."

"I already talked to Zac," Harris said. "He's still in ICU but will return to the Oval Office in a few months. I hope I can keep the country at peace until then. I know you just arrived, but I thought we'd take you back to Washington, D.C., with us."

"That's an honor, sir," Cordy said, remembering her mission. "Who will deliver the vaccine to Syria?"

"You can give it to Dr. Kim," Acting President Harris said. "He's the leader of Israel's healthcare research team, consults for the WHO, and looks forward to working with the CDC on this virus. He's waiting at baggage claim."

"I didn't dare part with the vaccine," Cordy said. "It's in my backpack, and I didn't bring any other luggage."

"Where are you now?"

"At the coffee shop located across from my arrival gate."

"I'll sign off and have an agent bring Dr. Kim to you at the coffee shop."

As they waited for security to escort the WHO consultant, Cordy's eyes darted around the crowded shop. The urgency of the situation was palpable. There was no room to sit, so she positioned herself at the end of a counter near the door, ready to intercept Dr. Kim.

Usher and Braun stood behind Cordy as she placed her backpack on the counter's edge and fished around to retrieve the vaccine stuffed at the bottom of her bag. It wasn't easy to reach. She removed the silver package, a bag of clothes, her laptop, and finally, the Styrofoam pack and set it beside her bag.

A woman in a hijab, sitting on a high stool beside Cordy in the bustling cafe, glanced up, slid her red purse over, and moved her water glass aside to make more room on the counter.

"Last call to place your order," the waitress said above the din. "We close in fifteen minutes."

Another plane must have landed because several backpackers swarmed the coffee shop's doorway, jostling Cordy as they entered the area.

Cordy placed her clothes in the bottom of the bag, wedged her laptop along the side, and rearranged items to stuff the vaccine box back into her bag to keep them safe, fearing the crowd might knock them off the counter during the mad rush to get refreshments.

Constant chatter echoed from the airport intercom, and the crowd closed in around Cordy.

Someone tapped Cordy's arm. She glanced up to find a man dressed in a white cotton tunic standing at her side. "Hello. I am most honored to meet you. My name is Dr. Kim." His raven-colored braid fell over his shoulder as he bowed.

Cordy returned his greeting. "I'm happy to meet you. One moment, She reached into her backpack. I have it right here."

The lady in the hijab bumped into Cordy as she hopped from the chair at the counter. "Excuse me. They just called my flight." She cleared the counter, stuffed a few items into her purse, wrapped the strap around her shoulder, and fled.

New patrons quickly moved in to fill the woman's vacated spot.

Cordy continued to rummage through her backpack, her heart pounding with the weight of the mission. She finally located the lumpy Styrofoam package with the precious contents inside. "Finally," she breathed, relieved that the vaccine was almost in Dr. Kim's hands. She handed the Styrofoam container, with its life-saving cargo, to Dr. Kim. "I'm glad this arrived safely and is now in your care."

He checked the box, which was still packed in ice. "Thank you, Agent Cordelia. I must go. My flight for Syria is already loading, and the agent at the gate is waiting for my return."

"Wait, I'll go with you." Cordy stuffed her laptop into her backpack and slipped a strap over her shoulder. "There are some details I need to share with you."

Cordy walked quickly beside Dr. Kim as he headed for the plane and passed along the information on how to use the vaccine. When they neared his gate, Cordy waved. "Have a safe flight."

Braun and Usher were two steps behind, darting around passengers and luggage. Braun called out, "Let's go, Cordy. Harris is waiting."

"I'm coming. I'll meet you on the plane."

"Okay, but hurry," Braun warned and talked with Usher as they walked away.

Cordy rushed to catch up to Braun and remembered she hadn't delivered all the information about the vaccine. She turned. "Dr. Kim. Wait up!"

He paused at the boarding gate.

Cordy dashed toward him. "I have Dr. Jennings' phone number in case you need more information on the vaccine. Call her with any questions and fill her in if there are more cases."

Dr. Kim nodded. "Thanks again, Agent Cordelia." He peered up at the security camera. It beeped approval of his ID, and he disappeared down the ramp.

Cordy glanced around the airport. *Where am I supposed to board Air Force One? There won't be a gate posted on a kiosk.* She dashed past the coffee counter. No one was around, and the shop had closed for the night. "Braun? Where are you?"

Cordy nearly missed the special gate when Braun stepped back off the ramp. "There you are. I was afraid you decided to go to Syria after all." He flashed a smile. "But I knew you would find me. You always do."

Cordy blew out a deep breath. "I have a solution for that." She beamed. "It's here in my backpack." Her heart thudded against her chest as she remembered the silver package. "Oh, no! I misplaced the present you gave me. I laid it down on the counter when I removed the box for Dr. Kim."

She dashed back to the closed coffee shop with Braun in tow. "How could I? I lost your gift." She searched the counter, moved cushions from the chairs, and looked in the trash can next to the area. The silver package was nowhere. A thought raced through her mind. "I think that woman with the red purse might have taken it," Cordy said. "I don't know why, but she seemed in a hurry to leave and nearly ran over me."

"It's not a problem," Braun said. "I can get another one when we return to the States."

"But…" Cordy protested. He stole her words with a kiss. "I mean it. Don't worry about the gift. Promise me."

"Okay. I guess."

"There's fresh coffee brewing on the jet. I'll get you a cup, and you can relax." Braun grabbed her hand, and they hurried to board.

Cordy sipped coffee and had settled in a cushioned chair on Air Force One when Harris walked over and sat in a luxurious leather seat across from her. "How are you feeling?"

"To be truthful, I'm exhausted."

Braun rounded the corner dressed in a full tuxedo, shoes shined, and every hair in place. "Too exhausted for…" his smile widened, and he cocked his head with a wink.

Cordy gasped as she gazed into the gray-green eyes of her ruggedly handsome fiancé. Her hands fisted. She took two deep breaths, stood, and stepped to him toe-to-toe. "Braun Hastings, what's going on? How can you ask such a question in front of the president, of all people?"

Braun turned toward the president. "See, I told you she would agree wholeheartedly."

Cordy glanced around the plane to chuckles and grins. "Is this an inside joke?"

"As usual, you didn't even give me a chance to finish. I was going to say, 'Too exhausted for a wedding?'" Braun drew her closer. He leaned his forehead on her soft strawberry-blonde curls and inhaled. "I never want to be separated from you like this again. Marry me!"

"Now?" Words tangled in her throat. "This very minute?" Cordy grabbed the lapels of his jacket and pulled him to her. "You're serious!"

"It's that, or you'll have to find another ride home," Braun said. "It's the only way to keep me from you tonight. I want to keep you an honest woman."

Cordy's heart fluttered like a bird trapped in her rib cage. The air seemed to have become thinner. She could hardly breathe. "I've always dreamed of a perfect wedding while wearing a perfect gown, being married to the perfect man."

"One out of three isn't too bad," Braun said. "And Acting President Harris is lending his quarters as our honeymoon suite tonight if you only say yes."

Without hesitation, Cordy wrapped her arms around Braun. "Yes. I'll take your offer."

"You were right," President Harris said. "She agrees wholeheartedly."

Cordy turned to President Harris. "Thank you for everything."

Then she turned to Braun. "Give me five minutes to freshen up. She started down the aisle, then asked, "Which way?"

Braun moved forward.

"Oh no, you don't!" Usher warned. "I'll show her to her room and stand guard outside. Remember, big brother is on duty."

Braun laughed, "Hurry back. I've been a fool to wait this long and can't wait a minute longer!" The usually confident man transformed into an eager teenager, afraid she'd say no.

"Why wait?" Cordy wrapped her arms around Braun's and turned toward President Harris. "I want this man to be my husband, and I vow to be a loving wife forever and ever."

Braun smiled. "I accept and promise to be your loving husband throughout eternity."

"Good enough for me. I now pronounce you husband and wife. You may…"

Too late, they were already kissing. When the plane shuddered and dipped a wing, Cordy thought she was floating on air before resuming level flight. *Life with Braun will be an adventure. I wonder what our honeymoon will be like.*

The End

Thank you for reading Rapid Response. I loved writing it and hope you enjoyed reading it. If you did, please tell a friend and consider leaving a review on Amazon. Your sincere feedback means everything to me.

There is nothing like a good mystery. Suspense novels get my juices flowing. Please visit me on my website *JillFlateland.com*. I hope to have another story to share soon.

The next book in this series is Crashing The Grid. Check out the first chapter below.

Preview of Crashing The Grid – Chapter 1
Barely A Bride

Agent Joshtine Cordelia's abrupt, unconventional marriage on Air Force One, after two days of travel and no sleep, made for the most romantic event of her life so far. The eccentric honeymoon that followed was equally unforgettable.

The previous month was a whirlwind of events. Undercover Agent Braun Hastings discovered that U.S. President Zac Spendorf was infected with Virus X by his best friend turned traitor, General Rutoon. Unable to lead the country, Zac sent Braun to rescue Vice President Tom Harris from Syrian peace talks gone awry and swear him in as acting president. Cordy met Braun at the airport to deliver an emergency Virus X vaccine intended for Syria, where the next epidemic outbreak loomed.

Strangely, in the middle of their two separate missions, romance flourished. Braun, in his usual way, cooked up a secret wedding. Everyone, except Cordy, was in on the preparations, with Acting President Harris stepping in as celebrant.

Cordy, dressed in worn blue jeans and a navy fleece jacket that covered a red silk blouse, hadn't prepared for a wedding. She didn't have a gown, bridal bouquet, wedding cake, or a wedding ring for Braun, but it was perfect. At one time, a traditional ceremony had been her dream. Now, it oddly didn't matter.

She was charmed by Braun's unknown romantic streak and thrilled to be his wife. Cordy's eyes journeyed over Braun's radiant face as he drew closer. Their lips met gently at first.

A Secret Service agent snapped a photo of the young couple with his cell phone. "I'll forward a copy to all of you."

Harris chuckled as team members on board applauded.

Cordy felt on cloud nine when Air Force One dipped its wing before resuming level flight. She pulled away in surprise. "Did the pilot mean to do that?"

A Secret Service agent laughed, "That's Old Burt for you," and the crowd joined in.

"Encore!" Braun's brother, FBI Special Agent Usher Hastings, poured a glass of champagne for each person. His light gray tux matched Braun's, but Usher had already removed the silver bow tie and loosened the top button of his burgundy shirt.

Braun lifted Cordy into his arms and whispered, "I love you, my adorably stubborn lady."

"You mean independent!" she insisted.

"Right, and you're beautiful even without that wedding gown I bought for you. I hope the lady from the coffee bar gets good use out of it."

Cordy's jaw dropped, and her eyes widened. "You bought me a wedding gown? Do you mean the silver package Usher gave me at the airport before we boarded? The one that lady stole?"

Braun nodded. "I knew you would expect more of a ceremony, and I wanted to surprise you with a stunning, sexy dress to match my tux. It's not every day we get married."

Cordy smiled. "Won't she be surprised? I think she planned to steal the Virus X vaccine."

Braun kissed her and set Cordy on her feet.

"Thank you so much for the thoughtful gift," Cordy exclaimed, lifting his left hand and gently kissing it. "I would love to see a picture of the dress. Maybe I can find a similar one and wear it on our first anniversary. And I'll definitely need to get you a wedding ring!"

"It's a plan." Braun hugged her.

"I have a gift for you, too," Cordy moved out of his embrace. "I designed it myself. Well, with a little help from Quint."

Usher stepped up to the couple with two glasses of champagne. "Congratulations. Now it's your brother's turn to kiss the bride."

Cordy gave him a peck on the cheek and took a glass. "Thanks."

Usher looked disappointed. Braun took the other glass and punched him in the shoulder. "Find your own true love!"

"Cheers!" Harris lifted a glass for a toast.

Cordy sipped her drink before retrieving her backpack from the luggage rack. After rummaging through it, she pulled out a package wrapped in light blue tissue paper. "Here it is. It'll make the perfect wedding present. I can't wait for you to open it." She kissed Braun on the cheek before handing over the gift. "May it keep you safe, forever."

The crew gathered in a semicircle, waiting to see what Cordy got him.

Braun paused as he reached for the present. "What is it?"

"Open it and find out." Cordy bubbled over with joy. "It's okay to open in front of everyone. The gift is personal but not embarrassing. I can't wait to see the look on your face."

"With a build-up like that, I'll love it." Braun tore open the tissue paper and exclaimed, "A gold pen and a tie-tack?" His right eyebrow crept up. "Cordy, they're gorgeous."

She laughed at his questioning look. "Here, I'll show you. You can set it to record by pressing the gem, which plays back everything over my phone." Cordy removed the clear studded tie-tack from the box and placed it on Braun's lapel. The stone turned a bright red and glittered in the light. "Huh? Why did this change color? I didn't write that into my specs." She studied the gem. "It should be a clear stone."

"I like red." Braun opened the satin-lined box. "I've never had a gold pen before."

"It's not just a pen." Cordy took it from his hand. "It's an electronic alert device. It also contacts me directly when you're near danger."

"What kind of danger?" Braun asked.

"When working with a hacked vital program or a malware inserted into a software system or near an explosive device."

Braun's lip curled up on one side. He tapped his right index finger on his chin.

"I can tell you're a skeptic." Cordy twisted the top and nearly dropped it when her phone chirped a warning alarm. "Oh, my!" She grabbed her cell phone and clicked open an app, flipping from one screen to the next. "This can't be right. Are we in danger?"

Braun stared at the phone over Cordy's shoulder. "Slow down. I can't read as fast as you're going."

Dark spots blossomed before Cordy's eyes as her heartbeat roared in her ears. She wavered and bumped against Braun. "It can't be."

"What is it?" Braun wrapped an arm around her, grabbed the phone, and stared at the screen. "Has your phone been hacked?"

"No, it's something more sinister. My phone tells me an insecure source is tracking this plane." Suspicious, she had to be sure the pen was working and that they were safe.

"Surely Air Force One's computers are secure." Usher's voice sounded like an echo. "We're on a Stealth B-21 designed to make it hard to spot on radar. FAA has blocked our flight plan from online public tracking."

Braun took one look at Cordy. "It must be from another source." Glancing toward Harris, he asked, "When did you last log onto your computer?"

He read my mind. Cordy turned up the power on the pen sensor.

Harris shrugged. "I hate those things. Maybe two days ago. No, it was yesterday, September 10th. I remember because I sent a message to Laurie." He blinked a few times as his eyes glistened. "It was my daughter's twenty-first birthday, and I couldn't be there to help her celebrate." He swallowed and added, "I probably never shut the computer down."

Cordy ran the pen over Harris' laptop. "No warning sign. Stay here with your guards while we check this out."

"A tracking device?" Braun didn't wait for a response. He headed straight for the cockpit.

Usher set down his champagne and followed.

Cordy's mind whirred as she pushed past him. No longer tired, numbers and codes raced before her. *What caused the pen to alarm? And why did the tie-tack gem turn red? Red must mean danger. Both devices are sending a warning—this can't be good. And who would attack Air Force One?*

Order Crashing The Grid for the rest of the story.

About The Author

Jill S. Flateland,
RN, BSN, CCRN, MBA

Sweet Revenge is the first in a series of action-packed thrillers introducing Agent Dr. Joshtine Cordelia-Hastings (Cordy) Crisis Series.

Her venture continues in *Rapid Response*, where Cordy fights a bioterrorist attack. An astronaut unknowingly transports a potent virus, created without gravity on the space station, back to Earth. This virus is more deadly than our recent COVID-19 epidemic. Not only does it devastate the lungs, but it also attacks the brain. Risking exposure, Cordy rushes to find a cure when U.S. President Spendorf, his key advisors, and many members of Congress become infected.

Next in the series, *Crashing The Grid*, sends Cordy and her team to reverse a cyber attack on NYC that shut down the power grid, water treatment plants, and more. Cordy's world becomes a massive planet of asynchronous electronic puzzles to be analyzed, decrypted, and decoded. It's a perfect fit for a woman and job, and she has honed her skills through past experiences as a research analyst and an FBI Intelligence Analyst, Always plotting her next strategy like a three-dimensional Chess game, she figures out five moves ahead of every play.

Cordy's adventures continue in *Combating Chaos: All Systems Down*. Cordy and her new husband, JSOC Braun Hastings, hunt down a Russian terrorist, General Okueva, who enlists student hackers to disrupt the New York Stock Exchange and major financial systems. Foreign forces have also attacked London and Rome. Cordy and her team risk their lives to stop the terrorists.

I'm currently writing *Caught Unaware*, where Cordy has been promoted to a new cabinet position to lead the Cyberspace Crisis Team. A massive cyber attack on Washington, D.C., challenges the team to pull out all stops to defend the president, especially when drones attack the White House. I hope you enjoy these fast-paced novels.

In 2006, I retired and ventured into the wider writing world. In 2011, I published *A Lightning Slinger's Tales of the Rails* which tells of my aunt, Dr. Vera E. Williams, life as a female telegrapher during World War II. She worked for the railroad to make enough money to get her degree in teaching.

In 2014, we published *Ding Dong! The Rural Schools Are Gone*, a story of my two aunts, Vivian V. Lund (age 97 at the time, died at 104 in 2022) and Dr. Vera E. Williams (age 88 at that time, died at age 90 in 2016), who were both teachers during the early twentieth century.

I entered my fifth novel, *Until We Meet Again*, in the 2014 Colorado Gold Contest at the Rocky Mountain Fiction Writer's Contest. The novel became a finalist in the suspense category. *Tobias McFitzroy's old tombstone lay cracked in half and sinking under its weight in a cemetery outside a Colorado ghost town northeast of Fort Collins. The old stonemason had carved his own epitaph. It read, "Until we meet again. 1830 – 1899." Unlike most people, it didn't mean when he'd meet them in heaven. He couldn't. He hadn't made it that far.*

Although my background is over 40 years in healthcare as a critical care nurse and the CEO of an Urgent Care Corporation, I've been a writer all my life. My husband, Byron, and I live in Colorado, and we travel extensively.

Sales Support a Worthy Cause

Byron and I are actively involved with two Non-Governmental Organizations (NGOs). The first is Angel Covers, who helped open Vill-Angel Medical Clinic in the center of a rural farming community in Katale, Kenya, allowing poor families to receive high-quality healthcare.

As Director of Healthcare Services, my goal is to help expand the clinic to offer maternal-child care. Many families have no car to travel to a hospital, the nearest being 17 kilometers from the clinic. Some have a motorcycle, others have a cart pulled by a donkey, but many walk on foot.

Most women deliver babies at home, but the infant mortality rate in Kenya is six times higher than in the U.S. (Kenya has 30 infant deaths/1000 births compared to the U.S., which is 5 infant deaths/1000 births.) Some women travel up to two hours on foot while in labor to receive care during high-risk pregnancies. Plus, children are at the highest risk for death within the first 28 days. Most die of pneumonia, diarrhea, and sepsis. Our clinic can treat these ailments, and provide follow-up care as needed.

The second is Seeds of South Sudan, where donations help rescue refugees from Kakuma Refugee Camp in Kenya, allowing orphans to attend boarding school in Kenya. Once these students graduate, they plan to return to South Sudan to help rebuild its economy, infrastructure, and create a stabilized country.

You, too, can help. Part of the proceeds from the sales of these books help support these causes, and I thank you from the bottom of my heart. We know you have many choices for purchasing mystery novels and methods of donating to worthy causes, so I'm grateful that you chose to help support these charities.

Other Books Written by Jill S. Flateland

Thriller Series:

Sweet Revenge

Rapid Response

Crashing The Grid

Combating Chaos: All Systems Down

Suspense Series:

Until We Meet Again

Secret Series:

Secrets & Chandeliers

Family Secrets & Betrayals

Secrets Lost Among Forget-Me-Nots

Secrets of Grayson Mansion

Family Memoirs:

A Lightning Slinger's Tales of the Rails

Ding Dong! The Rural Schools Are Gone

Chugs & Hugs: Growing Up In A Train Station Vol 1

Chugs & Hugs: Growing Up In A Train Station Vol 2

Chugs & Hugs: Growing Up In A Train Station Vol 3